"Action packed from beginning to end . . . I was on the edge of my seat with this one and even though I dreaded reading The End because the story would be over, it still did not make me slow down reading this book one iota! Linnea Sinclair is one author on my keeper shelf and her books are always rereads for me!" —Fresh Fiction

"Too many authors on the romance side forget the science fiction part and too many science fiction writers simply can't write the romance well. Sinclair blends them perfectly. . . . The pacing is fast, the dialogue is excellent, and the book is full of secondary characters who are so well drawn they could carry a novel on their own. Highly recommended, as are the rest of Sinclair's books." —Sequential Tart

"Once again Linnea Sinclair delivers. *Hope's Folly* is the perfect combination of an action-packed sci-fi space romp and a heart-warming romance. A keeper."
—The Book Smugglers

PRAISE FOR
SHADES OF DARK

Winner of 2009 PRISM Award for Best Futuristic
Winner of the 2008 *Romantic Times* Reviewers'
Choice Award for Best Futuristic/Fantasy Romance
Winner of the 2008 PEARL Award for
Best Science Fiction/Fantasy
***Romance Reviews Today* Perfect 10 Award**

"A rip-roaring tale of danger, passion, and hard choices. No one blends romance and science fiction like Linnea Sinclair, and *Shades of Dark* is another sizzling page-turner!" —MARY JO PUTNEY, author of *A Distant Magic*

"A masterpiece . . . Not to be missed . . . Linnea Sinclair is always an author you can count on for amazing stories and is one of the best in the business. *Shades of Dark* is going down as one of my favorite books of all time and well deserves RRT's Perfect 10 award for excellence!" —Romance Reviews Today

"*Shades of Dark* is one of those rare entities; a sequel that is as good, if not better, than the original. . . . This story is a compelling page-turner and a novel that firmly places Linnea Sinclair in my select group of must-have authors. Five cups." —Coffee Time Romance

PRAISE FOR THE DOWN HOME ZOMBIE BLUES

Honorable Mention for the 2007 PEARL Award for Best Futuristic Romance
Nominated for the 2007 *Romantic Times* Reviewer's Choice Awards for Best Futuristic/Fantasy Romance

"Linnea Sinclair invades Earth with a rip-roaring, genre-bending, edge-of-your-seat read that has it all: crackling action, monsters, double-crossers, unlikely heroes, and a fully realized love story. I loved it!"

—SUSAN GRANT, *New York Times* bestselling author of *Moonstruck*

"From its tongue-in-cheek title to its melding of romance and zombie-killing action, there's little in Sinclair's newest sci-fi romance that doesn't surprise, grip or entertain. . . . Fans of romance and fantasy hunting for edgier fare can stop singing the blues." —*Publishers Weekly*

"Quirky, offbeat and packed with gritty action, this blistering novel explodes out of the gate and never looks back. Counting on Sinclair to provide top-notch science fiction elaborately spiced with romance and adventure is a given, but she really aces this one! A must-read, by an author who never disappoints. 4½ stars. Top pick!" —*Romantic Times*

"Outstanding . . . Realistic characters, romance, humor, conflict and suspense, what more could a paranormal fan ask for in a sf/futuristic novel? . . . A keeper."
—PNR Reviews

PRAISE FOR
GAMES OF COMMAND

Winner of the 2007 PEARL Award for Best Science Fiction and Fantasy Romance
2008 RITA® Finalist for Best Paranormal Romance
AllAboutRomance.com Top Ten SF/Fantasy & Futuristic Romances

"Linnea Sinclair just gets better and better! *Games of Command* is not to be missed!"
—MARY JO PUTNEY, author of *A Distant Magic*

"*Games of Command* is a wonderful book. Linnea Sinclair has written a unique and utterly intriguing hero in Kel-Paten. Sexy, complex and devoted, he's a man to fall in love with."
—NALINI SINGH, author of *Hostage to Pleasure*

"When it comes to high-flying adventure, political intrigue and dark romance, Sinclair has it aced! This sur-

prising tale is filled with shifting loyalties, deception and
jaw-dropping flying maneuvers. . . . 4½ stars."

—*Romantic Times*

PRAISE FOR
an accidental Goddess

**Winner of the 2003 RWA® Windy City Choice Award
for Best FF&P Romance
2002 PEARL Award Honorable Mention for
Best Science Fiction Novel
Romantic Times BookClub magazine's 2002 Gold
Medal Top Pick Award**

"Entirely entertaining." —*Contra Costa Times*

"Proves once again why Sinclair is one of the reigning
queens of science fiction romances . . . This is a book
[with] bright, attractive characters, an interesting plot,
action, adventure, humor and romance." —*Starlog*

"A star in the making." —SFCrowsnest.com

PRAISE FOR
Gabriel's Ghost

**Winner of the 2006 RITA® Award for
Best Paranormal Romance
2003 Prism Award, 2nd place (tied with *An Accidental
Goddess*), for Best Futuristic Romance
2002 Sapphire Award, 2nd place (tied with *An Accidental Goddess*), for Best Speculative Romance Novel
Romance Reviews Today Perfect 10 Award**

"Both an exciting sci-fi adventure and a warm romance,
with deep characterization and meaningful relationships.
Highly recommended." —Romance Reviews Today

"There isn't a shadow of a doubt in this reviewer's mind that Bantam has a bona fide interstellar star in this author. Prepare to be star-struck, dear reader."

—Heartstrings Reviews

"How can a review do justice to a book that sweeps you away from the very first page? . . . Sinclair has managed to mix religion, politics, adventure, science fiction and romance into one of the best reads of the year. A true winner!" —*Interlude Magazine*

PRAISE FOR FINDERS KEEPERS

Finalist for 2006 RITA® Award for Best First Book
Winner of the 2001 Sapphire Award for Best
Speculative Romance Novel
Winner of the 2001 PEARL Award for Best Sci-Fi
Romance

"*Finders Keepers* is romance, but also science fiction in its truest form. Ms. Sinclair creates a complete and fascinating universe." —*Romantic Times*

"A riveting, tightly written, edge-of-your-seat tale that pulls the reader in from page one, never letting go until the poignant finish." —Romance Reviews Today

REBELS AND LOVERS

LINNEA SINCLAIR

BANTAM BOOKS
NEW YORK

Rebels and Lovers is a work of fiction. Names, characters, places, and incidents either are the product of the author's imagination or are used fictitiously. Any resemblance to actual persons, living or dead, events, or locales is entirely coincidental.

A Bantam Books Mass Market Original

Copyright © 2010 by Linnea Sinclair Bernadino

Published in the United States by Bantam Books,
an imprint of The Random House Publishing Group,
a division of Random House, Inc., New York.

BANTAM BOOKS and the rooster colophon
are registered trademarks of Random House, Inc.

ISBN: 978-0-553-59219-1

Cover art: Gene Mollica

Printed in the United States of America

www.bantamdell.com

9 8 7 6 5 4 3 2 1

acknowledgments

I'm hugely indebted to the following for their patience, input, humor, and support during a difficult time in my life, which included the writing of this book: author Stacey "Apple Cosmo" Kade; author Monette "Attorney Babe" Michaels; reader M. L. "Hit 'em Straight" Helfstein, USNR (Ret.); my editor, Anne "Sparkle Mommy" Groell; and my agent, Kristin "The Rock" Nelson; as well as my Groupie Loopies at the Intergalactic Bar & Grille. And special thanks to wonderful (cat-owned) authors Robin D. Owens, Susan Grant, and Mary Jo Putney. Thank you all for being there when I needed you, for when the words wouldn't come and the tears wouldn't stop.

Thank you also to Dr. Sisco at the Cat Care Clinic (Naples, FL), Doc Ellie Scott and staff at Stringtown Animal Hospital (Grove City, OH), Dr. Lisa Fulton at the MedVet Cancer Center (Columbus, OH), and reader and veterinarian Dr. Earmie Edwards for all your efforts on Daiquiri's behalf.

To my beloved angel-cat, Daq. You left much too soon and are always in my heart.

A big note of appreciation to my last-minute beta readers: Corrina Lawson, Debra Holland, Linda Burke, Melissa Nix, and Arwen Lynch.

And to my husband, Rob Bernadino, who after almost thirty years not only still finds me amusing but knows when I need to cry—and didn't hesitate to bring new furry typing assistants into our lives: Chester, Brady, and Jimmy-James.

"Now and Forever"—DJ Lithium
"Titicaca" (Firestorm remix)—Firestorm & Steve Allen
"Angel on My Shoulder"—Kaskade
"Infinity"—Guru Josh Project
"Move for Me"—Kaskade

"Our deepest fear is not that we are inadequate. Our deepest fear is that we are powerful beyond measure. It is our light, not our darkness, that frightens us most."

—Marianne Williamson

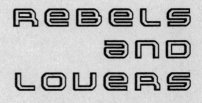

REBELS
AND
LOVERS

His family was sending one of their corporate star yachts through two major jumpgates—from Sylvadae to the port city of Tal Verdis on Garno—just for him. And that, Devin Guthrie knew as he sat in his spacious glass-walled office on the fifteenth floor of Guthrie Global Systems's financial headquarters, portended trouble.

Big trouble.

Devin nodded casually to his eldest brother's image on the main deskscreen, deliberately keeping his voice noncommittal, as if the disruption didn't matter at all. "A Trans-Aldan flight would be cheaper," he suggested to Jonathan. Even if he went first-class. It would also be slower. That was more than reasonable by Devin's way of thinking. He was in no hurry to have his life turned upside down.

But that only deepened his brother's frown on the large screen.

"You know better than anyone that the restructuring of the Empire hasn't hurt our portfolio." Jonathan was dark-haired and dark-eyed like their father—the indomitable Jonathan Macy "J. M." Guthrie, who, at almost eighty, was still the undisputed patriarch of Guthrie Global Systems. Jonathan also had J.M.'s intense, narrow-eyed gaze. "Your *time* is valuable. Additionally, using our own transport is safer. Especially with Philip resurfacing last month."

Devin pulled off his silver-rimmed glasses—another

thing his family found fault with—and rubbed at the spot between his eyebrows.

He couldn't argue the validity of Jonathan's statement. Privately, the family rejoiced that the second eldest of the Guthrie brothers was alive. But Philip's resurrection had repercussions. He was now no longer an Imperial admiral but had allied himself with the newly formed Alliance of Independent Republics—"traitor worlds," according to Imperial First Barrister-turned-Prime Commander Darius Tage. And, in spite of the fact that the Alliance was in the process of being granted "conditional" legitimacy, sources whispered that there was a price on Philip Guthrie's head.

Being a Guthrie—one of the oldest, wealthiest, and most established families in the Empire—might no longer be a guarantee of safety from a well-timed accident. And therein rested Devin's last salvo.

He slipped his glasses back on. "Actually, traveling by commercial transport *would* be safer. Tage isn't going to kill one hundred fifty passengers to get at one of us. But a Guthrie personal yacht malfunctioning at a jumpgate exit or never coming out of jump—"

"Would be viewed as suspicious *and* a direct threat, not only to us but to the Rossettis, Petroskis, Helfsteins, and Falkners." Jonathan ticked off the names of some of the Empire's more prestigious families on his fingers. "Tage is too smart to make a direct move against us."

No, the emperor's longtime adviser was crafty enough to cover his tracks first—or get someone else to do the dirty work.

Just as J.M. had Jonathan do his. "Devin . . ."

Devin held up one hand as a sign of capitulation, because he could hear his brother's impatience. "Fine. I'll check my schedule and call you—"

"I'll wait." Jonathan leaned back in the padded leather chair. A soft golden light danced in small sparkles through the elegant beveled-glass library window behind him, illuminating the hallmark Guthrie intertwined-Gs visible over his left shoulder. Devin's brother was at the Guthrie estate outside Port Palmero on Sylvadae—a world halfway across Aldan sector from Devin's offices on Garno. Most GGS offices had the luxury of a secure, near-instantaneous private comm link, which, at moments like this, Devin hated. The more common two-to-three-day communications delay afforded time to think things over and come up with a stronger argument.

He angled away from the screen where Jonathan's image waited and tapped up a small hologrid. The data floated in a green-tinged glow. He scrolled through his appointment calendar, noting what projects were of immediate concern and wondering how far he could stretch those that weren't. He was not looking forward to going to Sylvadae.

It wasn't because his current residence on Garno held any special appeal. It was a world known for its casinos, theaters, and restaurants circling the Tal Verdis spaceport, but he wasn't a gambler, he rarely went to the theater, and whatever fell out of his penthouse residence's chefmaster unit was fine by him.

It was just that crunching numbers, massaging financial data, and coding investment probability programs were what Devin did best. He was far more comfortable with data than with people—especially when those people were his parents, his older brothers, and his brothers' families.

And especially when those same parents had no qualms about using his eldest brother to force Devin to change his life.

Not that he hadn't seen it coming...

Well, then, get it over with. But he would do it on his terms, his timing. "The quarterly summary for Galenth needs revisions. And the stage six contracts from Baris–Agri are due in tomorrow with the Englarian Church amendments. If those unfold as expected"— and as he was senior analyst on both, there was no reason they shouldn't—"I'll be able to leave here by noon, Fourthday." That gave him three days to firm up the Baris–Agri deal—a project that had been his primary focus for more than two months. He had to be here to make sure these final contract negotiations went smoothly.

"Delegate the revisions and the contracts. The star yacht will be there at half-past six *tonight,* your time."

Half-past six? Devin's fist clenched out of sight of the deskscreen cam. "But Baris–Agri—"

"Father advises you to be on it."

It wasn't just the tone of finality in Jonathan's words. It was that no one—except Philip Guthrie— ever defied J.M.

"More tea, Mr. Devin? Or perhaps something stronger? Dinner will be ready shortly."

Nelessa's voice pulled Devin's attention from his microcomp, where nice, friendly, nonjudgmental numbers were keeping him company on his flight to Sylvadae and keeping his mind off the reason behind his trip—and the annoying fact that the Baris–Agri deal would conclude without him. His microcomp was a Rada—a top-of-the-line unit that he'd customized to do even more than function as a pocket comm and datapad. It had voice and holosim keyboard capabilities and could integrate seamlessly into any larger datacomp system. He'd already sent eight pages of notes to his assistants. And gone through three cups of tea since he'd boarded GGS's corporate yacht, the *Triumph*.

The chief attendant from GGS's private yacht waited with expert patience by Devin's seat. The dusky-skinned muscular woman was in her early forties, about six years his senior. Her voice was far softer than her appearance; she sometimes doubled as Jonathan's wife's bodyguard when Marguerite traveled outside acknowledged "safe" areas in Aldan. Devin didn't doubt there was an L7 laser pistol secreted somewhere under Nel's pale-blue GGS uniform jacket.

Her hands, however, held only a teapot and a linen napkin.

Devin glanced at his empty teacup on the low table on his right, its thin white porcelain edges banded with pale-blue circles meeting at the intertwined double-G emblem. The same emblem was etched into the double doors of his office on Garno. Where he should be now—and wasn't. "Tea's fine, Nel. Thanks."

He'd save the hard liquor for after the meeting with his father and brothers.

Nel refilled his cup, then moved silently back toward the galley just behind the cockpit. The *Triumph* was smaller than the *Prosperity,* GGS's 220-ton yacht, which held twenty passengers in opulent luxury, with ten large sleeping cabins. But the 130-ton ship could still seat ten on a day trip and sleep six on an overnight, not including the crew of three. And currently, Devin was the only passenger.

Devin thumbed his Rada off and put it down on the table as his mind—tired, frustrated—strayed from the Baris–Agri deal. Was Jonathan's choice to send the

Triumph deliberate? It had been *her* ship—or, rather, Makaiden had been the first pilot, though on longer trips she'd share that command with her husband, Kiler. But, to Devin, it was always *her* ship. He couldn't separate Makaiden from the *Triumph,* and when he'd first seen the ship's distinctive slant-nosed outline through the spaceport terminal's windows, all thoughts of Baris–Agri vanished. He couldn't stop his heart from racing, his breath from catching, and his hopes—illogically, stupidly—from rising.

His hopes where Makaiden Griggs was concerned were not only illogical, they were impossible. And not just because she'd left Guthrie employ almost two years ago, after her husband was fired.

Her husband had been one of the reasons behind the impossibility of Devin's hopes. Though a little thing like a husband wasn't known to stop Devin's brother Ethan from his conquests, adultery wasn't something Devin would do. Even if Makaiden had been interested.

He told himself that repeatedly.

The larger reason was that Devin was a Guthrie, and Makaiden Griggs was not the kind of woman a Guthrie admitted to having feelings for. She was a working-class woman, a jump-rated pilot whose family was out of the wrong end of Calth sector, whose education wasn't from a prestigious university like Montgomery or Valhaldan but at the hands of whatever freighter operator would take her on. She drank her ale straight from the bottle and probably couldn't name one decent vintage wine. Or even a marginal one.

She and her husband, Kiler, flew Guthrie yachts for more than five years. Devin found himself—not in love, he would never admit that—*irrevocably intrigued* by her within the first three months of meeting her. He was twenty-eight at the time, and she was—according to personnel records he memorized—a year younger. But Makaiden Malloy Griggs had a presence beyond her years—a light that sparkled in her eyes and a brassiness that hinted at an inner strength. A confidence. A dedication. She loved being at a stellar helm and made no apologies for it.

And she wasn't the least bit impressed by the Guthrie name. Around Makaiden, Devin felt like a real person. Not a Guthrie heir.

In that way, she reminded him of Philip's ex-wife, Captain Chaz Bergren. But in all other ways, she was different. She was short where Chaz was taller, her hair a pale tousled crop where Chaz's was a rich auburn that curled past her waist. And she laughed a lot more than he ever remembered Chaz laughing.

Even now, the memory of her infectious laughter made Devin Jonathan Guthrie feel things he didn't want to—couldn't *afford* to—feel.

But then, for Makaiden Griggs, life was good. She loved her husband, even leaving her career with GGS for him. And for all that Devin as a Guthrie could offer, he was sure she would have wanted none of it. She didn't need him.

Not that he ever tried to be anything other than a friend, a colleague—her employer's youngest son.

It was that friendship that drew his father's notice. And because J.M. suspected, Jonathan suspected. Which again made Devin wonder—as Aldan's stars flickered in the blackness outside his viewport—if that's why the *Triumph* was sent. A final, irrevocable reminder that his life would proceed according to the greater Guthrie plan.

"Dinner, Mr. Devin?"

He pushed himself out of the soft chair by the viewport and followed Nel's beckoning hand to the small dining table on the opposite side of the salon. He and Makaiden had played cards here many times as he was shuttled between GGS offices in Aldan and Baris sectors. There wasn't a lot for a pilot to do in jumpspace, and Devin always made sure he had a deck or three tucked into his briefcase. She'd taught him to play Zentauri, and, even though he was a natural cardcounter and could memorize five decks, she beat him now and then, her thought processes craftier and more creative than his.

Stop doing the expected. Surprise me! she'd challenged.

He'd wanted to. God and stars, how he'd wanted to. But—

Don't think about that now.

The sliced roast smelled good. The cream linen tablecloth and napkin were smooth to the touch. Nel poured a ruby-red wine into an etched crystal glass, then waited for him to taste the roast, in case adjustments needed to be made. Cooked a little more or some spices added.

He knew the routine. He was a Guthrie. "It's all lovely, Nel. Thanks."

"My pleasure, Mr. Devin."

He cut another piece of the fragrant roast. The last meal of a condemned man. Devin Jonathan Guthrie, thirty-five years old and sentenced to marriage, without parole.

"Seven more days. That's all I can give you, Captain Griggs." The thin-faced man in the cheap, shiny brown three-piece suit grabbed the railing of the *Void*

Rider's rampway and stared up at her with narrowed eyes. "You either pay what you owe or we'll settle it the hard way."

Kaidee Griggs leaned on that same railing and stared down at Horatio Frinks with equally narrowed eyes, ignoring the tall, wide-shouldered Takan body-guard hulking threateningly behind. "What about the two thousand I gave you last week?"

"That leaves thirteen—"

"Which you will get, Frinks, when I get paid. You know that. We discussed that. It's not my fault the Empire's dumped more slagging restrictions on cross-border trade. I'm not the only free-trader caught up in this."

"But this ain't no trader debt, and it's over a year old now. I don't like it. Orvis don't like it."

The Taka nodded slowly. He wasn't Orvis but, like Frinks, was hired muscle.

"And *I* don't like it, but damn it, I can't pay you if I can't haul goods. You have an issue? Go to slagging Aldan Prime and talk to His High-Whatever Tage. I would have paid that debt off four months ago if it wasn't for him." Well, maybe not *paid off*, but she'd be a lot less in debt if restrictions, fines, taxes, and penalties hadn't been slathered on to free-trader operations by His High Asshole Darius Tage. For the better-ment of the Empire. Of course. And at the command of Emperor Prewitt III. Of course.

It was always the emperor who commanded these things. Tage was just his obedient servant.

In a *crigblarg*'s eyes.

Sheldon Blaine's claim to the throne was starting to sound more and more attractive—the terrorist tactics of his Farosian Justice Wardens notwithstanding. At least Blaine—who even from prison still claimed to be the real heir to the royal Prewitt line—would want traders going to and from Tos Faros and other points in Dafir sector.

Now it was damned near an impossible task to get across the B–C border into Calth. And even traffic in the commercial space lanes in Baris was subject to "unannounced inspections." As if she had Philip Guthrie tucked in her cargo hold?

She *knew* Philip Guthrie—though she doubted many on Dock Five would believe her if she said so. And if she did have the man on her ship, she'd not waste his talents by stuffing him in a cargo hold. He'd flown right seat with her and Kiler a few times. The man was impressive. She could almost forgive him for being a Guthrie.

Frinks made a disgusted noise and turned away. "Don't say I didn't warn you."

She shoved herself back from the railing and headed for the *Rider*'s airlock, fear warring with frustration. Seven days. She couldn't get to Calth and back in seven days even if the Empire didn't have a destroyer sitting out there with Dock Five in its sights, inspecting and impeding traffic.

The best she could do in seven days was to get off Dock Five the minute the restrictions were lifted and never return. Let Orvis hunt her down. That could buy her a month, maybe three.

But it would also put her in a serious financial bind. One of the few intelligent things Kiler had ever done was to prepay the *Rider*'s docking-bay fees on a two-year contract and sign the ship on as part of the Cal-Ris Free-Trader Collective. The CFTC, its contacts, and its contracts—for all the annoying rules and restrictions—were the only things keeping her and her ship alive. Leaving Dock Five meant leaving all that behind and starting from scratch again.

Just like they did when they left Guthrie Global.

Another thing to thank Kiler for.

That and a twenty-five-thousand-credit gambling debt—with the *Rider* as collateral.

She'd always worried that it would be her heritage, her family history, that would derail her life. How damnably odd that the handsome, respectable—well, respectable back then—pilot she had married turned out to be the source of all her troubles.

And that the very family history she was so afraid of was the main reason he was interested in her. So much for true love or forever after.

She closed the airlock behind her and leaned on the bulkhead's hard edge, her back against the wall in more ways than the obvious.

Thank you, Kiler Griggs. What in hell am I going to do now?

It was almost dawn in Port Palmero when Devin's limo glided silently over the long, tree-lined drive leading to his parents' estate. Lights in the main house—an imposing four-story brick-and-streamstone mansion—glowed golden, as they would when a guest was expected; lights in the family and guest wings were more muted. Lights in the servants' quarters were bright, as always. One never knew when a Guthrie might want something.

No, to be fair, his parents were exceedingly good employers, but one never knew when a Guthrie Global Systems executive might arrive from the far reaches of the Empire, body clock and local clock out of sync.

Devin's body clock was definitely out of sync. He

was no night crawler, and his wristwatch and body clock told him he'd been traveling for eighteen hours. The local time was a quarter after five.

Another forty-five minutes and he could join his father for coffee in the informal dining salon adjacent to the patio that overlooked the eastern gardens. J.M. had his coffee promptly at six every morning. An hour later, his wife, Valerie, would bring her bowl of seasonal fruits and light cream to the table, and they would start another day with soft, companionable conversation.

J.M. never raised his voice before breakfast.

Devin wondered if today was the day the old man would break that rule.

"Welcome home, Mr. Devin." Barthol, the house's chief steward, met Devin on the southern patio, where the limo driver—knowing Devin's preference for unobtrusiveness—had pulled the vehicle up the rear garden drive. Devin made no move toward the suitcase the driver deposited on the brick walkway. Barthol, unlike J.M., *would* argue before breakfast.

A Guthrie did not lift luggage.

Neither, actually, did the balding, pale-skinned Barthol. At least, not any farther than the few inches from the walkway to the antigrav pallet humming by his black-clad legs.

"Thanks, Barthol. How's your wrist?" He fell into step with the man who'd been the Guthrie steward since Devin was a child.

"All healed. Thank you kindly for asking."

"No more basketball with Trippy and Max, I take it?"

Barthol's wide mouth stretched into a grin. "Your nephews keep me young, just as you and your brothers did. But my jump shot isn't what it used to be."

Barthol was somewhere between seventy and eighty—at least, that was the best Devin and Philip had been able to deduce. He never talked about his age, and to see his rangy form lunging around the estate's basketball court, it would be easy to shave ten or fifteen years off that total.

Or more. Barthol had seemed old to Devin when Devin was in grade school, as Max was now. He must seem ancient to twelve-year-old Max and his nineteen-year-old brother, Trippy.

Shame Trippy wasn't here. Of all his nieces and nephews—and there were currently seven—Jonathan Macy Guthrie III was his favorite. "Triple trouble," Valerie Lang Guthrie had intoned when her first grandchild was born. So Trip, or Trippy, he became.

Devin had been sixteen when Trip was born. He was almost as close in age to Trip as he was to Trip's father, Jonathan.

The patio's glass-paneled doors, sensing human presences with accepted biopatterns, slid open silently.

"Do you wish to retire to your suite for a few hours?" Barthol asked as they headed for the rear elevators. "Your father should be at the east patio shortly."

"I caught a couple hours' sleep on the ship." If lying on the soft bed and staring at the cabin's ceiling could be called sleep—and it wasn't just Baris–Agri keeping him awake. "I'll freshen up, then join him. Do you know if Jonathan's coming over this morning?"

Barthol glanced at the silver wristwatch edging out from beneath his white cuff. "He alerted security to his and Miz Marguerite's arrival in fifteen minutes."

So it would be J.M. *and* Jonathan over coffee. Devin loved his family, but not when they double-teamed him. Devin stepped into the carpeted elevator,

Barthol on his left and his luggage in front. His suite was third floor, south.

"We've been informed that Miss Tavia will be in around nine this evening," Barthol told him as they exited into the hallway. "Your father requested the Blue Lily Suite for her."

Right down the hall from his. How convenient.

Devin touched the palm pad at his door, which read his biopattern and opened immediately. The browns, gray-blues, and greens of his living room were familiar—his mother often threatened to redecorate to something brighter, more cheery, but somehow he was still winning that battle.

"I know it's a bit early, but the staff and I would like to offer our congratulations, Mr. Devin," Barthol said, as Devin tossed his jacket over the back of the dark-green three-cushioned couch.

Not condolences? Devin never had the feeling Barthol truly approved of Tavia Emberson. He wasn't even sure he did—other than that Tavia was one damned good handball player and didn't try too hard to reform his unsociable tendencies. And wasn't averse to a long engagement; neither was in a hurry to wed. "That's very kind. Thank you."

"Shall I unpack for you, sir?"

"I don't have much." He'd packed only what he needed for the flight. Anything else he could find in his closets, which held a smattering of things he'd left behind from recent visits but more so from his university and postgraduate days—the last time the Guthries' Port Palmero estate had been his home. Fashion—much to Tavia Delaris Emberson's dismay—never concerned him.

Barthol retreated, AG pallet in tow, the door closing behind him. Devin left his suitcase where the pallet had deposited it and trudged through his bedroom—his bed still sported the comfortably worn gray-and-blue quilt—then through his dressing room and into his bathroom. Lights came on around him as the rooms monitored his presence. He leaned over the expansive pale-green marble double sink and examined his reflection in the mirrored wall, then took off his glasses and rinsed them under the faucet. There were shadows under his eyes—which were a murky blue, not bright blue like his mother's and Philip's—but the shadows were to be expected from one who'd been traveling all night and part of the next day. He put his glasses on the marble countertop, then rubbed one hand over his chin. He should shave. He should probably even shower, because then, at least for a few hours, his short-cropped hair wouldn't stick up quite so haphazardly in spikes. But a warm shower would relax him too much, make him sleepy.

He needed to be awake to face J.M. and Jonathan.

He settled for shaving and changing from his cream-colored business shirt to a round-necked, somewhat misshapen soft sweater almost the same brown as his hair. It was his favorite sweater, and he'd annoyed himself by accidentally leaving it behind a few months ago.

The fact that Makaiden Griggs, working double duty as his bodyguard, had helped him pick it out at a spaceport mall on Aldan Prime three years ago had nothing to do with it. It was a comfortable sweater. He liked it. He'd bought it.

Makaiden was the one who told him the sweater matched his hair.

He always thought it matched her eyes.

He shut the closet door with more force than was

necessary, the hard crack of wood against wood spearing the silence of his suite.

Anger vibrated through his body, surprising him with its appearance and intensity. It had to be because he was overtired; the Baris–Agri and Galenth projects weren't his only duties. There were also several ventures tied to the recent restructuring of the Empire that had kept him working late hours the past few weeks, and now this last-minute summons and the all-night travel...He was tired, that's all. Not angry. Devin Jonathan Guthrie never permitted himself to get angry. It was a useless emotion that interfered with rational, analytical thought. It let others know they could get to you, manipulate you, hurt you.

Anger was a waste of time.

Moreover, he had nothing to be angry about.

Not even being told you're getting married?

He'd been in a relationship with Tavia for almost a year now. It had started on the handball court, had progressed to occasional dates at the symphony or dinner with other GGS executives, and had eventually ended up in bed. She was an Emberson—not old money like the Guthries, Petroskis, Tages, or Sullivans, but respected money, especially on Garno.

Tavia Emberson was, as his sister-in-law Marguerite would say, "a good match." Devin was, after all, the youngest Guthrie son. Marguerite, a Petroski, had landed the eldest Guthrie, a marriage the society vids deemed "an excellent match."

So yours is only good. That doesn't make you angry?

No, that made him a realist. But even a realist had rights. Yes, he would agree to a public announcement of his engagement to Tavia. He was Devin, not Philip.

He wouldn't rebel outright. But if and when he married would be on his terms, on his schedule.

Not, as Jonathan had informed him through the deskscreen of his Garno office, before their mother's next birthday several months from now.

J.M. and Valerie Guthrie wanted Devin settled and a grandchild on the way before Valerie turned seventy-seven.

Devin would give them engaged. The rest he was withdrawing from negotiation.

He would not end up like Ethan.

"Devin. Good to have you home." His father, already in business attire of dark pants and a pale-blue collared shirt, rose from his chair at the glass-topped table and clasped Devin's shoulder in a firm grip. He was only slightly shorter than Devin, his straight posture belying his years—as did the thick dark hair that he wore combed back from a craggy face. His brows were bushy, more silver-tinged than his hair, which Devin suspected benefited now and then from retouching. But his father was almost eighty, and if he wished to indulge in a little vanity, Devin would not be the one to take that from him.

Devin leaned into his father's half embrace, patting the old man on the back. That was about as demonstrative as the men in his family were known to get. He took the chair on his father's right.

"Mr. Devin, good to see you again, love!" Audra, the Guthries' longtime head chef, appeared at Devin's elbow with a pot of Mountain Gray, his favorite tea. Unlike the rest of his family, he wasn't a coffee drinker.

"I've missed your cheese biscuits," Devin told her honestly, and received a wide smile in answer. He turned to his father. "How are you?" For once, it wasn't an idle question. J.M. was never a muscular man, yet he felt somehow frailer, lighter, during their brief embrace. Devin reminded himself to ask Jonathan later if their father hadn't been well lately. He knew their mother would tell him nothing unless J.M. authorized it.

"Life's good," his father answered as the stocky head chef slipped back toward the main kitchen. "Your mother's busy with the latest yacht-club charity ball. It's getting to be that time of year. Ah, Jonathan!" J.M. turned as Devin's brother strode casually into the patio dining area. "Audra! We'll need more coffee."

Jonathan rested one hand briefly on Devin's shoulder as he walked by, then sat on J.M.'s other side. Like J.M., he was in business clothes, but his collared shirt was a darker blue and his blue-and-gold silk scarf was already threaded through the collar loops. Audra appeared silently, poured fragrant coffee—"Leave the pot," J.M. ordered—and disappeared just as silently.

A stack of sweet rolls already graced the middle of the table. Jonathan chose one, impaling it on an elegantly scrolled silver fork. Devin found he had no appetite.

"I know Jonathan explained we'd like to see you and Tavia married in the next few months," J.M. said without any preamble, as usual. "You *are* thirty-five, Devin, and while I know it's clichéd to say, 'It's about time,' the fact of the matter is, it is. With the recent turmoil in the Empire, it's important that Guthrie Global and our family appear in all manner united, strong, and respectable."

Intending to muzzle Ethan? Devin thought but didn't dare say. Although with Ethan, a chastity belt would be needed in addition.

But no doubt Ethan's excesses were one of the reasons J.M. needed another strong, respectable son to ensure the continuation of GGS as a force in the Empire.

"Additionally," J.M. continued, "your mother and I aren't getting any younger. She's pushing me again to retire. I'm giving it serious thought. So we have plans, not just for ourselves but for all of you. And it's time to set those plans in motion."

"But I don't—"

J.M. raised one hand, stilling Devin's words. "You know how much grandchildren mean to your mother. What happened with Philip almost killed her. He and Chasidah had no children. Your mother's grief at believing he—that any part of him—was gone forever was heartbreaking."

More than Valerie grieved over the early—and erroneous—reports of Philip's death. Devin took the news as if someone had sucker punched him in the gut. He was closer in age to Ethan than to Philip, but mentally, emotionally, and intellectually, Devin had attached himself to Philip since he was small. He went to Philip with his problems at school or at camp. He looked up to Philip, first in a Fleet cadet's uniform, then as a lieutenant, then captain.

Philip was, quite truthfully, more than his brother. He was Devin's close friend—a friendship that had expanded several years ago to include Trippy. Just as Philip had seemed to sense Devin's isolation as youngest son, Devin saw Trip's isolation as eldest grandchild. Different sides of the same coin.

The best times he had lately were when he, Trip, and Philip were together.

But now Trip was at Montgomery University, and Philip was somewhere over the Baris–Calth border.

There was an emptiness in the family circle, so Devin understood Valerie's fears. He only wished his parents didn't look to him for the solution.

"Your mother needs to see all her boys happy and settled," J.M. said with a nod to Jonathan. "Philip is always in our prayers. We respect his dedication to what we all know is inevitable—there will be changes in the Empire. But the life he's chosen is a dangerous one. Your mother needs a distraction from that."

Devin turned his teacup around on the saucer. "And Tavia and I are to be that distraction." It wasn't a question. It was a statement of fact.

"Tavia's a lovely young woman from a well-placed family. We approved of her from the first time you brought her here. Is there anything about her that you now find objectionable?"

"No." Tavia Emberson *was* lovely—a natural beauty made even more attractive by her family's money. Her shoulder-length black hair was thick and glossy, her dark honey-colored skin was perfect, and her tall, lithe body even more so. Like him, she had a passion for singles handball, and that sport plus her trainers kept her in top condition. Any number of men would trip over themselves to have Tavia Emberson. Devin wondered now and then what she saw in him: an antisocial number cruncher who had an annoying habit of inspecting his host's computer data systems rather than making small talk with the other guests at the high-profile parties she invariably dragged him to.

Then reality always kicked in. He was a Guthrie. And on the amateur sport circuit in Aldan, he consistently ranked as one of the top-five players in competitive handball. Plus, he was a better-than-average dancer—thanks to those lessons his mother had forced on all her boys. Three things he knew were important to Tavia Emberson.

She never realized that dancing with her rescued him from having to chat with her friends at those parties she so loved.

"My problem," Devin said, stilling his movements with the teacup, belatedly realizing he was giving away too much, "is the timing. For one thing, I have several projects in my department that can't be shunted aside while I participate in planning engagement parties or a wedding."

"Marguerite already offered to help Mother and Tavia," Jonathan said. "So has Hannah."

"Marguerite and Hannah aren't going to stand in for me at the parties," Devin answered. "You're talking not only Garno society but Port Palmero. And Aldan Prime, likely, if aunts and uncles get involved."

"You can have Nathanson and Torry handle the Webster merger, the Galenth Fund project, and the Baris–AgriCorp deal," his father put in smoothly. "I've already had them clear their schedules."

Devin's mouth opened but no sound came out. *Nathanson and Torry . . .* Shock roiled through him. Those were *his* projects, especially Baris–Agri, which had involved some delicate negotiations with the Englarian Church, whose farming cooperatives were a key producer. To be so summarily removed because he needed to appear at parties . . .

"But—"

"The reality is," J.M. continued, "you haven't taken a vacation in quite some time. Years. Take six months off. Enjoy your new bride. Start a family. Your brothers and I can handle everything else."

But . . . I don't love Tavia. And she doesn't love me. In desperation, the truth surfaced. This wasn't a guess.

Devin and Tavia had discussed the basis of their relationship, because she, too, was under pressure from her family to marry. Her relationship with Devin, their attendance at various handball competitions, their occasional nights together, were essentially damage control lest either set of parents hook them up with a partner neither could stand. At least he and Tavia didn't usually annoy each other. They had similar goals, similar outlooks on life.

He'd talked to her immediately after Jonathan's call yesterday. They agreed they had no problem being engaged, because it honestly wouldn't change their schedules much. She had her job in corporate legal in her family's business, her social circle, her friends. He had his. They'd get together for the next handball tournament, then likely not see each other for several weeks.

But six months—six months with no office to go to, no reason to challenge his mind, someone else handling Baris–Agri and Webster. Nothing but him and Tavia and the constant queries about babies . . . No. He wouldn't—*couldn't*—live like Ethan and Hannah, whose four children had to deal with a drunk, philandering father and a clinging, neurotic mother. All products of a loveless corporate merger termed a marriage.

A sharp trilling broke into his panicked thoughts.

Jonathan pulled out his pocket comm, then frowned at the comm's small screen. "Excuse me." Jonathan rose and headed for the patio. The doors slid open silently when he was a few steps away, then closed just as silently behind him.

Devin focused on his father. "With all due respect, Father, I think Tavia and I should be the ones setting a date for a wedding." *And for everything else.*

J.M. shrugged, but his dark eyes were unwavering. "I'm sure you feel we're rushing you, but there are other things you must consider, things beyond your mother's emotional state." J.M. pushed his breakfast plate away, then folded his hands on the table, pinning Devin with his gaze. "The Embersons have an excellent relationship with Darius Tage. Their very lack of social prominence, as compared to ours, has kept them out of the political realm until recently. Yes, we've had Tage as a houseguest here, but we've also had Mason Falkner. Many times. Too many times, I'm sure, for Tage's liking."

Devin willed all emotions from his face and his body. Mason Falkner, onetime Imperial senator from Dafir, was now the new head of the Alliance.

"But Falkner wasn't the Empire's enemy when he was a guest here," Devin pointed out. "And the Alliance will be granted legitimate political status by the council."

"That doesn't matter to a man like Tage. What does matter is that Philip is now under Falkner's command, heading Falkner's fleet. Inferences could be made that the plot to have the Calth and Dafir sectors secede from the Empire were hatched in this very house, because Philip was also here some of the times Falkner was."

So were dozens and dozens of other people. His parents' parties were gala affairs.

The suggestion that a rebellion was planned under this estate's roof was insane, almost paranoid. "I understand what you're getting at, but your solution is illogical. If my marrying an Emberson is an attempt to keep us safe, then why not insist Jonathan and Ethan divorce their wives and we all go seduce Tage's daughters and nieces?" Devin couldn't remember if Tage had any daughters, but chances were excellent the man had nieces. "Then we'd be one big happy family."

Something flashed in J.M.'s eyes. "Your sarcasm is not appreciated."

"I'm sorry, but your plan is flawed. If Tage has made direct threats against us, then not only do I need to know that, but our *security people* need to know that. I sincerely doubt that anything Tage plans will be halted by my being put out to stud to the Embersons. And if—"

His father slammed his hand against the table, rattling dishes and glassware. "Do not take that tone with me, Devin Jonathan!"

Well. His father *could* raise his voice before breakfast. "I'm not trying to upset you, Father. I'm trying to make you see reason. If the situation is—"

The patio doors slid open as Jonathan's voice—harsh, frightened—broke into the room. "That was Rallman. Halsey's dead. Rallman found his body when he came on duty. Campus security's on it. But they can't find—Trip's not in his apartment or anywhere on the Montgomery campus."

Devin stared. Jonathan's words and expression were so unexpected—so full of emotions—he couldn't quite process them. Beside him, J.M. stiffened, his hands clenching into fists.

Jonathan strode to the table and grasped the back of his empty chair, his face pale, his knuckles white. "I can't believe I'm saying this. My son's bodyguard has been murdered. And my son is missing." His voice cracked. "*How in hell* am I going to tell Marguerite?"

Devin, seated at the main deskcomp in his father's elegant study, was in problem-solving mode. It was something he excelled at. He had Guthrie security personnel and private bodyguards on high alert, electronic surveillance across the estate's palatial grounds in full sensor sweep, the house in lockdown, and the family physician on the way. His mother took the news of her grandson's disappearance and bodyguard Ben Halsey's death with frightening stoicism, the trembling of her hands as she clutched them in her lap the only outward sign of her distress.

Marguerite Petroski Guthrie collapsed, sobbing uncontrollably. Jonathan carried her to his old suite, which was where he was now, while Devin worked with single-minded efficiency, confirming the status of the rest of the family, especially Trip's siblings at their exclusive private school.

Thana and Max—Trip's younger sister and brother—were quietly whisked out of class by their bodyguards. The current question was whether to hold them in their own Port Palmero home or to bring them here, to the main Guthrie estate.

"Here," Devin told Petra Frederick, GGS's chief of security. Devin felt they needed to be with their mother, not sitting isolated and confused with only armed escorts to talk to. And their mother and father definitely needed to see them.

Not all Guthrie marriages were like Ethan's. Jonathan's demeanor might be aloof, but Devin never doubted his brother loved Marguerite and their children. His brother's barely concealed terror in the breakfast room wasn't feigned.

Guthrie men, when they loved, loved deeply. They were just horribly inept at showing it.

Petra Frederick nodded. "I'll have them on property in a half hour, Mr. Devin."

He signed off, turning his attention to Ethan, Hannah, and their children, confirming their locations with their personal security. From there, aunts, uncles, and cousins were alerted. And all GGS offices in Aldan and Baris.

A less specific message, with perfunctory regrets, was sent to the Embersons, as well as to Tavia's personal pocket comm: *Family emergency requires delay of your visit*. The Embersons didn't need to know details at this point.

Devin didn't need to add more people in the line of fire.

It hadn't escaped him that Trip's disappearance might be only the beginning of someone's move against them—corporately, politically, or both. He didn't share his father's paranoia, but threats had been made, even before Philip changed allegiances.

He also knew Ben Halsey wasn't one to go down without a fight. A burly man in his late fifties, Halsey was ex-ImpSec—and Imperial Security Forces had a well-earned reputation for excellence and ruthlessness. For someone to get a jump on him...Devin could only liken it to a handball match where an unassuming and unknown player suddenly decimates a known athlete with years of experience.

He needed to see Rallman's log and the Aldan Prime police reports. And he needed the holos of Trip's apartment at Montgomery. The answers to all the questions would be there.

Halsey was tough, experienced, but Jonathan Macy Guthrie III was no idiot. Trip had made a point of studying every combat holo then-Captain Philip Guthrie ever authored. Philip was more than the ship driver he often joked he was. He'd graduated top of his class in the academy and he was an acknowledged authority in several forms of combat and tactical reconnaissance. When Devin was Trip's age, Philip—ten years his senior and already a respected Fleet officer—had put him through a grueling boot-camp survival course on one of the Guthrie game preserves on Sylvadae. They'd both done the same thing for Trip, just last year.

Devin didn't have Philip's love of weapons, but he could handle a high-powered Carver laser pistol. So could Trip.

J.M. tried to protect the Guthrie clan through fortuitous marriages. Philip did so by teaching Guthrie boys how to survive. And, if necessary, kill.

If someone had come after Trip, Trip would have fought back; Devin had no doubt of that. So he needed to see the police holos. He needed to follow the trail of blood.

Kaidee threaded her way through the noisy crowd packed in Trouble's Brewing, looking for a seat at the bar. Hell, she'd be satisfied to even *see* the bar. The throng was easily four deep, in various shades of gray, dark blue, and green—all standard freighter-crew uniform colors. She waved to three gray-suited crew from the long-hauler *Wiznalarit*. Another few steps and she nodded at more familiar faces, including Corrina and Rae from the *Solarian Wolf*, and received raised ale

mugs in a silent toast. Tables in the popular pub on
Dock Five's Blue Level were packed, with patrons sitting on armrests, laps, anything.

Trouble was, it wasn't just Trouble's Brewing.

Dock Five was packed, with about every bay or
berth taken. Even the regular shuttle and passenger
transport docks were filled with cargo ships, captains
moving their freighters only to allow the next transport to unload or retrieve passengers.

As soon as the passenger transport departed, the
captains moved their freighters back into the dock
again.

No one she knew was out in the lanes.

Six hours ago, Tage had added another destroyer at
Dock Five's outer beacon and shut the lanes down—
again—to all traffic other than scheduled passenger
transports and the Imperial Fleet. Even the jumpgates
were blockaded.

So freighter captains and crew did the only thing
they could do when there was no work: they drank.
And Trouble's Brewing always had a more-than-
decent supply of ale, because it maintained a small
brewing facility in its kitchen.

But if Trouble's ran out of grain, real troubles
would begin. She could almost feel an undercurrent of
tension, ready to explode.

"Kaid! Makaiden Griggs! Over here!"

Kaidee turned at the sound of her name, recognizing the voice of the bald-headed, pale-skinned older
man whose hand splayed in the air. His brown coveralls bore the glowing-wrench logo of Popovitch Expert
Repair Service. She dodged a 'droid server with two
trays full of dirty glasses and headed for the corner
table where Pops, his office manager/daughter Ilsa,
and his repair techs often lounged.

Garvey—she didn't know his first name—was leaning over the back of a chair that was empty except for
one of Pops's scuffed boots. Next to him was Aries
Pan, a tech Pops had hired a few weeks back. A small
screwdriver tucked behind her right ear held her pink
and purple hair back from her face. She smiled as
Kaidee approached, her face impish yet intelligent.

"Need a seat?" Pops asked, motioning to the
bearded dark-haired tech. "Garvey was just leaving."

"Don't mean to put you out," Kaidee said to Garvey, as she returned Aries's smile.

Garvey wiggled his thick eyebrows. "Meeting up
with my little honey. It's yours, Captain Griggs."

"And he'll come back covered with love bruises and
a happy twinkle in his eye," Aries drawled teasingly.

Chuckles sounded around the table. Garvey looked
sheepish.

Kaidee nodded her thanks. "You could have probably sold this seat and made some money."

Pops dropped his foot from the chair to the decking
as Garvey disappeared into the crowd. "We're all
going to be needing a new business before long, if Tage
don't let up."

That was the truth. Kaidee liked Pops. She'd known
of his repair facility for more than a decade but had
dealt with him for only about a year now. Which
meant she didn't know him well enough to dump her
troubles on him. She snagged a bottle of ale from a
passing 'droid server, dropping a credit chip in the slot
in its left arm, and tried to focus on something other
than her personal problems. "You mean that with all
these ships on dock, Pops's Repairs doesn't have a cap-
tive audience?"

"With no one moving goods, no one's getting paid.

Which means captains don't want to spend money they don't have."

She understood that only too well. "They have to open the lanes soon." Real soon. She didn't want to see Frinks on her rampway again.

"Tomorrow." Pops looked around the table with a snort. "Isn't that what we hear every few hours? Lanes'll be open tomorrow."

Kaidee had heard the same line. Last time Tage pulled this, it had been almost a shipweek of tomorrows. And a shipweek would create serious trouble for her.

"Or we'll all starve to death, eventually," Ilsa was saying, leaning against a sandy-haired man's shoulder. Ilsa was about Kaidee's own age, the man perhaps a little younger. His hair was pulled back in a long tail, which he had draped over the other shoulder. She'd seen him in Pops's place before but didn't know his name. And he didn't wear tech coveralls but a spacer's black leather jacket.

She gathered from Ilsa's posture that this was her current lover.

"You'll have riots here before that," the man said. "Heard Trel's had a big bar fight. Stripers had to fire-hose the place to stop it. Next time they'll probably use gas."

Aries nodded. "No one in Aldan would cry big tears if we all got spaced or Dock Five imploded."

Aldan was the central hub of the Empire, with worlds like Sylvadae, Garno, and Aldan Prime, whose wealthy denizens would, no, not miss Dock Five at all. It had been a gathering place for pirates, mercenaries, and other ask-me-no-questions types for centuries, back when the Empire was just Aldan, Calth was first being colonized, and Baris sector was some unpronounceable Stolorth name.

Dock Five was also home to a lot of hardworking traders and spacers and ships that did the backbreaking runs the larger shipping companies had no interest in doing. So it was a place where a lot of careers started—and a place where many of them died.

Kaidee wasn't sure right now which end of the spectrum she was on. But if Frinks had his way, it would be the latter.

"We're not the only ones the Baris blockades have locked in," she said, after taking a swig of ale from her bottle. It was icy cold and had a bittersweet tang that suited her current mood perfectly. "There's Starport Six—"

"Which houses a military base, so they're getting supplies," Ilsa's lover said. "Lots of 'em, now that Corsau Station's gone over to the Alliance."

Corsau? She hadn't heard. That had long been an active and prosperous station on the opposite end of the B–C. She'd been there dozens of times. No wonder Tage was angry. "When?"

"Shipweek ago, maybe less," Pops put in. "Depending on which source you hear it from."

Aries turned her near-empty bottle in her hands. "I heard the Empire took it back again, but I think that's just what they want us to believe."

"Like I said, depends who you hear it from." Pops leaned forward, dropping his voice. "Right now I trust this new Alliance a hell of a lot more than I do our crazy emperor and his flunky. And sources I know *and* trust say Corsau joined up with Kirro, Umoran and the starports in Calth sector, and the rest of Dafir. Tage can't risk losing more of Baris sector."

"And locking us in helps him how?" Aries grumbled.

"The new Alliance has Ferrin's *and* the shipyards there," Ilsa said, with a vague motion of one hand, indicating something beyond Dock Five's hull. "That puts the Alliance in the position to build more ships and then move into Baris from both ends of Calth." She looked at her father. "Ain't that right, Pops?"

Pops sighed. "Sounds like you been listening in to my office when you were supposed to be working, girl."

Ilsa shrugged, then laughed lightly. "And you just figured that out?"

"Just watch what you say and who you say it to."

Another shrug. "Can they really expect we'll all sit here, happy as you please, without bitching? Without wondering what's going on?"

"My feeling is they're looking for certain people. And they're listening to the bitching to find out where those certain people are."

Kaidee could almost hear her father's voice: *Time to run, girl.* Except the Empire had found him and killed him almost a year ago. No, this was some new project of Tage's.

Maybe that was why Frinks was suddenly pressuring her for the rest of Kiler's debt. Orvis was smarmy enough to work for Tage as an agent. Kiler had probably blabbed about his "close personal contact" with the Guthries. It wouldn't be hard for someone like Orvis to check that out, to verify that they'd flown for GGS for five years.

But that didn't mean she had Philip Guthrie in her cargo hold and Guthrie funds in her account.

You're hallucinating, Kaid. This has nothing to do, personally, with you or your family. And the Empire knows exactly where Admiral Philip Guthrie is: in command of some Alliance warship that kicked the shit out of an Imperial cruiser out by the C-6 jump-gate. Or so she'd heard about a shipmonth ago.

So who did the Empire want badly enough to damned near bring Baris sector to a halt? Kaidee had a feeling Pops knew, but she wasn't about to ask him. The last thing she needed was to get involved with volatile Imperial politics. She had enough problems on her own.

She had to come up with thirteen thousand credits—and fast.

They pored over the police reports from Aldan Prime and Montgomery University security for the better part of two hours. Ethan even dug out vids of his and Hannah's visit to Trip's apartment only two weeks ago and painstakingly went over every scene of every room, comparing it to the police images, looking for something the police might have missed. They came up with nothing.

They viewed Rallman's logs, again, in detail. "Professionals," Jonathan said, as Ethan nodded in agreement. "It was done quickly, neatly."

Neatly, yes. But other than that, the data made no damned sense at all.

Devin scrubbed at his face with both hands, then slipped his glasses back on. "I'm not ruling out that Tage may have had Halsey killed," he said, leaning his elbows on his knees as he sat in the high-backed leather library chair near the polished gray stone fireplace. Jonathan, eyes still shadowed with worry, was in the matching chair on the other side. J.M. looked pale, his mouth pinched as he sat behind his large, ornately carved desk. Ethan lounged tiredly—one leg propped up on the sofa table—on a nail-studded couch catercorner to the desk.

Hannah was upstairs with Marguerite, Valerie, and the children.

A half dozen armed security personnel were milling about the house, their footsteps and occasional low conversations drifting into the library.

"But I have a hard time believing," Devin continued, "that kidnappers would have cleaned Trip's apartment, packed his duffel and his bookpad, but left his deskcomp behind. And where's his pocket comm? Why would they leave him with a means to contact us?"

"Stop playing detective, D.J.," Ethan drawled. He was the only one who called Devin that, and he knew Devin hated it. But everyone was strained, nerves taut. That was just Ethan's way of showing his frustration. "The police are trained for that kind of thing. You're not."

Devin shook his head and looked at Ethan. His brother's dark hair was tinged with gold from the sun, his face tanned from the hours he spent sailing. But all the fresh air and sunshine hadn't been able to remove the dark circles under Ethan's eyes, the result of hours of drinking. And—Devin often suspected—possibly worse. His brother was in no shape to handle this kind of stress from his family. "It has nothing to do with playing detective. It has to do with logic."

"People don't become criminals because they have an excess of logic."

"If they were criminals, Ethan, they would have taken Trip's vidcams, comps, everything. Nothing that happened there bespeaks a lower criminal element."

Ethan snorted. "Bespeaks?"

That rewarded Ethan with a slanted glance from his father. Ethan shrugged and fell back against the couch cushions. There were six years between Ethan and Devin, so for six years Ethan had been the baby of the family. Devin's arrival didn't seem to change that. If anything, it made it worse. Or so Devin had heard the servants whisper more than once.

But this wasn't sibling rivalry. This was something no Guthrie did well: feeling helpless. Ethan just did it worse than the rest of them.

"Explain to me why there's no sign of a struggle in the apartment," Devin asked again.

"To throw us off," Jonathan said grimly.

"But if they wanted to cover the kidnapping by making it look as if Trip ran away, then why leave Halsey's body behind? If they had time to get a cleaning crew in Trip's apartment, they had time to get someone to dispose of Halsey's body. Any other explanation is illogical."

"Tage wants Philip, badly." J.M.'s voice was tight. "That kind of hatred can make a man do illogical things."

Just as the horror over Halsey's death and Trip's disappearance was making Devin's father and brothers jump to illogical conclusions. "Tage doesn't kill people himself, Father. He farms that out to his ranks of ImpSec assassins. And ImpSec wouldn't be that sloppy."

Ethan waved one hand dismissively. "So you're an expert on ImpSec now?"

That earned him another warning glance, this time from Jonathan. "Try contributing instead of complaining."

"I'm not complaining. I'm as upset as the rest of you are." Ethan's voice rose to an almost petulant

whine. "Just because I don't have all the degrees you
and Devin have doesn't mean I'm stupid. Neither is
Father. We're Guthries. We have money. Lots of it.
And people who want that try kidnapping. All the
time." Ethan switched a look from Jonathan to J.M..
"You know that's true. There've been kidnap threats
against us before."

Devin opened his hands in a helpless gesture. "Kidnappers work against time and discovery. They're not
going to let a kid pack his duffel and his bookpad. It
would be of no use to them."

But it would be of use to Trip. That was something
Devin thought of as soon as he saw the police reports.
Trip never went anywhere without his bookpad,
which held his prized collection of Philip's training
manuals.

Ethan sat up straighter. "Kidnappers plan—"

"Father, Uncle Devin's right."

Startled, Devin glanced to his right. Sixteen-year-
old Thana stood in the library's wide doorway, a large,
long-furred black-and-white cat in her arms. Cosmo,
Devin remembered. Petra Frederick had evidently let the
children stop home long enough to retrieve Cosmo—
a source of comfort—but not to change their clothes.
Thana was still in the dark-blue pants and white tunic
that comprised her school uniform, her long dark hair
pulled back and tied with a white ribbon. "Trip takes
his bookpad everywhere." Her voice wavered slightly.
She sucked in a breath. "Not only because it has his
class work. It has all of Uncle Philip's stuff. If someone
kidnapped *him*...well, he'd make sure that was left
behind. Because then we'd know he really didn't want
to leave. *I'd* know." She held her father's gaze for a
moment, then looked at Devin. "He cried a lot when
we heard Uncle Philip was dead. I told him he should

talk to you or to Father, but he...he said no. He said...," and she hesitated, her desire to find her brother clearly warring with her desire to protect him.

"I know you're worried about Trippy." Devin prompted her as gently as he could. "I am too. But if you know anything that might help—"

"He said he was gonna join the Alliance and help them kill Prime Commander Tage," twelve-year-old Max said, stepping into the open doorway. Like Thana, he was in blue pants and a white tunic. But his dark curly hair was mussed.

"Maxwell Macy!" Jonathan shot to his feet. "If your brother was talking such nonsense, I should have been told. Immediately."

Max dropped his gaze to the carpet under his shoes. "I know. I'm sorry."

Devin stared at Max, then at Thana, seeing—*feeling*—their fear. And not of their father but for their brother's safety. Jonathan was stern, but he was fair. And, in rare moments, he could even be kind.

But Max and Thana, who knew Trippy better than anyone, were afraid. So was Jonathan. So was Devin. Trippy *had* spoken to him about Philip's reported death, but Devin hadn't taken the young man's rantings against Tage seriously. More than half the Empire was ranting about the new prime commander lately.

Jonathan looked at his daughter. "He told you this as well, Thana?"

"Something like that."

"Something?" Jonathan's voice rose as he stepped toward his daughter. She lowered her face into Cosmo's thick fur, cradling the cat more tightly against her. "Your brother's missing and all you can remember is 'something'?"

"That's because they're lying." Ethan cut in, his voice hard and angry. "They just want the attention—"

"That's not true, Uncle Ethan!" Max's hands fisted at his side.

"Enough." A deep voice that hadn't lost its firmness or ability to issue orders in almost eighty years halted them all in their tracks. J.M. splayed his large hands on his desktop. "Yelling and unconfirmed suppositions are unproductive," he said to Jonathan. He nodded at his grandchildren. "Thana, Max, please go to the kitchen and tell Audra we'd like some coffee brought to the library. Ethan." He pinned his third son with a meaningful glare. "Go see if your mother needs anything."

Thana let Cosmo slip to the carpet then turned, grabbing Max's shoulder as Ethan shoved himself off the couch. The cat on their heels, the children hurried away from the doorway, obviously glad to have escaped their father's wrath. Ethan followed, but not without one final glance back into the library, peevishness clear in the tight lines of his face.

"Sit down, Jonathan," J.M. ordered. Then, as Jonathan returned to his seat: "I understand exactly what happened now. If your son did in fact have some wild idea to harm Darius Tage, it stands to reason Imperial Security would have taken him into custody. It also stands to reason we will be hearing from them or Tage's office shortly. We will, of course, get our barristers working on the case immediately."

"But why kill Halsey?" Devin persisted. "Halsey wouldn't have stood in the way of a legitimate arrest warrant. And why remove Trip's bookpad?"

"Evidence, of course." Jonathan's tone was as hard as his father's was earlier.

"But they didn't take his deskcomp. Any research

Trip did—and I'm assuming we're all now thinking he hacked into plans for the palace or schematics for Tage's personal transport—would have to go through his deskcomp first. He could download things onto his bookpad, but how and where and when he acquired them would reside on his deskcomp."

"Maybe he erased them," Jonathan said.

"Trippy doesn't know how to permanently erase data. I would know if he did." If there was one thing Devin Guthrie knew, it was data. Data, computers, numbers. "ImpSec could recover erased data. If they believed Trip was involved in something subversive, they wouldn't leave a deskcomp behind."

J.M. dismissed Devin's argument with a sharp wave of his hand. "They probably have some specialist retrieving his deskcomp. They're not going to lug that and my grandson out the door at the same time."

No, but they had time to bring in a cleaning crew. The illogic of it all made Devin's stomach twist into a knot. He pulled his glasses off again and rubbed his eyes with the heels of his hands.

"You really should get your eyes fixed," Jonathan intoned. "It's a simple five-minute—"

A soft double knock halted his brother's relentless recommendation for eye surgery. The pungent, nutty aroma of coffee drifted into the room. Devin peered over his hands, expecting Audra's short, rotund form in the wide doorway but seeing Barthol's lanky one instead.

"Coffee, sirs?" Barthol asked as Devin straightened.

Devin glanced at his watch. It was almost one-thirty in the afternoon, seven hours since the discovery of Trip's disappearance. Twelve hours since Halsey's death. That had to mean Trip left to "join the Alliance"—he could still hear the excitement in Max's voice—twelve or so hours ago.

Ben Halsey's death was a separate incident. And J.M.'s and Jonathan's refusal to see that put Trip in increasing danger. Because Devin couldn't discount that whoever killed Halsey *was* after Jonathan Macy Guthrie III—and was likely still after him. And had a twelve-hour head start.

Obedience warred with responsibility, loyalty with protection.

There was Baris–Agri. The Galenth Fund. His parents...

And his nineteen-year-old nephew, with no idea that a killer was tracking him.

Devin shoved himself to his feet as Barthol placed the coffee tray on the low sofa table. "None for me."

His father's voice stopped him at the library's doors. "Where are you going?"

He turned slightly, as if not fully facing his father could somehow buffer the wrath he knew would come. "To find Trip. Somewhere between here and Calth sector."

"Devin Jonathan! You can't be serious—"

"I am. You can sit here and wait for Tage to contact you, but every minute you do is one more minute Trip is out there, chasing this crazy scheme of his, with whoever killed Halsey right on his tail."

His father's eyes narrowed. "I will not have you use this as an excuse to run out on your obligations."

Excuse? Obligations? "You already have Nathanson and Torry handling my projects—"

"And your wedding?"

Devin stared hard at his father. "I think Trip's life is more important."

"Our barristers will handle his arrest. Your job is to marry the Embersons' daughter."

His job. The ludicrousness of it almost made him laugh out loud. His job—the youngest, least important Guthrie son's *job*—was to be put out to stud to a social-climbing Garno family, while the next Guthrie heir's life was in danger.

He raised his chin and said a word he had never before uttered to his father. "No."

His father's lips thinned. "Devin Jonathan Guthrie, how dare you defy me!"

"I'll need the *Prosperity*. I assume she's fueled and we have a pilot available? That will get me there quicker." He wasn't one hundred percent sure where "there" was, but based on conversations he'd had with Trippy right after the erroneous news of Philip's death was released, he had a strong suspicion Trippy was heading for the border of Aldan and Baris sectors.

His father glanced at Jonathan. "Alert our pilots. Devin is banned from using any Guthrie stellar transport until I say otherwise. And you," his father said, turning back to Devin, "will stay here. And do as you're told."

Small tendrils of hot anger coiled beneath Devin's skin. It was an unfamiliar and uncomfortable feeling. He tried to tamp the anger down, but some escaped, adding a bitter note to his answer. "No. I will not."

He swiveled abruptly away and, ignoring his father's command to return to the library, headed doggedly across the grand salon for the closest set of elevators and his suite, his fists clenched so tightly by his side that his arms shook.

Devin was sealing his duffel when a soft rapping sounded on his door. He left the suitcase on his bed, then crossed his small living room, his footsteps hard even against the plush carpeting. Shoulders tensed, he yanked the door open, expecting Jonathan or Ethan. Or even Valerie, because he wouldn't put it past J.M. to use a mother's tears to try to stop him.

But it was Barthol, alone in the hallway.

"May I come in, Mr. Devin?"

"If my father sent you—"

"He didn't."

Devin stepped back warily, noticing a black box tucked under the chief steward's arm.

"I thought you might need this," Barthol said, as Devin closed the door behind him. He held out the box.

Devin took it, recognizing what it contained as Barthol named it: "It's a Carver-Twelve. Admiral Guthrie gave it to me."

"Philip gave me one too."

"But I doubt you brought it. And if you're going to catch up to Master Trip, you're not going to have time to stop at your residence in Garno to get it."

Surprise and relief surged through Devin. "You don't believe Tage has him either."

Barthol stepped by him, hands behind his back, pacing the room as he spoke. "Miss Thana wasn't the only person Master Trip confided in about his concerns for his uncle Philip. And ImpSec would not leave a deskcomp behind. Nor would they be holding a Guthrie for this length of time without contacting Mr. Jonathan or your father. It's simply not the way we— they—operate." He turned to face Devin.

Devin didn't miss the deliberate correction from *we* to *they*. "You were with Imperial Security?" That didn't totally surprise him. Many of GGS's security personnel had been. But Barthol?

"Yes and no. My division was Special Protection Service: SPS."

That surprised him. "Executive protection and political assassinations."

"Yes."

Devin's eyes narrowed. "Are you working for Tage or for my father?"

A corner of Barthol's wide mouth quirked up. "Barrister Tage lost my allegiance years ago. The man is a dangerous and despotic megalomaniac. As for your father, more than twenty years ago I took an oath to protect the Guthrie family. It's one I still follow—your father's firing of me ten minutes ago notwithstanding."

"He—"

"Also banned me from GGS transports. However, I took the liberty of booking passage for two on a commercial flight that leaves the spaceport in one hour fifteen minutes. We have not been banned—yet—from any of the ground vehicles. If you pack a duffel now, we may well make it to the spaceport before your father realizes that oversight."

"Barty . . ." Devin hadn't called the man that since he was a child. "I'm appreciative. Touched, honestly. But do you have any idea of what we could be getting into here?"

Barthol adjusted his jacket, which, Devin realized, was black with a black shirt underneath—not his uniform. The edge of a shoulder holster peeked out. He acknowledged Devin's appraisal with a slight nod. "A lot more than you do, Mr. Devin. Shall we go? We have at least two days of travel ahead of us."

Pops was right. "Tomorrow" was now well into day four. And Frinks's Takan thug had taken to following Kaidee damned near everywhere, as if she didn't realize she had three days left to come up with thirteen thousand credits. She refused to flinch every time she saw him behind her, but her insides churned like an old sublight drive gone bad. Her appetite was gone. Just as well. Food cost money.

Kaidee considered selling the *Rider*'s prepaid docking bay space, but that would mean she'd have to put the *Rider* somewhere else, and she couldn't drift aimlessly off Dock Five. There were fuel costs and fees associated even with that. She had to breathe air, she had to eat food when her ship's meager stock ran out, and she had to make sure her ship's toilets flushed.

There were also abandoned docking rafts out in the 501, a mined-out asteroid field about a half shipday from Dock Five—if the Imperial grunts let her get that far. There wouldn't be any food, but there might be some power she could filch. If she didn't get raided by pirates first.

You're going to get raided by pirates either way, a small voice warned her. The irony of that didn't escape her.

She damned the fact that Kiler had never renewed the passenger certification for the *Rider*. They'd discussed it, but it took money—a lot of money.

Hauling cargo's a hell of a lot more reliable, he'd

said. *And you don't have to worry if the containers are comfortable.*

No, but a passenger certification would have provided her with an alternate means for an income. *And* a means to be long gone from Dock Five by now.

But she didn't have even the funds to pay Frinks. She was sure, with the current situation on dock, the cost for certification had probably tripled.

She stopped again at the Free-Trader Collective offices and tried not to look desperate.

"We don't know any more than you do, Captain Griggs," the round-faced man at the front desk said. His gray shirt bore the CFTC logo. His pale eyes looked tired. "The lanes open tomorrow. That's all we're told."

But they wouldn't open tomorrow. The Imperial destroyers were still out there. She was still stuck here, along with hundreds of other increasingly unhappy and agitated stationers—many also in financial straits.

But none, as far as she knew, with a hulking eight-foot-tall Taka shadowing them.

Her last chance would be to hop a commercial passenger shuttle to Starport 6. It would mean losing the *Rider,* but, if it came to that, it was honestly better than losing her life. But she was saving that for her very last-chance effort. She'd hate to be on board a shuttle only to see the lanes open and freighters streaming away from Dock Five.

Her ship was all she had left. Even her pride was gone. Hope had fled more than a year ago, with Kiler's death in Port Chalo.

She hit the next—perpetually nonworking—bank of escalators and used them as stairs down to Green Level. Four Englarian clergy—two shorter humans, two taller Takans—in their usual sand-colored robes were in a circle, holding hands, praying a few steps from the base of the stairs. Maybe it was some special religious holiday—she never could keep up with the Englarian ones—or maybe, like everyone else, they just needed answers. She knew the feeling. She hadn't talked to Pops since Trouble's Brewing. She didn't want to bother the man. But she knew he had connections—connections that should scare her.

Still, Frinks and Orvis scared her more.

There was a job board at the other end of Green— hourly odd jobs and daily work. Postings were filled as soon as they came up, but maybe today there'd be something no one else wanted. At this point, providing it didn't require her to remove her clothes or someone else's, she'd do anything. A couple hundred credits wouldn't satisfy Frinks, but it might buy her another day. She needed that day.

The corridors were crowded—they were always crowded—and, as was happening more and more, people in the corridor were arguing. Kaidee slowed her pace, hearing the shouts before she saw the pushing and shoving. She tried to sidestep the problem, but the ring of onlookers was large and growing as some people shouted encouragements, others laughed, and someone actually threaded through the crowd taking bets as to which one of the malcontents would hit the decking first.

The lunatics are running the asylum. She was skimming the bulkhead, looking for a place to squeeze through, when a familiar face caught her attention. A face that shouldn't be on Dock Five—not ever. She blinked, staring. She could be wrong. She had to be wrong.

She wasn't.

What in hell was Trippy Guthrie doing on Dock Five?

She recognized him immediately, even though it had been almost two years since she'd last seen him. He was around seventeen at that time—a friendly, intelligent kid. The young man she stared at now was a little taller, a little more broad-shouldered, but he was definitely Trippy. She'd know the Guthrie good looks anywhere, and Trippy had them by the handful, from his shiny dark hair to his lean, square-jawed face to the long dark lashes that shaded bright-blue eyes.

Plus, with his light-tan suede jacket and what looked like a leather backpack, he was far better dressed than anyone on the docks.

Was one of Guthrie Global's yachts stranded here? There was no other explanation. Because Guthries didn't belong on Dock Five.

She scanned the crowd around Trip, looking for Ben Halsey. If a GGS ship was here, then Halsey would be right on Trip's heels. Or Rallman, if Halsey was sleeping. But she couldn't spot Halsey. She couldn't spot anything that might be GGS security.

A trickle of alarm ran up her spine.

"Trippy!" she called ineffectually through the shouts and jeers. She tried to elbow her way past a knot of drunken spacers, but they pushed back, and for a moment she lost sight of him. She shoved harder, squirming through, and saw him again, because he *was* tall—over six feet, she judged. She picked up her pace, trying to keep up with his long-legged gait as he suddenly moved away from her—or from someone coming after him?

His wide-eyed expression said as much.

Shit. Where in hell was Halsey? Or Rallman? Or whoever was assigned to Trip now?

She flicked the safety off the L7 laser pistol at her side. Something was very wrong.

He turned the corner into a cross corridor and, moments later, so did she, but she slammed against a wall of spacers moving in the opposite direction and had to backtrack and then dodge sideways. By the time she reached a clear spot in the corridor, he was gone.

She spun around, hand still on her pistol. Dark-haired men were common, but there was something about a Guthrie, something in the set of their shoulders, in the straightness of their spines.... It was as if they were hand-fed prowess for breakfast from the time they were born. Even ten-year-old Max had had it. Even *Ethan* had it—though on him, it was a waste. Jonathan, being the eldest, practically oozed it, as did Philip. And Devin... Trippy had his father's mien, but he had his youngest uncle's shy smile and intense, penetrating gaze.

Of all the Guthrie brothers, Devin was the enigma. Part of her might even admit she missed him. The other part of her—the realist, the one who barely survived a fiasco of a marriage to Kiler—would tell her she was clearly out of her mind to even let Devin into her thoughts, let alone her fantasies.

Idiot. This was no fantasy. This held the potential for very real trouble, unless... She scanned the crowd. Not a Guthrie anywhere in sight.

Shit. That was not good news.

She was probably wrong. It probably wasn't Trippy. But she knew it was.

And with Imperial destroyers sitting out there and the likes of Horatio Frinks in here, that fact worried her. She changed direction back to Pops's with more than her own troubles on her mind.

"A luxury star yacht?" Pops looked up from his deskcomp as Kaidee crossed her arms over the high back of the empty chair opposite his desk.

"There can't be that many on Dock Five."

"Actually, there are four or five here regularly—not that you'd know what they are. Most are pirate rigs, heavy-duty conversions."

Actually, she would know what they were, but that wasn't the topic. "No conversion. This would be either a PanGalaxus Splendera or a BGR-750. Or something top of the line like those."

"I don't have access to every ship that makes dock here, Kaid. Just my clients'."

"Don't know why, but somehow I thought you'd hear if there was a Splendera on dock."

Pops sighed, but he was grinning. "I'll take that as a compliment."

"It is."

"The answer's no. I'm sorry. And, yes," he continued, because Kaidee did little to hide her disappointment, "I would tell you. You're good people, and I know you wouldn't be asking if it wasn't important." He glanced back at his screen, then up at her again. "There are two pirate rigs stuck here with the rest of us, but no PanGals or BGRs or anything of that caliber. So." He raised his chin. "Why is it important?"

Kaidee leaned a little more heavily against the back of the chair. Pops trusted her. She had to do the same. "I saw Trippy Guthrie on dock not fifteen minutes ago, and not a GGS bodyguard in sight."

"I get the Guthrie part. Who's Trippy?"

"Jonathan Macy Guthrie the Third. The old man's grandson—*eldest* grandson. Son of the eldest. All that stuff."

Pops let out a low whistle. "How do you know the Guthries?"

"Kiler and I flew for them for five years." Pops's eyebrows shot up into his bald pate as Kaidee continued. "Trip used to like to hang out in the cockpit of the BGR, to get informal flying lessons. He's a good kid. A *real* good kid. He doesn't belong here. And it looked like he was just figuring that out."

"You think he's a runaway?"

Kaidee narrowed her eyes, thinking. "He'd be in his first year at Montgomery University. So, no, I can't see him running away. He'd have too much freedom there, even with his required bodyguards. Granted, he has a strong adventurous streak—he's like Philip Guthrie in that. That's why they put Ben Halsey on him. Halsey's ex-ImpSec and real seasoned."

"You're worried."

Kaidee nodded reluctantly. Like she didn't have enough problems? "Yeah."

"Young men his age often do stupid things."

"Like borrowing one of Grandpa's sailing yachts, loading it with friends and beer, and partying for three days straight? Absolutely. But they don't end up on Dock Five alone."

Pops blew out an exasperated sigh between thinned lips and poked at his compscreen for a few minutes more. "Nothing, Kaid. Sorry. Not a ship that I'd think would be associated with GGS or even a university transport. He must have gotten here by freighter or commercial passenger shuttle."

"Can you, um, access passenger records?"

Pops snorted. "You do have a too-high opinion of my abilities. But if I hear anything, I'll let you know."

She nodded her thanks. She in no way saw herself as the savior of wayward university students, but people had watched after her when she was that age and crazy and had saved her unruly ass more than once. And if there was a problem with Trip's over-domineering family, Kaidee felt fairly sure Trip wouldn't see her as one of the oppressors. She'd get him to tell her what the problem was, and they'd solve it together.

Then she'd deal with the rest of the thirteen thousand credits Frinks wanted.

Maybe Trip would give her a loan. Then again, given the trouble Kiler had caused, maybe not.

She threw one last question at Pops before she left his office: "You have any need of a Welcran data-booster system? Slightly used? Or"—she hesitated, her mind running over how much of her ship she could gut without putting herself in a serious hole—"a Gartol sublight regulator? It's only two months old." It made her sublights run so sweetly, but it could also garner her a couple grand. She still had the older unit. She could reinstall that. And hope it didn't break down again.

"Not right now. But if someone comes asking..." He let his voice trail off, and she could see troubled thoughts clouding his gaze as his eyes narrowed. Yeah, she was broke, and yeah, it was tough admitting that. But Pops wasn't the type to dole out pity.

"You know where to find me. Thanks."

"They'll open the lanes soon, Kaid. Hang in there."

"Working on it," she replied with a halfhearted salute as she turned away. Soon. It was always soon. She just didn't know if soon would be soon enough.

Devin Guthrie had never been to Dock Five.

He'd heard stories—some from the various GGS pilots over the years, and some from Philip—and all had highlighted the aging station's decrepit condition, unsavory denizens, and general air of impending peril. Along with any number of other things that defied identification.

In Devin's estimation—as he and Barty threaded their way through the bedraggled, unkempt stationers and the whirring, blinking, barely functioning servobots filling the corridor on Green Level—the stories paled in comparison to the actual experience.

It wasn't the acrid tang of sweat or the torn and greasy coveralls that made him itch. Dirt didn't bother Devin. Like the rest of his brothers, he loved competitive sports. Handball was his choice, but he'd spent years on basketball courts and ice rinks. He'd taken his spills in the mud and dropped his gloves on and away from the blue line. But even the worst locker room didn't have a fragrance quite like Dock Five.

"The air recyclers," Barthol said, as Devin again raised his hand to his nose, far less discreetly than he thought, "aren't one of Dock Five's strong points."

Neither was the shuttle flight here—a very long two and a half shipdays, even in first class, or what passed for first class on a spaceliner that serviced Dock Five. Devin slept through the six hours in jumpspace, though dreams of a woman with short, tousled pale hair kept intruding. During the time in realspace, he grabbed what data he could from whatever Imperial data beacons' frequencies he could snag with his Rada and tracked Trippy's financial withdrawals—which were all small amounts so as not to raise any alarms.

Except that Devin knew what he was looking for.

Dock Five was where he'd thought Trip would head, anyway, based on his previous conversations with his nephew. Plus, if one wanted to get somewhere illegally, Dock Five—a convenient distance from the Calth and Stol borders—was the most logical port of embarkation in Baris.

Chances were good that whoever was trailing the Guthrie heir knew that too. All Devin could hope was that he and Barthol got to Trippy first.

"It appears accommodations might be a bit difficult to come by with the current trader embargo in effect," Barthol said, glancing at his microcomp as they threaded through the crowd. "My first two hotel queries have come back negative." Barty's microcomp wasn't a Rada like Devin's but a military-issue DRECU. Given Barthol's ImpSec background, Devin suspected Barthol's microcomp might be as sophisticated as his own, but he could never remember what the acronym stood for other than Decode, Reception, and Covert.

Traveling by GGS transport that included the usual elegant cabins would have solved the lodging problem, but they hadn't traveled by GGS transport. That was one of the many Guthrie rules already broken. Devin adjusted the weight of his duffel on his shoulder. Another Guthrie rule to fall by the wayside. He was carrying his own luggage, despite the fact that Barthol wasn't happy about it. "If we find Trip quickly enough, that won't matter."

Barthol shot him a sideways glance. "Do you have any idea how large and convoluted Dock Five is?"

He'd looked over the schematics—and, yes, they were highly irregular—but not yet committed them to memory. "I know it ranges from six to ten levels, all coded by color. And it utilizes numbered corridors in an odd–even sequence. But it's a station, essentially. How many places—"

"Dozens, Mr. Devin. And all are equally within play. Yes, I know you're used to thinking city, region. A station's contained environment seems more manageable. But consider Mr. Ethan's twin girls chasing each other around the main living area of your parents' estate, going in concentric circles—or, in this case, rectangles—each never quite catching up to the other. Then imagine that there's a bank of elevators on either side, so that they're now not only going in continuous rectangles but on different levels. That's not unlike what we have here."

A bark of laughter followed by a high-pitched squeal halted Devin's response. He turned toward the sound and saw a squat, balding man and a taller woman with bright yellow hair leaning against an area of gray bulkheading next to what appeared to be a bar or dining establishment, judging from a flashing menu on the right of the doorway. The woman's pink shirt dangled from her fingers; the man's hands massaged her bare breasts. The woman giggled. Devin, embarrassed by the crude display, looked away.

"Nor can we," Barthol continued, "expect assistance from the local authorities."

The groping man wore brown pants with a stripe down the side and a gun belt. Those facts surfaced in Devin's mind as he followed Barthol down the corridor. Security striper. No, the local authorities seemed to have their hands full.

"At the very least we need a hotel room," Barthol said. "Someplace we can secure. When we find Master Trip, we may not be able to book passage back to Aldan immediately. I would not want to wander these corridors with him until transport becomes available."

They'd be targets, likely more than they were now. Devin didn't miss some of the appraising—as in, *your clothing is worth far more than mine*—glances sent his way. He'd already pulled down the cuff of his sweater to cover his wristwatch. It wasn't that he felt he couldn't defend his person or his property. It was just that he didn't want to be in a position where he had to do so.

A soft pinging sound came from Barthol's DRECU. "Ah, good," Barthol said after a moment. "We've acquired rooms. One level up on Blue. If memory serves me, there should be an escalator around the corner here . . . Well. Something of one."

It was an escalator, Devin noted. Only it no longer moved, and more than a few stair treads were missing. People hurried up and down it anyway—human people and nonhuman people. Tall, furred Takans in grimy coveralls. Almost as tall bluish-skinned Stolorths in nondescript shipsuits.

GGS had been considering a trade deal with a respected Stolorth merchant clan as recently as four months ago. Devin exchanged messages with their senior financial officer. But he couldn't remember the last time he was in the same vicinity as a live Stolorth— no, he could. He was twelve years old and felt distinctly queasy upon realizing the imposing woman's neck was ringed with gills and her fingers connected with webbing. The fact that she was his aunt's friend and colleague at the university did little to reassure him. When he was twelve, his aunt Pelagia—Dr. Pelagia Lang Javeiro, head of his family's multisentient Harmony-One Project—had the ability to disconcert him too.

He'd thought he'd outgrown that. But as he approached Dock Five's version of an escalator, a female Taka in dockworker's coveralls leered down at him, her thin smile revealing a row of sharp, pointed, and very stained teeth.

Devin tightened his grip on his duffel. Maybe not. "Lead the way," he said, with far more enthusiasm than he felt.

What little enthusiasm he had left died when he saw the entrance to the hotel, which could easily be mistaken for a cargo bay, in Devin's estimation. In fact, as he stood before it, inspecting the wide double doors and the triple-thick plating over which *The Celestian* was stenciled in three Imperial languages, it looked— and smelled in an oily, musty way—as if it had at one time been a cargo bay.

Wonderful.

An antigrav pallet loaded with small duro-hards blocked their way. The pallet was malfunctioning, a painful whirring noise coming from underneath as two human workers—dockworkers or hotel employees, Devin didn't know—pushed and pulled on the pallet's arched handles.

"Goddamned slag-headed piece of shit!" the taller worker rasped loudly.

"The primary differential regulator's jammed," Devin said, stepping closer, recognizing the pitch of an AG unit in distress. "It—"

"You here to fix it?" The frizzy-haired woman on the other side of the pallet barked out the question.

"No, but I—"

"Then get the hell out of the way." She lifted her chin toward the man. "Sergey, push!"

"Mr. Devin." Barthol touched his shoulder. "It's probably best if you don't—"

The high whine of laser fire interrupted Barthol's words. Devin jerked around as a scream sounded somewhere behind him, back in the direction of the escalator. A few people reversed course, heading for the commotion, but most kept walking away, intent on their own business and not interested in anyone else's.

"Don't," Barthol repeated, his grip tightening on Devin's shoulder.

Devin shrugged him off. Any commotion could potentially center on Trippy—or draw his nephew's interest, just as it drew his own. "I'll be right back." He strode forward, breaking into a trot as a knot of stationers near the top of the escalator came into view. There were voices, hard shouts, and someone speaking rapidly in a clipped, odd-sounding language. A Stolorth male and two Takan women stood heads above the rest of the crowd, the Stolorth hanging back, the Takans—in dockworker brown coveralls—pressing forward.

Devin craned his neck, scanning the crowd, hoping to see his nephew's dark head but also discerning the crowd's focus. He didn't see Trip, and almost everyone was glancing down. Except for a staggering, wrinkle-faced man who, as Devin watched, tried to slip his long fingers into the back pocket of a shorter man's sagging coveralls.

The short guy spun. "Hey!" He grabbed the old man's arm. A creased green wallet fell to the decking, and now there was a new commotion—new shouting, new shoving and pushing.

Devin sidled his way through the raucous crowd until he leaned against the metal railing overlooking the open area around the escalator. Two stripers stood on either side of the body of a red-haired woman who was sprawled facedown, her left arm bent at an angle human arms didn't bend. A third striper was locking cuffs on another woman, whose short black hair held a wide streak of white on the left. Both women were in what appeared to be black leathers—typical spacer attire. A battered cylindrical security servobot circled the scene's perimeter about four feet off the decking, orange warning lights flashing around its middle.

"Looks like Nula finally caught up with Gudrin," the man standing next to Devin told the woman on his left.

"Drugs or weapons?" the woman asked.

The man shrugged. "Probably both. Or could be gambling again. Nula's done work for Orvis before."

The woman said something low and harsh that Devin couldn't hear, then the pair moved away.

Barthol took their place. "Any sign of Master Trip?"

Devin shook his head.

"Chances are good," Barthol said, dropping his voice, "that whoever is after him will not chance a public confrontation. Master Trip is not like them." He jerked his chin to the scene below. "People here know who belongs here and who doesn't. In that lies one of our best chances of finding him."

"We don't belong here either."

"In that lies one of our biggest problems." He touched Devin's arm. "We should return to the hotel now, before the price for accommodations climbs any higher. Or before that rather unsavory fellow leaning against the pylon—no, please don't look—erroneously decides we're easy marks and tries to relieve us of our duffels. I believe this area has had enough excitement for one day."

Devin had a feeling the kind of excitement he'd just witnessed happened more than once a day on Dock Five. He followed Barthol. It was time to check Trip's accounts again and try to pin down where his nephew was accessing his money. That would mean hacking into the bank's datagrids—something he'd never done.

But he had designed security programs to prevent exactly what it was he would attempt to do, so all he had to do was outsmart someone like himself. And pray that someone smarter than he was wasn't watching.

As she moved around the edges of the crowd gathered at the escalator, Kaidee caught a glimpse of the morgue personnel in their light-blue biohaz suits, sealing the shiny black body bag around Gudrin's corpse. A chill ran up her spine like a warning. She didn't know Gudrin Vere personally, but she'd heard of the itinerant navigator—and her gambling problem—only because any mention of that kind of thing caught her attention these days. She didn't know Nula either. At least, she didn't know the name. Not everyone on Dock Five used their real name, though, and as the reported shooter was no longer on the scene, Kaidee didn't know if her face might be familiar. But Kaidee heard enough in the conversations around her to note that Frinks's and Orvis's names were mentioned along with Gudrin's and Nula's.

That made her close her fingers around her L7 and quicken her pace past the crowd, including a pair of robed Englarian nuns whose heads were bowed in prayer—for the dead, she guessed with fair accuracy. The Englarians had been busy lately. Orvis was collecting his debts, and she could feel her name rapidly inching its way to the top of his list. It made her palms sweat and the back of her neck prickle.

And made her rethink the wisdom of trying to find Trip Guthrie. Being associated with Captain Makaiden

Griggs, ex-wife of Captain Kiler Griggs, might not be the safest option for him at the moment.

Better she get back to the *Rider* and see what else she could sell. A galley table and chairs, maybe. They were in decent condition and deck-locked with only a latch system, not bolted. She loved the small over-stuffed couch in the captain's cabin, but, hell, maybe she could get a few hundred for it.

After a quick check over her shoulder to be sure her Takan shadow wasn't following, she cut down a side service alley. At its end was a set of lesser-used stairs that led to freighter docks two levels down on Orange.

Two human women in yellow shipsuits were lean-ing against the bulkhead by an open office door, talk-ing and laughing. They glanced disinterestedly as she passed, their voices fading as a coverall-clad balding man and a wheezing AG pallet approached.

Kaidee sidestepped out of the way, her mind refus-ing to let go of the problem of Trip Guthrie. She could at least send his father a transmit that she'd seen the kid on dock. She still had Jonathan Guthrie's office comm code. Devin Guthrie's too—somewhere. If not, there was always the main GGS office comm code. She could leave a message—

A loud thud, then another, then a hard grunt slowed her steps. A fight in a cross corridor just before the stairwell, or another of Orvis's henchmen doing his job? She palmed her L7, flicking it to low stun as more grunts and thuds echoed. She'd make a dash for the stairwell doorway but at least be able to counter any-thing that might come her way—without incurring a fine if she had to defend herself. Stripers let you off with a warning if you zapped someone with low stun. Full stun meant fines and jailtime.

If that's Orvis, it might almost be worth it.

She bolted through the intersection, skittering to a halt at the last moment—heart leaping to her throat—because she saw Trip Guthrie and he saw her. Just as he delivered one hell of a good punch to some bearded guy's face.

Fuzz-face staggered back, slamming against the bulkhead. But Fuzz-face had a friend—big and bald—who even now reached for Trip's shoulder.

She fired the L7.

"Trippy!" she called, as the guy next to him hit the decking like a bucket of bricks in max-G. Even low stun put you flat out, though not for long.

"Captain?" Trip's blue eyes were wide in surprise. A thin trail of blood leaked from his nose. He swayed slightly.

She lunged the three steps it took to reach him, grabbed his wrist, and tugged. "This way!" Fuzz-face was straightening, shaking his head, reaching for a pistol holstered to his thigh.... But there was another sound coming closer. Boot steps. Stripers or backup, she didn't know. Either was big trouble, and with a dazed, bleeding kid by her side, she didn't want to wait around to find out.

"Now!" she yelled, jerking harder on his arm. That got him moving as the boot steps pounded louder.

The whine of high-powered laser fire hummed through the air just as she yanked him through the stairwell entrance. Why was it only the good guys who set their weapons to low stun per station regs? She shoved Trip ahead of her. "Down!" She had to lose their pursuers before heading for her ship.

But judging from the clatter of boots, their pursuers liked *down* too. So she pushed Trip through the stairwell doorway at the next landing and out into the corridor again. They needed someplace busy, a crowd to blend into—a crowd that knew her and would defend her. And she could think of no place busier—and more craving a good bar fight—than Trouble's Brewing.

If they could get there without the kid passing out on her. Or their being shot in the back. Whichever came first.

Kaidee never liked Yellow Level on Dock Five. Years ago, someone had spray-painted *Welcome to Pisstown* on a bulkhead near the main lifts, and though the paint had faded, it was still legible. She didn't need to see the words. The sharp odor from the freighter bay waste-recycling system one deck below engulfed her as she and Trippy Guthrie barreled out of the stairwell and into the corridor.

Trip was coughing as they stepped quickly sideways, almost knocking over a trio of dockworkers.

"Hey!"

"Sorry," she called. *Keep moving. Keep moving.*

Trip coughed again, then dragged his sleeve under his nose, blood staining the tan fabric of his jacket.

"We'll fix that in a minute," she told him. She still had her fingers locked around his wrist, though he was trotting pretty well now, darting through the crowds and around the occasional wobbling servobot as easily as she did. She wanted to move quickly without running. Running attracted all kinds of attention. They needed to blend in, then disappear.

"Keep your head down," she added. His height wasn't an advantage at the moment—not unless she could insert them both into a trio of Takas. But with Frinks's friend on the loose, that held trouble too. A group of Stolorths, maybe...

"This way!" She dragged him abruptly into a side corridor, took the first left, then the next right into a service alley. She had to be careful she didn't double back and run into their pursuers. Dock Five—which had grown out of several enormous mining barges— wasn't unlike a large rectangular maze.

Now, if they could get *behind* their pursuers...

"Any idea who's trying to kill you, Master Trip?"

He snuffled. "Not sure."

Not sure or not willing to admit it? She thought of all the trouble she'd gotten into—and *could have* gotten into—when she was nineteen. Filching kegs of ale and joyriding in station maintenance flitters were the least of it. "You do something to piss off the local stripers? Or," and it sounded crazy but she had to ask, "ImpSec?" Stripers she could likely outsmart. ImpSec would take a lot more work. "Someone after your family's money?"

"Not stripers."

Footsteps banged loudly against the decking behind them. She shot a quick glance over her shoulder. "Shit." Fuzz-face and friends. Running noisily. Attracting attention.

Stationers filled the corridors left and right. She and Trip could play duck-and-hide, but if their pursuers got smart and came at them from opposite sides, they were dead. And so were a lot of other people who just happened to be in Pisstown at the wrong time.

A flash of white light caught her attention. Lifts, off to their left. The blinking light meant a car was arriving. There was a line waiting...

Fuck the line.

"Trip, when I tell you, groan really loud. Like you're going to die, got it?"

"But I'm not—"

"Do it, or you *will* be dead." She shoved him toward the lift banks.

"Got it," he said over his shoulder.

"And don't wipe any more blood away! Lean on me." She snaked her left arm around his waist as if she held him on his feet. "Now!" she said as they neared the end of the line.

"Owww," Trip moaned. "Ohhhh."

"Medical emergency!" Kaidee shouted. "Clear the way!"

"Owww! Ohhhh!"

The line shifted slowly—except one woman, with eyes narrowed. "He don't look like—"

"Body-fluid biohazard!" Kaidee barked at her. "He's got the red scum. Move or—"

The woman jerked back. Trip moaned again, thrashing his head left and right as the lift doors opened.

"Medical emergency! Biohazard!" Kaidee bellowed, glancing over her shoulder. Fuzz-face and two others were at the edge of the corridor, pistols in hands, surging toward her and Trip. The lift emptied quickly. Kaidee pushed Trip inside. "Against the side wall!" she hissed, slapping blindly at the pad to close the doors. He was too big of a target.

Through the slowly closing doors, she saw Fuzz-face elbow an elderly man aside, then claw his way past more people toward the lift. Heart pounding, Kaidee punched the *Close Door* pad again, then jabbed the icons for Violet, Pink, and Black Levels. Anything up, away from here, quickly.

C'mon, c'mon! Close, damn you!

The doors sealed and the lift shuddered, hard. She could hear someone shouting on the other side of the doors, then she and Trip were moving up. Away from Fuzz-face. Relief cascaded through her, forcing Kaidee to drop her hands to her thighs and bend over at the waist. She sucked in gulps of air as she looked up to study Trip, who leaned against the opposite wall, his face pale, blood-streaked. But he was grinning.

"That was full apex, Captain Makaiden! Um, I mean, Captain Griggs."

"That was...?" She shook her head in disbelief as she straightened. "Wipe your face. It's not over yet. We still have a ways to go."

And Jonathan Macy "Trippy" Guthrie III better have a damned good explanation of just what in hell was going on when they got there.

Two lumpy beds with threadbare green coverlets, a narrow black desk, and two matching black metal chairs did not, by any stretch of the imagination, qualify as the "luxury" hotel room promised by the 'droid clerk behind The Celestian's lobby desk. But all Devin cared was that he had a place to work. And this was, if nothing else, that.

Part of him wanted to bolt back out into the grimy corridors of Dock Five and locate Trip. But Barty was right—the place was a maze of cross-connecting corridors, many of which dead-ended without warning because that particular section of the dock had ceased to exist, either from neglect or by accident.

An ore tanker with a drunken captain at the controls could put a fairly large hole in the side of any station, and Dock Five had had more than its share of those.

They needed to define locales and establishments where Trippy had been or was likely to be, based on his credit usage or withdrawals. That meant Devin had to sit in their "luxury" hotel room for now and confine his investigations to dock- and banking-computer pathways via his Rada. Its highly sophisticated sensors poked holes into the local datagrid while its thermal-sensitive holographic screen—an adjunct to the unit's embedded main one—floated in front of Devin's eyes like a square green-tinged cloud.

He was peripherally aware of Barty prowling about the small white-walled room, poking his bald head into the closet, thunking and clunking something around in the lav. He was just as aware when, with a sigh, Barty pulled up the remaining hard-backed chair and sat at the other side of the narrow desk, tapping on his own microcomp.

Then there was silence again, broken only by the breathing of two men working and the occasional grunt or stomach growl. At some point they would need to track down a restaurant that wouldn't fatally poison them. But right now...Devin jerked his hand back from the Rada's holographic screen as a series of numbers flashed in the upper right corner and then was gone. "Shit!"

"Something?" Barty looked up from the DRECU.

"Not something. *Someone*. Someone else is looking at Trip's accounts."

"Someone from GGS security—"

"Not like that. This is someone hacking, like I am." And damn it, he should have expected that. He should have taken more precautions. Or had a trap running for just this situation.

"Did they see you?"

He pulled up two more filters, ran a bit of code that had worked for him in the past. "Not unless they're better than I am."

Barty coughed lightly. "Which means...?"

"Likely not, but we can't rule it out." Damn it, whoever it was was gone now. It could be they saw him. But it could also be that they'd tripped one of the bank's alarms he'd deftly avoided. Either way, he shouldn't hang around. This was part of Dock Five's data pathways. He had no idea of the overall level of security of the system. He had to assume it was less than he'd like and more problematic than he wanted to consider.

He dumped out of the system with a bit less grace than he'd have normally used, but speed at that moment was more important than skill. Getting caught wasn't the issue. Getting flagged was. He didn't want the account locked down and more people watching for intruders.

Mouth pursed, he reviewed the data he was able to save. He could feel Barty watching him, impatience hanging in the air as strongly as the musty metallic odor that he was already associating with Dock Five. But this was not something he could rush, even though he wanted to.

Trip's life hung in the balance. Accuracy was essential. Especially because now Devin had proof that others were tracking the Guthrie heir. He had to locate Trip before they did. He damned the fact that the entries had to be screened chronologically, oldest first, or else the data would skew and he'd lose it all.

And lose the only clues they had to Trip's whereabouts.

"It looks as if he arrived about fourteen hours ago," he said after several minutes of intense focus. "I'm guessing whatever transport he used disembarked him in Orange, because that's where his initial purchases for food and drink were." He brought up a diagram and angled the floating screen so Barty could see it. "I'm not showing any lodging charges. That could indicate he's staying with someone."

"Someone he met in transit?" Barty suggested. "Or

someone who convinced him to leave the university campus—either through persuasion or force?"

"And is using Trip's credit chips to throw us off track? I can't discount that." But he didn't like it; it made his jaw tense and his stomach sour. It also kept him from sending a message to Port Palmero that they'd found Trip. They hadn't. Yet. They'd only found usage of his financial account.

"Did he ever mention associating with any political groups on campus? Blaine's Justice Wardens have had underground meetings there for years."

Devin nodded. "They were there when I was on campus too. But, no, Trip didn't seem to go for that kind of thing."

"Reports of Admiral Guthrie's death could have changed his thinking."

Devin sucked in a slow breath. Reports of Philip's death had changed a lot of things. "He idolizes Philip. And I know he felt Philip believed Blaine and his group are dangerous. Were you in the library when Max said Trippy ran off to join the Alliance? As crazy as it sounds, it makes the most sense."

"Thana and Max told me first. I was the one who suggested they bring that information to their father."

The fact that the children trusted Barthol more than their own parents didn't surprise Devin. He remembered feeling that way when he was younger. Hell, he still felt that way.

"I didn't know," Barthol continued, "if Master Trip gave you any further insight into his feelings."

Devin shook his head. "You know Guthrie men don't discuss feelings," he said absently, moving down the data again as quickly as he safely could. Small expenditures. His nephew hadn't sat down for a meal but was buying small foodstuffs. Eating on the run?

Or just cautious when it came to Dock Five's sanitary procedures? He couldn't blame him if it was the latter. He—

"Wait, we have a small credit transaction seven minutes ago. But, damn it! I lost half that string when I had to dump out."

Barthol stood, leaning over Devin's shoulder. "Blue Corridor Twelve. Tidymart Pro?"

The vendor name made no sense to him either, especially without a more specific location code. "That's all I could get."

"That's enough. Grab your jacket and your Carver. I fear we're not the only ones with that information."

Devin shoved the Carver into his shoulder holster, then snagged his jacket from the bed, praying he and Barty got to Trippy first.

Kaidee waited outside the door to the male-gender lavatory in the far corner of Trouble's Brewing, arms folded across her chest, and endured the disparaging glances from the various males striding by.

The similar facility for female gender was on the other side of the bar. So there was only one reason she'd be on guard here.

"Can't trust him out of your sight, eh?" she heard one brown-suited dockworker say with a snicker.

She smiled wanly in return and played the part of the overpossessive lover, knowing the dockworker had no idea that the center of her impatience was a runaway nineteen-year-old. But, no, she couldn't completely trust Trip to wash the blood off his face and make some attempt to clean the stains from his shirt without doing hell-only-knew what else. Nor could she trust that Fuzz-face and his friends might not have tracked them here—even though she'd pushed Trip out of the lift at Violet Level, then dragged him through two different stairwells to Blue and *then* came into the bar through a service-alley supply-room entrance.

She'd hoped Pops might be at his usual table, sucking down an ale. Hell, she'd have settled for Ilsa. Aries would have been a boon—Trip would have deemed her "apex"—but none was here. Still, she'd make do. There were other faces and ships' patches Kaidee recognized, and she felt more than fairly sure that in a standoff with Fuzz-face, she'd find most of Trouble's Brewing on her side.

She hoped.

Trip emerged, face damp and somewhat ruddy from scrubbing, jacket sleeves pushed haphazardly up—though not enough to hide the water stains trailing to his elbow. She stepped toward him and stopped abruptly, as if hitting an invisible wall.

She sniffed. "What in hell?"

He ducked his head slightly and loped two long steps over to her, smelling like a twenty-credit prosti.

"Antiseptic dispenser was empty," he said, with a shrug that sent another wave of noxious fumes wafting under her nose. "But aftershave contains alcohol, and it didn't cost much more. I figured it was—"

She sneezed. "I get it. I get it." Maybe it would wear off. Or maybe if Fuzz-face grabbed Trip, it would knock the bastard unconscious.

It certainly made a few patrons back away, eyes slitted in defense, as they returned to the main area of the bar.

"Sit," she told Trip when, by some miracle of the bar-and-space gods, three patrons suddenly vacated a nearby table that bordered the bulkhead.

Maybe not a miracle. The Takan one was sneezing.

"Put your back to the wall," she ordered him, then dropped into the seat on his left, where she had a clear view of the bar's front entrance and a decent one of the two exits behind the bar. Either the bar's air recycs were sending Trip's noxious scent away from her or whatever he'd liberally applied to his skin was fading. She palmed her L7 and then noted, with a small start of surprise, that her charge was also taking stock of his surroundings. Actually, his mostly calm demeanor through this whole ordeal surprised her.

Then again, he was a Guthrie.

"So tell me in detail this time," she said, her gaze drifting over the bar's inhabitants, her voice low but audible. "You didn't see Fuzz-face until after you hit Dock Five. And you've never seen him before."

Trip had already said as much, in his brief recounting in the lift and then in spurts and gulps as they ran up and down stairwells. But she needed the whole story. Kaidee also desperately needed to believe that Jonathan Macy Guthrie III's appearance on Dock Five had nothing to do with the Imperial warships out there, or with Frinks and company in here.

Or her delightfully dead ex-husband.

And there were other questions she wanted answers to, like why Trip was on Dock Five in the first place. Was there a problem at home or at school? They hadn't delved into that, because her immediate concerns were the people who'd almost succeeded in grabbing him. No matter how bad a problem was at home, his parents wouldn't send someone to harm him—and they wouldn't send strangers. That meant Fuzz-face worked at someone else's commands.

"Didn't see the bearded guy on my flight, no. But like I said, I slept. Or was reading." He patted the leather backpack hanging off one shoulder. "I didn't think to be looking around. Stupid, I know." He glanced at her, then back at the throngs of people standing around the bar—gray shipsuits, green shipsuits, humans, and Takas. Two dark-haired women were laughing loudly, one wiping tears from her eyes. A group of five dockworkers—three human and two Takas—seated at a nearby table had their heads together, intent on something a thin-faced young human male had on the datapad in his hand. No one seemed to be looking at her and Trip. Yet.

"Uncle Philip would hand me my head for not keeping track of my surroundings," Trip continued. "'Specially because I ditched Halsey. None of us is supposed to be out without security, you know?"

"When did you first notice the guy?"

"Not long after I got off the shuttle. I was hungry. The snack stall has this polished metal wall, almost like a mirror. I saw this guy...behind me, sort of. Then I remembered he was the same one who'd bumped into me a few minutes before. Something just wasn't right, so I pulled my pack around, like I was looking for credit chips. But I was really checking it because that's where he bumped me. And I found a tagger. A Lockpoint, I think."

A Lockpoint tagger. A tiny tracking device that easily latched on to fabric or, in Trip's case, expensive leather. Not much more than a small metal bump, which could feel to inexperienced fingers like a slub in the material. But Trip had known what it was.

She wondered if Kiler had shown him. She couldn't see Trip's father being aware of those kinds of things, but Ben Halsey would have known and quite possibly educated Master Trip. Halsey would know a Lockpoint from an Alphoid RLM.

"Where'd you leave it?" If he knew what it was, then he knew it was important to ditch it.

He shot her a quick grin as if he heard her confidence in him, then let his gaze sweep the crowd again. *Definitely Halsey's training,* she thought. "I put enough space between him and me, and then I latched it on to a cleaning servo's towel rack. I figured that was the end of it. The guy—well, this is Dock Five, and I know what my pack costs. I thought he was going to wait until I hit an empty corridor, then rob me."

She studied him as he spoke. Smart enough to know what a tagger was and that it was a Lockpoint but naive enough to believe the whole thing was over his two-hundred-fifty-credit leather backpack. Not experienced enough to recognize that a goon like Fuzz-face was far beyond petty thievery. And spoiled enough *not* to know no one was going to waste a high-tech piece of equipment like a Lockpoint tagger for a two-hundred-fifty-credit leather pack.

At least not until Fuzz-face showed up with reinforcements.

"Yeah, I kind of figured at that point it was more than just my pack," Trip admitted with a grimace. "Plus, the bearded guy knew my name. Kind of."

"Kind of?"

"He called me Jonathan. No one calls me that. Well, sometimes Grandpa J.M. does." He shrugged. "Some of my professors do. And Uncle Ethan when he wants to annoy me."

Ethan, Kaidee remembered clearly, excelled at annoying people. But Ethan wasn't the problem here.

"What else did you hear the bearded guy say?" She watched a server 'droid roll its way toward them. They'd have to order something to eat or drink, or the 'droid would issue the ubiquitous warning that this was a pub, not a hotel. "Not just what he said to you. Anything that might indicate what he wants."

Trip was shaking his head as the 'droid arrived. Kaidee ordered two coffees and let the 'droid swipe her credit chip. Ale was for relaxing, and this wasn't time to relax.

"I remember hearing some guy say, 'Get Jonathan,'" Trip said, as the 'droid pivoted on its base. "Paid it no attention 'cause I don't think of myself that way. Only when he grabbed me and said, 'Jonathan, you're coming with us,' did I put it together. Well, that and the fact that he had a gun. An old Carver-Eight. He was going for it when I hit him."

"And you don't know why he grabbed you?"

"Honest, Captain Griggs, I don't."

"He didn't mention your parents or your grandfather? Ransom? GGS?"

"Not that I heard."

She fingered the small L7 and scanned the crowd again. The laughing women had quieted, but the group of dockworkers was still focused on the young man's datapad. She saw them without seeing them, her mind going in worried circles.

Damn it, there were too many variables, from a disgruntled ex-GGS employee to something personal with Trip's parents. Or grandparents. The Guthries had money, they had economic power, they had social standing, they had political power. It could be anything or any combination.

The only thing she knew for sure was that it was trouble.

"And you left the university why? Were you meeting someone here on Dock Five?" It wasn't like Dock

Five was the usual party locale for wealthy college students.

Trip glanced at her, lips parted, then clamped them shut. He glanced away. He shrugged.

She felt her own jaw tighten and had to remind herself he was not only male, he was nineteen: a young man with a large dose of child inside. But a young man...

"Is this over a girl?"

That got him to look at her but didn't gain her an answer.

"Trip, I'm not judging you. Damn it, I'm trying to keep you alive. Someone's pissed off—either at you or your family or your family's business or all of the above. I can't solve this if you don't tell me what's going on."

"It can't have anything to do with—Nobody knows I'm here."

"*Someone* does." She pinned him with a hard stare. But not for too long, because Trouble's Brewing was packed with people coming and going. And any one of those coming in could be looking for Trip Guthrie.

Or Makaiden Griggs. She'd forgotten that for the past hour, as involved in Trip's situation as she was. But Frinks was out there, and someone had ordered Gudrin Vere's death.

Which made her realize she hadn't seen her Takan shadow in a while. Slag it. She hadn't exactly been looking for him either, but that didn't negate the fact that he was out there. Or, worse, that Frinks had put someone else on her tail.

"This doesn't have anything to do with someone named Orvis? Or Horatio Frinks?" she asked him.

The confusion on his face looked genuine. "Who?"

She waved the question away. "People who belong

here. You don't. But you didn't end up here by accident. Neither did those guys who jumped you."

His expression darkened, his brows coming down in thought. "But I purposely didn't tell anyone where I was going—and why—for that very reason. I didn't want to put Uncle Philip at risk."

"Uncle Philip?" That was not remotely the answer Kaidee expected. Philip Guthrie? *Admiral* Philip Guthrie?

"Even he didn't know I was coming here," Trip continued, as images of Imperial warships stationed off Dock Five blossomed in Kaidee's mind. Was this whole thing some kind of trap? Any citizen of the Empire knew that Tage wouldn't mind at all if Philip Guthrie was captured. Or killed. But she couldn't believe Trip would be party to that.

He's just a kid. A big nineteen-year-old one, but a kid. And not beyond being manipulated by a professional. Tage has offices full of those. "Who told you to meet your uncle here?"

"I'm not meeting him here."

Kaidee fought the urge to pound her head on the bulkhead behind her. The kid should be a politician, for the way he used evasive answers. "Trip." She paused, knowing that would make him look at her. It did. "What in hell are you doing on Dock Five?"

"I think it's important that . . ." His voice trailed off again. Then he huffed out a hard sigh. "You know Uncle Philip was reported killed, right? But he really wasn't?"

When she nodded, he continued: "That's when I knew I had to join up. With him. With the Alliance." Passion crept into his last few words, and his shoulders straightened.

God and stars. Kaidee went from wanting to pound

her head to wanting to smack Trip's. The damned kid had *hero in training* written all over him—from the tilt of his chin to the stiffness of his spine. "What does Dock Five have to do with—"

"Everyone knows you can get anywhere from Dock Five. Or buy the documents to get you there." He shot her a glance that had clear echoes of his father, Jonathan Guthrie II, in the way the dark brows dipped and eyes shifted slightly downward. As in: *You left your brains on the floor.*

She bit back her initial retort that *everyone* is usually an ass. *He's a kid. He's a kid.* "As in illegal transport into Alliance territory? And you know, of course, how much that would cost? And you know how to bargain for that without getting caught by stripers or, worse, ImpSec?"

He shrugged, but some of the bravado that had kept his shoulders straight dissolved. He leaned back in his chair, slumping slightly.

"Throwing a lot of money around on a place like Dock Five," she said softly, "can get you killed."

"I thought—"

"Be straight with me, Trip. Were you telling me the absolute truth about how you had this run-in with Fuzz-face? Or were you dealing with him to try to go out-system?" *That* would change everything. Fuzz-face could well be an undercover ImpSec agent. Or worse.

"No. I swear—"

She suddenly sat up straight, seeing movement by the side door that set her internal alarms pinging. Two large human males. Not Fuzz-face but the balding one she was sure had been with Trip's attacker earlier. Dark jackets were too large, and hands were snaking underneath or being tucked behind at the waist. Armed, definitely. Clutching weapons, definitely.

Looking for Trip Guthrie? Too damned likely.

They sure as hell didn't look like they were looking for an ale.

Her pulse spiked. She nudged Trip's boot with her own. "Side door," she said quickly, quietly. "Guy on the left?"

Both men—Baldy and Curly, she dubbed them—were scanning the busy movement in the bar but hadn't fixed on the spot where Kaidee and Trip were seated. Or else they had, she realized with a sinking feeling, and were too well trained to reveal that fact.

But not well trained enough to hide their imposing predatory appearance. She crossed ImpSec off the list. ImpSec was cagier than that.

"You shot that one earlier," Trip said, confirming her recognition of the balding man.

"Stunned him," she corrected him. Station rules. She tried to abide by them. Not everyone did, as Gudrin Vere had found out when Nula caught up with her. "You see Fuzz-face anywhere?"

Trip slouched down in his seat and raked the bar with just a glance and only the slightest movement of his head. She wondered again how much Halsey had taught him.

"Nope. You?"

"Nope." She'd used the same method. Movement drew attention. They didn't need that right now. "We need to get out of here. Front door's closest, but it's also the most obvious." Just to the side of the front door, though, was a little-known maintenance access to what was now the CFTC shuttle bay. Scenarios and options ran through her mind. So did a penchant for safety. There were far too many innocent patrons between here and that access way. "There's a back exit to your right, behind the bar. Provides more cover." And fewer innocents in the line of fire, should stupidity make an appearance. Bar 'droids were replaceable.

"I know how to use a gun, if you have a spare," he told her.

"Only my L7. With luck, we won't need it." She nudged him again. "Big group over there is getting ready to leave. When they start moving, so do we. Keep your head down. Don't run unless I tell you to. Just make for the back of the bar. Then get down to Green Ten. Got it? Green Ten. Popovitch Repairs. Tell Pops I sent you. You can be straight up about who you are. He'll help you."

Trip blinked, an emotion flickering through his eyes. She wasn't sure if he was afraid or affronted. His mouth thinned. "I'm not leaving you here alone."

Affronted. And with a short memory of who had rescued whom earlier.

"We're leaving," she stressed the word, "*together*. But if I don't tell you where we're going, and we get separated—"

"Oh. Right."

"The group's moving." But so was the armed trio. "Try to use one of the Takas as cover. I'll watch our friends. You head for the bar." She swiveled her chair around, spying something on the decking as she did. A short-brimmed dockworker's cap under the table. Discarded or forgotten, she didn't care. She snatched it and, ignoring the grimy stains on the tan material, shoved it over her hair, tugging the brim down. She didn't know how good a look Fuzz-face and friends had gotten at her, but if they were convinced Trip was again alone, they wouldn't be watching for her coming up from behind.

Trip swiveled in the opposite direction, pulling himself to his feet as she eased around the table's edge. Hands shoved in pockets, shoulders hunched with his telltale leather pack stuck under one arm, he plodded parallel to the tall Taka in brown coveralls moving with the group from the table. Kid *was* good, when he wanted to be.

She followed a few paces behind, with the safety off the L7 and her face angled just enough to keep the burly men in her peripheral vision. They were weaving through the crowd, heading for the bar as she was, but she was sure they hadn't seen Trip. The shorter, curly-haired guy was in the lead, and he was looking quickly left and right in an almost nervous fashion.

She could appreciate nervous. Her palms felt slick and her heart was hammering in her chest. She was a cargo pilot, for God's sake. Granted, she'd grown up on freighter docks and knew how to fight as dirty as any dock brat did. Dirtier, thanks to some of her father's crew. But that was more than fifteen years ago. She'd been hauling corporate executives and cargo for seven years now, and neither execs nor cargo ever shot at you. Well, almost never.

Shit. Baldy was hanging back. Slowing down. And seemed to be watching the Taka—Trip's cover—with the same sideways method she was using to watch him. But he was six, seven tables away, with a lot of patrons in between.

Then she remembered Fuzz-face elbowing the old man without remorse. *Innocent bystanders* wasn't in this group's vocabulary.

The Taka slowed, turning to say something to the human male behind him. Trip slowed, too, but in those few seconds when the Taka angled around, Trip was in

full view. She knew he was, because Baldy suddenly
straightened and grabbed Curly's shoulder.

"Trip! Cover's blown!" she ground out between
clenched teeth. Then Baldy's hand slid out of his
pocket. And his hand wasn't empty.

She pushed against Trip's back, hard. "Run!"

Trip lunged, sidling around the stalled and startled
Taka.

But Curly was already moving, shoving dockworkers and freighter crew aside, shouts and curses flowing
in his wake. Baldy was a few steps behind him. Curly
took a different axis, heading for the bar, palming a
small laser pistol from his pocket as he went.

Bastard hopes to cut us off, trap us. She couldn't let
that happen. She scanned the crowd quickly, praying
for Pops or one of his techs. Someone to help, someone to cause a diversion long enough for her and Trip
to get away—or serious enough to get the crowd to
turn against the duo, who were now annoying patrons
with their pushing and shoving but not yet doing anything to cause a really workable problem.

This was, after all, Trouble's Brewing.

Then, in the midst of it all, a solitary 'droid ambled
toward her, two capped coffee mugs on its tray. Their
coffee.

Kaidee watched, astonished, as Trip grabbed one
mug and flung it—no, *pitched* a perfect throw, bean-
ing Curly on the side of his head. The man roared, hot
coffee splattering and spilling down his face and neck.

"Look out! He's got a gun," Trip yelled.

People dove out of the way, their drinks tumbling,
clattering against tabletops. Someone shouted, hard
and harsh. A few turned for Trip, but then Baldy
jerked his weapon up and fired—a low whine that told
her his weapon was set for stun. She doubted it was

compliance with dock regs. It was simply that Baldy wanted Trip Guthrie alive.

With the appearance of the weapon, the focus of the crowd changed. Kaidee hit the deck just behind Trip. She heard more shouts, more thuds. She wasn't the only one in Trouble's Brewing who knew the sound of a stunner.

They had their diversion. She also hoped they had the patrons of Trouble's Brewing on their side. Bar fights were one thing. Guns fired in the bar were another. Although once someone started...

"Stay down but go, go!" She shoved Trip's ass, getting him crawling forward quickly. She chanced a peek over the top of the table, L7 out. She didn't have a clear shot. The two laughing women at the bar had separated. One had unlocked a chair and swung it at Baldy. The woman was too far away, missing him by more than inches, but it made Baldy turn and snarl something. It was the distraction Kaidee needed.

"Up! Run!" she yelled.

Trip bolted forward through the obstacle course of tables, chairs, and patrons. Drinks flew. Kaidee's boots slipped on puddles of frothy ale, and suddenly she was two, three people behind Trip as others moved to join the melee or lunged to get away from it.

Curly, jacket still glistening with coffee, stepped onto an empty chair, then up onto the middle of a table, evidently deciding the decking was a less-useful route. Trip changed course, veering away not only from Curly but from the bar exit.

Damn it! That move would trap him against the corner bulkhead. It looked as if Trip's smarts just went down the recyc.

"This way!" she shouted, but he obviously wasn't listening as he dodged around a small—and unrelated—

fight between two brown-suited mechanics. The taller man reared back to level a punch. Trip ducked under his fist and up again, then ducked again as the opponent lunged, swinging.

If the situation wasn't so goddamned serious, Kaidee realized, it would be goddamned funny.

Curly jumped to the next table, but before Kaidee could get him in her sights, two ship's crew clambered up on the table in front of Curly, as they tried to escape from the ruckus. They blocked her shot at Curly.

She swore harshly as she turned to look for Trip. Her heart clenched. He was gone.

Under a table? He had to be, she hoped, crawling toward the bar. She sidled past another chair and the fighting mechanics, shouts, curses, and thuds sounding around her. She raked the decking with her gaze, then looked back at Curly and—

Thwack! The woman with the chair finally connected, catching Baldy between his shoulder blades. Kaidee watched just long enough to see the man flail and fall forward.

Down but, she was sure, far from out. But it was one less thing she had to worry about for the next five—

Shit. A familiar form appeared between two 'droid servers standing rigidly behind the bar. Fuzz-face was back.

"Got something." Devin glanced up from the embedded screen on his microcomp just in time to avoid running into an elderly couple shuffling quickly down the main corridor on Blue. He sidestepped and only then realized that Barthol's hand already pressed against his shoulder, guiding him away from the near collision and around a zigzagging servobot. "Tidymart Pro is a toiletries dispenser service. Common in public lavatories."

Barthol nodded. "Makes sense. There is no lack of facilities on station. However—"

"It's not something Dock Five would necessarily provide for its denizens, yes. I thought of that." Considering Dock Five barely provided breathable air. "Cross-referenced the corporation with product news feeds. Client base is generally hotels, restaurants."

"There are a number of possibilities on Blue. Blue Twelve, however, holds a couple of small hostels, a take-out eatery, and—"

Two women and a man suddenly tumbled through an open doorway about fifty feet down the corridor, as if they'd been jammed by a billiards cue. They rolled, flailing, cursing. Another man followed—a brown-furred Takan in dockworker coveralls. He sprinted past them, dodging around a black-and-silver squat servobot on some unknown errand, and kept running, not looking back.

Through that same doorway—more of a double-wide rectangular airlock complete with faded yellow-

and-black safety striping—came the low whine of laser fire in several short bursts. Devin's adrenaline spiked. In Tal Verdis, that would have stripers and private security converging on the location. Here, it barely garnered more than a few raised eyebrows from passersby.

"Trouble's Brewing," Barthol said.

"That's an understatement."

"No, that's where we're headed. Bring up corridor schematics. You'll get its merchant codes."

Devin quickened his pace, poking rapidly at the database queries on his Rada, peripherally aware of a metal chair sailing into the corridor, then skittering across the grimy dark-gray decking with a grinding squeal. "They're licensed for Tidymart dispensers on premises." If Tidymart's on-site distributor wanted to file charges against him later for hacking into their client database, so be it. Right now it was the best lead they had on Trippy. And they were only fifteen or so minutes behind his last credit usage for shampoo or soap or whatever he'd used. They would have been only five minutes behind, but repairs blocking a section of Blue Corridor had forced them down one level to Green, then back up again, all via the damnably slow and erratic lifts and nonfunctional escalators that seemed to be Dock Five's consistent landmarks.

"Side entrance." Barthol pointed to a dimly lit, narrow corridor on Devin's left. "Less likely to be in the direct line of fire."

"Trip knows better than to—" Devin pivoted on his heels. He kept pace with Barthol, but his protestation halted. Trip might not seek out a place known for violent encounters, but someone had killed Halsey. Someone who was also after Trip. And that someone was no stranger to violence.

The side entrance to Trouble's Brewing was a similar rectangular hatchlock design but with only a single doorway, over which illuminated letters proclaiming the pub's name blinked sporadically. This entrance was only slightly less in the direct line of fire. Bottles and glasses flew, crashing against tables. Voices shouted, bellowed, groaned, and swore. Devin stood transfixed for a few seconds by the frenzy and sheer cacophony filling the cavernous bar. It was like nothing he'd ever seen—at least, not outside of an action vid or sim game. The bar—judging from the ceiling height, rickety overhead metal-grid walkways from which an odd assortment of light fixtures dangled, and round hanging maws of exhaust-fan ducts—had obviously at one time been a docking bay. Faded berth numbers were still stenciled in red on the far wall, along with the perfunctory open flame and fume warnings in all three languages.

In between or on top of all that were lighted advertisements for a variety of alcoholic drinks.

With a determined shrug, Barthol pushed into the fray. Devin caught up, ducking as something round and silver—a tray?—flew by. He readjusted his glasses as he straightened. "Damn it, Barty. If he's in here, there's no way we'll—*Shit!* Trip!" He raised his voice over the din, shouting his nephew's name as his adrenaline kicked into overtime.

He'd been right. God and stars, his analysis, his hunch, had been right. Trip *was* on Dock Five.

"Where?"

It had been a glance, half a glance; that was all Devin had been able to see and process through the jumble of forms careening through the bar. More of an impression of height and gait and profile. But it was

Trippy. Devin was positive. More than that, he recognized his nephew's expensive leather backpack tucked under one arm. He'd already come to know that you didn't see very many of those on Dock Five. "In the back. Bar area, right side," Devin called out over his shoulder. He doggedly pushed past people—his brain didn't bother to register sex or species—because when he'd spied Trip, he'd spied something else: weapons. Including one in the hand of a wide-shouldered man using tabletops as a walkway. Most of those in the bar—well, those who weren't punching someone— were heading for the exits. This guy was heading for the far corner of the bar. Just where Trip was.

Devin stepped over an upended chair as he unlatched the safety strap that held his Carver securely in his shoulder holster.

But when he scanned the area again, Trip had disappeared—ducked under a table or slipped out a secret doorway. Devin didn't know which and wouldn't until he reached the other side of the bar—because of a 'droid server wobbling back and forth, two male Takans arguing, and a drunk woman laughing hysterically, all blocking his view. He had to get to where he saw Trip before the armed guy did.

He had no idea if his nephew was the cause of the commotion or was the armed guy's target. But given his determined direction, he couldn't rule out the possibility.

He also had no idea where Barty was. Nor could he risk turning around to look for him. He had to maneuver through the mob to where he last saw Trip and trust that Barty hadn't lied about his own expertise and training and could hold his own in a bar fight—or whatever else this turned out to be.

Devin pushed past two men in brown coveralls

slugging it out and caught a glimpse of figures disappearing around the far end of the bar; he was certain one was Trip. The others . . . It was too quick, too jumbled, too much going on in front of him, behind him, on his left—

"This way!"

He heard Barty's command over the grunts and groans and saw the lanky, black-clad form a few feet behind where Trip and three humans of various sizes—his memory kicked out a clearer image now— had vanished.

Devin nodded his acknowledgment, grimly recognizing that one of those who'd vanished was the table-climbing armed thug. "Keep Trip in sight!" he called back as he shoved his way past a scuffle, then pushed himself up and over the bar, landing a few feet behind Barty's retreating form.

The movement skewed his glasses. He pushed them back up as he darted around the back of the bar into a narrow service corridor. The oily smell of frying foods mixing with something like a cheap perfume assailed him. The passageway led to a small kitchen through one opening on his left and what appeared to be a storeroom farther down. He quickly followed sounds of thuds and something slamming, metal on metal, and realized what it was when he surged into the empty storeroom: an emergency blast door opening and closing. He shoved against the crash bar and stepped quickly out into an unfamiliar cross corridor, just in time to see Trip plant his fist in the middle of a bald guy's face. The guy's gun flew from his hand and skittered across the decking, disappearing and reappearing in patches of dark and light from nonworking overheads. Devin lunged for it at the same time that another attacker appeared, as if from nowhere, on his left. He collided with the shorter guy, knocking him to the decking, and shoved his knee hard in the guy's back—a move he'd practiced many times with Philip. Confident that his attacker was pinned against the decking, he reached over the guy's head for the bald guy's gun: a Stinger laser pistol. But the guy bucked and squirmed, throwing Devin off balance and making him suddenly realize two things.

The guy wasn't strong enough to dislodge Devin's weight.

And the guy wasn't a guy but a woman, with narrow shoulders and a well-padded...hindquarters.

Real manly, Dev. Pick on a girl, sounded in his mind, making Devin's conscience and, okay, his ego squirm almost as much as the female in the threadbare gray spacer's jacket and flight suit was squirming underneath him. His conscience flinched, but the hard ugly fact was this female wanted the Stinger, wanted to hurt Trip. Devin was not going to grant her either luxury. He shoved the Carver's muzzle through the wisps of unruly blond hair sticking out under the edge of her cap and against the back of her neck. "Move and you're dead."

It was a lie. Aside from the fact that Devin had never killed anyone, he wanted her alive and talking. He wanted to know what happened back at Montgomery University, who killed Halsey. Who wanted Trip Guthrie and why?

But the woman underneath him didn't know all that. She went suddenly still.

Devin snatched the Stinger with his left hand, then shoved it into his pants pocket. "Trip!" he shouted, as his nephew pounded a right cross into the bald man's solar plexus. Baldy hunched over, sucking wind noisily. Trip jerked his face toward Devin, eyes widening, mouth opening in amazement.

"Uncle Devin?"

There wasn't time to answer. Off to Devin's left, Barthol wrestled in the shadows with a curly-haired man in a dark-gray jacket. The man wrenched around and jammed his elbow into Barthol's midsection. Barthol doubled over with a hard groan, clutching his stomach. The man pushed past him, heading for Trip.

Fuck. Devin swung the pistol at Barty's attacker. "Freeze, asshole!"

The asshole froze. Devin reached in his pocket for the Stinger. Trip knew how to use it. But before he could toss it to his nephew, Trip's balding thug kicked Trip's feet out from under him, then bolted toward the main corridor in a shambling run. Swearing, Trip scrambled to his feet, clearly wanting to follow the guy.

"Trip, stay here!" Devin swung his Carver toward the thug's retreating form but checked fire as Trip spun, unknowingly stepping directly into Devin's line. By the time Devin shifted position, the thug had reached the crowded main corridor, easily blending in and using stationers for cover.

Shit.

A hard thud sounded behind him. Devin whipped around to his left, but he was too late. Barty's attacker had taken off in the opposite direction down the dim corridor, boots pounding on the decking.

They still had one attacker left, under Devin's knee. He didn't know if he'd trust station stripers to interrogate the woman, but there was always GGS security. Or Barthol, who had been with ImpSec but was now down on all fours, wheezing.

Trip stepped toward Devin. "Uncle Dev—"

"Not now." He tossed the Stinger to Trip. "Check on Barty."

"But—"

"Help Barty now!" Whatever explanations his nephew had, whatever excuses he wanted to offer for this crazy scheme that put him on Dock Five, could wait.

Keeping the Carver's muzzle against the back of the woman's head, Devin removed his knee and grabbed her left arm. "Up!"

He lifted the woman easily, then spun her. Her filthy cap tumbled off as Devin pushed her against the bulkhead and, in a move he'd learned from Philip, shoved the Carver under her chin. He glared down at her.

Makaiden Griggs, eyes narrowed, face smeared with grime from Dock Five's decking, stared back up.

"Makaiden?" He was surprised by the hoarseness of his own voice, suddenly thick with emotion. *Makaiden* was trying to hurt Trip? Questions—damning, horrible questions—raced through his mind and constricted his heart with an unexpected pain. There'd been whispers of some kind of trouble after she and her husband left GGS, but nothing he could trace. He'd never have believed them, anyway. Not about Makaiden Griggs.

"Mr. Devin," Makaiden said, her voice soft but noticeably tense. Understandably so. He held a gun under her chin. "I'm not the problem here."

He frowned. He didn't like this, not one bit. He was suddenly without explanations, without information. And if Makaiden was here, where was her hus—

The high-pitched whine was the only warning. It lasted a second—*half* a second—but it was enough for Devin to flatten Makaiden against a recessed area in the bulkhead as someone took a shot at them from down the corridor on his left, beyond the bar's store-room exit. The bad guys hadn't run away. They'd re-grouped and come back with a vengeance.

He punched out two shots with his Carver, periph-erally aware that, off to his left, Barthol had yanked Trip down and then rolled to one side behind the wide protective arch of a bulkhead support, dragging Trip with him. Then Barty, too, was returning fire.

"Shit!" That from Makaiden, wriggling against him. She ran one hand between their bodies, which—for another brief second—sent shocks through his sys-tem that had nothing to do with ordinary electricity. *She's a married woman,* surfaced briefly in his mind, as her hand came up with an L7 pistol he didn't know she had and hadn't thought to check for. Philip would have a lecture for that. "Fuzz-face has reinforce-ments," she said tersely. "We need out of here now!"

"Captain Griggs! We'll cover you!" That was from Trip, who evidently was far less surprised by Makaiden Griggs's appearance than Devin was.

Devin glanced down at her, returned her quick nod with his own. "Go!" Questions as to what Makaiden Griggs was doing with his nephew and where Kiler Griggs was would wait. Survival was more important.

He'd found Trip. He'd found Makaiden. He didn't want to think about why the latter made him inexpli-cably happy.

He was too busy trying to keep from being shot in the ass.

When they reached Barty, the older man was rising, waving one hand. "Main corridor!" Barty fired off an-other round of shots, the last one hitting a seesawing servobot following a preprogrammed course that un-fortunately brought it into the fracas. It exploded, sending metal fragments pinging off the bulkheads and decking. Buying them some precious time.

Trip raced ahead of Devin, skittering around the corner just as Makaiden pushed by. "This way," she said, waving toward the bar's main entrance.

Back into Trouble's Brewing? But there was no time to question. She had Trip by the arm and was propelling him along with her, and Devin had no intention of losing sight of Trip.

For a fleeting moment, the thought that she and Kiler were working with the thugs, that she was leading them into a trap, surfaced in Devin's mind. He shook it off but kept the safety off his Carver.

He *hated* not having complete data.

He and Barty slipped through the pub's wide hatchway behind Trip and Makaiden, stepping quickly to the right to shove past a trio of cleaning 'droids mopping the floor and locking chairs and tables back into the decking. Makaiden moved behind them, glancing around the bar.

"Why—" Devin started, but she was shaking her head.

"Blue's blocked up a ways, due to a water main break."

"I know."

"We go around it. There's a back access to the CFTC docking bay through here." She spoke rapidly, her gaze still zigzagging over the twenty or so patrons now milling about, drinking what others had left behind. Looking for her husband? "Fuzz-face will be checking for us at the escalators or lifts. But we need to move now."

"Where's—"

"Let's go." Makaiden sidled past a stack of chairs toward the corner of the bar, stopping at a panel on the bulkhead where faded letters appeared to spell out *Recycler Maintenance* in red. A recessed keypad was on the left. She tapped at it as Barty came to stand next to her, his narrowed gaze searching the bar. A short square section of bulkhead swung inward, creaking. Makaiden waved her L7. "Now!"

Trip ducked in—the panel was little more than four feet in height—and Barty followed. Devin found himself staring at Makaiden Griggs—a former GGS captain who apparently knew about some very odd ways of getting around Dock Five.

"*Now,* Mr. Devin!"

He crouched down and stepped through, aware of the sudden warmth of Makaiden's hand on his back. He angled around to look at her as the panel shut. His world went black, his grip on the Carver tightened. His heart rate spiked. Then a small green glow flared between them, brightening and turning to white.

"Be careful standing—"

"Ow. Shit!" That was Trip.

"Up," she said, raising her voice slightly. "Low ceiling."

"I thought Dockmaster Stulesk closed off this access ten years ago." Barty's voice was low but audible. He hunkered down next to Trip, who was rubbing the top of his head.

Makaiden snorted out a short laugh. "Welcome to Dock Five."

"It's good to see you, Captain Griggs."

"Good to see you, too, Mr. Barthol."

"Captain Griggs knows a lot of back ways around this place," Trip said.

And had already shown Trip a few? Devin glanced at Makaiden, waiting for her comment but hearing only tense silence.

"Spent some time here as a kid," Makaiden said finally, and waved her small handbeam down the passage. "Once we hit the secondary tunnel you'll be able to stand up."

Devin couldn't remember any mention of Dock Five during his study of the personnel jackets on Makaiden Griggs. "You grew up here?"

She had already shuffled away from him. "Relatives had a concession here," she answered without turning around. "Let's keep moving. We have a long way down to Orange. Or wherever you docked your ship."

"We don't have a ship. We arrived by commercial transport."

She stopped, switching a quick glance from him to Barty and back to him again. "Commercial transport?"

She knew the Guthrie fleet as well as he did. More than that, she knew Guthries never traveled by commercial transport. That was written in the slight parting of her lips, in the slight dip of her brows. Even with the dim, uneven lighting and sweat smears on his glasses, he could see her surprise.

"We have a room at The Celestian," Barty said. "If memory serves me, we should be able to get access through these same tunnels. Unless anyone has a better idea, I suggest that we head there now. I think we all have a lot of questions."

Devin knew he had questions. He just had an increasingly bad feeling about the answers.

Kaidee didn't know what shocked her more: Devin Guthrie's appearance on Dock Five or Devin Guthrie's appearance on Dock Five without the usual luxury yacht and GGS pilot in tow. She would never have let him wander around a place like Dock Five when she'd been his pilot, unless he had a security escort—and even then, she would have been with him, because, well...she usually was.

She understood why at the spaceports—Devin had a penchant for exploring local cuisine, and she knew where not to eat or drink. But more than that, there were times when she sensed Devin Guthrie was a loner who was simply lonely. When the detail work of whatever business meeting she'd flown him to was done—detail work that kept his mind absorbed and occupied—he'd end up on the *Triumph*'s bridge, pressing her for stories—"hangar flying," as the old-timers called it—until she'd nudge him toward a game of Zentauri to distract him.

Because there was only so much of her past she could talk about, including how she knew about these tunnels, which had prompted Devin's *You grew up here?*

Where and how she grew up was a question she didn't want to answer—especially not to Devin Guthrie. With luck, she wouldn't have to.

She quickened her pace down the shadowy maintenance tunnel, handbeam off, Devin, Trip, and Barthol trotting behind her in an enforced silence. This part of the access tunnel had airflow grids on one side, which were the source of the weak and intermittent lighting but also a potential liability. She could clearly hear the rumble of voices and thudding of boot steps from Blue Corridor through the grids and knew well that, at certain points, someone next to a grid might be able to hear them. These old maintenance access tunnels weren't well known, but they *were* known. She didn't want anyone out there to suspect they were in here.

And it wasn't just Fuzz-face she was worried about. It was that Fuzz-face might somehow know Frinks and that Devin Guthrie's appearance might be somehow, some way, tied in to it all.

As idiotic as that sounded. She had a hard time imagining Devin Guthrie—*any* Guthrie—being involved with the likes of Frinks and Orvis. But then, she never thought Kiler would get himself killed in an explosion in a repair hangar and leave her with the mess he did. She was coming to learn that a little paranoia was a healthy thing.

A familiar configuration of pipes on her left caught her notice and she halted, evidently surprising Devin, because he bumped up against her back, left hand cupping her shoulder with a firm grip. Then he quickly stepped back, almost as if he found touching her distasteful. No, that was stupid. Devin was nothing if not overly polite—and considerate and respectful. The way Kiler used to privately and condescendingly refer to Devin—*Mr. Perfect and In Control*—always grated on her, but the assessment held an element of truth. Devin Guthrie *was* the quintessential gentleman, and not in a stuffy, off-putting way either. She shrugged a *no harm done* at him, but he looked away, his expression unreadable.

Okay, so maybe he could be a little stuffy.

Not your problem, Kaid.

She raised her hand as Trip and Barthol stepped up next to her and Devin, and, when she was sure they all could see her, she pointed to the cluster of pipes and conduit overhead. Then she lowered her hand sharply. Big drop in ceiling height ahead.

The three men nodded.

She turned, crouching down, and hoped Trip had enough sense to crouch even farther. He'd already hit his head once and had been none too quiet about it.

Then her mind returned to the puzzle that was Devin Guthrie.

Quite honestly, the possibility of his being involved with Frinks made no sense—she had no problem adding *honorable* to the list of Devin's attributes—but it made even less sense that Halsey or GGS Security Chief Petra Frederick would send Devin Guthrie to find Trip, not even with Barthol at his side. Over the years she'd heard a few mentions from Halsey and Frederick about the wiry old man's "other skills." But other skills or not, he had to be looking at the ass end of seventy. Devin was, yes, only mid-thirties, definitely fit, and very possibly the most intelligent one in the whole clan. But he wasn't security, had never served in the military.

Though he damned near proned her out like a pro.

She winced as the sore spot in her back chose that moment to remind her just how fit—and fast—Devin "Perfect and In Control" Guthrie was.

So maybe Halsey had trained him. It had been two years since she'd flown for GGS. For all she knew, Devin had security training. He . . .

She shook herself mentally, could almost hear Kiler's deep voice chastising her for her *perpetual looping suppositions*.

God and stars, Kaid, can't you just let it be?

She could. She had to. Once she got them back to
The Celestian, she was washing her hands of the
whole affair. Trip was back with his uncle and a longtime family employee. *She* was no longer a GGS employee, so this whole situation was not only not her
job, it wasn't her problem. There was probably a good
explanation why Devin was here and Halsey wasn't.
Maybe Halsey *was* here, or maybe he was on his way
here in one of GGS's star yachts. Even if he wasn't, she
had no doubt Devin had enough funds to get them all
back to Sylvadae. Passenger transport was still operating out of Dock Five, though they might have a few
days' wait for a reservation. If they got hungry, they
could order room service. They had money for that
too.

She didn't. The only thing she had was trouble, and
they didn't need any of hers.

It took them five minutes to move through the narrower tunnel. When they cleared it, Kaidee's back
wasn't the only sore thing. Her knees ached and she'd
damned near impaled her left shoulder—twice—on
corroded conduit brackets jutting out from the wall.

She straightened, rubbing her shoulder, and noticed
she wasn't alone in her grimacing.

"Was this place built for miniature sentients?" Trip
asked quietly, massaging one elbow.

There were two patches of grime on Barty's face.
"Servobots used them. Blue used to be a main docking
level." He, too, kept his voice low, even though there
were no airflow grids here and no one in Blue Corridor could hear them or see them.

Devin's face was also streaked, likely from where

he'd touched the decking or walls to keep his balance while hunched over and then rubbed the sweat out of his eyes. He rolled his shoulders, straining the fabric of his dark-brown jacket, then looked around the small square room lit only by Kaidee's handbeam. "How much farther?"

She played the handbeam over the near wall. "Through that hatchlock, then down a ladder. Comes out at another hatchlock that leads into the hotel's storeroom. If anyone's in there, let me do the talking, okay?"

Trip was nodding when she turned back. Devin seemed to study her.

It hit her then that—her own paranoia be damned—he didn't trust her. She could see that in the way his eyes narrowed behind the lenses of his silver-rimmed glasses, in the way his wide mouth formed a thin line. Mr. Honorable was seeing a very less-than-perfect Captain Griggs, who was far too knowledgeable about a place like Dock Five.

For a moment that hurt, because memories surfaced: playing Zentauri with him on the *Triumph,* laughing—she always thought he had a low, sexy chuckle. Walking by his side through various spaceport malls on Aldan Prime or Port Sapphire. He invariably seemed to find a reason to need her *shopping expertise,* as he called it.

Mother frets I'm fashion-blind, he'd teased, blue eyes twinkling. There were times when Mr. Honorable could also be Mr. Charming, and she'd wondered more than once why he hadn't charmed his way permanently into some young woman's heart. If she had a sister ... but she hadn't. And even if she had, there was no way a Guthrie would be interested in a dock brat.

Though that had never stopped him from treating

her with respect. Okay, he was the youngest of J.M.'s sons but still a Guthrie, who didn't have to offer honor and respect to a dock brat like Makaiden Griggs. Even if she flew his yachts. *Especially* because she flew his yachts.

But he had, and that had made her, well, fond of him. He brought something into her life that she'd come to realize she'd never get from Kiler: Devin Guthrie made her feel valued. So seeing the undisguised wariness and distrust now...hurt. She'd graduated from dock brat to Dock Five scum.

She shoved the pain away. *Welcome to my world.* Hurt was nothing new. Thank you, Kiler Griggs.

She tapped in the code to open the hatchlock, then shoved the heavy door sideways, surprised when a masculine hand appeared next to hers, helping. But it wasn't Devin's hand. It was Trip's. Of course.

"Thanks." She stepped through and headed for the black-and-yellow striped ladder on the far bulkhead.

The ladder ended at another hatchlock that responded to her coded input, but she opened this hatch more slowly. Only a crack at first. Listening. The room beyond was a shipping-and-receiving station for The Celestian Hotel; had been for as long as Kaidee knew. But she also knew that when Blue was Main Dock—a good fifty years before she was born—this had been a cargo staging area.

She heard voices. Two. One male, one female, though the female sounded Takan, with the guttural tones and clipped words. If they knew her, this would be easy. If they didn't, she needed an explanation they would accept.

"Trouble?" Barthol's low question was in her ear.

"Times two," she answered. "But we don't know how much until we get in there." She angled around slightly, caught the outline of Devin's Carver under his brown suede flight jacket. "Stow that," she said in a loud whisper. "Yours, too, Trip. We go in..." She hesitated, thinking. "They may have heard about the fights in Trouble's Brewing. We act as if we just ditched out from that, okay? It's basically the truth."

"Sounds easy," Trip said. Devin nodded.

"Okay." She put her L7 in its holster on her utility belt, then shoved the hatchway open. There was about a two-foot drop to the decking below. She jumped down, landing with a thud.

"Hey," she said, holding her hands out at her sides as the Takan female rose from behind her desk. The human male standing on her left turned quickly. The Taka was middle-aged, gray-furred, with three silver hoops hanging from her left ear. The man was not much older than Trip, his red hair slicked back from a low forehead. He and the Taka both wore the dark-blue coveralls of a hotel maintenance worker. Another human—a female in her early forties, with chin-length black hair—reached for the Mag-5 on her hip. Kaidee hadn't known a striper was in the room. "We're not the problem," Kaidee explained. "Trying to get away from the problem. Couple of slag-heads went crazy in Trouble's Brewing."

She heard the muted thumps of the Guthrie trio behind her, but she kept her focus on the female striper and did a quick assessment of the Taka's desk. Coffee mugs. Three. This was a social gathering, then. Break time. If she was lucky, the reports of the firefight with Fuzz-face and friends hadn't reached this striper yet... or it had all been lumped in as part of the trouble at the pub.

"This young lady," said a weak and halting voice

behind her, "said she could get us out. Me and my nephews here. Saved our lives."

Barthol? Damned if it wasn't Barthol, sounding every year and then some of however old he was. She chanced a quick glance over her shoulder. He was leaning on Devin, panting, his face pale against his black shirt and jacket, his posture hunched. Correction. He looked every year of at least a hundred.

The striper relaxed her grip on her gun. "Heard the report go out on main comm. But how did you know how to get through the tunnel?"

The red-haired guy perched a hip on the Taka's desk. His name tag read *Gustav*. "And how'd you know the hatch codes?"

Shit. She hated specific questions about the tunnels. But at the very worst, they'd implicate only her. Barthol was smart to make it clear that he, Trip, and Devin had simply followed her. As Devin was already figuring out, associating with Captain Kaidee Griggs wasn't the best idea.

"My uncle used to work maintenance here." Well, that was partly true. Her uncle had worked on Dock Five—just not in maintenance. "Whenever my mother had a . . . friend visit," and she shrugged, adding to the innuendo that sounded in her words, "she stuck my uncle with me." She huffed out a short, deprecating laugh. "She had a lot of friends."

Gustav snorted. The Taka sat back down and folded her arms across her chest. "Your uncle worked for the hotel?" Her gruff tone was easy. Her eyes were hard. She was older than the guy or the striper. She knew what those tunnels had been used for and who used them.

Kaidee looked over her shoulder at Barthol. "You all are safe now, okay? You don't need me." She switched her focus to the striper. "And you don't need them, right? I brought them through the tunnels because, well, someone was going to get hurt." She didn't know if Barthol wanted it known they had a room here.

The striper took a step forward. "Can't have you wandering—"

"We're hotel guests." That was from Devin, in a tone Kaidee recognized as Guthrie Imperative. "I have my room card in my pocket. If you'll permit me, Officer?"

The striper nodded. Kaidee couldn't see what Devin was doing, but she prayed it wasn't something stupid like drawing his Carver. She heard the slight rustle of fabric and watched the striper watching Devin. When alarm didn't show on the woman's features, Kaidee relaxed an inch.

"Bring it here," the striper ordered.

Devin brushed by her, a cream-colored plastic room card between the outstretched fingers of his left hand. Keeping his right hand free, she noticed. Someone *had* taught him a few things.

The striper took the card and stepped back, motioning for Devin to stay in place. She swiped the card over a small reader attached to her belt. A green light flashed along with data Kaidee couldn't see but knew was there. She wondered if the Guthrie name would mean anything to the woman.

"Mr. Barvin," the striper said as she eyed Devin. "Just checked in today?"

"Yes."

Barvin? Kaidee wondered where the pseudonym had come from, then it hit her: Barthol and Devin. Barvin.

"Out of Aldan Prime?"

She knew Devin lived on Garno, but the location was probably part of the disguise as well.

"Yes."

"You have an open-ended reservation. Looking to relocate to Dock Five?" The tone of her voice said she clearly knew no one from Aldan Prime would do that.

"I had some personal business with no definite timetable."

The striper poked at her reader again. "You and your family are free to go. Sorry for the inconvenience." She focused on Kaidee. "Your ID?"

"Griggs, captain of the *Void Rider*," Kaidee said, as she reached under her jacket and pulled her ID chip's small case from the upper left pocket of her flight suit. A false ID would be nice, but she didn't have that kind of talent or money. "I have ID and my CFTC chip." Many stripers had a lenient attitude toward CalRis Free-Trader captains because of a long-standing practice of "free samples"—that was really what the *free* in *Free-Trader* stood for, Dock Fivers always said—that made their way from freighter holds to stripers' hands. But there were always those who looked down upon the practice—or felt their free samples were never large enough or often enough.

The striper accepted the case, then studied Kaidee's data on her reader. "You're not rated to transport passengers, Captain."

"I know," Kaidee said. "I—"

But the striper was glancing to her left, frowning. "Mr. Barvin, I said you're free to go."

Devin had moved only a few steps away and stopped. Barthol, leaning heavily on Trip, waited behind him. "I just want to make sure there are no problems."

"You're a registered guest—"

"Problems with the captain," Devin continued smoothly over the striper's explanation.

The woman's frown deepened. "If she offered you passage off station, yeah, there is a problem. Because she's not rated for that."

"I didn't—" Kaidee began, but this time Devin cut her off.

"She offered us a way out of a bar fight where my elderly uncle was about to get his head bashed in or worse. We're grateful—enough that I'm concerned with what appears to be a misinterpretation on your part over Captain Griggs's role."

He should have been a professor. Or a barrister, Kaidee thought. Granted, Devin was taller than the striper, but he wasn't using his lean height so much as his voice and his gaze. Steely-eyed? She almost laughed. She'd been watching too many of those low-budget action vids Kiler had loaded into the *Rider*'s library.

Except those vid heroes never wore silver-rimmed eyeglasses. Or spoke with a cultured Sylvadae accent that clearly didn't belong on Dock Five. Or belong with her. And the sooner he made that clear to the striper, the better off he'd be.

"Maybe you don't understand what we got here on dock," the striper replied. The woman reset Kaidee's chip into the ID case, then tossed it to her. She turned back to Devin. "We got a lot of freighters on lockdown and a lot of captains who would easily risk a *misinterpretation*," and she stressed the word, barely concealing a sneer, "to get back in the lanes. Including lying about what they were rated to carry."

Kaidee bristled. Not that she hadn't thought about it. "I didn't—"

"Especially," the Takan female spoke out, her voice

carrying to where Kaidee stood, "when they have a lock lien on their ship from Z. M. Orvis." She leaned back from her deskscreen and, with a satisfied grin on her thin lips, crossed her arms over her chest. Gustav, still perched on the desk's edge, continued to study the screen. "In the amount of twenty-five thousand," he added without looking up.

"Thirteen thousand," Kaidee said quickly. Too quickly. *Shit. Next time you open your mouth, make sure your brain is in gear first.* She'd just aired her financial dirty laundry, not only to the striper but to Devin Guthrie.

She had no idea how or why the Taka had pulled up that information on her, but then, this was the hotel's supply office. It wasn't unlikely they'd have access to ship schedules, manifests, and, yes, financial status, which could affect a freighter's ability to deliver contracted goods. Or else—her luck—this Taka was the sister of the one Frinks had tailing her.

"Thirteen thousand," Kaidee repeated. "I've paid it down." She found Devin staring at her, eyes narrowed behind the clear lenses of his glasses. And her mind, with disgusting clarity, filled in the gaps: Makaiden Griggs had a lock lien on her ship and was found in the company of a missing Guthrie heir. Extortion, anyone?

Slagging wonderful. But she couldn't say anything to Devin without giving away who he was—something the striper and the Takan shipping clerk would no doubt find even more interesting. And damning.

"Look, Mr. De—Barvin. I'll get this all straightened out on my own. Okay? You're guests here. You're safe." She shrugged. She was rambling. She wanted them to leave. If the Taka had uncovered the lock lien, there was no telling what else she might dig up. Stuff on Kiler. Stuff on Makaiden before the Griggs surname granted her what she thought was safety and legitimacy.

None of this was Devin's, Trip's, or Barthol's problem.

Go away. Leave.

Her telepathic prodding failed. Devin didn't move, and Trip was frowning. Did the kid think she meant to use him? That hurt almost as much as the coldness in Devin's eyes. Only Barty seemed unconcerned, but then, he was playing elderly and infirm.

"Stay put, Captain Griggs," the striper said as she walked over to the Taka's desk. Hand on one hip, she stared at the screen. The Taka said something in a low voice that Kaidee couldn't hear. The striper nodded. Gustav nodded.

Kaidee glanced over her shoulder. *Go,* she mouthed to Trip, because he was the only one looking at her.

Then Barty sighed a pained, wheezing noise. "I do think it's time for my nap. This is a bit more excitement than I'm used to."

That seemed to accomplish what neither the striper's assurances or Kaidee's mental pleadings could. Devin and Trip turned to Barthol.

"Of course," Devin said. "Uncle." He put one hand under Barthol's elbow. "Officer, if you need a statement from us, leave word at the front desk."

So that was it, then. She was on her own. "Good luck, gentlemen," she called after them, as if they really were strangers, people thrown together by happenstance: a bar fight, a chance proximity of their table and hers. Not as if she was someone who'd been in their employ for several years, who'd shared meals, laughter, shopping excursions...

That was a different lifetime. A different Kaidee.

This Kaidee's life was in shambles. She imagined Devin was now very glad that Captain Makaiden Griggs was no longer in GGS employ.

She turned back to the trio at the deskscreen, ignoring the retreating steps of the trio behind her, the scrape of a hatchlock door. Then the sounds faded. Her sadness over losing Devin's respect flared to anger, adding a sharp note to her words. "I wasn't trolling for passengers."

The striper shot a quick glance at the closed hatch door, eyes narrowed, then back at Kaidee. "I have witnesses here," she said, "who say you were." She took a step toward Kaidee, hands on both hips now, chin lifted in defiance.

What in hell? "You have no proof of that."

"We have plenty." The striper looked over her shoulder at the Taka. "Let her hear it, Norga."

The Taka tapped at the deskscreen.

"If she offered you passage off station, yeah," the female striper's voice said clearly through the unit's speakers, "there is a problem. Because she's not rated for that."

"She offered." That was Devin's voice. "Yes."

A chill raced down Kaidee's spine and settled, hard, in the pit of her stomach. Norga had been doing more than researching her ship's status on her deskscreen.

"This young lady said she could get us out. Me and my nephews," Barty's voice said.

Then from Devin: "Officer, if you need a statement from us, leave word at the front desk."

The striper's smile was slow, confident, and damning.

Kaidee met her gaze without flinching. "What do you want?" Her voice was deliberately flat. Inside, she was screaming, kicking over the Taka's desk, pounding smarmy red-haired Gustav to a pulp, and smashing the deskscreen over the striper's head.

The smirk widened to a smile. "What do you think? Nice, law-abiding captains don't go around owing money to the likes of Orvis. Even before Norga found that info, you gave yourself away with those hatch codes. That guy from Aldan, what is he? A new buyer? He sure wasn't happy to find out about the lock lien, was he?"

"What," Kaidee repeated, "do you want?"

"That ship of yours is a sweet Blackfire. Fast. Probably got some even sweeter modifications."

Gustav snorted out a laugh at the striper's words.

"Or you wouldn't even be working for Orvis," the striper continued.

I'm not working for Orvis, she almost said but stopped. One, she knew the woman wouldn't believe her, and, two, if the striper or Norga dug deep enough into their obviously less-than-legal databases, they'd find proof that, yes, at one time the *Void Rider* did have ties to Orvis's pirate enterprise.

Kiler's death severed that connection but not the debt.

"If you think I'm going to turn my ship over to you rather than face charges of illegal passenger transport, I'll take my chances with the latter," Kaidee said.

"No, no, you got it all wrong!" The striper chuckled. "I don't want your ship, Captain Griggs. We're here"—and she flashed a quick look at Norga and Gustav—"to offer you our special services. *Protection.*" She stressed the word. "You know how it works. We'll keep your little secret, keep the authorities from hassling you so you can continue your, uh, lucrative business. All we want in return is a small fee. Say, four thousand a month."

It was a shakedown. No wonder the striper hung out at Norga's desk. Just like Pops, Norga had the data on ships docking here. The striper had the muscle. Kaidee wondered how many other captains were already paying a "protection fee" based on words gleaned from ordinary conversations in Norga's office, then twisted into incriminating statements.

She also wondered if the CFTC knew about this. Or, not unlikely, was in on it.

"And if I say no?"

The woman's eyes went hard and cold. "Then illegal-passenger-transport charges will only be the beginning. Trust me on that."

"We'll keep your little secret, keep the authorities from hassling you so you can continue your, uh, lucrative business." The striper's voice, sounding a bit hollow, echoed into the room, and not from Norga's deskscreen. Kaidee jerked around, looking for the source. So did the striper, Norga, and Gustav.

The hatchlock to the old access tunnel swung open. Devin Guthrie crouched on its edge, microcomp in his left, Carver in his right. Shock surged through her. Why had he come back? Surely not for her sake.

"Two can play at this game, Officer." His voice was light, but he wasn't smiling.

"All we want in return is a small fee. Say, four thousand a month," the woman's voice continued, but from a different direction.

Kaidee spun. Barthol stood in the main hatchlock to the hotel corridor, also with a microcomp and a Carver. "I would advise against any sudden movements," he said, all traces of age and infirmity gone from his voice and stance.

Devin's boots hit the decking. "Back away. Over there." He waved his weapon at Norga and Gustav.

"Now." He clipped his Rada back onto his belt as he took the seat Norga vacated.

Barty moved toward Kaidee. "Captain Griggs, I could use your assistance."

She was already reaching for her L7. "Gladly." She didn't know why Devin and Barty had returned, but she was damned glad they did.

"Hands out, turn, face the wall," Barty ordered.

The trio grumbled but complied.

Barthol pulled the striper's pistol from its holster and then tossed it across the decking toward Devin.

Out of the corner of her eye, Kaidee watched the weapon skim the floor. She could see Devin's Carver on the desk, his focus and fingers on the deskscreen as he altered or erased whatever data Norga had on Kaidee and, possibly, others. The Guthries were known to be generous, but she wasn't sure how far their generosity extended in this situation or how long it would extend to her. She knew what Devin had heard; she could guess at what he was thinking. That made her consider for a moment why he was even helping her. But then, she'd been associated with GGS. Scandal of any sort—especially with Philip Guthrie's current renegade status—wasn't something GGS wanted.

Suddenly the striper dropped down, swinging out with one leg, her boot making contact with Barty's ankle. He stumbled, falling backward. Kaidee fired, her shot hitting the striper in the hip. Not center mass—not enough to fully stun the officer—but enough to put her flat on the decking, her eyes blinking rapidly as her body went limp.

Barty rolled onto his back, Carver gripped with both hands. "Freeze!"

Norga froze. Gustav bolted, throwing himself at Devin as Devin turned in the desk chair. They crashed against the desk, grunting, swearing, the chair's deck lock keeping it and them upright. Kaidee took aim, but there was too much movement for her to get a clear shot. Devin grabbed Gustav's shoulders. Gustav shoved him back. Coffee mugs flew, spattering liquid. A basket of datatabs upended, clattering as they hit the sides of the desk, then the decking. Gustav tried to pin Devin against the desktop, but Devin swung at him, his fist catching Gustav's left ear with a smack. Gustav fell sideways against the desk, then sprang just as Barty fired. Barty's shot grazed the desk where Gustav had been a second before.

Someone shifted in Kaidee's peripheral vision. She switched her aim from the struggle at the desk to Norga. The tall Taka held still, all but radiating with intensity. The striper near Norga's boots groaned, swearing, but her limbs were motionless—at least until the effects of the stunner wore off.

Which could be any second now.

Oh, hell. Kaidee flicked her stunner to full charge and fired again at the striper, catching her center mass this time. Then, before Norga could react, she hit the Taka with a blast in the chest. The Taka collapsed next to the unconscious striper.

Kaidee swung around toward Devin, aware of Barty now on his feet. A high-pitched blast zinged by her. Gustav arched back, his right hand splaying outward, a knife Kaidee hadn't seen until that moment falling from his fingers.

Devin angled himself up from the desk, his glasses skewed, blood staining the left shoulder of his sweater where his jacket had pulled away.

Kaidee's heart caught in her throat. God and stars, no, not Devin.

She shoved her L7 into its holster, then grabbed his arm, steadying him as he tried to stand. "Devin!"

"Fuck. That hurts." His voice was low, his words slurring.

"I suggest," Barty said, grabbing Devin's other arm as he swayed toward them, "we get him up to our room, quickly."

Kaidee shot a glance at the unconscious striper as she put one arm around Devin's waist. He leaned heavily on her—all lean, wiry muscle. "But she knows—"

"Nothing. The room card he gave her was bogus— an old trick I've used dozens of times. Plus, I erased her datapad, and he should have deleted any traces they did on you."

"But she . . . They know my name, my ship's name."

"You hit them on full charge, didn't you? Then we have at least four hours before they wake up. With a little luck, given what we know about them, that's not a lead they're going to want to follow."

A little luck? How about an enormous, galactic-size dose of luck? Something Kaidee never had, not in her entire life. She only had Kiler. Then Orvis and Frinks. And now one very pissed-off striper.

And one very injured Devin Guthrie.

Fucking slagging son of a bitch! A dozen more epithets crossed Devin's mind but not his lips as he lay on the bed in his hotel room, with Barty working what he called "field medicine" on the wound in Devin's shoulder. Field medicine meant antiquated methods of dealing with the deep gash, because getting to a med-tech right now would require answering questions they didn't want asked—considering there was an unconscious striper in The Celestian's supply office three floors below.

Field medicine also meant pain—in spite of the copious amounts of Lashto brandy Barty had poured down Devin's throat—but it was a pain Devin would not voice, because Makaiden was a few feet away in that same hotel room, her soft brown eyes filled with worry and compassion.

At least he hoped that's what it was. With his glasses off and the brandy in his gut, he couldn't be one hundred percent sure.

So he was taking it like a man, just in case it was compassion. Just in case she might be as...irrevocably intrigued by him as he was by her.

She's married, his conscience reminded him.

But that doesn't mean she couldn't feel compassion, he argued back. Maybe she'd even grant a dying man his last wish. Except he should save that for when he was actually dying. Not just feeling as if he was dying.

"Did that hurt?" Barty the torturer asked.

"Not really," Devin lied through clenched teeth.

"I need another towel." Barty glanced up to where Trip—looking a bit pale and tight-lipped himself—stood next to Makaiden.

His nephew nodded and loped quickly for the lav, then returned as quickly, towel in hand.

"Put pressure on his shoulder right here," Barty instructed. "I have to dig those barbs out."

Oh, yeah, the knife the bastard shoved into his shoulder was barbed. Lovely.

Trip paled even more.

Makaiden grabbed the towel. "I'll do it."

Then she was next to him on the bed, arms reaching across his bare chest, hands pushing on his shoulder, her hip against his side. He liked her close. He could see her face more clearly. Her eyes, her mouth, the column of her neck, and the swell of her breasts against the gray fabric of—

"Fuck!" Pain jolted him, blinding him momentarily, leaving him gasping for breath, his right hand fisting against his chest.

"That's one," his torturer said.

A small, warm hand slipped into his. "Hang on to me, Devin. Squeeze my hand tight."

His panting slowed. He focused on the feel of her fingers wrapped around his and was ashamed by the way his arm trembled. Ashamed he couldn't be stronger, braver. And she was leaning so close . . .

"Come here often?" His voice was a low rasp as his mind sought for a diversion from the pain. The pain in his shoulder. The pain in his heart.

She was married—

"Only by special request." Her smile was soft but didn't reach her eyes.

—to Kiler Griggs, who obviously had thrust them into a world of financial shit. The name Orvis meant nothing to Devin, but he knew what a lock lien was. The old whispers about Kiler Griggs surfaced again through the haze of brandy fogging his mind. Gambling? His mind couldn't focus, but it had to be something like that. So Kiler Griggs had gambled away their money and their ship, and here was Makaiden, toughing it out. Because she loved her husband and stood by him.

He probably should suspect her of involvement in the plot to get Trip, but he couldn't. Not only had she saved their asses twice over, but... she was Makaiden. All he wanted to do was take her shopping. Buy her the galaxy, wrap it in ribbons, just for her.

"Need new sweater," he managed. His old one was in shreds on the floor.

"Yeah, you do."

"Help me find—" He choked on the word, pain searing, flaring down his chest, his arm, exploding into his brain. He was sure he was crushing her hand, but the only groans he heard were his own.

"That's two," said a voice as Devin's world dropped into darkening shadows.

The lights came on behind his eyelids. He slitted them open. "Makaiden?"

Pressure on his fingers. No more pressure on his shoulder. She was there, yes, still beside him, still holding his hand. Barty was...

...a blurry figure across the room, talking to another blurry figure he recognized as Trip.

Devin licked his lips. His mouth was dry. He had a blistering headache.

"Welcome back," she said.

He must have passed out. *Oh, real good, Dev. Big, strong, manly thing to do.* Philip, he knew, would never pass out from pain. "How long... what time..."

"Not long. Fifteen minutes or so. Barty got the rest of the barbs out and sent a transmit to your father that Trip is safe."

His ego gloated for a moment, visualizing his father's, Jonathan's, and Ethan's surprise that, yes, Devin rescued Trip and they were all—somewhat—safe on Dock Five. Depending on how the transmit was sent, it could be anywhere from hours to days before they heard back from his family. His imaginings would have to do for now. He made a mental note to send an update himself and to request an update back on the Baris–Agri deal.

"You want something to drink?" Makaiden reached for a translucent white plastic cup on the nightstand.

Devin's stomach rebelled, and all thoughts of his sweet victory fled from his mind. "Don't ever want to see Lashto brandy again."

She laughed and passed the empty cup to Barty. "I meant water."

He heard Barthol snort. Then the thud of footsteps and Trip's face came into view. His nephew looked as tired and pained as Devin felt.

"Uncle Devin? I'm sorry, really. I didn't mean ... I didn't think any of this would happen. I'm sorry."

Barty appeared behind Trip and held out the cup of water. "I told him about Halsey."

"Halsey was fine, alive when I left. I swear." Trip's wide eyes held confusion and pain.

Devin angled up to accept the water. It was cool, went down easily, and didn't make noises about coming back up.

Barty was shaking his head slowly. "Trip last saw Halsey alone in the kitchen, slicing an apple for a late snack. Trip said he was going to study in his room, then go to sleep. Using a loud music vid for cover—

Trip's done this before, you know—he climbed out his window, then into a friend's apartment. They'd swapped security codes."

It sounded as if Trip had been taking lessons from his uncle Ethan. Except Ethan always got caught.

"I left a message on Halsey's private comm before I boarded my flight," Trip said, a defensive tone in his voice. "I didn't tell him where I was, just said not to worry, that I'd contact him in a couple days." He hesitated, the foolishness of his actions now very apparent to him. "I only wanted to reach Uncle Philip before they could stop me."

Something surfaced through the fog that was Devin's mind. "We checked Halsey's comm messages. There was nothing."

Barty was nodding. "Someone listened and erased it. And either got someone to the spaceport or had someone waiting here on Dock Five. We don't know because Trip didn't realize he'd been followed until Captain Griggs questioned him."

"Kaidee," she put in, correcting him.

"Kaidee and Trip," Barty continued, taking the empty cup from Devin, "got a good look at the men—Fuzz-face is what she calls the ringleader. He tried to tag Trip with a Lockpoint. Trip ditched it, but they found him again anyway. So did Kaidee. She got him to Trouble's Brewing, which is where we found them."

It was a quick, concise recounting. And, Devin suspected, far from the full story. But his brain honestly couldn't handle much more.

"We don't think our striper friend and Norga are a related problem," Barty said.

"That was my error," Makaiden said softly. No, Kaidee. She always called herself Kaidee. Why? Makaiden was such a beautiful name. He had a hard time thinking of her otherwise. He decided not to try.

He squeezed her fingers, which made her look at him and made him realize how irrevocably lost he was. His head was spinning, and not just because of the brandy. He cleared his throat. "The lock lien. Have...tell Kiler I can—I need to talk to him about that." He stumbled over the words, not sure where assistance became insult.

Her brows dipped, her eyes narrowed, and he knew he'd gone too far. A couple's financial issues were personal. Their problem. Not some stranger's, even if that stranger was a former employer, a friend who was irrevocably—

"Kiler's dead. He was doing repair jobs for extra money and was killed in an explosion."

Devin stopped breathing. He stopped breathing, thinking, *anything*, because the only thing he was aware of were her words. And they encompassed his entire world at that moment.

Kiler's dead. Makaiden's husband was dead.

She was...not married. Not anymore.

His heart surged. But laughing with joy, he suspected, would not be an appropriate response. "Makaiden. I'm sorry."

She looked away from him with a half shrug, half sigh. Her fingers slid from his and, after a few seconds, she pushed them through her hair. He wanted to pull her hand back. He wanted her warmth.

"Sorry doesn't begin to cover it," she said, and he desperately tried to read the odd tone of her voice. Grief? Fear? Grief would make sense. Fear didn't, unless it was fear of being alone and destitute.

He could fix that.

"My condolences." Barthol's voice held exactly the

right amount of respect and concern. But then, he was Barthol. The enigmatic Guthrie steward and former ImpSec assassin with impeccable manners.

Makaiden shoved herself to her feet, then paced away from the bed, shoulders hunched. "Everything Norga told you is true. We had financial issues. Kiler...got involved in things, with people he shouldn't have. My fault. I just thought he...Well, I didn't ask enough questions. But that's my problem." She turned back. "You have to get Trip somewhere safe until you can get him home and find out who killed Halsey and why. And safe, obviously, is nowhere around me."

"I was very safe around you," Trip said slowly. "And, uh, I'm sorry. About your husband. I liked him."

"Thank you." Makaiden slid her hands into the pockets of her pants, looked at Trip for a moment, then down at her boots.

She's bailing on us. Devin knew the signs, read the discomfort and capitulation in her body language in the same way he had in dozens of financial negotiation meetings over the years. Except in those same meetings he was completely sober and fully alert. Not muzzy-headed and half blind.

All he knew was he couldn't lose her. Not now. He'd just found her again, after all those years. The fact that his reason for being here was to find Trip and bring him home slid into the background. Kiler Griggs was dead. Makaiden suddenly was a dream within reach. He painfully pushed himself up on one elbow. "Makaiden—"

"There's a guy who has a repair shop on Green Level. Popovitch Expert Repair Service. You can trust Pops, and he knows things, people who might be able to help you. I don't know," and this she directed to

Barthol, "how much you know about Dock Five. How current your info is. Pops has been here a long time."

"I appreciate that. And your concern for our safety."

If Devin could have managed it, he would have hurled his pillow at Barty. *Don't tell her you appreciate her concern. Tell her she has to stay!*

"But, Captain Griggs! What if that striper tries to blackmail you?" Trip stepped toward her, hands splayed, and Devin thanked God and the stars that someone in the room had a modicum of sense. "You need our help."

"I need, Master Trip, to get my ship working so I can pay off Kiler's debt. Tage has to lift that embargo soon, and if I'm anywhere but on my ship when that happens, I'll miss a bunch of opportunities." She reached out and took his hand in an affectionate gesture. "I'll be fine. Nobody gets on board the *Rider* unless I let them. You take care of Barthol and your uncle."

Trip's uncle didn't like the sound of that. "Makaiden..."

But she'd released Trip's hand and was headed for the door, determination in the hard set of her shoulders. She thought she was protecting them. But he couldn't lose her now.

"Makaiden, wait."

She reached for the palm pad, clearly with no intention of waiting.

Devin sucked in a hard breath and pushed everything out of his mind except that he was a Guthrie. "Captain Griggs."

That got her attention. She turned.

Please stay wouldn't work, even though that was on the tip of his tongue. *Please stay* might have her asking why, and he wasn't ready to answer that out loud, if she even believed him—

I've been irrevocably intrigued by you for years.

—and especially not in front of Barty and Trip. Moreover, *please stay* didn't erase Kiler's debts or her shame over them. But that did provide him with something workable. He jerked his chin toward Barthol's DRECU on the small table. The room spun. He closed his eyes for a moment, then opened them. "Get me the exact figures on your ship's . . ." His mind hazed. What was the term? Oh. "Lock lien." That was it. "It won't take me more than fifteen, twenty minutes to transfer the funds to pay it off."

She stared at him.

He waited for a smile, something that said she realized how brilliantly he'd solved her problem.

She stared at him.

He'd been too abrupt. He saw that now. It was so easy for him to talk about money that he often forgot not everyone felt that way. "I—we owe you. You helped Trip—"

"You think I did that for some kind of reward?"

He wished he had his glasses on. She sounded angry, but without them he couldn't see the small nuances in her expression. "I'm sure that wasn't in the forefront of your mind—"

"What was in the forefront of my mind was that a bunch of thugs were beating the crap out of some kid. A kid I *like*, and not because of his bank account."

"That doesn't preclude the fact that you helped him. Therefore, we owe you." It seemed logical enough to him. Why couldn't she see that?

"Mr. Devin. Say thank you."

"What?"

"Say 'Thank you, Captain Griggs.' "

He didn't understand her point. "Thank you, Captain Griggs."

"You're welcome. Now you don't owe me anything." She slapped at the palm pad, then disappeared through the opening door into the corridor, leaving him bereft and thoroughly confused.

He sat up straighter, only to have Barty's hand firmly force him back down. "You're bleeding again. I need to redo that dressing."

Devin's head hurt. Actually, more than his head hurt if he wanted to be honest about it, but he didn't want to be honest about it. He also didn't want to be listening to Barthol detailing plans to leave Dock Five, as much as he knew his primary responsibility was to get Trip safely back to Sylvadae. Instead, Devin wanted to be tearing down the corridor after Makaiden.

He doubted he could walk across the hotel room without falling over. Pulling on a clean shirt had left him gasping.

Then Barty said they were leaving. Now.

"It's been two hours forty-five minutes." Barty had a duffel open and was quickly but neatly putting things inside. "We need to be far away from here by the time that striper or her friends regain consciousness and, if they're so inclined, give out descriptions of their attackers."

"How far away can we possibly get?" He gingerly pushed himself into a sitting position, dragging the bed pillows behind him as he did. His desire to be with Makaiden warred once again with his obligation to Trip and the family. That made his tone turn petulant. "This is Dock Five. The flight you booked doesn't leave for two days."

"Exactly my point. We only need to keep moving for two days. There are a few hotels—that's a loose description, of course—that have a room available. One for tonight. Another for the following night."

Trip had taken over one of the desk chairs and sat backward on it, his long legs out to either side, his arms folded across the chair's back. His chin rested on his hands. "That means Captain Griggs is in danger. They don't know our real names, but they know hers, what she looks like."

That thought had plagued Devin ever since Makaiden walked out the door ten minutes before, ever since his money failed to keep her with him. He had two more days to keep trying.

"Aside from the fact that her ship is in a defensible position," Barty was saying, "they're not going to challenge Orvis to get at her. In a convoluted way, her debt—"

"Her husband's debt," Devin said.

"—assures her safety."

Did she know that? Was that why his offer angered her? His thoughts turned in circles so that he was only peripherally aware of Barty digging around in a small blue med-kit—until something stung the side of Devin's neck.

"A small stimulant," Barthol told him, tossing the thumb-size hypo back into the kit. "It should kick in in about three to five minutes." He lifted his chin toward Trip. "Help your uncle get on his feet. I'll get his jacket."

Devin waved away Trip's outstretched hand, already feeling the stim's surge of energy. Teeth gritted, he swung his legs around to the edge of the bed. The room tilted, but only slightly. Not bad.

"Please let Trip help you up. You're far from one hundred percent right now."

"I can do it." Devin leaned on his good arm and tried to push himself off the bed. His left knee buckled.

"I may have to shoot your uncle if he doesn't listen to me," Barty grumbled, grabbing Devin around the waist.

"Trust me. The way I feel right now, it would be a great kindness."

"Trip, take our duffels, will you? We're not going far. Just down two levels to Yellow."

"Yellow? Oh, hell." Trip slung the duffels' straps over one shoulder with ease. "We're going back to Pisstown."

Kaidee shoved through the stairwell door at the far end of the hotel corridor, anger and shame roiling through her as she listened for footsteps behind her and tried hard not to listen to the running commentary in her head. *He offered you a way out of debt. A legitimate way out. And you turned him down. Rudely.*

Well, yeah, she was fairly good at being rude when she wanted to be. Another thing she'd learned from Kiler.

The problem was that Devin had once again proved how decent and honorable he was by trapping the striper at her own game, saving Kaidee's ass, and then taking a knife in the shoulder as a thank-you. And Kaidee felt like a complete shit for wanting to be rude to him. But, yeah, she did want to, because, truth be told, his offer hit too close to home port. Too close to her own inner desires. Too close to things that ran through her head when she stumbled over Trippy Guthrie: maybe the kid would give her a loan.

Okay, she'd discounted that idea quickly. But it had surfaced and then Devin had echoed it, and it felt as if he'd read her mind or, worse, the darkness of her soul—something she never wanted him to see.

She needed money—but not that way, not from Devin guessing almost so accurately at her motivations. How long, then, before he believed she was involved in the whole "get Trippy" scheme? Not long, if he probed any deeper into Kiler's debts.

She had to stay away from him. She couldn't bear the further disappointment in his eyes when he found out. He already knew far too much about her, and none of it was good.

She reached the main lobby level and stopped, catching her breath. She leaned her hand on the stairwell door. For three seconds she reversed her decision completely, thought of turning around, running back up three flights of stairs and admitting, *pleading*, that, yes, a loan—she'd make sure it was only a loan—would really help at this point. She could get Frinks off her tail and maybe even renew the *Rider*'s lapsed passenger certification. That would give her options besides cargo, help her through the lean times, which she knew were far from over.

But she couldn't do it. She pushed open the stairwell door—slowly enough to be cautious but firmly enough that there was no doubt as to her direction. Out. Back to her ship. Away from Devin Guthrie and his smoky-blue eyes and strong firm fingers that held hers with surprising tenderness.

Idiot. The man was half drunk and thoroughly in pain. There was no tenderness, and she was a fool to even think there could be. He was a Guthrie, probably tagged to marry some socialite from Sylvadae, just as his brothers had. If he wasn't married already.

And Kaidee Griggs was an itinerant freighter operator and a thief's ex-wife. At best, she was a former GGS employee—and one not worth rehiring. She heard that clearly in the harsh way he'd said "Captain Griggs" as she left his hotel room.

Sounds from the lobby filtered in past the door's edge: a man's voice, high-pitched, whining about systems errors slowing down the slagging computers again. A soft thud, then a barked command: "Put that suitcase back on the pallet!"

A scraping noise of something dragging over the decking. A muted thud of a door closing. A soft laugh.

She shoved past the partly open door and slipped down a dimly lit side corridor leading away from the lobby, praying there were no stripers scanning the crowds on Blue for her likeness. Orvis, Frinks, and now a Dock Five striper all had reason to view Makaiden Griggs with an unhealthy interest.

What a lucky girl she was.

Hand on her L7 stunner, she exited and cautiously wove her way through clumps of freighter crew and dockworkers. If there was trouble, it would be at the *Rider*'s hatchlock. If there wasn't, there was no way she was leaving her ship again. The Empire had to lift the embargo soon. She wanted to be in the pilot's seat filing her flight plans out of here when they did. If they didn't, she could starve just as easily on board her ship as in Dock Five's corridors. And a lot more comfortably.

Though she had lied to Trippy: the *Rider* wasn't as secure as she'd said it was. Her ship could be breached, because she'd been forced to strip out and sell that top-end security system Kiler had installed.

That bought her some fuel, some water, and

allowed her to make an additional cargo run a few months back.

She hoped now it hadn't also sealed her death warrant.

Pisstown. Devin had wondered about Trip's odd descriptive and wondered even more when Barty neither contradicted nor corrected Trip's crude phrasing. Now he wondered how people—well, humans—even breathed on this level without falling to the decking, retching.

He pushed down the bile rising in his throat. It tasted all too familiarly of Lashto brandy. His chest hurt, his shoulder throbbed, and as a headache hovered somewhere between his eyes, he realized his glasses' frame must have twisted during the fight in the hotel's cargo office, and his eyes were forced to strain to adjust to the now-crooked lenses.

Yet, in spite of all that, he couldn't stop thinking about—*worrying* about—Makaiden. Once they had Trip settled in wherever Barty was leading them, he'd—

"Uncle Devin." Trip's voice was soft, but his grip on Devin's arm was tight. "I think that's one of Fuzzface's friends. Over there by the escalator."

Shit. It was the curly-haired man in the dark jacket who'd wrestled with Barty earlier. Only now he sported the beginnings of a black eye—an eye that, fortunately, wasn't looking at them. Yet.

Barty plucked his DRECU from under his jacket and brought it up in a quick motion, then down again. "There are databases I may still have access to," he said, nudging Trip toward a corridor on the right.

"We'll run this image once we obtain our new hotel room. This way. Now."

Devin kept his hand on his Carver as they twice had to backtrack and try an alternate route to the hotel Barty had chosen. They spotted the curly-haired man once more. A group of stripers, talking and laughing, forced their other rerouting. By the time they hurried through the hotel's narrow doorway, Devin had almost gotten used to the stench that was Pisstown.

The hotel lobby—if it could be called that—was a brightly lit enclosure a bit larger than the living room of his suite at his parents' estate on Sylvadae. But there the similarities ended. The lobby decking was covered in a stained dark-yellow carpet. The walls, also yellow, were bare. One industrial-looking spotlight dangled over a lumpy bright-red couch that flanked the wall to his right. Another illuminated the registration counter.

"No vacancy." The woman behind the counter— the lobby's only occupant—had short-cropped orange hair and purple stars tattooed down the left side of her wide face. Devin judged her to be somewhere between twenty-five and forty-five in age and easily triple his weight. Her short-sleeved white shirt—oddly pristine— had *Happy Hours Hotel* stenciled on the front. Her gaze was glued to a mini-vid player just below the level of the counter.

Barty stepped closer to the edge of the counter. "I'm Bart Mikmin. I reserved a room an hour ago under Mikmin Repair and Supply."

Purple Stars glanced up, her gaze darting from Barty to Trip to Devin, then back to Barty again. "No vacancy."

Devin pursed his mouth in frustration, suddenly understanding the game. He palmed a twenty-credit chip from his pocket, then leaned on the counter, realizing too late that the countertop had large sticky patches that pulled at the edge of his jacket sleeve. He let the blue edge of the chip peek through his fingers, careful not to let his skin come in contact with whatever coated the counter. "Maybe the computers are slow again and the reservation just came in."

With a sigh, Purple Stars swiveled toward the deskscreen.

Barty angled slightly so that the hotel's narrow doorway was in his line of sight. Devin fought the urge to keep one hand on his Carver. So far this had been a frustrating, exhausting, and damned near deadly day. And it wasn't over yet.

Purple Stars was poking disinterestedly at the touchpad in front of her. "M-I-C-K-M-A-N?"

"M-I-K-M-I-N," Barty corrected.

Devin let the chip drop onto her desk's touchpad.

Fleshy fingers with bright yellow-painted nails snagged the chip in a practiced move. "Yeah, slaggin' system's slow today. Room 109." Something whirred behind her. She plucked the keycard from the tray and dropped it on the counter in front of Devin. "Corridor on the left. Checkout's at first shift bell or you'll be double-charged."

Devin grabbed the keycard. "Thanks."

"My pleasure, cutie. I'm here for the next six hours, if you need me." She winked, her smile showing off broken teeth.

The Lashto brandy in Devin's stomach threatened to rise again.

The room was smaller than the previous one, and its cleanliness was definitely in question. It held one narrow bed with a red coverlet, a wooden nightstand with a lamp bolted to the top, and a low two-drawer black metal chest. The lav was closet-size. The only positive, as far as Devin could see, was that in here no one was trying to grab Trip or shoot at them.

"It's arguably one of the safest places on dock," Barty explained, pulling one of the duffels out of Trip's grasp. "This level of the hotel has three hidden exits. All connect to old service tunnels. Two go down to Orange. One goes up to Green. Pirates love this place. And if it was good enough for the likes of the infamous Captain Nathaniel Milo, or Screech and her band of merry thieves, then it will serve us well."

Fighting pain, weariness, and, he realized with an odd start, hunger, Devin sagged down on the bed. The decking was probably softer. "You call that safe?"

"I call it 'nice to have options.'" Barty retrieved a small data cradle from the duffel and plopped his microcomp into the slotted stand. "Let's see if one of my former colleagues recognizes a face."

"Any chance these guys after Trip are ImpSec? Tage's people?"

"ImpSec doesn't—or didn't—bother kidnapping people. Plus, there's a sloppiness here, a desperation that doesn't smell like the Empire to me." Barty grimaced at his screen. "The Farosians are easily excitable. I just don't know why they'd target Trip."

Devin didn't either. But he did know that the suppositions J.M. and Jonathan had made about Trip's uncovering some politically sensitive material were wrong. "What if it's not political but financial? Corporate?"

"It still comes back to the question of your nephew as the target. If someone's after GGS, it would make more sense if they'd try to take out your father or Jonathan. Or you."

"Want me to unpack, Uncle Devin?" Trip asked while craning his neck at Barty's screen.

"Leave it. I doubt we're staying long." Though Devin felt as if he could sleep for a year in spite of the stim.

"We'll move to a new hotel tomorrow. But right now we need food, and we need rest." Barty echoed Devin's concerns without looking up from his hand-held. "Especially you, Mr. Devin. I need to check that knife wound—"

"Later." Devin was already pulling his own micro-comp from the duffel. *You can sleep when you're dead,* he remembered Grandmother Guthrie saying. "Since this place comes highly recommended by your pirate friends—"

"I never said they were my friends."

"—can I also assume I can get a secure data connection here?"

"You can. Use this code."

A series of numbers and letters flashed on Devin's screen. He grabbed the data, shunted it into his security strings, brought up the holographic display, and went information-hunting to see who else was still looking for Trip Guthrie. And anything he could quickly find on Kiler and Makaiden Griggs.

He wanted only the basics. He didn't have a lot of time to waste. Regardless of who was looking for Trip, his nephew was now ostensibly safe. Barty would make sure they were on one of the Compass Spacelines flights back to Aldan in two days. He included that information in the brief message to his father about Trip's recovery and remembered to ask about Baris–Agri. It even was possible that GGS security could meet them at an intercept point. Compass Spacelines had stopovers at Marker.

Makaiden was another matter, but he wasn't about to go charging into her life without knowing what he was up against. He didn't have ImpSec training like Barty or military training like Philip. This was pure corporate strategy, where information created leverage. And when it came to Makaiden Griggs, Devin Jonathan Guthrie knew he needed all the leverage he could get.

Fifteen minutes later he was frowning at the data on his display, wishing he had Guthrie Global's powerful high-tech systems to work with and not this small, albeit top-notch, microcomp. He found no more traces of anyone poking into Trip's financials, which could be good news. Or it could mean they were stealthier and craftier than he was.

Slim chance, but he couldn't discount it.

What troubled him more was the information he was able to unravel on Kiler Griggs's livelihood post-GGS. There was something odd about an apparently lucrative and well-funded—and it *was* well-funded—cargo and transport business suddenly spiraling toward financial ruin. The *Void Rider*'s client list showed more than twenty excellent firms, including Mapper–Corden out of Marker. Hauling cargo for Mapper–Corden alone could have kept Kiler and Makaiden comfortable. Yet mechanics' liens filed even before Kiler's death indicated that funds were going out faster than they were coming in. The *Rider*, according to specs on file with Dock Five, was a Blackfire 225 and wasn't old enough to incur those kinds of repair costs.

Illegal upgrades, as in pirate? He didn't discount that. Nor did he discount the possibility that Kiler gambled to excess.

But those things didn't explain it either.

He also couldn't explain the inordinate amount of activity the *Rider* handled for a firm called Nahteg Galactic. Devin had never heard of Nahteg, but given its stated volume in Dock Five's records, he should have. Nahteg, it appeared, was almost single-handedly keeping Kiler Griggs in business.

A silent partner? A front for a pirate operation?

On its surface, Nahteg looked completely legitimate. Its headquarters were in Port Chalo on Talgarrath. All the proper corporate legal papers were on file. But Devin quickly pierced the surface and superficial. And found himself going in circles.

Familiar circles. *If I wanted to set up an illegal operation, this is almost how I would have done it.* Nahteg was a front, and a damned good one. He just didn't know what it was a front for, or why Kiler Griggs was chosen as its main transporter. And with only Dock Five data as his resource, Devin was having a damned difficult time finding out.

"Nahteg Galactic." He looked at Barty. Trip had seated himself on the decking, back against the wall, with his head resting against his folded arms. Dozing or sleeping, probably. Devin felt a commiserating wave of exhaustion wash over him.

"Hmm?" Barty glanced up from his microcomp.

"Ever heard of them?"

The older man's brow furrowed. "No."

"Can you ask your, um, friends?"

"Send me the data."

Devin tapped his screen. "Sending. Anything yet on Fuzz-face's thugs?"

"Dock Five's databases hold nothing. My queries to Aldan and Calth could have an answer back in as little as three to four hours. Or it could be days. We might well be back on Sylvadae before we know."

Devin would have preferred an answer now, but he knew the vagaries of intersector communication, especially in an area as remote as Dock Five. But the delay

gave him more time to concentrate on what he really
wanted: Makaiden Griggs. Too bad he couldn't just
buy a ship and hire her to fly it for him.

Then again...

"Captain Griggs."

Kaidee heard the now-familiar voice call her name
as she reached the top of the *Rider*'s rampway. She let
her hand rest on her L7 but didn't draw it as she
turned, arguing with herself that only desperate people
took desperate actions. And she wasn't yet ready to be
perceived as desperate—even if she was.

"What do you want, Frinks?" She forced a bored
tone into her voice.

The thin-faced man rocked back on his heels, grinning. "Just a friendly reminder. You have two days left
to repay that debt."

"Two days as of tomorrow."

"It's damned near that now."

It was, and she felt every goddamned minute of it.
She was tired. She was hungry. And, as much as she
didn't want to admit it, she was scared. "As soon as the
lanes open, I'll have work. You *know* that. Orvis—"

"Wants payment. Two days."

She watched him leave the bay, the hard soles of his
pointed-toe boots slapping crisply against the metal
decking, the sound fading along with her racing heart.
Two days or...what? She'd be dead like Gudrin Vere?

She had a feeling that would be too easy. Orvis had
other ways of "working off a debt." It was rumored he
owned casino operations and several high-class nighthouses, though she doubted she was pretty enough to
service the kinds of wealthy clients his places attracted. Not that she wanted to, but at least in the

nighthouses, the perversions and brutality would be—if not halted—discouraged.

But there were other establishments Orvis was rumored to own—places where nothing was discouraged and no one cared what a prosti looked like.

She sealed the *Rider*'s airlock behind her and headed for her ship's small bridge. Maybe she should talk to Pops again about any spare parts she could sell. Trouble was, she didn't have thirteen thousand worth. But then . . . every freighter hand knew ways to break dock and leave a berth without permission, without filing a flight plan. Though often not without some damage to the ship.

She slumped down in the pilot's seat and wondered just how far her ship would get before the Imperial warships guarding the lanes opened fire.

At least a hull breach would be a quick death.

And if nothing else it would give her a chance to see Kiler again and beat the crap out of him in hell.

Kaidee woke, the dim light of her cabin turning shadows into familiar shapes, the hushed wheeze of her ship's enviro the only sound.

She opened her eyes and, with a groan, rolled over. Her bare feet hit the decking. She padded to the lav across the narrow hallway from her equally narrow bedroom, stripping out of her well-worn gray sweatpants as she did. She pulled her baggy thermal nightshirt over her head, the cabin's perpetual chill wrapping around her body. A long hot shower would be wasteful, given the cost of water. But she wanted one.

She had only two days left to live anyway.

Melodrama doesn't suit you, Kaid.

The shower sluiced off the last remnants of sleep. A mug of hot tea from the built-in beverage and food dispenser—the standard "slurp-and-snack"—in her main room's galley unit quieted her rumbling stomach. Clad again in her usual freighter grays, she headed down the corridor past the small Deck 1 cargo hold, past her ship's sole lift, for the bridge. As in all Blackfires, with their distinctive V-shaped bow, the *Rider*'s bridge was almost triangular, with piloting and screens that monitored all ship's systems at the front U-shaped console, navigation on the right, and communications on the left. She settled into the black swivel chair in front of the *Rider*'s comm panel to check transmits, dock news, and to see if her name appeared on any arrest warrants yet.

If my ass is in jail, will Orvis still expect payment?

She toyed with that thought for a few moments, then realized that someone like Orvis probably had both corrections officers and inmates on his payroll. There was nowhere she was safe from him.

Except that Devin offered...

She shoved the thought away. She couldn't risk seeing him again. Couldn't risk that he might ask about Kiler being fired from GGS for misuse of corporate property—he'd used the *Prosperity* and a GGS vacation villa to entertain his gambling "friends"—and why she'd willingly given up her position. Part of her wanted to tell him that Kiler had blackmailed her, that he'd threatened to tell J.M. who her father was if she didn't leave with him. But that would mean admitting who her father was, and she couldn't risk seeing *that* disillusionment in Devin's smoky-blue eyes when he found out.

She wasn't even sure how much he knew about Kiler's firing. Jonathan had handled it. She knew Kiler's official personnel record said only *dereliction of duties*—not that he'd hosted drunken orgies at the villa. Something she didn't find out until weeks later.

It was almost an omen that the sweater she'd helped Devin pick out that day at the spaceport mall was now in shreds.

Her comm screen flashed with the CFTC logo. Updates were in. She wanted nothing more than to read the headline EMBARGO LIFTED! But she knew that hadn't happened, or freighter crew and captains she shared pints of ale with—like Mikey, Corrina, or Rae—would have contacted her. And she would have skipped the shower, thrown on her grays, and been long gone.

She scanned the updates, then dock news, then

trade stats and reports. Passenger transport reservations were clogged. Trade was at a standstill. Five more bar fights during the night shift. Nothing had changed.

At least there was nothing about problems at The Celestian Hotel. That omission didn't surprise her. Even murders didn't always make headlines. A lot of residents on Dock Five preferred anonymity or, as in that striper's case, wouldn't want such a lucrative scam exposed.

She still had options, she reminded herself as she grabbed her empty tea mug, needing a second cup. Pops might find a buyer for her Welcran data-booster system. Or the Gartol regulator. She had other feelers out as well, but then, so did a lot of other haulers. The list of stuff she could buy—cheap—was bordering on astounding. But even cheap was too much money.

She refilled her tea mug at the slurp-and-snack, then, breaking her own promise not to leave her ship, headed for the *Rider*'s main airlock just forward of the Deck 1 cargo hold. The freighter bay that housed the *Rider*, the bay that Kiler had so thoughtfully paid advance rent on, had to have emergency overrides to open the external bay doors.

Now all she had to do was find them, figure out how to operate them while firing up the *Rider*'s engines at the same time, and do so without setting off any alarms. Such a move would probably land her on the dockmaster's shit list for a long time—and make her liable for any damages.

As for the warships, she'd figure something out. Later.

It took her fifteen minutes to find the emergency panel inside a dark maintenance tunnel at the back of the bay. Of course. That made sense. In an emergency, crews couldn't count on getting directly into the bay through the main airlock. But the maintenance tunnels—like the one she'd used to go from Trouble's Brewing to The Celestian—created a maze of access points all over Dock Five. This tunnel led to the bay next to hers and to ones above and below hers. All would have code-locked doors. The codes she knew might work, but that wasn't her problem. She didn't want to go to another bay. She wanted access to the manual controls for the external doors. She played her handbeam over the interior bulkheads. The controls should be somewhere near these for the enviro—

"Having a problem, Captain Griggs?"

Shit! She spun, heart pounding, her right hand flying to where her L7 should be. And wasn't. She stared at Frinks and, hulking behind him, his Takan muscle, clad in stained coveralls with all sorts of metal objects hanging from his utility belt. And damned herself for leaving her ship unarmed with only her tool belt.

Where in hell was her mind?

She knew where it was: on a certain smoky-eyed business magnate, heading back to Sylvadae with nineteen-year-old Trip Guthrie in tow.

She considered stabbing Frinks with her screwdriver or hitting him on the head with her handbeam. But by the time she did that, the Taka would have her in a stranglehold.

"Routine maintenance," she answered Frinks blandly as she stepped out of the tunnel entrance, flicking the handbeam off. But she didn't slip it back into its strap on her utility belt.

"As in the exterior-door manual release?" Frinks made a *tsk*ing sound with his tongue. "Don't you worry your pretty head over that, Captain. We've already taken care of that for you. We wouldn't want them to accidentally open and you to accidentally leave before you had a chance to pay Orvis what you owe him."

What Kiler owed him. "I'll have a nice payment for you within a shipweek of the embargo being lifted. You know that. If you'll tell Orvis—"

"I did tell Orvis." Frinks stepped closer, and she could smell something sour and oily coming from his skin and his cheap flashy suit. Her stomach tightened. "And being the sincere gentleman he is, he said to tell you he fully understands your predicament. You being a widow and all alone."

Here it comes. You can work off your debt on your back or on your knees. You don't mind a little rough play, do you, Captain Griggs?

"That's why Orvis, being a gentleman and all," Frinks continued, "wants you to know there is one thing you could do for him, one special favor, and he'd wipe that debt clean. You'd be free and clear. He'll even pay to fill your ship's tanks with water and fuel."

The whole debt? And fill her tanks? Hell, Kiler never complained about her bedroom skills, but she wasn't *that* good. And there were certainly far prettier women around. Warning bells sounded in her mind, but she knew Frinks expected her to ask. So she did.

"What does Orvis want me to do?"

Frinks made a sharp move with his left hand. The Taka stepped forward, and she suddenly noticed a small vidcam in his large hand. Her heart hammered against her ribs as she closed her fingers around her handbeam. She knew there were certain types of slime who paid for vids both sexual and brutally violent. And that the women in those vids generally ended up dead. Then the *Rider* would be—according to Orvis's promise—a well-stocked ship but with a dead captain.

But the Taka tapped the vidcam's screen and an image flashed to life. Her breath caught. The image was of her, Devin, and Trip, right before they ducked into the maintenance tunnel at Trouble's Brewing. The cleaning 'droids could have recorded it.

"There were two very important people here on Dock Five yesterday," Frinks was saying. "People Orvis wants to . . . meet. Sadly, they're no longer at The Celestian. Orvis thinks you know where they are."

"I have no—"

"You and Kiler were GGS pilots. The Guthries know you, trust you."

"They're not on my ship. You can look."

"We already scanned."

"Then you know as much as I do."

"I think you know more. A great deal more."

Why do you want them? She almost asked that out loud but stopped herself. To show concern, to show emotion, was to be trapped. One thing Kaidee knew for certain: Orvis was not here to help the Guthries.

"Okay, so I ran into them briefly at Trouble's Brewing." She pointed to the vidcam. "You can see that yourself. There was a bar fight and I showed them a back way out. End of story. So as much as I'd like to help Orvis"—*in a* crigblarg's *eyes*—"that's all I know."

"Where are they hiding?"

"I don't know."

"Captain Griggs—"

"Frinks, I don't know. I'm an ex-employee. Ex. I don't run in their social circles and they don't confide in me."

Frinks's disbelief was clear in the narrowing of his eyes and the slight quirk of his fleshy lips. "Then maybe it's time you renewed your acquaintance. Just for old times' sake. Orvis, in his generosity, is giving you six hours to do so. Six hours. Bring them here, to us, and all your debts will be forgiven. Got that, Captain Griggs?"

He nodded sharply, the Taka clipped the vidcam back on his utility belt, and the two walked side by side toward the corridor airlock without waiting to hear her answer.

Which was, yes, she got it. But, no, she wouldn't cooperate. Not even to wipe out all of Kiler's debts. Not even for full tanks of water and fuel.

But for a moment she could almost hear Kiler's voice: *Guthrie's armed. And that Barthol, he's had training. Hell, they might even be able to kill Orvis. That would be great, wouldn't it? All you have to do is put them together. If Orvis dies, you're free. If he doesn't... you're still free. It's a win–win.*

No, it wasn't, and whether Devin and Barty could kill Orvis wasn't the point. The debt was *her* problem, not theirs. She wasn't going to walk to her freedom across their backs.

They were probably long gone off dock anyway. The Guthries had money, and money could buy a seat on any passenger transport out of here. So they were on their way home. She'd never see them again. Never see Devin...

She sent a prayer in his direction. *Please be safe.*

She trudged back to her ship in search of her L7. Her options were dwindling. She was going to need it.

Devin took a slow sip of his tea, because with his mouth full he couldn't unleash the stream of expletives he wanted to say. But it really did seem like this goddamned fucking place in the middle of goddamned fucking nowhere conspired against them. He swallowed and instead thought of an answer to the problem. A typical Guthrie answer. "Offer them twice the price."

"Already did," Barthol replied, putting his DRECU down on the bed, then reaching for the plate of breakfast pastries. He took one, then passed the plate down to Devin, who, like Trip, was seated on blankets folded on the floor, back against the wall. It was, if not more comfortable, at least roomier than the small bed. "Compass's position is they're overbooked on all passenger transports. Our reservations are canceled. And they don't have three seats available on the same flight for another four days."

"Try for two seats." Devin bit off a piece of sugared bread and chewed thoughtfully. "You and Trip. You can protect him as well as I could if anything goes wrong." Probably even better. His shoulder still throbbed, limiting his range of motion. And in spite of getting several hours' sleep, he was tired. Bone-deep tired. And worried about Makaiden. But if Barty escorted Trip home, Makaiden was a worry Devin could do something about.

"They don't even have one seat. Not at any price."

Devin handed the plate to Trip, who'd become increasingly quiet, almost glum. Devin guessed that Halsey's death and all the subsequent problems were finally registering. Including the fact that, because of Trip, they were stuck on Dock Five. And had to be out of this hotel room in another hour.

It was dangerous out in the corridors, and they all knew that. Fuzz-face's thugs were out there, and Barty's contacts had yet to come back with any answers or identification. The enemy was an unknown. Not a pleasant position.

"We'll simply have to deal with this delay," Barty said. "Yes, it will mean changing hotel rooms again. I'll start working on that right away. But it also gives GGS more time to respond to our messages. They might even be able to get the *Prosperity* out here. Or the *Triumph*."

The *Triumph*. It had to be the *Triumph,* because in those four days—if they were forced to spend them here—he would find Makaiden and get her back on her ship again. The *Triumph* had always been *her* ship.

"In the meantime, we have another room waiting for us on Green. Pack it up, boys." Barty pushed himself off the bed. "We need to be on the way out of Pisstown in forty-five minutes."

"My ass hurts," Trip grumbled, shoving himself to his feet. "Can I shower first?"

"Five minutes," Barty said, and then there was a discussion about clean clothes and who wanted the last of the sugar bread, but Devin only half-listened. The crazy idea he'd played with all night surfaced again.

Maybe it wasn't so crazy. He snatched his Rada from the floor. Maybe his mind was clearer this morning, or maybe he'd just gotten used to the pain. But it all came together with the cancelation of their flight and the image of Makaiden at the controls of the *Triumph*.

She was down on Deck 2—the *Rider*'s largest deck, comprised almost fully of cargo holds—when the ship's comm link chimed. Not the usual news-and-trade-report download chime but the personal chime, a triple bell-like sound that meant someone who knew her ship's personal comm codes—

God and stars. It had to be Rae from the *Solarian Wolf*, or maybe Mikey. The embargo was lifted. She was free.

She ignored the lift and ran up the cramped stairway behind it, shouting, "I'm coming, I'm coming!" as if the comm panel could hear her. She should have had it segued into the panels in the main galley—also on 2—but it had been weeks since she'd been down there. She'd even shut off lights and enviro, to save power.

So she had to run to answer the comm, then threw herself over the black swivel seat and slapped at the flashing icon. "*Void Rider.* This is Griggs." Her voice was breathless.

"Captain Griggs. This is Dabberly from CalRis Free-Trader Collective," said a familiar voice. Okay, not Rae. Not Mikey. But CFTC would know if the embargo was lifted, wouldn't they?

"Dabberly. Sorry. I was belowdecks."

"Understand, Captain. Apologies if this is a bad time, but your presence is required at our offices as soon as possible."

Her presence? "This is, uh, about the embargo?"

"Sadly, no. Apologies again. But we need your authorization to finalize the ownership transfer of your ship and your membership in our collective."

Ownership transfer? Frinks. That goddamned slag-assed Horatio Frinks. She still had two days, more or less. But even at less, she still had time. That's what she'd been doing down on Deck 2: taking inventory of everything and anything she could sell. She intended to hand out flyers all over Dock Five, take first offer on anything. She doubted she'd get thirteen thousand, but she'd get something.

And now Frinks, so smug, so sure, had called in the

lien on her ship and claimed it under default of payment.

Goddamned slag-assed bastard.

"Could you be here in the next half hour?" Dabberly asked.

"Oh, absolutely," she said with teeth gritted. "I'm on my way right now." Spitting fire, kicking ass, and taking names.

She'd use her inventory list as collateral and force CFTC to give her a loan. It was an option she'd considered before but always dismissed because their rates were exorbitant—almost as bad as Orvis's. And because CFTC required detailed record-keeping, triple-checking of manifests, strict adherence to hauling regulations—all things no normal freighter captain wanted to do. In essence, it was almost impossible to comply with their restrictions.

But she had to comply with them for only a week, just until the embargo lifted. And it was a week during which she wasn't hauling cargo anyway. Oh, they'd inspect the *Rider*. They'd present her with a list of violations and demand correction.

It would be annoying. No, it would be a major pain in the ass. But it would buy her time with Orvis. And it would get Frinks's name off her ship's ownership papers.

That's all Kaidee wanted. That and a fully charged Norlack laser rifle.

But she doubted CFTC would approve of that expenditure.

It took her fifteen minutes, with nonfunctioning escalators and ovecrowded lifts, to make her way to CFTC's offices on Blue. She recognized Dabberly's dark bushy hair and angular face as he turned at the front desk. He smiled as she approached, his teeth white against his dusky complexion.

"Always good to see you, Captain."

"You too, Dabberly." She let some of the ire drain from her voice. She liked the middle-aged man. What was happening here wasn't his fault. "Where do you need me?"

"Executive offices." He waved toward a door on the left. "We have a barrister and a licensed certifier just finishing up the paperwork. And congratulations, by the way. I know you've been worried. This, along with the renewal of your passenger-transport certification, will really help."

Renewal of her passenger certification? She couldn't see Frinks or Orvis getting into the passenger business. What in hell were they going to do with her ship? Turn it into a flying brothel?

"Right," she said, frowning as she slipped around his desk, then past a row of storage cabinets. She would have loved to barge into the office with her L7 drawn and primed, but that would be bad form. Still, she flicked off the safety. Frinks rarely went anywhere without his Takan muscle. She was entitled to her own security blanket.

The door was partly ajar. She knocked on it anyway and, when a female voice said, "Come," stepped inside, schooling her features to somewhere between furious and neutral.

And found herself face-to-face with smoky-blue eyes behind silver-rimmed glasses.

"Devin?" To her shame, her voice squeaked.

She glanced rapidly around the room. No Frinks. No towering Taka. Just Devin, standing, and, seated behind a wide desk, a dusky-skinned woman wearing a neatly pressed light-blue business suit, her dark curly hair shot through with silver.

"I'm Barrister Layton," she said, rising, holding one hand out. Kaidee realized she'd seen her in CFTC's offices before, but they'd never been introduced.

Kaidee accepted the woman's hand as if on autopilot. "Makaiden Griggs."

"Yes, Captain Griggs. Have a seat, please. We're just waiting for the certifier to return with the retinal and bioprint scanner."

Certifier. Retinal scanner. For the transfer of ownership of her—

"Just what in hell do you think you're doing?" she blurted out. Devin had taken the only other chair opposite Layton's desk and sat with his hands loosely folded in his lap, his features a mask of perfect professionalism.

"Fixing things," Mr. Perfect and In Control said calmly after a moment's silence.

"Fixing things? You shouldn't even be here! Do you have any idea—" She clamped her mouth shut and fought the urge to scrub at her face with her hands. God, he was supposed to be on a shuttle out of here. She didn't see Trip or Barty, but she prayed they were far away from Dock Five, because all that had to happen was for Frinks to see her with Devin. "You have to leave." Her voice was harsh. "Now, Mr. Devin."

"Barrister Layton, if you'd be so kind as to give us a few minutes?" Devin asked in that smooth, well-schooled, and so very Guthrie-in-charge voice she remembered well. It matched the businesslike effect of his cream-colored shirt and blue-and-gold silk scarf with the signature intertwined Gs peeking out from under the edge of his suede jacket. No hint of a knife wound or struggle. Though his slight beard shadow added a hint of rakish charm.

"Of course, Mr. Guthrie. I'll check on the certifier and bring us all some coffee."

"Tea," Devin said. "And thank you."

The door closed.

"Makaiden—"

"You gave her your real name? Are you crazy?"

"There wasn't time to set up a corporate shell."

"People are trying to *kill* you. Or haven't you noticed? And now you're going to put your very well-known name out there on a ship registration? On Dock Five?" She shook her head in frustration. "Tell me Barty and Trip are safely on a shuttle and heading back to Sylvadae."

"They're down the corridor at Trouble's Brewing, having lunch."

She stared at him. "You're out of your fucking mind!"

Something sparked in his eyes briefly, but his demeanor didn't change. Calm, collected, in-control Devin Guthrie. "Barty's armed. So is Trip."

"So are Fuzz-face and his friends, and they outnumber Trip and Barty." Especially when you added in Frinks. But Frinks was her problem, not Devin's.

"Exactly. That's why I bought your ship. There were no seats available on flights out for at least four days. We very much need off Dock Five as soon as possible. The *Void Rider* is now certified to carry passengers. All you have to do is transport us back to Sylvadae."

And what happens after that? I'm stuck on Sylvadae, a destitute cargo captain on a luxury-yacht world, with no ship and no job. She wanted to throw that at him, rattle his calm façade, but Barrister Layton returned with the certifier—a nervous young pale-skinned man in his mid-twenties—and a dark-wood tea tray with two red CFTC mugs.

"Everything settled?" she asked brightly. Too brightly.

"This is for the best, trust me," Devin said quietly as Layton set the tea tray on her desk.

She stared at him. How many times had she heard exactly those words from Kiler? She turned away, then looked up at Layton. "Let's get this over with." She suddenly felt the pressure of time. She had to collect Barty and Trip and get back to the *Rider* before Frinks or the Taka saw them. Before Orvis found out. But the *Rider* was low on fuel and water.

The passenger-transport certification permitted her to leave Dock Five. But without fuel they weren't going to get very far. And Devin had already spent— she quickly scanned the docupad Layton handed her— more than thirty-five thousand just paying off her debt and renewing her passenger certification. Another twenty for his CFTC registration as owner—

The figures almost leapt off the screen at her, jolting her as much as if there had been physical contact. She swallowed, hard, her throat dry. Devin Guthrie had paid off her and Kiler's purchase loan on the *Rider* of two million seven hundred forty thousand. In full.

"Captain Griggs?" The young certifier waited in front of her, scanner in hand.

She was out of options. She stared at the small blue retinal-reader light as he waved it past her face, then closed her eyes and put her palm against the cool surface of the screen.

It was done. Devin Jonathan Guthrie now owned the *Void Rider*. And he also owned her.

Kaidee waited until they were outside the CFTC office and heading for Trouble's Brewing before speaking, even though she knew this wasn't the time to vent her frustration. There was too much at stake, too many problems nipping at their heels, and she strode down the corridor as if she could feel their tiny pointed teeth tearing at her flesh.

"You need to listen, Mr. Devin, and listen good."

"Makaiden—"

"*Listen,* damn you! You have no idea what you just got yourself, or me, into. You may think this is for the best"—God, how those words rankled her!—"but in buying my ship, you also bought yourself all my troubles. There are other issues here you know nothing about. If you'd even—"

"What issues?"

God, where did she begin? How do you give someone like Devin Guthrie a crash course in real life, dockside? Could she even do so without admitting things she did not want to admit? "Issues that say we have to get off Dock Five, fast. But I'm low on fuel—"

"I've already paid for the *Rider* to be refueled."

The ease with which he spent large amounts of money stunned her. Almost as much as the ease with which he made decisions without consulting her. Not that fueling her ship was wrong, but, damn it, did he even *know* what kind of fuel? She stared up at him, losing track of her surroundings for a moment and almost mowing over a pair of Takan women in long white aprons, who guided a wobbling antigrav pallet between them.

He owns your ship. He owns you. She bit back the next angry barrage that was on the tip of her tongue and wrenched on the employee demeanor she'd worn so successfully first at Starways spacelines, then at GGS. "Thank you. That's...that's efficient." She almost said *kind of you,* but he wasn't being kind. He was acting as an owner should. "However, someone needs to be there to unlock the fuel ports. And no one is." The last few words came out through clenched teeth. Owner or not, he had no clue as to what was waiting for them just around the corner. Which—with Frinks or Fuzz-face—was a statement that could be taken literally.

"We will be there shortly."

Shortly might not be soon enough. Not with Orvis's network of paid eyes and ears. She sucked in a hard breath. "There's another problem. The minute Frinks—there are certain people who will get nasty if they find out I'm fueling my ship. Preparing to leave."

"The debt to Orvis is paid off."

"The financial one, yes. But nothing with Orvis is ever that simple." She quickened her pace; Devin easily kept up with her as they threaded through clusters of freighter crew and overall-clad dockworkers. "This is not two corporations playing nice while jockeying for market position. The man's a criminal."

"I know that."

"No, you don't. Your kind doesn't know what Orvis is like. The threats he makes. The people he controls." She stopped at the wide doorway to Trouble's Brewing and grabbed his arm. "He sent Frinks to my bay a few hours ago with a vid image and a demand. The image was of you, me, and Trip yesterday, in here. The demand was that I deliver you to Frinks in the next three hours. I ignored it because I thought you were gone! You're *supposed* to be gone, on your way back to Sylvadae or Garno or to wherever in hell you could buy passage. Instead..." And she tore her hand from his jacket sleeve, then flung both hands wide in frustration. "You're here. Still on Dock Five, buying my *ship*! And in so doing you have put all of our lives at risk, because if Frinks finds you with me or in my bay, he may kidnap you and Trip. Or kill you. Now do you understand what you've done?"

The lean face in need of a shave and the smoky-blue eyes behind silver-rimmed glasses showed no emotion as he looked down at her. "That does make things slightly more complicated."

"Slightly?" The word came out in a harsh whisper because she was that close to screaming at him.

"We'll collect Barty and my nephew, then deal with what needs to be done." He swept one hand out in a courteous gesture, motioning her into the pub.

She strode through the doorway without further comment, not only because she knew she was running out of time but because she knew that if she hesitated one minute more, she was going to punch Mr. Perfect and In Control right across that lean, chiseled jaw of his.

The pub was busy but not overcrowded. She spotted Trip and Barty seated along the side wall, remnants of a meal on their plates. Trip was shoving the last of a piece of bread into his mouth as she approached. Barty tapped the younger man on the shoulder, then looked at Kaidee. "Everything went smoothly, I trust?"

"We need to move, and move quickly," she said without any preliminaries. "We may have big trouble waiting for us at my bay. If not, it's real close behind. Keep the safeties off your weapons."

Trip wiped his mouth with his napkin. "Sounds like fun."

"It could be fatal, Master Trip," she said tersely, as

Barty shot Trip a warning glance. For a fleeting second Kaidee wondered what Devin was like at that age. Did he have Trip's sense of adventure and excitement? Or had he always been a quiet loner, calculating and distant?

"We're paid up," Barty said with a nod to Devin, now standing—looming, in her estimation—at Kaidee's side. "I suggest you follow with Trip. I'll take point with Captain Griggs." He grabbed the strap of a duffel tucked under his chair. "She can fill me in on the details as we go."

It was easier talking to Barty. Probably because, Kaidee mused, he was an employee—as she had once been. He knew an employee's need for approval, the desire to perform, the importance of knowing how and why and when to cover your ass. And while he shared Devin's calm demeanor, there was an intensity, an emotion, in Barty's questions that Devin "Perfect and In Control" Guthrie lacked. An excitement tempered by a dry humor. He understood the urgency and the irony.

Plus, she didn't have a soft spot for Barty.

Devin was . . . calculated. Quantified. Redacted. Though he wasn't always that way. In the last two years she worked for GGS, she'd seen Devin thaw, open a bit with her. She'd glimpsed his shy smile, heard the deep rumble of his laugh. Sometimes the employer–employee line blurred a bit. Those times felt good.

But that was then. This was trouble—a trouble partly of her own making, but, damn it, Devin had just made a huge contribution. At least it wasn't a trouble Barty was unfamiliar with.

"ImpSec watched Orvis for years. Still does," Barty told her, as they wove their way through freighter crew, shop workers, and the occasional pair of robed Englarians moving at various speeds down the corridor. Despite the tension of watching for unfriendlies, Kaidee relaxed infinitesimally. For all his outward pomposity, Barthol was a soldier, and one with sources of information. She didn't have to explain about what Orvis had done or could do. Barty knew—enough that he kept his hand on his Carver's grip as they hit a set of lesser-used stairs on the way down to Green, then across several corridors to another set leading down to Yellow. They stopped there because Barty's microcomp pinged. They tucked themselves behind a support strut while Barty checked the data.

Trip was grinning, and she could almost hear *Full apex!* running through his mind. Duck-and-hide with weapons primed appealed to him. Devin's expression was his usual inscrutable mask, but when she looked up at him, his gaze locked on hers and something hot and electric shot through her veins, startling her. It had to be her imagination.

Don't be an idiot, girl. He's a Guthrie.

"Nothing. Another dead end," Barty said with a shake of his head.

Kaidee saw the first sign of emotion from Devin— other than when he was flat-out drunk with Barty digging a hole in his shoulder. Something akin to anger and disappointment flashed over his features, his mouth thinning, his eyes narrowing. Then it was gone, like a cargo-bay hatch slamming shut.

They moved on.

Kaidee could feel Frinks's eyes on her at every cross corridor, could hear his Takan cohort's boot steps just above them in every stairwell. Barty's expertise might be reassuring, but the closer they got to the *Rider*'s bay on Orange, the harder her heart thumped in her chest.

It couldn't have been more than twenty minutes since she'd been forced to sign the *Rider* over to Devin, but that might be enough time for one of Orvis's people to alert him to the change of status—and the name of the new owner. It would look to Frinks and Orvis as if she'd known where Devin was all along, sought him out, and cut a deal behind Orvis's back. She couldn't imagine that Orvis wouldn't react. And if by some miracle they got off Dock Five unscathed, she knew she was going to spend the rest of her life looking over her shoulder, waiting for that telltale whine of a laser pistol—the last thing she'd ever hear.

Thank you, Kiler Griggs.
And thank you, Devin Guthrie.

The good news—when they exited out of the narrow stairwell onto Orange Level—was not only that the dingy gray corridor was empty of humans or other sentients but that they found themselves conveniently behind a trio of boxy cargobots slowly guiding an overloaded antigrav pallet in the direction of the *Rider*'s bay. Devin recognized the units as older-model Varrods. GGS had used Varrod cargobots years ago; Devin was about Max's age when he used to tinker with them at one of the Garno warehouses, reprogramming them to dance in crazy circles. Bulky, lumbering, and slow, they now provided decent cover. If Devin stepped slightly left or right, he could get a glimpse of what was farther down the corridor without letting whatever might be farther down the corridor have a clear shot at him.

Unless, of course, whatever was farther down the corridor was behind them. But that wasn't the bad news.

The bad news was that Makaiden was still furious. She was keeping up a low conversation with Barty, with an occasional comment to Trip, as they headed down the wide corridor, but she barely glanced in Devin's direction. Admittedly, her fury wasn't an unusual reaction to high-handed tactics, and he'd be the first to confess what he did with her ship neatly fit into that category. He could explain, but he didn't think she wanted to hear it right now—even if he could figure out what to say that wouldn't make him appear even more the bullying idiot than she already thought he was.

What he hadn't expected was her "your kind" comment: *Your kind doesn't know what Orvis is like.* That hurt, because although rationally he understood the belief behind it, emotionally he found it stung. He didn't view Makaiden as a different "kind" than himself, though he knew Jonathan or Ethan would. But he wasn't Jonathan, and he sure as hell wasn't Ethan. He had always *believed* Makaiden knew that.

Evidently not, or maybe the pain in his shoulder made him oversensitive. Or her fears about this Orvis made her overly sharp. It was something he knew he'd have to work on, but not now. He had more-pressing problems. Like the fact that the cargobots suddenly slowed, veering to the right, guiding the front of the pallet toward the next orange-striped airlock. Their change of direction revealed a pair of stripers—human males—just past the next cross corridor, maybe fifty feet away. The darker-skinned older one leaned against the bulkhead. The other, shorter and red-faced, waved his hands left and right as he talked, his words unintelligible.

Shit.

With a quick motion and mumbling a similar epithet, Barty tugged Trip against the bulkhead and behind the stalled cargobots' container-laden pallet. Devin had already moved to shield Makaiden and didn't miss the narrow-eyed glance she sent him as she sidled next to Trip. Another error on his part. Yes, Captain Griggs understood the problem and could take care of herself.

But there were also things he could do. He sandwiched himself between Makaiden and Trip, slipped his Carver back under his jacket, and pulled out his Rada.

"It's pretty common for them to patrol through here," Makaiden was saying, her voice low as she indicated the stripers with a quick jerk of her chin. "If they're not waiting for me—*us*—they should move on. With luck, down the cross corridor."

With no luck they'd continue straight on and have his, Barty's, and Makaiden's images in their *wanted for assault on an officer* database.

One of the 'bots beeped shrilly, a familiar sound. Two red lights on the airlock's upper left corner flashed. Good. Evidently little had changed with Varrod 'bots in the past two decades. His attempt to reroute their course had worked. Their codes—

A lower-pitched chirp sounded and, even before he glanced at the lights, he knew the airlock's indicators had flashed green. Hell's ass. The 'bots were back on their original course. He sent the reorientation codes again, damning the fact that even though the 'bots were only a foot or two in front of him, he couldn't hard-link in and change their program manually. He had to come in on a secondary greenpoint wireless linkage, and that, he was learning, was less than reliable.

The cargobots wanted inside that bay. He wanted them out here in the corridor, playing defensive shield so they could get to the *Rider*. At the moment, they were stalled and the lights blinked yellow.

Footsteps and male voices cut into his thoughts and made him lift his face toward the sound: the stripers, heading this way, not turning at the cross corridor. Devin's mind raced, then caught on a scenario he'd seen dozens of times in GGS warehouses. A scenario that would fit unobtrusively with their current circumstances and maybe deflect suspicion. "Trip, you're a cargo apprentice." He spoke quickly, his voice low. "Barty, use your microcomp like a manifest recorder. You're training him. Makaiden, you're, we're..." Nothing came to mind. She was in freighter grays—a captain's uniform, if someone looked closely enough. That was workable given their location, but he was too well dressed. And the stripers were too close now for Devin to slip away unnoticed.

For a wild, crazy moment he considered flattening her against the bulkhead and kissing her. That's what the actor playing the super-spy always did in those adventure vids when the spy and the heroine needed to hide in plain sight.

But for Devin, it wouldn't be playacting. He caught Makaiden's glance, her eyes narrowed, lips parted slightly, and suddenly—even though he knew it was the most irrational thing to do—he wanted nothing more than to do exactly that: kiss Makaiden until the stripers went away, and then keep kissing her. For hours. He stepped toward her, closing the short distance, hesitant about doing something so insane and yet so damned wonderful—and was shocked when she reached for him, her hand resting firmly against his forearm. Maybe—

"Trouble," she said harshly. "Behind you."

Devin whipped a glance over his shoulder, caught sight of a Taka in faded coveralls loping doggedly down the corridor, a shorter human male in his wake. They weren't close enough for him to see faces or details, but evidently Makaiden recognized them.

"Orvis?" he guessed.

"Close. Frinks. And friend," she added, bringing

the L7 in her right hand higher. "We need to get out of here."

No, not out. "In," he said, motioning to the airlock hatchway with his microcomp.

"That's not my bay," she said, as he brought up the 'bots delivery program again. "I don't have the lock or unlock codes."

"Not an issue." He took a moment away from his work on his Rada to thrust it in the cargobots' direction. "The 'bots do."

Her eyes widened slightly, understanding dawning. Then: "And if Frinks figures a way in?"

"We will have figured a way to be someplace else," Barty said before Devin could answer, which was just as well, because the cargobots that so desperately wanted into that bay a minute before now were stubbornly resisting his attempts to permit them to do so.

"Uncle Devin?" There was an undercurrent of panic in Trip's hushed words.

"Hey, you there!" The man's shouted command came from the stripers' direction.

A 'bot chirped twice. "Got it!" Devin said through clenched teeth.

Trip was leaning against the double doors when the green lights flashed, and he almost fell inside the bay when they slid open. "Go, go!" Devin shoved Makaiden ahead of him. The cargo pallet wobbled. The 'bots made a low thrumming noise and crept forward by what seemed to be an inch at a time. He had to get the 'bots inside or the signal to lock the doors wouldn't work.

"Get clear!" he said hoarsely, not wanting Frinks or the stripers to hear his warning. But he couldn't risk Makaiden, Barty, or Trip getting injured. He keyed in the emergency jettison-cargo command just as the high whine of laser fire filled the corridor.

The pallet and the cargobots surged forward. Devin dove through the hatchway next to them, cradling the Rada against his chest as he caught the side of the pallet with his hip. He stumbled, then hit the decking, knees and elbows impacting painfully. Swearing, he rolled onto his back, Rada screen in front of his eyes, and hurriedly initiated the lockdown command. The pallet halted with a jerk, the 'bots' thrumming increased, then, with an audible groan, the airlock doors slammed closed.

Lock, damn you, lock! He stared at the green signal lights over the hatchway, aware of Trip crouching on the decking behind Makaiden and Barty, who had weapons drawn and aimed.

The doors shuddered again. Then the lights blinked red. Locked.

Devin let his head drop back against the decking with a thud. His heart raced and he didn't remember the last time he'd breathed. He did so now, drawing in a long breath, then letting it out in a noisy exhale.

Makaiden's voice cut through his few seconds of respite. "The stripers can get override commands from the dockmaster's office. Five, maybe ten minutes."

"Unless they're busy wondering why Frinks was shooting at us," Devin offered, pulling himself off the decking and briefly surveying his surroundings. He clipped the Rada back onto his belt. He was in a medium-size bay with the usual arched metal struts lining the side walls. There were three banks of overhead lights but only the middle one was lit, throwing the edges of the bay into shadow.

"Willing to bet your life on that?"

He wasn't. Neither, obviously, was Barty, who was

already prowling about the shadowed regions of the bay—which was, Devin suddenly realized, curiously empty of a ship. An oddity, considering the current lack of dock space on Dock Five.

"Bellfire Cargo has this bay," Makaiden said when he voiced his observation. She was watching Barty, then looked back to him. "They got off dock just before the most recent embargo and are smart enough not to come back right now."

"Then why would someone deliver cargo here?" Devin asked, as Barty motioned Trip over to where a wide metal grate covered an opening about four feet square.

A thump and then a thud from the airlock halted all conversation. Devin tensed and was aware of Makaiden straightening. Then the thump and thud moved away, fading. Whatever it was had nothing to do with them. He hoped.

"Mistimed shipment, probably," Makaiden said, answering the question he'd posed before the interruption set everyone on edge. "Bellfire would have been back by now, if everyone's schedule wasn't interrupted."

"If we use the service tunnels, how far to the *Rider*?" Barty asked from the far left side of the bay. He had one hand supporting the access grating while Trip wriggled it loose.

Makaiden turned from her inspection of the pallet's contents. "I'm three bays past the cross corridor. But that corridor keeps it from being a direct route. We have to go under it in a subtunnel that's not much more than a big square pipe, with only one way in and one way out. We could get trapped in there if Frinks has people behind us as well as coming in from my bay."

"You don't lock your bay?" Trip asked.

She nodded. "Sure, but Orvis, as lien holder, had a legal right to my lock codes. Which means Frinks knows them."

"He's not lien holder now," Devin said.

"But I didn't know that when I left my ship, did I?" she shot back. She met his gaze evenly, but there was fury in the tightness of her mouth and the slight downturn in her eyes. Then her expression shifted, her mouth softening. She looked tired. She shook her head. "Sorry."

"I understand."

"No, you don't." The accusatory tone was back in her voice. She turned away from him and headed for where Barty and Trip stood by the open access grating.

"Unless the stripers have joined Frinks," Barty said as Makaiden approached, "there are four of us, armed, to the two of them. Those aren't bad odds."

"Frinks has more muscle than just the Taka. He could easily get half a dozen armed thugs to take us on when we get to my ship. And if the stripers are working with him, they could get behind us in the tunnels, herd us toward Frinks, and—"

A loud hammering made Devin spin around. Someone or something was pounding on the hatchlock doors. There was no question this time, and the noise didn't go away. The hatchlock lights flashed but—for the moment—stayed red.

He was already tapping in overrides via his microcomp when Makaiden asked, "Can you keep them out?"

"I've got the hazardous-substance-leak lock activated. That doesn't mean they can't bypass it." He knew Varrod 'bots' programs were prone to glitches. He was using one now. "It will just take them longer."

"Devin, do these 'bots have a self-destruct sequence?" Barty asked.

"Levels one through three that you can set on a three-, five-, or ten-minute delay."

"Set it for ten minutes, level one. A good diversion with minimal damage."

"Five minutes, level two," Makaiden said. "That should activate the blast doors without blowing a hole in the outer bulkhead." She stepped next to Devin while he worked the microcomp.

"Decompression is a problem we don't need," Barty said tersely as the hammering grew louder.

"Decompression, if it happens, will trigger the blast doors and panels in the accessways," Makaiden pointed out. "It shouldn't affect us and, providing we can clear the subtunnel, won't hamper where we go. But it could keep them guessing as to whether we're dead or alive."

Barty nodded. "Agreed."

Devin looked up from the Rada. "It's set." Then he focused on his Rada again and didn't stop his transmissions even when Makaiden grabbed his arm.

"What are you doing? We don't have time—"

"Moving the 'bots away from the hatchway so they don't blow a hole in the doors," he said as the pallet hummed. "I don't want to make it any easier for whoever is out there to get in here."

"Three minutes before you get a hole blown in you."

"You're not getting rid of me that easily, Captain Griggs." The flippant remark was out before he even realized he'd said it. *Where in hell did that come from?* There was no time to ponder this new personality quirk. He tapped the microcomp off, shoving it in its holder on his belt as he jogged quickly after Makaiden.

Their boots hitting against the decking made a hard, sharp sound in counterpoint to the hammering on the bay's hatchlock door.

Two and a half minutes later, shock waves from the explosion sent them all stumbling, falling to their knees in the cramped confines of the narrow subtunnel. Kaidee lost her grip on her handbeam. It hit the flooring with a clunk, and suddenly they were surrounded by darkness.

Sirens whooped. Another wailed in a staccato-like tempo.

"Blast doors closing!" Kaidee shouted, her heart rate spiking. There were a lot of warning noises on station, but the rapid pulse of a blast-door siren was hard to forget. "Move, move!" They had to clear the next reinforced panel—which served as a blast door in the accessway—and get out of the subtunnel or they'd be trapped between the blast panel behind them and the one ahead for anywhere from minutes to hours. Or longer.

Trip and Barty—she knew the sound of the older man's wheezing rasp by now—clambered ahead. Devin...damn it all! She could feel him down by her ankles, groping around for her handbeam. She reached out in the darkness until she found a fistful of his jacket. "Leave it, damn you. Move!"

She yanked hard. He bumped against her, his arm snaking around her waist, and then he was dragging her forward. "Got it." His voice was a deep rumble. Light flared weakly—something must have broken when she dropped it—but it was enough to see Trip and Barty, enough to see the rough ribbing of the tunnel jutting out at measured intervals. One of those ribs was a panel. It should be closing by now. She should be able to see...

There! She grabbed Devin's hand and jerked the handbeam up and to the right. Shit! They were too far away, the tunnel's low ceiling and uneven flooring littered with piping and conduit slowing them down.

"We have to clear that! Go, go, go!" Her voice rasped, her lungs burned, and her shoulders, arms, and hips were hit, poked, and impaled by all sorts of flanges and protuberances, but she couldn't slow down.

Barty shoved Trip ahead of him, and she heard his breathy command: "Keep going. I'll get there." The man had to be tiring, his age catching up with him.

"I've got him," Devin said, shoving the beam at her with one hand, his other against Barty's back.

There was no time for argument or hesitation. She was smaller, lighter, and even with the pipes jutting out from the tunnel walls hampering her, she could move faster than the men.

She might also—with Trip's help—be able to block the blast panel with something, keep it from closing. The panels had no manual overrides. She pushed ahead, the beam zigzagging as she ran.

The panel, sliding from the right, was almost at the halfway point. She saw Trip sidle around it and skitter to a stop.

"C'mon, Captain Griggs!" He held out one hand toward her, as if he could pull her along.

She wanted to turn around, wanted to know where Devin was, wanted to know he'd make it, but she couldn't waste a second.

"Jam the panel!" she shouted to Trip. "Keep it open!"

He twisted around, pulling at various protuberances on the wall, but nothing came loose.

She reached him just as he turned back. "The floor.
Even something small. Slow it down." She aimed the
beam downward, illuminating conduit, junction boxes,
and...yes! Trip dropped to one knee, grabbing the
discarded squares of metal before she could tell him to
do so. He shoved a thin square under the front of the
sliding panel, then sat back quickly, hands against the
floor, and kicked at the square, using the heel of his
boot as a hammer.

The blast panel made a grinding, squealing noise,
and for a brief moment Kaidee thought they'd jammed
it. Then the metal square slid sideways. The panel
jerked forward, with less than two feet to go to seal
the tunnel completely.

Trip grabbed another metal square, wedging it in
place with his boot as Kaidee followed his attempts
with her handbeam. She kicked the plate back into position when it twisted sideways, sweat trickling down
her face and the back of her neck. "Damn it!" Devin
and Barty were still in the first part of the tunnel. Her
heart pounded, her fury at Devin dissolving under the
very real fear that he'd be trapped, injured. And
Barty—

"Grab him!" It was Devin, Barty stumbling in front
of him. She had Barty's wrist, then Trip was on his
feet, thrusting his arms under the older man's armpits,
lifting him through the narrowing gap.

Kaidee jumped back. They needed room, Devin
needed...

Devin plowed into her, knocking the handbeam
from her grasp again. There was the loud clunk of the
panel meeting the wall, a flicker of light, then nothing,
complete darkness, as a hard, muscled body pinned

her against the tunnel wall and its row of lumpy piping. Her face was crushed against Devin's chest.

She angled around. "You okay?" She could feel Devin breathing hard, the rise and fall of his chest moving the soft suede of his jacket against the side of her face.

"Yeah," he said after a moment. His other arm tightened across her back. "Trip? Barty?" He stepped away from the wall, taking her with him.

She went willingly. She couldn't see, and staying with him was preferable to flailing around in the dark, stumbling over his feet.

"Here, Uncle Devin." Trip's voice came from somewhere to her left and below her knees.

"I think...I need...to sit for a minute or two." That was Barty. And he didn't sound good.

"Are you hurt?" she asked him.

"No. Just...not as young as I'd like to be." He rasped out a soft laugh.

Guilt shot through Kaidee. Barty had asked for ten minutes to clear the accessway. She'd insisted on five, not even thinking—*yeah, use your brains next time, Kaid*—that Barty would need more time. It was easy when around him to forget his age. But the past several days had to have been hard on him. And she'd damned near killed him.

She pulled away from Devin. His arm around her waist felt too comforting. She was supposed to be angry at him, but more than that, she didn't deserve comfort. Not from him.

A small glow flared on her right, barely piercing the darkness. She recognized it immediately: Devin's microcomp, its screen emitting a soft green light. *Good thinking.* Hell, he wasn't Mr. Perfect for nothing.

A moment later, a second glow: Barty's microcomp.

Then a rustling noise and a whiter light from a unit in Trip's hand.

The gloom receded somewhat.

Devin squatted down in front of Barty and angled his microcomp toward the older man. "Can you make it?"

Barty snorted, shoving himself to his feet. "It wasn't so long ago I beat you on the basketball court."

Devin and Trip rose along with Barty, shadowy forms with small luminescent centers.

"It's not much farther," Kaidee said, "and we will be getting some light in through the gratings as we get closer."

Devin stepped up next to her, with Barty behind him and Trip at his side. Kaidee wondered if either Devin or Trip saw what she did when Devin aimed his microcomp's light at Barty—a small capped vial peeking out of Barty's jacket pocket. A medicine vial, she was fairly sure. It hadn't been visible before. In the darkness, he probably was unaware that it wasn't fully concealed.

Barthol may have been able to challenge Devin at basketball a few years ago, but there was something wrong with the former ImpSec operative now. Something more, she suspected, than just his age.

And she had no idea what they would yet have to face to get to the *Rider*.

"It's too quiet," Kaidee whispered, flat on her stomach and peering down through the narrow grating of an even narrower air duct, which offered her a decent view of the *Rider*'s starboard side and main ramp. She was shoulder to shoulder and hip to hip with Devin, her gaze raking the familiar bay, her mind wrestling with how damned difficult it was to be furious with someone she'd always had so much respect for. Trip and Barty—who still looked in pain despite his protestations otherwise—were twenty or so feet below, in the larger main access tunnel. Her ship's bay had seemed too quiet and too empty from there. Hence, her and Devin's current position—a means to provide a more complete view.

She wasn't totally sure something was wrong. But something definitely wasn't right.

Frinks, the stripers, Fuzz-face... someone should have made a move and staked out the *Rider*'s rampway. But no one had.

"It's not impossible that our diversion worked," Devin said, his voice equally low. "Which is all the more reason we need to get on board. That diversion won't last forever."

She knew that, and she'd almost gone charging into the bay five minutes before when they'd cautiously approached the access grating—and heard and saw nothing that could remotely be construed as a threat. Even the *fuel available* light on her bay's utility panel glowed green. Something she'd not seen in several weeks.

"And you said if someone had breached ship's security, you could tell at your airlock."

She had. She could.

"Makaiden."

She nodded. "Okay, okay." It was a whisper, but a whisper through clenched teeth. Which she forcibly unclenched when she reminded herself that Devin Guthrie owned her ship. And her. Her job was to take them home, not argue security strategy.

And not be so aware of Devin that she could feel the heat off his body.

Not good, Kaid.

She pushed herself backward, slithering out of the air duct as slowly and quietly as she could, until she was sure she was far enough away from the grating that her thunks and bumps couldn't be heard in the bay.

Devin moved as quietly as she had, and not for the first time she took a moment to appreciate the lean muscle tone of his body. He played handball competitively, she remembered. Though right now he clearly favored his injured shoulder.

Her boots dangled suddenly in midair, and she knew she'd reached the ladder. A little farther and her feet found the rungs, then she was climbing down, still keeping noises to a minimum. Devin's boots appeared when her own hit the accessway flooring.

He took the rungs two at a time.

"Keep the Carver on stun," she said when he faced her. "I'll change the lock code on the corridor hatchway. Get Trip on the fueling; he's done it with me before. I need to find out how soon traffic control will grant us a departure slot." *Providing we're not ambushed the minute we enter the bay.*

She and Devin were first through the accessway into the bay; Trip and Barty followed. The *Rider* sat— a hulking deltoid beast with a narrow rampway jutting out—on landing struts that, planetside, would deploy wheels for taxiing. Good hiding places. Heart pounding and pistol out, she swept the bay, left to right, as Devin moved right to left.

"Clear," he said, after a minute.

She wasn't convinced. "Cover me." She sprinted for the hatchway to the corridor, and twice her fingers slipped as she recoded the lock. Finally it took. The dockmaster's office could still get in, but it would take them longer.

It occurred to her that if Frinks had someone in the bay, she'd just locked them in.

She turned. Barty was leaning against the base of the ramp, not looking well at all. She trotted toward him, pistol still out. "Trip, do you remember how to fuel—"

"Sure do. On it!" He sprinted to the fuel port.

She reached the rampway base and checked the ramp codes and ship's security status on the control panel, aware that her heart had yet to slow down. Everything looked exactly as she'd left it.

Luck, or a trap? She headed up the ramp, with Barty following behind.

After all the troubles they'd had, things couldn't possibly go this smoothly, be this easy. All she needed now was for traffic control to say they were cleared for departure in the next thirty minutes and she'd really get nervous.

Traffic control cleared the *Rider*'s departure in twenty.

Trip and Devin locked down the fuel port and showed up on her bridge with thirteen minutes to spare. She and Barty had already searched both decks of her ship for intruders—or any devices they might have left behind—but her trip alarms were undisturbed, biothermal scans were negative, and, as far as it appeared, it was just another shipday hauling cargo. Or, in this case, passengers.

Except Orvis had to be frothing at the mouth, and more than several someones wanted Trip Guthrie in their clutches—or sights. Yet no one was pounding down her airlock's door.

Nervous didn't even begin to describe it.

"Maybe Fuzz-face and friends shot Frinks, and the stripers hauled 'em all to prison," Trip offered, no small amount of glee in his voice as he settled into a chair in front of the navigation console.

Kaidee glanced at Barty sitting at communications—he assured her he could operate the console—and at Devin next to him.

"From your lips to God's ears," she replied, powering up the docking thrusters. "Ship shows secure. Sending signal to open bay doors. If you're not already strapped in, do it now. We're going to leave this bay at max allowable speed the moment I get the go sign from traffic control."

She intended to shadow anything larger and longer than the *Rider* the minute she cleared the bay. She didn't believe for one moment that trouble had given up on finding her. She feared it had just changed location and now waited with weapons primed somewhere between here and the jumpgate to Aldan.

Kaidee held the *Rider*'s position just short of Dock Five's inner beacon and listened to the monotone words of the departure-control 'droid. She didn't know whether to laugh or cry—and in relief or in anger. Or both, for both reasons. "Acknowledged," she said when the 'droid asked for her response. "I'll have an amended flight plan filed with you in"—she checked the data on her screens—"five minutes. Maintaining course and heading as directed."

The Imperial ships babysitting Dock Five were tiny blips on her long-range scans, but she knew they could pinpoint her easily. *Don't shoot at me; don't shoot at me.*

She half-swiveled in her chair and faced Barty and Devin. The older man still looked a bit pale. She'd have to deal with that once she figured out where they were going. Because they were not going back to Sylvadae. Or even Garno. Their bad luck had returned.

"Baris Central Traffic refuses to grant us clearance to cross the border into Aldan," she said without any preamble. Barty sat up straighter. Devin had been poking at his microcomp. He raised his face now, frowning, eyes narrowed behind glasses sitting crookedly on his nose.

If she wasn't so slagging annoyed at him—and if he wasn't a damned Guthrie and her damned boss to boot—she'd have found him endearingly attractive right then. But she was annoyed, and he was all of the above.

Trip was the first one to speak out. "Why?"

"Tightened security procedures, coupled with the fact that we have a shiny new passenger-transport certificate, which places us on some kind of temporary watch list," she said, with a nod to Trip. "We've not been cleared through the central databanks at Starport Six yet. All that usually means is the ship has to file more-detailed docs until clearance comes through. Usually."

"But now they're restricting where we can go," Barty said.

Kaidee nodded. "Now they are. Baris Sector only."

"For how long?" Devin asked.

"Forty-two to seventy-two hours was the usual delay. But I was just informed the delay is now one shipweek, minimum."

"A shipweek?" Devin clearly wasn't happy.

"We've been given clearances for Calfedar and Talgarrath." Oddly, both were close to the Calth border. It was almost as if someone wanted to see if they'd make a run for it, into Alliance territory. "Or we can return to Dock Five. That's it." Devin started to speak, but Kaidee held up one hand. "Hear me out, because traffic control is keeping me in a holding pattern out here until we file a destination, and that doesn't make me happy."

Devin sat back and nodded. Kaidee continued: "Calfedar is out of the way, quiet. It doesn't have a major commercial spaceport like Garno, just three minor ones, and one of those is controlled by the Englarian Church. But they have a spacedock—a small station—and we'd have the option of tethering out there on an external bay if it's available. It's about a quarter of the size of Dock Five, pretty basic, but it's

clean and, I think, safe. If we have to hole up somewhere, it's a good place to do so. An external bay
means we can leave quickly. But if someone's looking
for a Blackfire 225, we're spotted pretty easily. Pros
and cons." She splayed her hands.

"Talgarrath is another story, especially Port Chalo,"
she added. "It can be dangerous." She glanced at Trip,
then back at Barty and Devin. Port Chalo probably
meant nothing to them, but to her it was always the
place where Kiler's luck ran out—though this wasn't
the time to tell them that. "A lot of...stuff runs
through Port Chalo. And, unlike Calfedar's, the Port
Chalo spaceport is someplace I don't enjoy going. It's
expensive, overpriced. And the portmaster there isn't
shy about inventing fees to up your costs."

"You have a major client on Talgarrath," Devin
said.

His knowledge startled Kaidee. Then she remembered feeling—more than once—that he didn't trust
her. He did more than not trust her. He'd done significant research on the *Rider*.

*Of course he did, you idiot. He bought it. What do
you think he was doing before you showed up at the
CFTC offices—sipping tea?* CFTC kept financial and
client files on all member ships.

"That was Kiler's deal, Kiler's contacts," she explained. "I don't do business with them anymore." Actually, she never did. Kiler wouldn't let her meet with
anyone from Nahteg. Considering he usually came
back from meetings with them drunk and bragging
obnoxiously—and obviously untruthfully—about the
untold wealth Nahteg would bring them, she had no
interest in doing so.

She watched Devin glance back at his microcomp,
frowning. He was tapping the screen, scrolling with a

quick stroke, then tapping again. Research mode, probably. Comparing Talgarrath to Calfedar. She didn't have time for that. Cruising out here at Dock Five's beacon made her feel like one big target. She glanced at her scanners—again—even though she had them set to max sensitivity. Nothing barreling toward her—not an ion torpedo from an Imperial ship, not an ore tanker linked to Orvis, not a security scout ship full of stripers. But that didn't mean there couldn't be in another minute or three.

"Gentlemen, I need a decision."

Devin looked up. "Calfedar appears the better choice. Unless Barty has an objection?"

"We could more easily get major transport back to Aldan via Port Chalo," Barty said. "But, all things considered, the risks are less on Calfedar. The Englarian Church has a fair amount of influence there, which is bolstered by the Empire's long-standing 'hands off' policy in regards to the Church. It could give us a chance to catch our breath, make wiser decisions that aren't fueled by various nefarious types looking to do us harm."

Though his tone was light, Kaidee didn't miss his mention of "catching our breath." Barty was feeling his age and limitations. She also didn't miss his comment about "wiser decisions." She wondered what he thought of Devin's decision to pay off the lien on the *Rider*. It sounded as if that might be a point of contention.

But then Barty, like herself, was a Guthrie employee. Devin made his own decisions.

"Calfedar," Devin said.

She swiveled around, tapped her nav screen, and brought up the preprogrammed flight plan. "Filing that now. One hour twenty to the jumpgate, once we get clearance to leave. Until then, there's a passenger cabin with private lav starboard side, one deck down," she continued, aiming her voice over her shoulder but watching her scanners closely now. Her notice of departure would signal the last chance someone would have to take a couple of shots at them. "And crew bunks with a shared lav portside. You three can fight out who sleeps where. There's also the galley—at some point we need to think about dinner. And behind that, a small sick bay. Barty, you might want to familiarize yourself with it in case you need to work on Mr. Devin's shoulder again."

There was the squeak of chairs and soft thump of boots on decking behind her.

"Excellent, Captain Griggs," Barty said. "I'll do that."

"I'll give you all a half-hour warning to jumpgate transit." She automatically checked fuel and enviro levels as she spoke, tapping in adjustments as needed. "I want everything stowed and secure, and I'll need all three of you strapped in—either up here, in your bunks, or in one of the mess-hall chairs—at that time."

"Captain Griggs?" That was Trip. "Can I be on the bridge for jump transit? It's been a while, and that would be full apex...."

She glanced at him. Trip had stopped by Devin's chair at the comm console. He fingered his backpack strap nervously.

Behind him, Devin gave his head a slight affirmative nod. Uncle approved.

Kaidee smiled at Trip. "If you want to help take her through jump, you'd better get moving. Stow your pack, get something to eat. I'll call you on intraship just before we hit the first beacon."

"Apex!" Trip turned to leave. Devin's hand shot out, thumping his nephew at the hip. Trip glanced down at his uncle and received a raised eyebrow. "Oh, uh, thank you, Captain Griggs," Trip added. Chastised.

"Help Barty with our duffels." Devin used the toe of his boot to nudge the larger one in Trip's direction.

"Sure." Trip hefted it easily, as Barty grabbed the straps of the smaller one.

A soft ping followed by two low beeps had Kaidee turning back to her console. Approval of her flight plan, transit codes, and the ubiquitous dockmaster's bill flashed down her screen. She studied the data and, as footsteps receded, powered the sublights to full. The nav comp, now on auto, directed the *Rider* toward the primary space lane and the gate.

Kaidee tapped open intraship. "We're cleared." And no one had shot at them or rammed them yet. Amazing.

"It's a slagging miracle," she murmured softly, then caught herself. Alone on the ship for the past several months, she'd fallen into the bad habit of talking to herself. She'd have to stop that before Trip, Barty, or, God forbid, Devin—

"That the flight plan was cleared? Or that we've made it this far?"

Yes, God forbid, Devin. Who was still on the bridge. She felt her face heat in embarrassment.

He has a right to be on the bridge. He owns the ship, ran through her mind as she swiveled her chair halfway. He was still at the comm console, his microcomp in hand. But he wasn't looking at it. His gaze was fixed on her.

The intensity startled her. And made her cheeks flame even more.

She looked away, then rubbed her face lightly with her hands, hoping he'd think that was why her cheeks were red. "Sorry. It's been a stressful day. And I tend to make inane comments when I'm tired."

"You're worried about Barty." Devin's voice was deep and quiet. "The reason you told him to inspect your sick bay wasn't just because of my shoulder."

She let her hands drift to her lap. "No."

"He was running out of energy," Devin said. "But as you noted, it's been a stressful day. More than he's had to deal with in over a decade, I'd guess."

She'd wondered if he knew Barty was on medication. Evidently not. "He has a small bottle of medicine in his shirt pocket. He doesn't know I saw it. It was right after you almost got chopped in half by that blast panel. When we were in the dark I think he took something, but because we were in the dark he didn't realize he hadn't pushed the bottle all the way back down. Then you used your microcomp screen for light, and I could see the bottle with what looked like a pharmacy label on it."

Devin nodded slowly. "I'll keep an eye on him. Thank you." He gave her a wistful smile.

Suddenly he was the Devin Guthrie she remembered: the soft-spoken man with the cultured accent, the gentle smile, the quizzical gaze behind silver-rimmed glasses.

Then his gaze went from quizzical to something else again. Something intense. Heated. Almost as if . . .

Her console pinged. She turned, grateful for the distraction. They'd cleared the last Dock Five beacon without incident, nav comp automatically segueing over from Dock Five Traffic to the signal from Baris Central Traffic. The Imperial warship images on her scanners were now much smaller. And boot steps behind her told her Devin Guthrie had finally left her bridge.

No, *his* bridge.

She turned around to be sure she was really alone, then let herself sag back into her chair. The intensity of his gaze replayed in her mind. It could mean anything or it could mean nothing. Or it could mean that Devin Jonathan Guthrie had realized that he not only owned this ship, he owned her. Not legally, of course, but he certainly had bailed her out of a serious situation.

And might just be expecting repayment for all the trouble she caused him.

Devin stepped out of the *Rider*'s large lift—obviously meant more for cargo than passengers—and followed the sound of Barty's voice through the galley, then toward what Makaiden had said were the crew cabins on the ship's port side. Like the little he'd seen of the upper deck, this lower one had dark-gray decking and lighter-gray bulkheading, without the benefit of the carpeting or decorative wall panels found on the *Triumph* or other GGS ships. Rivets, beams, pipes, and conduit were in evidence. The galley held two square metal tables—also gray—ringed by bench seats, all welded to the decking.

There was nothing remotely attractive about the *Rider*.

Her captain, on the other hand . . . Devin gave himself a mental shake. Makaiden had caught him staring at her. Again. He had to stop that before she labeled him as some kind of lunatic, but he couldn't help it. He'd fantasized about her for too many years: all the usual stuck-on-a-ship with her, deep in some uncharted area of the Empire, and all the ways he'd make her forget about her husband—except she no longer had a husband.

His life had just taken an extraordinarily interesting turn, and all because his nephew had decided to embark on a fiasco of an adventure. An adventure that, from the sounds of it, was earning him a long-overdue lecture from the inimitable Barthol, who was sounding much better, his voice stronger. He'd ask Barty about his health later, when they had some privacy. Right now Trip was the focus.

"You will, of course, have to face the consequences," Barty was saying, "as set out by both your father and grandfather."

And so will I. Trip wasn't the only one who had broken the Guthrie rules. The fact that Devin had found Trip notwithstanding, he would have to face not only J.M. but, he realized with a start, Tavia Emberson.

Tavia. He knew his mother had asked Tavia for an engagement-party guest list, as well as her help in wording an official announcement for the society pages. Those plans would have to be canceled. He'd also found Makaiden. He'd have to face J.M. over that too.

He followed the path that wound to the left between the galley tables and spied a wide doorway, open, as Barty's voice continued: "And as we still don't know who killed Ben Halsey or why..."

Devin rapped his knuckles on the doorway's edge, then stepped into the sparsely furnished cabin. Barty was sitting on the corner of the bunk closest to the door; Trip sat in the middle of the one parallel to that. A third bunk, on the right side of the room, was empty. All had identical dark-blue blankets on them, and each had a small pillow with a light-blue cover.

Devin leaned against the doorjamb and folded his arms over his chest. "You've heard nothing from your contacts?"

Barty shook his head. His voice might sound stronger, but there were shadows under the older man's eyes. Illness, as Makaiden suggested? Worry? There was still plenty to worry about. It was more difficult to avoid your enemies when you were not really sure who they were. Or what they wanted, other than your nephew. Over and above the usual *the Guthrie family has money,* he couldn't even begin to address the why. Because *the Guthrie family has money* would have required neither the killing of Ben Halsey, nor the kind of maneuvers against them he'd witnessed on Dock Five.

"I've not heard back from Petra Frederick either," Devin told Barty. "Or J.M. Given where we are, that's not completely unexpected. I'm hoping for some kind of response before we make the jumpgate. I'd hate to be on the way to Calfedar only to find out GGS is sending a ship to Dock Five." Which was where the family would think they were, at least until they received his brief update that they'd found transport—though he didn't mention Makaiden or the *Rider*—sent just after the *Rider* received clearance to depart for Calfedar.

"Your father might not respond, fearing your message is a hoax," Barty offered, and Devin agreed. That was one of the reasons he'd been vague in his message. He didn't want the details falling into the wrong hands.

Barty leaned forward on the bunk, forearms on his thighs. He definitely looked tired. "But Frederick has the ability and the equipment to authenticate...to authenticate..." Barty gasped, his arms suddenly going limp.

As Barty crumpled toward the decking, Devin lunged, managing to catch Barty's shoulders in an attempt to break his fall.

"Barty!" Trip was down on one knee at Barty's side, his voice holding the panic Devin felt all too well. But Barty didn't answer.

Devin rolled the unconscious man carefully onto his back, making sure his throat was unobstructed and that he was breathing. He felt for a pulse in his neck, found it. It was weak, fluttering. Devin had seen players collapse on the handball courts over the years. He knew basic procedures, but there his medical expertise ended. "Trip, there has to be a diagnostic unit, portable, in sick bay. I don't want to move him until—"

"Captain Griggs will know where."

And be able to relay its location in less time than it would take him or Trip to find it. Devin shot to his feet. "Stay with him in case he has a seizure." Damn it all, he felt so helpless. He spied the intraship panel by the door and, fueled by a rising fear, punched the comm button with more force than was necessary. "Makaiden, Barty collapsed. Where's the—"

"Portable medalyzer's on the starboard wall of sick bay." Her words overrode his, and she spoke rapidly. "Left of the door. Silver and green cover. I'm on my way down."

"Understood." He slapped off the comm as he left the room, not knowing if she heard his affirmative. He darted around the galley tables, suddenly aware of the clatter of boot steps behind him, coming closer. A stairwell. Of course the *Rider* had to have one. If he ever got a minute's rest from emergencies, he'd use it to study this ship's layout. Right now he had an emergency.

He hit the main corridor, then skittered to a stop at the third doorway as Makaiden called out, "In there!"

A quick appraisal showed two diag beds with a display screen in between and the medalyzer right where she'd said. He unlatched the rectangular unit from its wall case, then moved back into the corridor, catching a glimpse of Makaiden heading toward the galley. It seemed as if an hour passed, but he knew it was only minutes before he had the unit in Makaiden's hands and she was taking readings on Barty's still unconscious form.

"It's safe to move him," she said, looking up from the screen.

"You have an antigrav stretcher?"

"Manual. Had to sell the AG one." She pushed herself to her feet with a glance at his nephew. "Trip? Give me a hand getting the stretcher." She held the medalyzer out toward Devin. "He's stable," she said as he took it, glancing at the pulsing lines on the green-tinged screen. "We shouldn't be a minute. See if you can't find that medicine vial. If we know what he's taking, it can save a lot of time. And his life."

"I ran his biostats and medication through your sickbay computer." Devin took the chair in front of the comm console, then swiveled it toward Makaiden as she turned the pilot's chair to face him. Behind her, endless blackness broken by only a few points of light filled the forward viewports. The bridge console screens flanked her right and left, pulsing and beeping in a low, erratic syncopation. That reminded him of the medalyzer he'd just spent the last ten minutes with. Not the best unit; nothing like the ones on GGS ships.

But it told him what he needed to know. "It's Gamdrel's Disease. There's a more formal medical term, but Gamdrel's is what most people call it."

"And veterans of the Boundary Wars are most often afflicted. He was ImpSec and at some point exposed to the toxins." She paused, studying him. "I'm guessing your family didn't know?"

"My father might have." But would he then have fired Barty—a longtime employee, a trusted member of the household staff—the way he did, simply because he'd challenged J.M.'s decision? It seemed heartless, but then, J.M., instead of softening in his later years, seemed to have toughened.

"Is he conscious yet?"

"According to the medalyzer, he's let his medication levels get too low. The recommendation was to keep him unconscious for at least another hour so his body will assimilate the drugs more quickly."

"He'll sleep through jump. I probably don't need to ask this, but—"

"Is he strapped in, secured?" Devin gave her a half smile. "Yes, Captain."

"We're forty-three out from the gate. Just passing a data beacon, if you want to use my comm to check for messages."

He tapped the microcomp at his side. "Already running a sweep—"

As if on cue, the unit trilled softly. Despite the fact that he was used to the noise, it startled Devin. For a moment he thought he'd activated something by mistake when he tapped it, but the icons flashing on the small screen when he pulled the Rada from its holder showed incoming messages.

"Ethan," he said, relieved and yet puzzled. He'd sent his messages to GGS Security and his father's private comm—including the latest, which his father wouldn't have received yet. This must be a response to an earlier one—maybe one Barty sent. He double-checked security on the incoming message. It was genuine and originated from his family's home but through Ethan's private link, text only.

Great that you found Trippy, D.J. Devin could almost hear Ethan's bored drawl. Some of his concerns abated. J.M. evidently told the family the news and appointed Ethan to send a message. *You missed all the panic here. Mother's in the hospital. Father and Jonathan are handling your division's contracts. The* Prosperity *will head to Port Chalo for you, Trippy, and Barthol. Change your reservations on Compass. ETA at Port Chalo is four days from date of this note. Reply back to me only. The main house link has been compromised. I'll explain when I see you.*

Devin's head swam. Now he knew why Ethan was the sender. His mother in the hospital. His father handling Devin's financial deals. The Guthrie estate's communications compromised. Port Chalo...and no ability to ask questions and get answers in real time.

He looked up from the unit's screen to find Makaiden regarding him quizzically. It took a moment to reorient himself.

"Port Chalo," he said, because that was the only thing he completely understood. "The *Prosperity* will be there in four, no, three days." Three because the date of Ethan's missive was yesterday. "We need to change course." Suddenly he wanted to bypass Port Chalo altogether and head straight back for Sylvadae. He couldn't—or, rather, Makaiden couldn't. He knew that. But something about Ethan's message was... wrong. It was nothing he could immediately define, only that there were problems, big problems. He needed to be there and couldn't be.

"You're sure?"

Devin glanced down at the words on his screen as if they might somehow miraculously hold more answers. "My mother's in the hospital. My father's handling the financial division—my division—and Ethan warns there's something wrong with the security at the house." He realized he was rambling. But this time, saying the words, he saw the first big problem. J.M. wouldn't become involved in GGS Financial. J.M., for all his brilliance, had no head for numbers. Jonathan was only slightly better, but Jonathan had his own division to handle. It had to be that Ethan misspoke—that J.M. and Jonathan had Devin's assistants, Nathanson and Torry, overseeing his projects.

But that's not what Ethan said, and that troubled Devin as much as what Ethan did say. Maybe J.M. hadn't given Ethan the full story. Given Ethan's lack of involvement with GGS—J.M. learned early on that his second-youngest son had no talent for business—that wouldn't be unusual.

"Changing course," Makaiden said, turning away from him. "Filing amendment of flight plans to Talgarrath." She was quiet for a moment—concentrating on something on the screens before her, he guessed. "That gate's about another hour from here. If Baris Central decides they don't want us going to Talgarrath, they have plenty of time to respond. But since we were initially cleared for either destination, I think we should be fine." She angled around toward him. "I'm sorry about your mother. Do you know what's wrong?"

"I'm guessing stress but, at her age, it could be anything. The thing with Philip hit her hard. And now this with Trip. She keeps too much inside, has to always appear in control." And he wondered where he learned it from. J.M. was more explosive. Never before breakfast, true, but he had a temper. Much like Ethan. "But Ethan's note didn't say what was wrong."

"At least she knows now that your nephew is safe," she said, turning back to her console, tapping one finger against a blinking white square icon. It vanished after her touch.

Devin nodded to the back of her head, his mind still turning over Ethan's words. Since Ethan received his messages, the family would know Trip was safe, yes. So his mother should be recovering—if that was her problem. But Valerie Lang Guthrie was not only in control of her emotions, she could be secretive. Definitely a need-to-know person, like Barthol. Devin scrubbed at his face with his hands. Like Barthol, his mother could have any number of medical issues she chose not to let "her boys" know about.

Why in hell didn't Ethan say what was wrong?

Devin tamped down the mixture of fear and anger that welled up unbidden. Just as his mother would do. He huffed out a hard sigh of frustration. He knew he had to meet the *Prosperity*. It was right, logical. But . . .

He couldn't define the *but*. Only that it loomed there, perplexing and fraught with problems. But there were no other options. If nothing else, the *Prosperity*'s communications equipment would provide him a direct means of contacting his family and, if need be, Petra Frederick.

"Mr. Devin?"

He raised his face and found concern written all over Makaiden's, in the downturn of her brows, the softness of her mouth.

"It's just Devin," he said quietly. With all the things suddenly going wrong, he didn't want that wall of formality between Makaiden and himself. He knew she still had issues with the way he'd acquired her ship. All the more reason he had to narrow that distance he felt she'd constructed between them. Something was very wrong with GGS, with his mother. He couldn't—*wouldn't*—add losing Makaiden to that list.

"And it's just Kaidee. Or Kaid," she countered.

He shook his head. "Makaiden. Don't short yourself. Don't shorten your name. Both are . . . extraordinary."

He watched her eyes widen at his blatant compliment. It wasn't like him. He knew that, and she knew that. And he knew he was staring at her again.

Her lashes dipped, her mouth parted slightly. Uncertainty? He was horrible at reading her. He hoped she believed him.

"Are you going to tell Trip about his grandmother?" she asked finally.

He started to say, "Yes, of course," then he caught himself. Trip already felt to blame for Ben Halsey's death, for Devin's injury, and for all the troubles chasing them on Dock Five. He was only nineteen. If Valerie Guthrie had collapsed because of her worry over Trip, then the news that Devin and Barthol had found him would restore her, and Trip didn't need to add that to his list of faults. If the reason for her hospitalization was something else, there was nothing Trip could do right now and the knowledge might only hamper him.

"I'll update him when we're on the *Prosperity*, headed for Sylvadae. My mother might even be out of the hospital by then. Until that point, he has enough to worry about with Ben Halsey's death and Barty's illness. And facing his father and grandfather."

She was nodding as he spoke, but he needed to hear it.

"I take it you agree?"

"He's your nephew, but, yes, I do. I spent a fair amount of time with him a few years ago. What you said about your mother holding things inside—so does Trip. If he didn't, someone would have known about this whole crazy scheme of his to meet up with his uncle Philip." She hesitated, then continued. "Maybe there's a lesson in this," she said softly. Then something on her console trilled, and she swiveled back before he could admit he'd thought that same thing. But he was beginning to believe the lesson was also his.

"We're cleared for Talgarrath," she said, with a quick glance over her shoulder.

He rose. "I'll tell Trip we're meeting up with the *Prosperity*."

And try to think of more ways to knock down those walls he felt Makaiden was building between them.

Kaidee silently blew out a long sigh between her lips when she was sure Devin was off the bridge and— judging by the muted ping—on the lift to the lower deck. She did not want to go to Port Chalo, and her reasons went beyond what she'd told Devin . . . was it only an hour ago? The place was ridiculously expensive. And corrupt. Though Dock Five could also fit that description.

But Kiler's involvement with something or someone in Port Chalo had gotten him killed. She never truly believed the repair-bay explosion was an accident. Accidental explosions didn't obliterate all traces of a body. There were too many safeguards in repair bays: alarms, fire suppressants. Injuries were common. Total incineration? Someone had helped that explosion along.

She hadn't been to Talgarrath since. She was going there now only because... Devin had ordered her to do so.

Right?

No. Even if Devin had left it totally up to her, she'd have agreed to take him to Port Chalo. His family was at risk. The same beliefs and values that had driven him to go against his family to find Trip were now driving him home again. She could see that in his eyes, in the thinning of his mouth.

She not only respected that, that kind of devotion damned near put a lump in her throat. She remembered only too well how her father had been abandoned by his brothers and sisters when he'd decided to do the right thing with his life. Even some of his crew had walked off. Only Kaidee and a handful supported him. And then, on Moabar Station, he was killed—likely because a former crew member, or even his own sister, had turned on him.

Maybe being owned by Devin Guthrie wasn't such a bad thing—except it would put her in regular proximity to him. And that, she was learning, was dangerous. Around him, it was too easy to let her guard down. She'd already made the mistake of encouraging him to call her Kaidee, not Captain Griggs or even Captain Makaiden. She couldn't afford that kind of familiarity. She couldn't afford to open her heart, because the results would be only pain—again.

She'd have to correct her mistake, keep that chasm between them wide and impassable.

It was the only way to keep her sane. And the only way to keep him safe.

11

They cleared the outer beacon for the Talgarrath jumpgate with no further communications from Baris Central, no strange and threatening blips on the *Rider*'s scanners. Devin was in sick bay with Barty; Trip was on the bridge at navigation, listening intently as Kaidee explained how to snag a news-and-message feed from the beacon—always a good idea before going into jump, because, if nothing else, it gave you something to read in transit. Then she showed him how to take the sublight engines off-line and segue over to the hyperdrive. In between explanations, he peppered her with questions.

Some seemed overly simplistic, but Kaidee didn't mind. She needed to keep her thoughts off Devin and knew that Trip needed something to keep from worrying about what would happen when he got home to Sylvadae.

Or else he had no intention of returning to Sylvadae at all but still intended to find his uncle Philip—and believed her instructions could land him a berth on a freighter bound for Calth.

Hell, Trip was a Guthrie. If he wanted a freighter, he could follow in his uncle Devin's footsteps and buy one in Port Chalo.

"Watching me pilot this ship isn't the same as doing," she said, shooting him a warning glance. "Just so you understand."

"I remember some of this from when you flew for us," Trip said, "but this isn't like the *Triumph*."

"A freighter handles differently from a passenger yacht. Part is design, part is weight distribution. That's a consideration on docking and a huge issue if you go dirtside. The other difference is that passengers complain if jumpgate transit is too stressful, if the hypers shimmy too much as they come online. Cargo doesn't."

"What did you learn to fly first?"

"Cargo. I didn't get my passenger rating until I went to work for Starways."

"That's where you met Captain Kiler, right?"

His comment startled her. "How do you know that?"

"Captain Kiler told me. Said the prettiest girls always worked for Starways. That's where he found all his girlfriends, and if I wanted one, that's where I had to go to work."

All his girlfriends. Kiler already had quite a reputation by the time Kaidee came to work at Starways, but he always swore that was because he hadn't met her yet. It was a charming line; Kiler was a charming rogue. And as wary as she was, she was flattered by his interest. They dated; six months later, they married. And for the first four or five years, she thought they had a great marriage. But what she'd seen as ambition in him soon was unmasked as greed and jealousy. Whatever they had wasn't enough or wasn't good enough.

His obsessions had escalated when they went to work for the Guthries and GGS. *That* was the lifestyle Kiler not only wanted but felt he deserved. Right away, not in the five-year plan he and Kaidee had developed toward their goal of owning their own transport fleet, starting with the down payment they had on the purchase of a newer Blackfire 225. He wanted it *now*. And Kiler didn't care what he had to do to get there.

That included using GGS executive vacation residences to run an illegal prostitution ring. Kaidee felt as if her life had been thrust back twenty years, to when her aunt had the nighthouse on Dock Five and Kaidee's father was forever trying to come up with funds to pay off the stripers or get his beloved older sister out of jail. Again.

Within a month of Kiler's firing from GGS, Kaidee filed for divorce. But the *Rider* was in both their names, and neither she nor Kiler had enough capital to buy the other out. So her soon-to-be ex-husband became her business partner.

And just as the divorce became final, she became his widow.

A triple chime. They'd reached the jumpgate's inner beacon. Kaidee abruptly pulled herself out of her memories, double-checking the screens before her. For the minute or so that she'd been lost in thought and time, her pilot self had continued to log in the necessary preparations for jump.

"Yes, we met at Starways," she told Trip, wondering if he'd noticed her momentary lapse and hoping, if he had, he'd assumed she was simply busy piloting. "But I don't think you need to get a job there to meet girls. I'm sure between the university and your family's business, you'll have plenty of opportunities to meet someone." A lot of someones, actually. Trip had the Guthrie charm and good looks.

And he was nice—a genuine niceness. It was something she sensed from Philip Guthrie, and from Devin—

She pushed the thought away. "I want you to watch how coolant levels spike on the hypers as we transit the gate. Blink your eyes if you have to clear them.

Blurred vision isn't an unusual reaction to gate transit on freighters of this class." GGS ships, she knew, had top-grade comfort dampers and other expensive hardware she couldn't afford. "You'll get used to it. But watch the pattern in the spikes." She caught his nod and tapped open intraship. "Two minutes to hard edge. Secure."

It was a standard warning. Ships under her hands rarely shimmied on gate entrance or exit, but there was always the chance of an odd hyperdrive surge, and she didn't need Devin or Barty taking further injuries.

The *Rider* flowed through the jumpgate, hyperdrives thrumming smoothly, communications links falling silent as the here and now of realspace was replaced with the neverwhen timelessness of hyperspace.

For the first time in weeks, Kaidee felt completely safe. All hell might wait for them at gate exit, but for the next three days they were, for all intents and purposes, inviolate. She leaned back in her chair with a soft sigh and with a practiced glance confirmed that all was as it should be on the *Rider*.

For now, a little voice said in her head.

But it was true. Her life lately seemed to go from one tailspin to another. And just because no one could shoot at them in jumpspace didn't mean a whole phalanx of ships didn't intend to do exactly that when they exited.

Some could be after Trip. But some could arguably be after her.

"Trip—"

"I saw the spike pattern, Captain Makaiden!" He sounded excited, dropping the false cool polish he'd adopted in the past two days. "I didn't think I did, at first," he continued. "But it's just odd, even, even, odd. A pattern that mirrors itself. Isn't that right?"

She nodded over her shoulder at him. "I've had people watch through five jumps and not figure that out. You've earned yourself dinner and dessert. Go hit the galley." She knew she'd told him to get something to eat right after they left Dock Five, but when Barty fell ill, those plans were sidetracked. Now she was hungry and guessed everyone else would be too. And it was...later than she thought. The time stamp on her pilot's console still reflected Dock Five time— which would stay as shiptime until they hit Talgarrath—and it told her dinner should have been two hours ago.

She was hungry *and* tired.

Trip rose. "Can I bring you something?"

"I'll be down in a bit. There's a secondary pilot's panel just off the galley, if something does need my attention." And one in the captain's cabin on this deck as well. She'd run the ship in her nightshirt and sweatpants before. As she was the only qualified pilot on board, it looked as if she might be doing that again.

Trip left with the thumping boot steps so common to tall young men still getting used to the height and weight of their bodies. Kaidee rechecked ship's status, then shunted the routine duties over to autopilot. Despite the fact that she wasn't needed on the bridge when in jumpspace, she might bring her dinner up here. She didn't feel up to sharing a meal with Devin, trying to figure out what was going on behind those silver-rimmed glasses of his. Let the Guthries have their privacy, and let the division between employer and employee be glaringly obvious.

Besides, she needed some private time herself. She

had to figure a way to buy her ship back from Devin Guthrie.

Devin steadied his Rada microcomp in Barty's hand. The older man was awake and demanding updates but still weak. And he was as unhappy as Devin with Ethan's message—other than the fact that a GGS star yacht would be available to take them home.

He brushed away Devin's concern over his condition—"It's manageable when I don't make stupid mistakes with my medication"—and concentrated instead on the immediate Guthrie problem.

"The main house link being compromised is almost inconceivable." Barty inched himself a little higher against the raised back of the diag bed, adjusting the pillow as he spoke. "Not impossible, mind you. I helped Petra Frederick make updates to the system, oh, eight months or so ago. There is no such thing as an impenetrable security net, but we thought we caught all the glitches." He frowned. "Evidently not."

"Was Halsey in on any of this? Could someone have gotten that information out of him before he died?"

"You're thinking a *Ragkiril* mind-ripper, I take it? That's always a possibility, and if so, that would lead me to think Tage's people might be behind this. Except, to the best of my knowledge, Halsey wasn't involved in the updates."

"Who was?"

"Your father, obviously. Frederick handpicked the technical staff, and I cleared them as well: Chelle and Hu. But neither worked on the final interface, and you'd need knowledge of that in order to break it."

Devin's mind churned. He leaned one hip against

the side of Barty's diag bed, then crossed his arms over his chest. "When you came to my suite after Trip disappeared, you said my father fired you because you'd disagreed with him. Why would he do that, when you're not only an integral part of our household but you're also involved in Guthrie security?"

Barty let out a long sigh. "This isn't the first time he and I have had words or been on opposite ends. I thought last week that he'd simply had enough of this pushy old man. And, honestly, I knew you were right, and I was too worried about Master Trip to consider it much more than an opportunity to get to Trip before someone else did. But now," and he shook his head slowly, "it's like . . . someone wanted me out of the way. I just can't fathom why your father would want to sabotage his own company, his own *family*."

"Unless he's not well?" Devin's voice was soft.

"Senility?"

"Or a brain disorder. Or other medical problem that would put him so on edge, make him so paranoid, irrational."

"Then you've noticed that too?"

Devin uncrossed his arms and ran one hand through the short spikes of his hair. "He wanted me out of my office, out of GGS Financial altogether for the next six months. To spend time with my new bride, take her to parties and get her pregnant."

"That was something else your father and I disagreed on."

Devin shot him a quizzical glance. "Parties or pregnancy?"

"Miss Tavia. A lovely young woman. Pardon my bluntness, but not for you."

Was there anything his father hadn't discussed with Barty? "Because she's much more sociable, you mean?" His father and mother had mentioned several times how they hoped Tavia's outgoing personality might rub off on him.

"Because you're not in love with her, and she's not with you. That's no way to spend the rest of your life."

Devin straightened abruptly. "I didn't know it was that obvious."

Barty arched one eyebrow. "I've spent more than two decades with Guthrie men who excel at failing to acknowledge their feelings."

Failing to acknowledge. Concise, factual, and a point Devin was not going to argue. His recent mishaps with Makaiden made the case for him. Amazing that he could be so clumsy with something so important. Then again, maybe not. "Given all that's going on, I think Father will understand my canceling wedding plans with Tavia."

"Given all that's going on," Barty countered, "that's the very reason your father may push for them. The political instability right now—plus Admiral Guthrie's, shall we say, notoriety—weighs heavily on your father. He knows he can't trust Tage, but he can't afford to alienate the man either. At the same time, Tage has to tread carefully around Guthrie Global. Your family's been influential for a long time. Other captains of industry look to GGS for leadership, for trends."

Devin shrugged, though Barty's comment worried him. "I told Father last month that we could pull out of Aldan, operate out of Calth and Baris, and do fine. Most of the raw materials for our manufacturing come out of places like Umoran and the Walker Colonies. Trade and export can operate anywhere."

"Mark my words, Tage knows that. The man may be despotic, but he's not stupid. He knows that if GGS pulls out of Aldan, others will follow. I think Tage is scared that Admiral Guthrie took his military knowledge to the Alliance, but I think he's more frightened that Philip Guthrie took the Guthrie name to the Alliance, thereby giving it credibility. That's why his people are working so hard to depict your brother as some kind of half-crazed traitor."

"When in reality, Tage is the crazy one," Devin said, his voice low and bitter.

"Ah, but he's the crazy one in power, calling himself the prime commander now, and with a watered-down Admirals' Council as the only check and balance, there's no way to stop him."

"Which is all very worrisome but doesn't explain Ethan's message."

"It might if your father somehow got Tage involved in Master Trip's little fiasco. You know he was fixated on his belief that Tage's people had Trip. If he acted on that or confronted Tage's people, it could have had repercussions—personally and corporately. Tage is well known for pushing for more government control over private industries like GGS. Philip was the first defection. Trip's could be seen as the second, and you, out here, could be named a third. That might be all Tage's people need as a reason to take over control of Guthrie Global via an Imperial mandate. For security reasons, of course." The smirk in Barty's voice was clear.

Devin slumped against the edge of the diag bed.

"If you weren't so busy worrying about Trip, Captain Makaiden, and me, you would have figured this out for yourself," Barty said softly. "I could also be totally wrong."

He could be, but Devin had a sinking feeling he wasn't. And there was no way to confirm or deny

those suspicions as long as they were in jumpspace—
for another three days.

Devin retrieved his Rada from Barty's outstretched
hand. "It's past dinner. Are you hungry?"

"Tired, mostly," he said with a sigh. "Send Trip
with soup and tea in two hours or so. These"—he
tapped one of the med-broches peeking out from the
edge of his T-shirt collar—"are programmed to supply
a fair amount of nutrition. I need a nap more right
now."

Devin felt suddenly guilty. The *Rider*'s sick-bay systems had yet to give Barty clearance. The older man
needed rest and here Devin was, peppering him with
problems and suppositions. With a nod, he headed out
into the corridor, needing a cup of hot tea and the
presence of one Makaiden Griggs. And not necessarily
in that order.

He found Makaiden in the galley with an empty tray
in one hand, waiting before the rectangular white
panel that served as the ship's food dispenser—a basic-
model chefmaster with three square delivery chutes.
She was already looking over her shoulder in his direction as he came around the corner.

"Trip just finished his dinner," she said, glancing at
the blinking cooking-time readout over the middle
chute, then back to him again. "How's Barty feeling?"

"Tired, and more than a little ashamed at misjudg-
ing his own medication schedule." He stepped toward
her, disturbed that when he did so she took her gaze
from his. Around him, she vacillated between anger
and annoyance. He wasn't sure which this was right
now. But then, as Barty so wisely noted, feelings
weren't a Guthrie male's strongpoint.

"Just getting a casserole," she said quickly. "I'll be out of here in a minute."

"Stay." He leaned one shoulder against the dispenser wall, because at least he could see her face, even if she wouldn't look at him. "Have dinner with me. Or whatever meal we're at right now." He ended his words with a small smile, trying to ease the source of her discomfort. He didn't know what it was—though he could make a few wildly accurate guesses having to do with the past forty-eight hours—but he sensed it clearly and wanted it gone.

The dispenser pinged twice. The delivery chute's translucent cover slid sideways. The aroma of melted cheese wafted past his nose.

Makaiden slid the casserole onto her tray. "Thanks, but I have some things I need to do on the bridge. Plus, shouldn't you be with Barty?"

"He's napping. He asked that Trip bring him some tea and soup in a couple hours. I think Barty wants to finish his 'this is what's going to happen when you get home' remonstrative chat." Devin studied the list of dinner items illuminated in blue on the screen in the corner of the dispenser. "So, what's good? What do you suggest?"

He didn't want her to leave. He wanted her here, talking to him, keeping him from going crazy over thoughts of GGS, Tage, his mother, and inexplicable security breaches. There was something about Makaiden's presence he'd always found reassuring. And even more so now.

"There's not a lot to choose from. I'm sorry. I stock what I like, and I like—"

"Cheese." Cheese and vegetable casserole, cheese soup, and egg and cheese pie were a few of the items on the list.

"It's dairy, protein, and the nutritional components are reasonably priced," she said with a shrug. She put the tray on the counter, then slid back the silver metal cover of the cooler unit.

"That's okay. I like cheese too. Actually haven't had a good egg and cheese pie since I was in college." He tapped in his order as she pulled out a bottle by its top. Juice? Water? Water, he noted, seeing the label.

"Want some?" she asked, holding the bottle in the air.

"I'll have hot tea."

She pointed toward a smaller silver-fronted dispenser to her right. "There should be some tea bags in the drawer underneath."

"Thanks. I'll..." But she'd turned away, heading for the galley's small dining area, and he was speaking to her back. "...get one."

He hesitated only a moment, then, mouth grim, followed her, hoping she was setting her meal at one of the two tables in the dining area. She wasn't. She was slipping around the corner into the corridor when he stopped at the closest table. He stood there, hands jammed in pockets, until the dispenser behind him chimed.

He snagged a tray, retrieved his dinner, and decided he'd give it another try.

She turned, eyes slightly widened in surprise, as he stepped onto the bridge, tray in hand.

"Tell me this is off limits and I'll leave." He offered her an excuse he didn't want her to use but would accept if she did. Because he was a Guthrie.

She seemed to study him for a few seconds, during which time he wondered if he could take back his offer to depart. "Both nav and comm have pull-out tray tables to the right of the chairs, like this." She tapped the one that held her tray. "I take it you have something you want to discuss?"

He took that for an invitation to stay. "Thousands of things, with all that's gone on," he said, dropping into the seat at nav as it was closer to her. He found the edge of the recessed tray and swung it toward him. "But actually I'd like to hear what you've been doing the past two years."

"Working, hauling cargo," she said, her gaze on the spoon stirring her casserole. Her tone sounded carefully neutral. Maybe not the best choice of topics. One of the things that happened in the past two years was the death of her husband.

He sought something positive. "You have some good clients."

"Tage's embargos have made that tougher lately."

Devin nodded. "For everyone. But now you're passenger-certified."

Makaiden sighed. "The *Rider* is not going to be a moneymaking venture for you, Mr. Devin."

"Devin," he corrected her.

She hesitated, then: "No, sir. You're my employer."

"I'd prefer to be your friend," he said softly.

"With all that's gone on," she said, echoing his statement of moments ago, "I don't think that's wise." She lifted her chin slightly. "Your dinner's getting cold. Sir." Something beeped on her console. She grabbed a spoonful of casserole as she turned away from him.

He took a few forkfuls of his egg pie and watched her work, spoon in her right hand, left hand tapping or nudging at various things blinking before her.

"With all that's gone on," he repeated, "I think knowing who my friends are is essential." If that's where they had to start, so be it. He wondered, though, what part Kiler played in her aversion. Did she still love her husband? Did she see Devin's acquisition of the *Rider* as somehow infringing on that?

There was a flash of pain in her eyes as she glanced at him. "Your family has always had not only my loyalty but my respect."

What about me personally? He almost asked that but for the soft whooshing sound of the lift doors followed by the hard, loping boot steps that could only be his long-legged nephew.

Makaiden's expression shifted, her brows relaxing. Obviously, she liked Trip and didn't have any problems with considering his nephew her friend. If only—

But her brows dipped again, and Devin shifted his gaze from Makaiden's face to Trip's and found matching frowns.

"Uncle Devin?" Trip held his pocket comm in his outstretched hand as he strode onto the bridge. "Something's wrong."

"You can't get messages in jumpspace," Makaiden said before Devin could respond. He knew Trip knew jumpspace was a communications null, so that wasn't the problem.

Trip nodded. "I wasn't trying to. I just turned it on to compose my apologies, like Barthol told me to. That's when I found this message in my unsent outbox. But I *swear* I didn't create it." He paused, darting a worried glance at Devin, then to Makaiden, then back to Devin again. "Why would I send my father a message demanding fifteen million credits for my safe return?"

Kaidee wasn't overly happy with having Devin in her quarters. The two small rooms and private lav were sacrosanct, her personal retreat, and watching his tall form stride in made her feel as if her last defensive shield had been breached. But since her quarters were originally the ship's ready room and data lab and contained direct access to the *Rider*'s commdat analytics program, there was no way she could keep him out.

Besides, she wanted answers as badly as he did.

Devin had his Rada out on her dining table—*damn, that was one impressive unit*—and had it synched to the smaller pocket comm and to the commdat panel on the bulkhead wall behind him. A green-tinged holographic display hovered in front of him, data flickering rapidly across its surface. But his investigation was proceeding slowly.

Too slowly for Trip, who was obviously nervous, jiggling one leg as he sat on Devin's right. "Anything yet?"

"Someone with the capability to break Guthrie security has the capability to thwart, even attack, incoming probes." Devin squinted through his glasses, mouth pursed, his attention never wavering from the display. "Right now I'm erring on the side of caution."

"Sorry," Trip said, his voice a low, tired rumble in his chest.

Kaidee, on Devin's left, changed her gaze from the Rada's display to Trip across the table. "At least the message was never sent, and you found it when it could do no harm."

"Seems like the only thing I've done so far that's done no harm." Trip scrubbed at his face with one hand. "I'm sorry. This is such a mess—"

"Can you get us some tea from the galley?" Kaidee interrupted him. "The unit in here doesn't work well."

That wasn't all that far from the truth—her quarters held only a basic slurp-and-snack—but Kaidee also felt that Trip needed to be doing something more than sitting glumly, listening to his uncle swear softly under his breath.

"See if Barty's awake and wants anything," she added as, with a nod, Trip headed for the corridor.

"Mind reader." Devin's low comment as the door closed behind Trip's retreating figure brought her attention back to the table and the man seated inches from her.

"Pardon?" His words confused her.

He glanced at her briefly, then back at the holographic screen. "Trip really has no idea what's going on, other than that whatever he does seems to cause trouble. Keeping him busy right now is a good move."

"I can't believe he'd leave his pocket comm around where anyone could access it."

"He wouldn't. At least, I've never known him to do so." Devin poked at a line of code, dragging it to the right. "But it wouldn't matter if he did. It's a secure unit. No one can use it unless they know his personal passwords."

Suddenly she understood the reason behind Devin's low epithets. "This isn't some outside operation. This is someone in GGS."

"Or in my parents' direct employ." The look he shot her was bleak.

He didn't have to say it; she could guess at the rest of his thoughts: someone who might be in the Guthrie home, even now. "Former employee?" For a chilling moment, she thought of Kiler. He often amused himself by creating password-encryption programs. Had another employee copied his codes, or had Kiler taught someone his methods before he died?

"If so, then someone in the last twenty-three days." Devin touched a square databox and pushed it next to the line of code. Numbers and symbols moved rapidly in and out of it. "We change passwords frequently for that very reason."

Kiler had been dead for a lot longer than twenty-three days. And if someone had filched one of his programs, why would they wait until now to use it? "So as much as twenty-three days ago, someone intended to kidnap Trip and send this message through his pocket comm. But if they had Trip, or even just had his pocket comm, why preprogram the message? They have the password. They could create a message and send it anytime they wanted to."

"I can only assume that the person who knew the password wasn't going to be the person or people holding Trip hostage. They might have even intended to leave his pocket comm somewhere else. That would be logical, since law enforcement would be tracking the comm's location."

"It is possible to determine the send date?" That should tell them something. Was it keyed to send the day Halsey was killed? Or was Halsey's death unrelated?

"More than possible. Almost there."

Kaidee glanced at the hovering display again. Her experience with datacodes was confined to what she needed to know to run her ship and what she'd watched Kiler and, when she was younger, her uncle or her father create. She wasn't remotely in Devin's league but knew enough to recognize his skill. And that not all of it was university-issue.

Then something flickered.

"Damn!" He swiped quickly at a pair of databoxes, positioning them around a wavering line of symbols. "Okay." He let out a long breath. "Let's try that again."

"Problem?"

"I hate self-destruct filters. Especially when they're sloppily set." He sat back from the display, then ran one hand through his hair, making it stick up in short spikes on the right side. "Whoever did this has just enough training to be dangerous but not enough to know how stupidly he could fuck—" He shot her an embarrassed glance. "Sorry."

"Fuck things up?" Kaidee snorted softly, amused by his discomfort. "I grew up on the docks, Devin. I've heard worse."

A half smile played over his mouth. "So I guess we're friends?"

It took her a moment to catch the line of his thought. Devin. She'd called him Devin. She damned her lapse and the heat she could feel creeping across her cheeks. It had always been so easy to be with him. And so easy to forget why she shouldn't be.

"I respect all the Guthries. And that includes you." But that sounded lame, even to her ears, and he was still smiling.

Then his smile turned wistful. "I hope that respect doesn't fade when I ask you to be my partner in crime."

For a moment alarm flared. But he was pointing to the Rada's display, and she knew it had to do with Trip's pocket comm and not her heritage.

"I need to do a little, um, creative coding here to disarm that self-destruct. But it will involve altering, temporarily, your ship's comm link relay—"

"You want to create a Corrinian parabola." She didn't try to keep the slight but noticeable smug tone out of her voice. She might not have his talents, but she wasn't ignorant. Especially of things less than legal and more than helpful, thanks to her uncle. Knowing those kinds of things improved your chance to survive, as long as you didn't get caught. "I grew up on *freighter* docks," she reiterated. "I've spent a lot of time on Dock Five."

He arched one eyebrow. "Maybe GGS should have hired you as security, not a pilot."

Except a security position would have required a deeper background clearance. Something she couldn't afford. "Those were my uncle's skills. Not mine."

"Why do I think I'd like your family?" he drawled. Then, before Kaidee could voice her disbelief, he pointed to the suspended display. "In the meantime, we have work to do."

That work—much of which would have drawn praise from her uncle and Kiler—took a little over an hour. Trip brought tea and bottles of cold water, but Devin wouldn't let him help with the programming.

"He doesn't need to know this at his age," Devin said, after sending Trip down to sick bay to watch over Barty.

"How old were you when you learned to hack system codes?"

"That's not the point."

Younger than Trip, then. She wondered if Philip had taught him, but, no, she never remembered Philip Guthrie having much of an interest in that area. Laser pistols, yes. Computers and data pathways, no.

She returned to the bridge, the last bit of encryption on a datapad in her hand, and dutifully sat at the communications console, entering it on cue. As before, she knew enough to know that a professional had programmed this, bypassing security traps and hard walls that were supposedly impenetrable and wrapping it all around and into the smaller but equally complex systems of Trip's pocket comm.

Or something like that. She knew it was used to extract security-locked information, but since it had little to do with piloting a ship, she'd never paid much interest to it or to other hacks her uncle had excelled at.

Now, in a way, she wished she had. It might have made her feel on a bit more of an equal footing with Devin.

Why? So you could be friends, like he said? Do you really think you could be friends with Devin Guthrie? His pilot, his bodyguard, sure. His mistress? Hell, what was it Kiler always said? If it pays well enough...

But anything more than that, you're kidding yourself, Kaid. J.M. would find out about your family and have you fired and spaced. And not necessarily in that order.

A noise in the corridor by the lift made her turn from the console: Devin, alone, his fingers wrapped so tightly around Trip's pocket comm that his knuckles were white. His mouth was a tight line.

Kaidee's gut went cold.

He took the seat next to her at the comm, then tossed the pocket comm with a careless ferocity onto the console's wide work area. The rectangular unit hit with a sharp clink, spun three quarters of the way around, then stopped, wedged against the edge of a keyboard.

"What?" she asked, meaning who, where, and why as well.

He seemed to understand. And the answer, she could tell, wasn't easy for him.

"My father," he said finally, putting a hard pause between the two words. "The indomitable Jonathan Macy Guthrie the First. The man who always has the right answer. The man who will not be disobeyed." He dropped his gaze for a moment and clenched his hands together, elbows on his knees. "I can't believe I'm saying this."

"Your father wanted Trip kidnapped, Halsey killed?" It sounded bizarre as she said it, but she understood his grief. As a child, she loved her aunts and uncles. Then she found out what they did for a living.

He looked up, pain on his face. "I don't know about Halsey. But the ransom message on Trip's pocket comm was originally created on my father's personal system. There are... hallmarks. Telltales. And they're there."

"Why would he do that?"

Devin barked out a harsh laugh. "Because he will not be disobeyed. And if he had to create a crisis to ensure that, he would. Except Trip's leaving ahead of schedule completely skewed his plans. As for the purported kidnapping, I'm guessing it would have been something easily solved but it would have manipulated certain people into the positions he wanted. Instead, he had a real crisis. And no easy solution."

"How would Trip being kidnapped make people do what he wanted?"

"Maybe he saw that as a way to force Philip to come home. Or maybe he thought that would encourage Tavia and—"

Kaidee waited for Devin to finish his sentence. He didn't. "Tavia?" she prompted.

He shook his head. "Another minor family problem. Non-problem, actually." He shoved himself to his feet.

Kaidee thought he was leaving the bridge, but he paced over to the empty pilot's chair and stood there, hands loosely on the chair's back, staring out the blanked viewport. There was nothing to see in jumpspace. It didn't matter. She had a feeling Devin was seeing things he didn't want to see.

His father setting up some childish game with Trip's supposed kidnapping? All because he wanted Philip Guthrie to return home? Or was it over some other family problem Devin hinted at? It didn't matter. It was a stupid and dangerous thing to do, and Devin knew that better than she did.

"There's more." He angled around and looked at her over his left shoulder.

Kaidee leaned forward in her chair, the grimness in his voice making her gut clench.

"There was a stealth pointer embedded in Trip's pocket comm."

A stealth pointer was an expensive and complex long-distance locator program. For the Guthries with a rambunctious teenager, it could make sense. "Trip's parents probably thought it was necessary—"

"It doesn't report back to Jonathan or Marguerite. It goes back to a location on Aldan Prime. Actually, an Imperial aide's office. Does the name Pol Acora mean anything to you?"

"No."

"He works for Tage. I didn't recognize the comm address, only that it was a government one. But because we've handled supplies for various Imperial shipyards, GGS has a listing of key contacts. I ran it through my Rada to confirm it."

"Why would Tage or this Pol Acora care where Trippy is?"

"You'd have to ask my father that." He turned back to the blank viewport. "The stealth program was uploaded when the ransom note was."

Kaidee sat for several moments in stunned silence, the implications of Devin's information circling in her brain. "Your father's sending the *Prosperity* to Port Chalo. Do you still think it's wise to meet up with the ship?"

"Reading my thoughts again, Makaiden?" Devin answered without turning around. His shoulders were stiff, his posture radiating pain. "My gut instinct is to say no, we shouldn't. But maybe this is what Ethan was hinting at. Maybe this is the real reason my mother's in the hospital." He shook his head slowly. "And for the next three days, all we can do is chase suppositions."

Kaidee glanced at the time stamp on the comm console. It was late and, considering all that had happened today, felt even later. "No. For the next two and a half shipdays, we can go over what we know and make well-thought-out plans. Contingency plans." She had one, but it was hugely risky. It could save them, if this was indeed a trap. But it would also damn her.

She shelved it for now. There had to be other, safer options. "We'll need them if your father's playing some kind of game."

Devin twisted around to face her. "If my father's playing some kind of game where he's willing to risk his own grandson's life, then any contingency plans we come up with won't be good enough. Trust me on that." He jammed his hands into his pants pockets and looked at her levelly. "Can you leave the bridge?"

"Why?"

"We need to go see if Barty can give us a crash course in ImpSec tactics. If my father and Tage are planning another crisis, Port Chalo would be an excellent place to stage it."

12

The dim lighting in the *Rider*'s sick bay told Kaidee that there would be no strategy session with Barty for several hours yet. They found Trip half asleep as well in the armchair near Barty's bed. A tray with an empty soup bowl was on a table behind him.

"His levels dropped," Trip said quietly after Devin roused him. "The unit said he needed another regeneration sleep period, and it knocked him out"—he glanced at the wall console—"about forty-five minutes ago."

"Looks like you need downtime too," Kaidee told him. "We all do. There's nothing that has to be solved in the next few hours, unless..." She glanced at Devin. He'd made no effort yet to tell Trip about his grandfather's scheme.

Devin gave his head a small negative shake. "Things will seem clearer if we're all rested."

Trip must have heard the weariness and frustration in Devin's voice. "What's wrong?" he asked, rising.

"Makaiden and I have been playing with a bunch of scenarios, that's all." He cuffed his nephew lightly on the shoulder. "Tired minds doing too much thinking. Let's get some sleep."

Kaidee followed Trip and Devin into the corridor, stopping when Trip turned left into the small mess area that led to the crew bunks. Devin hit the palm pad for the larger passenger cabin on her right. The door slid open, but he stood there watching Trip, then turned his gaze to her when the door to the crew bunk area thumped closed.

"Are you going to tell Trip about the message source?" She kept her voice low, even though Trip couldn't hear her.

Devin nodded grimly. "Eventually I have to. He needs to know that...things are not as they seem. That people he's trusted all his life may no longer be trustworthy." His eyes narrowed for a moment, then he shrugged one shoulder, as if pushing off the burden Kaidee very clearly felt he carried. "But not tonight. It's been a very long day. For all of us."

It had, but it wasn't just fatigue she sensed from him. She tried to put a hopeful tone in her voice, because she knew Devin was worried. "Tomorrow Barty will be awake and able to help."

Another slow nod. Then a sigh. "Makaiden..."

There was something about the way he said her name, something about the low rumble of his voice underscored by the quite thrumming of the ship's drive. It caused a little flutter inside her, a flutter she couldn't afford.

She took a step away from him. "It's late. Everything you need should be in the cabin-or here in the galley." She made an aimless motion with her left hand.

The way he was looking at her was far more direct. "Thank you."

She took two more steps toward the lift. "Good night," she said, and turned quickly, before his smoky gaze and her growing flutters compelled her to stay.

Kaidee's eyelids drifted open into darkness that shifted—as her muzzy mind looped in perplexing circles—to a not-quite-so-dark darkness. There was a faint glow coming from the lav across from her bed, as there always was when she had her quarters set to shipnight. The low-pitched humming of the jump-space drive was an ever-present reminder of her ship's location. No alarms wailed, chirped, or beeped.

So what was wrong?

The dream came back to her, a jumble of images and emotions. Fleeing down dimly lit tunnels. The narrow-eyed gazes of suspicious stripers. These were dreams she'd had before, but, this time, Devin was there. Devin of the quiet strength, the unshakable surety, the deep loyalty . . .

Devin who owned her ship.

She rolled over with a groan. She'd slept only two and a half hours. Her mouth felt like tacky sandpaper and she craved a cold bottle of water or, perversely, a mug of hot tea. There was an ache growing between her eyes, and her mind would not stop. *Devin. Trip. Barty. Orvis. Dock Five. Frinks. Stripers. Devin.* Sleep was not going to return at this rate.

The hell with water or tea. She needed a beer.

She slept in an old long-sleeved gray thermal shirt that was several sizes too large. Normally she'd head down to the galley just like that, barefoot as well. But she had guests. The ship's owner was on board. She rummaged through a drawer, found a pair of dark-blue sweatpants, then pulled them on. She should check on Barty while she was down there.

She doubted he'd care that she was barefoot.

After a perfunctory perusal of ship's status from the console in her quarters, she stepped out into the corridor, then padded down the stairs. She didn't want the rumble of the lift to wake Trip or Devin and, besides, the stairs led directly to the small mess hall. No need to pass Devin's door. But halfway down the stairs she hesitated. There was a noise that didn't belong. She frowned, listening more closely. A click or a snick; a small sharp sound. Another. Then a quick series of three.

Then silence.

She moved softly, damning the fact that she wasn't armed, but, hell, this was her ship. In spite of the spike in her heart rate, she knew an intruder or stowaway wasn't a possibility. But something leaking, a loose piece of power conduit tapping against the wall—*that* was always a possibility and could be equally dangerous.

Another series of soft snicks. Then a ruffling sound, as if someone shuffled a deck of playing cards.

Shit. She peeked around the corner of the bulkhead wall adjoining the mess hall and stared straight into smoky-blue eyes framed by silver-rimmed glasses. Devin, alone at the table next to the galley entrance, shirtsleeves rolled up haphazardly. Playing cards were fanned between his fingers. A bottle of beer was on his right.

The only consolation was that he seemed as startled as she was. A few of the cards fluttered away from him, falling to the tabletop. Then the stiffness of his shoulders relaxed. He scooped up the wayward cards. "Trip's had a hard enough day. Barty's sleeping peacefully," he said, his voice low. "His stats all look fine."

That would explain why he was awake; it didn't explain the cards or the beer. Then she realized he was giving her an excuse. Not *I'm worried, I can't sleep, I'm upset.* All of which were arguably true for herself as well, but not something she was comfortable admitting—and he seemed to know that, damn him.

At least he didn't know that his appearance in her dreams was also a cause of her restlessness.

"Thanks for checking in on him." She matched his tone so her voice wouldn't carry beyond the mess area and stepped toward him, the layout of the cards catching her eye. Zentauri. But Zentauri-Jir, the solo game, set up in casinos as player versus banker. Not the multiple-player version she'd shared with him so many times in transit.

Devin had been blind-dealing, acting as both player and banker. She eyed the positions of the cards, doing a quick tally. Something told her that was better than discussing why else they were both awake and in the mess hall with very little sleep. "You should have held back the two and put the six here instead." She pointed to the shorter line of cards on his right, just under the half-empty bottle of beer. He'd been here for a bit. Long enough to roll up his sleeves and unbutton his shirt halfway. Or else, like her, he'd failed at sleep and tossed on some clothes before heading for the galley.

"The gate shows a three low," he said, using one finger to tap the middle stack of cards, in between the stack called the orbit and the one called the dock.

"Right, but you can double on a low gate in Jir." She slanted him a glance, not missing the fact that Devin actually did disheveled well. "So much for all my lessons."

He peered up at her over the rim of his glasses. "It's been a while. Refresh my memory."

Her mind screamed *no*. Her body and heart considered what was right and rational and pushed those all away. She held his gaze for a moment longer than was prudent. "Let me get a beer."

"The whole concept of Zentauri-Jir is control, not competition like regular Zentauri. The banker is a position, not your adversary." She dealt the newly shuffled deck as she sat across from him, watching the cards and not his face. *Two, three hands,* she made herself promise. Enough to be social, yet not enough time to get talking about anything other than the game. But three hands went quickly and he was asking questions—good ones.

She'd forgotten how much she enjoyed playing cards with Devin Guthrie.

One more hand. But one more meant one more cold beer.

When she returned from the galley, grasping two chilled bottles, Devin was standing. "Let's move to my cabin. I don't want our chatter to wake Trip."

Her steps slowed.

Devin spread his hands in an innocent gesture. "Or not. Sorry. If you feel threatened—"

"Threatened?" She didn't hide the derision in her voice, because she knew it was expected. It wasn't that she felt threatened exactly, but—

"Uncomfortable," he offered. "I can leave the door open."

The look on his face was so guileless, she had to smile. "Leave it open, because if alarms start wailing, I don't want to be looking for a palm pad to find out what's wrong." That wasn't exactly factual. She knew where the palm pads were in every compartment on this ship. And since the passenger cabin Devin now occupied used to be the captain's quarters, there was a command console integrated into the main panel in the desk to the right of the door.

He gestured to the other side of the corridor,

retrieving his beer from her as she padded by, the decking cool under her bare feet.

The door to his quarters was open. She put her beer down on the circular plastiwood dining table in the far corner of the small living area. He tossed the cards on top and chose a seat with his back facing the aft bulkhead. She sat across from him and sifted through the deck, choosing specific cards before she dealt a hand. "Okay, now consider this..."

By the next hand, he'd developed strategies of his own, winning the solo game quickly without any of her previous hints. She had to remind herself that Devin was a linear thinker but that once he had that down satisfactorily, he opened up his more creative side.

"That's two in a row," she said, after he won the next hand in ten moves. Damned near pro status, that. "One more and I'm letting you loose in the casinos."

He grinned. "Bet I can do five in a row."

She snorted softly. "Maybe. But not each in less than ten moves."

"Bet I can."

She tilted his empty beer bottle and peered down the neck. "No more for you. You're hallucinating."

"You doubt me?"

"I can win five in a row. Sometimes. But not in less than ten moves."

"So you doubt me."

"I think...the game can surprise you. You're a good card counter. But no one's that good."

"What's it worth?"

"Pardon?"

He leaned forward, elbows on the table, then picked up a card and tapped it lightly against the polished tabletop. "What's it worth to you? Make a bet with me. I lose and . . . you name the prize."

My ship back in my name. It was on the tip of her tongue but she couldn't say it, not in jest, which is what he had to be doing. "Seriously . . ."

"Seriously. What do you want? Your heart's desire. Name it. I lose, it's yours."

Her heart thumped hard in her chest. This time there was no holding back. "My ship." The rasp in her voice surprised her. "Clear title in my name."

He nodded slowly, his face tilted slightly, not so much in puzzlement as in amusement. "Deal."

Shock sizzled through her. "You have to win the next three hands in less than ten moves. You understand? Not just three hands but less than ten moves."

"Understood."

This was too easy. This was . . . Trepidation replaced her shock of a moment before. "And if by some fluke of the stars and heaven *you* win?" she asked, keeping her voice carefully neutral.

"Besides the fact I get to say 'I told you so'?" His grin was calm, nonthreatening, but it didn't decrease her wariness one bit.

He tossed the card on the pile, then leaned back, his expression shifting to thoughtful. He lifted one shoulder in a dismissive gesture. "I don't know, Makaiden. What I want, you can't put a monetary value on." His smile faded slightly. "So given that . . . dance with me," he said softly. "You taught me to play Zentauri. If I win, I get to teach you to dance."

"Dance?"

"Don't you remember? Two, three years ago we were on Aldan Prime. A meeting Jonathan scheduled with Donalt Eurek. We took the *Triumph,* made the meeting on time, but afterward they had this big party."

She remembered. A lavish affair—the Eurek family owned a number of upscale restaurants and supper clubs. She'd argued she was an employee, just a pilot, but the invitation included everyone. Even Makaiden Griggs, feeling definitely out of place even in her formal GGS uniform.

There was a band—really more of an orchestra. The music was slow, soft, lovely. Devin had asked her to dance. And she'd confessed she didn't know how.

"I remember," she said.

"Have you learned since then?"

She huffed out a laugh. "No."

"Well, then." His smile widened. "It's about time. Deal?" He held out one hand.

She eyed his open palm. So he'd try to teach her to dance. Besides being embarrassing, it wasn't going to happen. He'd have to win the next three hands in less than ten moves. It wasn't going to happen.

She took his hand, let him close his larger, warm fingers around hers. "Deal."

His smile warmed her and worried her at the same time.

She withdrew her hand and shuffled the cards, then stopped. She pointed to an area below the edge of the table. "Your Rada. Over here, by me. It's not permitted in casinos."

Grinning, he unclipped it from his belt, then pushed it across the table toward her.

Kaidee had experienced tension before, but nothing like this. Part of her applauded Devin's skill at the game and wanted to see him win five in a row, just for the sheer pleasure of watching it happen. Yet with the soft slap of every card against the tabletop, she knew she was that much closer—or not—to regaining the *Rider*. And regaining the *Rider* meant getting her life back—for good, for real.

He won the next hand in less than ten moves easily.

"That's three down." He held her gaze for a moment.

"You had a couple of lucky sequences," she admitted, shuffling the cards a bit more intently. Three in a row—less than ten—was hard but not impossible. She'd done it.

She cut the cards, shuffled again.

Game four took longer, the orbit and gate stacks showing high cards when he needed low. She longed to know what cards he was holding, but then he might read approval or disapproval in her face. This had to be his game, his way.

He had to start losing.

He won.

"Damn," he said, one eyebrow arched. His surprise sounded genuine. "One more to go."

She shuffled the cards, very aware now that they were more than plastic-coated symbols. They were the *Rider;* they were her life and her dreams. She cut the deck, shuffling again, her mind and heart racing. Years ago she'd learned how to cheat at just about any card game, especially if she sat as dealer or banker. She could palm a card or three, hold them back or never use them altogether. If she managed that now, it would throw him off. It would guarantee her a win.

It would gain her the *Rider,* free and clear.

She fanned the cards across the table with her right hand, then folded them up again with her left. The table was slick, not cloth as in the casinos. Even easier to slip a few cards out.

Devin was taking a long pull on his beer. "Empty,"

he said. He reached for her bottle. "Yours too. I'll get us two cold ones. To celebrate," he said as he pushed himself to his feet. "For whoever wins."

"Thanks," she said, feathering the cards through her fingers as she watched him rise.

Then he was out the door, his boot steps heading for the galley.

She fanned the cards on the table again in a wide half-moon, her breath suddenly fast. He'd left her alone with the cards. She could set their order so that one or two shuffles when he came back would look legitimate but in reality she'd control the flow. Or she could simply take out a few key cards, hold them back. There were ways, methods...

The *Rider* would be hers.

He'd never know. The chances of someone winning five hands in a max of ten moves were so rare. He'd never know.

It would be so easy.

She scooped up the cards, their edges cutting into her skin as she held the deck tightly in her fingers. It would be so easy.

And it would be so wrong.

If it were Orvis or Frinks, she'd do it. No question. But this was Devin Guthrie. Forget that he owned her ship and, in essence, owned her. This was Devin—who risked his life to save his nephew, who pushed Barty ahead to safety in the tunnel, and who came back for her when the striper and the Takan clerk tried to trap her in a scam.

This was Devin, who was, she sensed, a loner by his own choice. Yet he'd asked for her friendship.

She put the deck of cards in the middle of the table, then folded her hands in front of her because they were shaking. She wanted her ship back, badly.

But not that way.

Devin returned, placing a tall bottle on her left. "I peeked in on Barty. His readouts are all good." He took his seat, his own beer on his right.

"He's a fighter," she said, pushing the stack of cards toward him. "Count them."

"Hmm?" He frowned.

"Count them. You left the room. Make sure that's a complete deck."

He picked up the stack, tapped the edges on the tabletop, his gaze on her. Then he slid them back in her direction. "I trust you."

Her heart lodged in her throat at his words. Her eyes threatened to mist. How could three simple words have such power? Maybe because trust, right along with love, were casualties from her marriage to Kiler. She knew how rare and precious they were.

Damn you, Devin Guthrie.

She gave the cards one more shuffle, then, fingers trembling slightly, dealt the final hand.

The orbit and dock stacks' top cards were midrange, which, damn it, created an easy setup that opened a number of workable options. Fate taunted her. But the gate card was a high card, and suddenly she knew, by the way his mouth tightened slightly, that Fate wasn't taking sides and it was anyone's game.

He played his first two cards—one high, one low, being cautious. She was only the bank, so she had no choice in which cards she put down in answer to his move. But she prayed they were low cards, boxing him in further if he indeed had a poor hand.

One low, one high. It was still anyone's game.

He had eight moves left in which to win. She was eight moves away from ownership of the *Rider.* She had to remind herself that it was his skill being tested, not hers. She was simply an observer. But that didn't stop her throat from going dry.

She took a sip of her beer as he pulled out a card and put it in line with the dock stack. Okay, she saw a pattern, or the beginnings of one. The next card he played should be high, if that was the pattern.

He played a low card.

What was he doing? She almost asked him that, then realized that neither of them had spoken for more than ten minutes. Was he nervous? For the first time, she considered the possibility. He'd invested considerable funds in her ship. What would happen if he lost it, and in a card game? J.M. would probably deem it irrational and unacceptable. Likely Jonathan would agree. Would this be one more thing to put Devin at odds with his family?

He's turning out to be something of a rebel. The thought surprised her and amused her. Not just Devin "Perfect and In Control" Guthrie.

Because, somehow, the moniker no longer fit the man seated across from her, hand fisted against his mouth as he concentrated.

Then there were two moves left and, from the line of his cards and the spread of the three stacks, there was no way he was going to make it. A thrill of joy shot through her, followed by a twinge of regret. Devin's family was going to make him pay in hell's hard work for losing the ship.

Maybe there was some way they could hide the truth. She could pretend she was working off the debt. Something that—

He pulled a card from those in his hand and put it under the gate stack.

Her heart stopped. It was high on high. Suddenly the numbers shifted. So did her luck.

He was watching her over the rims of his glasses. "This is it."

She turned over the next three cards from the stacks in order: orbit, gate, dock. A high card would win at this point. Her gaze raked the cards in the spread. There were a lot of high cards out already, and he'd just played one. His last? She didn't know but had to suspect, yes, it was. Which meant he had only low cards left, and he would lose, and she—

He played the next card.

It was high.

She sucked in a hard breath, part of her astounded at what she'd just seen, at his skill. But the rest of her felt deep-space chilled. The *Rider*. Her ship. It *was* her ship, and, damn it, she deserved to win! She deserved to own the ship that had been the sole focus of her life for the past two years. Her sanity. Her lifeline.

And she'd just lost her best chance at getting it.

She reached for her beer and, forcing a smile, raised it in acknowledgment. "Congratulations. That was... amazing." She took a long swig, wishing now the bottle held something stronger. Lashto brandy, maybe. Not that she could afford it.

Devin took a sip of his beer, then put it down. "I know you're disappointed."

She shrugged. "It was only a silly game. A way to pass the time tonight." And time had passed—almost two hours. "We both should get some sleep." Her day officially started in another five. She pushed herself to her feet.

He rose also, then tugged the empty beer bottle from her grasp. "Makaiden." His voice was low, almost gentle. "You owe me a dance."

No, she couldn't do that. Not after everything today—the shock of Devin buying her ship, of being pursued through Pisstown, detonating cargobots, and then Barty collapsing. No, she could not let herself lean into Devin's arms, because if she let herself get that close to him, she honestly didn't know if she'd punch him or, God help her, kiss him, seeking solace because he was warm and male and solid. And she felt, literally, adrift. "Look, it's late—"

"Not lessons, not tonight. Just one dance." He stepped closer. "To celebrate."

"I can't."

"Please." He held his hand out toward her in such an elegant gesture it made her laugh nervously.

"Devin, look at me." She swept one hand down her front. "I'm in an old shirt and sweatpants."

"And I'm not about to win any gentleman's fashion award."

She almost debated that. His half-open shirt offered a peek at a muscled chest sprinkled lightly with dark hair. His face had a slight beard shadow; his hair was tousled. If a man could ever pull off sexy and vulnerable at the same time, it was Devin Guthrie.

"There's no music."

He tapped at his Rada on the table, next to the stack of cards. The soft, lilting notes of a piano filled the small room.

"This is silly," she protested.

"I think, after the past few days, we both could use a good dose of silly." He held his hand out again. "One dance."

Damning her rapidly evaporating willpower, she stepped—not without a huge dose of trepidation—into his embrace.

Devin circled Makaiden's waist with one arm, then enfolded her hand in his. He put his lips near her ear and, for a moment, lost himself in the sweet scent of her soft hair. But no, no, that wouldn't do. She was wary, suspicious.

He didn't blame her. He'd done just about everything wrong since he found her. And this likely was one more thing on the list.

But his life was crumbling around him. His father was behind some kind of mad and dangerous scheme, his family's home had been threatened, and Barty, his friend and mentor, was ill. In two and a half days they would come out of jumpspace and head for Port Chalo. He had no idea what they'd find there, but he suspected more trouble.

And this time, escape might not be so easy.

So he needed to dance with Makaiden. He needed her in his arms, he needed the heat of her body against his.

"It's not difficult, really," he told her. He could feel her breath against his neck, and the desire to pull her more tightly against himself warred with the knowledge that that would only drive her away. And he would lose the only thing of real value to ever come into his life.

"I'll step forward with my left foot, you step backward with your right. Try not to think about it too much. Just listen to the music."

"*You* try not to step on my toes, okay?" Her voice

was small against his chest but held a note of defiance. "I'm barefoot."

"Wait." He pulled back reluctantly. "I can fix that." He released her hand, sat on a nearby chair, and quickly pulled off his boots, then padded back to her in his socks.

"You could still do some damage," she said as he drew her back against him.

"The last thing I want to do is hurt you." He watched her face as he spoke. There was a double meaning to his words. He hoped she understood.

She lowered her lashes but made no comment.

"Now," he began, because it was late and he didn't want the silence to grow between them. "Listen to the beat of the music. One, two, three. For you, right foot, left, then together. Right, left, together."

"Going backward?"

"Going backward."

She sighed, then, under her breath, "Right, left, together."

He chuckled, waited for a few notes to pass, then swayed her gently backward. "Right, left, together," he repeated with her, moving lightly against her at first. Then, as she seemed to fall into the cadence, he turned her mid-step. She made a small stumble but caught herself. He pulled her back to him and they again moved as one, closer this time.

He needed that.

The melody rose and fell smoothly—it was a classical tune he'd heard since childhood, clear, simple, and elegant. Nothing at all like the woman in his arms who was alternately amazing and frustrating, mischievous and intense, forthright and damnably secretive. By the fourth turn around the passenger cabin's small main room, he felt her relax. She was following the music, but she was also synchronizing with him, her body strong and lithe, yet fluid.

In the part of his mind where his fantasies lived, they weren't in the cabin's main room but in his bed, her body moving in time to his, her breath stuttering against his skin as his hands caressed her curves. The heat between them simmered slowly, building with every brush of a fingertip, until his mouth covered hers with a kiss that finally let him taste her, a kiss that let him groan her name in need, in desire. And she—

"Devin. No." Makaiden pulled her face back from his. Her hands splayed against his chest.

He was suddenly aware of the silence in the room—the music had stopped—and that they were no longer dancing. The rising heat in his body and the tightening in his groin told him they'd stopped dancing a while ago, though their bodies had never stopped touching. The rapidness of their breathing told him they'd started doing something else.

Her face was flushed but her lips were still parted. He knew then that not all of his fantasies had been in his imagination. They'd touched. They'd kissed. God, yes, they'd kissed. And he wanted more of that, more of her. But now she was backing away from him, slipping out of his embrace.

He'd failed. He was going to lose her. "Makaiden, I—"

"Don't. Please." She raised both hands defensively. The sadness in her eyes tore at him. "Let's just forget this ever happened, okay?"

He tried again, stepping toward her, hand outstretched. "Makaiden—"

"I'm sorry." Her voice was a harsh whisper. She turned quickly and fled through his open doorway, her small footsteps breaking the silence in the corridor, her sudden absence breaking his heart.

Kaidee stared at the ceiling of her cabin in the darkness and tortured herself by going over and over the last ten minutes of her so-called dance lesson with Devin, cringing at her weak protestations. Why hadn't she slapped him? Hell, why hadn't she clocked him one right across that lean jaw of his?

Because he's a good eight or nine inches taller than you?

That had never stopped her in various bar fights or dockside skirmishes.

Because you wanted to know what it was like to kiss him?

Yes, she had. And that was the reason she couldn't justify cracking him one in the face. She wasn't sure she wasn't the one who had started it. Worse, she wasn't sure he might have thought her slight stumbles were an excuse to get closer to him. He might even now be wondering just what else he'd bought along with her ship.

Which led her tired and mortified mind down another path: maybe Devin Guthrie was very aware of what he owned and what Makaiden Griggs owed to him. And this was his way of collecting it.

She should have flattened him. She should have never...

Her cabin lights cycled painfully to morning, the glow through her eyelids increasing along with her headache. Finally, she slitted her eyes open and glared at the bedside time stamp. She'd slept for a little over three hours.

With a groan, she pushed herself out of bed, padded out of her bedroom into the main cabin, and called up ship's stats on the auxiliary console. They were on course, all systems normal. Nothing needed her immediate attention—at least, nothing that couldn't wait for another hour. Or two.

"Reset wake-up, two hours," she told the cabin monitor. Then she collapsed back into bed, burying her face in her pillow.

The next time her bedroom lights brightened, her eyes were already open and she felt marginally better— physically. Emotionally...

She shoved herself out of bed and headed for the shower, then dressed, cajoled a cup of coffee from the slurp-and-snack in her quarters, and headed the twenty or so feet down the corridor, past the lift, to the bridge.

It was only a kiss. One hell of a kiss, okay, but she was a grown woman. It was just a kiss.

She considered shutting down the lift and closing the airlock at the stairs. Her passengers could survive quite well on the lower deck, thank you. Far better than she could with only a slurp-and-snack in her quarters. But as much as the thought appealed to her— *running away from your problems again, Kaid?*—she knew it wasn't a workable option. There were Trip and Barty to consider. They'd want to know why. And she didn't want to explain.

She wanted to drop them off at Port Chalo and then hit the lanes as quickly as she could. Except that would probably get the three of them killed, especially with Barty being ill. She knew Port Chalo. They didn't.

She sighed and initiated a routine systems check, then, coffee mug in one hand, pulled up the standard

Imperial news feed that Trip had watched her upload through that last public data beacon before the jump-gate. For the past few months she'd been ignoring the news; it rarely changed. The Empire continued to complain about the Alliance and its president, Mason Falkner, a former Imperial senator. The Alliance continued to declare its legitimacy. In between all that, various political types said various nasty things about one another, and everyone hated the Farosians.

Makaiden always reviewed trade and commercial news, and already had. But now she wondered if the problem with Guthrie security wasn't a Guthrie problem but rather something happening on Sylvadae. Or in Port Palmero. Maybe Devin really didn't have a reason to be worried and she could dump them in Port Chalo with a clean conscience, confident no harm would come to them.

In a *crigblarg*'s eyes.

She pulled up the Aldanian sector news feeds anyway. It was something to do.

She found nothing worthwhile out of Sylvadae or Port Palmero, unless the list of various parties or weddings or engagements—or disengagements—counted for something. To her, they didn't. She scrolled past without reading them. More political machinations out of Aldan Prime. Tage blaming Farosian terrorists for something. Farosian terrorists blaming Tage back. Nothing new there—

EXPLOSION GUTS GUTHRIE OFFICES ON GARNO—TERRORIST INVOLVEMENT SUSPECTED.

Kaidee almost dropped her coffee mug. The GGS offices on Garno were Devin's headquarters. She pulled up the vid report and, clutching her mug with both hands, hunched over in her pilot's chair to watch.

Five minutes later, she shoved the mug onto the

command console, then bolted off the bridge, heading for the stairs and the lower deck. And Devin Guthrie.

Devin was on his second cup of tea when Makaiden came barreling down the stairs, and for a moment he feared there was a ship malfunction. Being stuck in jumpspace for the rest of his life wasn't his first choice, though being stuck with Makaiden was infinitely more appealing. He rose from his seat at the wall table as she thudded to a stop, her face flushed, her mouth a tight line.

He knew it didn't involve Barty. He'd checked on the man not twenty minutes before.

"There was an explosion at your offices on Garno," she said, with no preamble. "The newshounds are talking terrorists."

Devin stared at her. He'd rehearsed a dozen things to say to Makaiden when she finally made an appearance on the lower deck come shipmorning. None of them involved the words *explosion* and *terrorist*.

Then his mind kicked back into gear, doing a quick analysis of the information and their current location, which shouldn't have afforded access to any news reports. "We're in jump—"

"It uploaded in the regular data feed just before we crossed the gate. With everything else going on, I didn't bother to read it." She motioned to the Rada clipped to his belt. "Plus I thought you might have snagged the feed."

He hadn't. As she said, with everything else going on, including the message from Ethan, news feeds were his last concern. And why hadn't Ethan told him? Because it had happened after his brother sent the message?

"I need to see the clip."

But she was already moving toward the stairwell, one hand motioning for him to follow.

So much for his rehearsed heartfelt expression of his feelings, which he'd spent the past two hours composing in his head. *Explosion* and *terrorist* rather ruined the mood. And added to his growing feeling of frustration and helplessness.

He sat at the comm console and watched the original report Makaiden had found, then two more she'd unearthed while he was watching the first. The good news was that no one was hurt—the explosion happened at night, when the twenty-one-story building in Tal Verdis was empty of all but a few security and cleaning 'droids. The bad news was that not only was the building's main data server now slag but so was the backup server, located on a different floor in a separate part of the building.

"They were after the data, not people. And they knew where that data lived." Devin leaned back in the chair, swiveling it slowly back and forth, much like the thoughts going back and forth in his mind.

"Why would a group of crazies who want Sheldon Blaine on the throne care about GGS data?" Makaiden asked, echoing his primary concern almost word for word.

"No salient reason I can think of," Devin answered, "and therein lies a problem."

"You working on any big Imperial contracts?"

"We're always working on an Imperial contract somewhere. We're an approved supplier for Marker shipyards. We handle various hard-goods contracts for the starports." Devin ran quickly through a list of recent business deals with the Empire. None stood as significant in any way.

"What if it's not Farosians but some splinter group, some fanatic with his own agenda?"

There was that. "We've always avoided controversial commodities for that reason." Devin was glad to have someone to brainstorm with and moreover was glad it was Makaiden Griggs, who, as a former GGS pilot, might have heard something of value, even if it was two years ago. He'd see if Barty was awake in a few minutes. Barty, too, might be able to provide a perspective that Devin, being a Guthrie and a corporate officer, might not have.

"I have to look at what someone would achieve by destroying our data servers," Devin continued. "Considering any data of value is also backed up off-site, I can't think of any useful reason. This will slow us down for a few days, maybe even a week. But that's all."

"How about data of lesser value?" Makaiden asked. "What wouldn't be saved off-site?"

He shrugged, his mind probing. "Minor schedules, noncritical in-house memos, personal communications. Things like that."

"What if someone was using in-house memos or personal messages to . . . I don't know, sell your secrets to a competitor?" Makaiden leaned forward, resting her elbows on her knees. "I know that rules out the Farosians, but I'm looking more at the act than at who the newshounds are insinuating to be responsible. Rather than figure out why the Farosians would do this, I'm trying to figure out who would gain by slagging your servers."

Devin sat up straighter, her words sparking ideas he didn't want to consider but had to.

"Don't look only at what someone has to gain," she said, "but at what someone has to lose."

That pushed him to his feet. "We need to talk to Barty."

Barty was awake, his readouts improving, though he'd developed a rasping cough that worried Devin. "Reaction to the medication. And my stupidity," Barty said with a wave of his left hand. His right hand held a mug of tea. Trip had just left, headed for the shower. "It should be gone by tomorrow or the day after."

Makaiden was angling a wall screen toward the older man. "I picked this up from a news feed we received before we crossed the gate yesterday." She played the vid clips from the three different news stations. Only one mentioned the tie-in between GGS and Admiral Philip Guthrie. None mentioned Trip's disappearance.

Devin summarized his and Makaiden's concerns.

"You missed another possibility." Barty raised his mug slightly, pointing it at Devin. "Your data systems may have been thoroughly raped. Their destruction was simply a means of covering those tracks. Someone doesn't want you to know what he was looking for. Or possibly even found."

Would Petra Frederick and her security teams come to these same conclusions? He hoped so. According to the news vids, Tal Verdis law enforcement was concentrating on the terrorist angle. He felt more strongly now that wasn't where they'd find answers.

"We have other problems," Devin told Barty.

"You mean the ransom message on Trip's pocket comm? He told me he found it and that you were trying to unlock the source code. If you haven't been able to, I might—"

"I did. I just didn't tell Trippy." Devin glanced back at sick bay's open doorway, making sure Trip wasn't lurking there. He sucked in a hard breath. "The source was my father. And there was a stealth pointer uploaded into Trip's comm at the same time."

Barty's eyes widened. "That's insane!"

"My thoughts exactly. But it's his codes. Hidden, of course. Decent encryption that likely would have fooled Port Palmero law enforcement, but it bothered me that someone had accessed Trip's comm. So I kept digging." Devin shook his head slowly. "All I could think of is that this is some kind of convoluted scheme of his to bring Philip home."

"Which office in GGS was the end source for the stealth pointer?"

"Location data wasn't coded to be sent to GGS. It was coded for the adjunct judicial offices on Aldan Prime."

Barty put his empty mug on the nightstand. "Devin, your father couldn't code an encryption if the fate of the galaxy depended on it, and he sure as hell couldn't manage to negotiate a stealth pointer. Nor would he even know Imperial codes. Now, that doesn't fully preclude possible complicity. But it certainly makes it—in my book—much less likely. This smells more like ImpSec to me. Except ImpSec would have no reason to create a ransom note." He pursed his lips. "Damned puzzling."

Suddenly Devin knew what had been bothering him, clanging harshly but indistinctly in the back of his mind like a muffled warning bell. Data encryption and systems codes weren't remotely the area of his father's genius, and that's why Ethan's message had struck such a wrong chord as well. Numbers, data, and J.M. did not mix. His father's genius was more in the creative end of business, in sensing market trends and in surrounding himself with the very best people who could do everything else. His father was a visionary, not a number cruncher.

Relief soared, then crashed. "If my father didn't do it, then whoever did has access not only to GGS's innermost systems but our personal Guthrie ones as well." That admission was almost staggering. "There are fail-safes, but if they have his codes"—he shook his head as if he could deny the facts—"they can gain entry to every level of every division. And all our personal, medical, and financial records."

"This is something Petra Frederick should be able to catch," Barty said.

"Unless she's part of it, working for Tage." Devin hated saying it but he had to.

Barty nodded. "You're starting to think like me." He chuckled, then coughed.

Makaiden handed Barty a glass of water. "Are you sure the message from Ethan *was* from Ethan?" she asked Devin.

Devin opened his mouth to say he'd recognized the comm codes and caught himself. "I was," he admitted. "I'm not now." He pulled off his glasses and scrubbed at his face with one hand. "Makaiden, I need to borrow the commdat in your quarters again."

Devin worked through lunch, analyzing all incoming and outgoing messages on his, Trip's, and Barty's pocket comms, as well as his Rada. He scanned Trip's bookpad. And he damned the fact that that was all he could do. Jumpspace was, in essence, a closed system. There was no way he could access GGS, and he had to. That's where the answers resided. All he could do now was make an educated guess.

At least he didn't have to tell Trip that his grandfather had been scheming to kidnap him. Because while he couldn't fully rule it out, the more he thought about it, the more unlikely it seemed.

Unless J.M. was so desperate for Tage's approval that he was cooperating with ImpSec. But Devin wasn't going to bring that up to Trip yet.

The sound of footsteps in the corridor caught his attention. Then Makaiden stood in the open doorway, tray in hand.

"You have your choice of vegetable cheese casserole or cheese toast and..." She hesitated, peering at the dishes on the tray. "...fruit. I can't be sure. Your nephew insisted on tinkering with the galley unit."

"Casserole."

"Wise choice." She slid the tray onto the table.

His annoyance lessened. Even though Makaiden could be annoying, it was a different kind of annoying. He felt better in her presence. *That's what happens when you're irrevocably intrigued by someone. And in love with her.*

That thought should have startled him. It didn't. He'd been more than half in love with her for years, but those were feelings he'd never let surface except in his fantasies. Now fantasy was reality, and it was—*she* was—better than he remembered. Annoyances and all.

She sat in the empty chair on his left, picked up a piece of toast, and bit gingerly into it, completely unaware of the emotional turbulence she had created in his heretofore well-ordered life. She chewed. "Not bad. A little soggy."

"Since when does my nephew play chef?"

"Evidently it's something his friends at college like to do: mess with the university slurp-and-snacks. Mostly it's to turn all the food green one day, purple the next. Pranks. But in order to do that, they had to learn how the damned units worked and how to customize nutritional components."

Devin found himself grinning. "For me, it was cargobots, though I was a bit younger. My father used to make me accompany him to various warehouses; then he'd get embroiled in some long meeting and I'd be left to amuse myself. I once programmed an entire cargobot floor-hockey game."

Now Makaiden was grinning, too, and that warmed him more than the casserole.

"So," she said, "the message to meet at Port Chalo was honestly from Ethan?"

He swallowed his bite of casserole, nodding. "It was sent by someone in possession of Ethan's codes. It was also sent by someone who writes a message like Ethan. I can't say it couldn't be copied. But I'd be less sure if the message had been stilted or formal."

"But someone who works for your family would know that, right? They could mimic him?"

"You worked for us for five years," he pointed out. "You've piloted Ethan and his family. Could you right now create a message that sounded authentically like my brother?"

"I don't know." She tilted her head in puzzlement. "Maybe. I know how he speaks. Short sentences. Impatient."

"True. So, you've received a message that Barty and I have found Trip on Dock Five and all's well, ostensibly. You want to tell us you're sending the *Prosperity* to Port Chalo and we're to meet it there. How would you phrase it?"

Makaiden had picked up a slice of pale fruit. She took a small bite, then pointed it at him. "Apple. Your nephew's a genius! But, no, that's not what I'd say. Okay, it would be an informal note. Brother to brother. Maybe..." She took another bite of the apple slice, then chewed a moment. She sat up straighter. "Great news, Devin. Father's pleased. We're sending the *Prosperity* to Port Chalo. You need to set a meet point with it in four days." She paused. "Something like that."

Devin shook his head. "That's the public Ethan. Not my brother Ethan. The dynamics between us..." And he pulled in a short breath, not knowing how much he should say. "Ethan and I don't get along as well as we should. Yes, we're brothers, but there's a tension between us and, whenever Ethan talks to me or writes to me, I can hear it in his tone. Plus, he doesn't call me Devin—at least, not when we're alone. In public—at GGS—it's always Devin. But in private, he insists on calling me D.J."

"D.J.?" Makaiden's eyebrows went up. "Why?"

"Because he knows I hate it."

"Why do you hate it?"

"Because that's what Ethan calls me." He half-sighed, half-laughed. "That, you see, is the gist of the problem."

"And in the message you got, he calls you D.J.?"

"Exactly."

"Who else knows this?"

"My immediate family. I'm sure Trip's heard him. Thana and Max too. But none of them has a reason to impersonate Ethan. And I'm not his only victim. He calls Philip 'Scruffy.'" He stirred the casserole. "Still, I can't unequivocally verify the message is from Ethan just because he calls me D.J. It simply increases the probability that it came from him."

"Is that probability high enough that you feel comfortable with the meet point at Port Chalo?"

There was something unsettled in Makaiden's voice

and posture. Devin studied her for a moment, remembering her unflappable calm in the cockpit of GGS ships. But here she was, hands clenched a little too tightly, her gaze on him in almost the same manner that his was on her.

Studying me?

"Makaiden, what is it?"

She started to speak, stopped, then: "Since, lately, people are either trying to shoot at Trip or blow up your office, I thought you might want to consider some optional landing sites."

"Optional . . . ?"

She was quiet for a moment. "Smugglers' ports. If Ethan's message isn't legit, then whoever did send that message won't be able to shoot the *Rider* out of the skies on approach to the spaceport."

He knew Port Chalo had a reputation and a large black market. It would never occur to him that Makaiden was part of that—GGS was known for their thorough background checks on all their employees. But she wouldn't have entry to those "optional landing sites" if she wasn't. "Sounds like you've had an interesting past two years." He said it lightly but had a hard time keeping the surprise out of his voice. She must have heard it, because she dropped her gaze, her fingers tightening. He flinched. "Sorry. I didn't mean—"

She looked up at him, her eyes hard. "I've had an interesting *life,* Mr. Devin. And I knew about systems hacks and smugglers' ports long before Kiler Griggs screwed me over, got himself killed, and left me with a shitload of debt. Okay? And, no, it's not in my personal records and no one at GGS knew. *You* wouldn't even know, except that, because I've had an interesting life, I can smell something really wrong here. And it's spelled A-M-B-U-S-H." She flattened her hands on the table and pushed herself to her feet. "I'm just trying to save your respectable Guthrie asses."

She was halfway to the door by the time he got to his feet and called after her. "Wait!"

She stopped, shoulders tensed, but she didn't turn.

"I know you had a different upbringing than I did," he said quietly. "That doesn't change how I feel... that I value you. Respect you." *That I've fallen in love with you,* he wanted to say but couldn't. He was dancing dangerously close to "emotions Guthrie men don't discuss" as it was.

Her shoulders dipped slightly. She glanced over her shoulder to where he stood, then turned. "Ever hear of Nathaniel Milo?"

That wasn't what he expected her to say. The question caught him by surprise, and he was shaking his head before something about the name seemed familiar. But nothing he could immediately place.

"How about a ship called the *Diligent Keeper*?" Her tone was still cautious.

Milo. *Diligent Keeper.* "Vaguely," he admitted. "I think Philip may have mentioned it when the *Loviti* was assigned to break up some piracy syndicate out in Baris or Calth." His brother had been captain of the Imperial ship the *Morgan Loviti* back then. Not an admiral, and not with the Alliance.

Makaiden locked her hands in front of her. "It was both. Six to eight ships operating under Captain Milo's command, with the *Keeper* as flagship, going in and out of Baris and Calth, docking at Dock Five and Talgarrath, because that's where the buyers were. Arms trafficking, mostly, but if Imperial supply ships were carrying something else, they'd take that too. *We'd* take that too," she amended. She lifted her chin. "I'm Nathaniel Milo's daughter."

It took a moment for the impact of her words to hit him. His first thought was that GGS security was obviously flawed in its background-checking methods. His second was that he was glad they were. He'd never have met Makaiden otherwise.

That's irrational. She's part of a smuggling syndicate family. He could hear a clear warning tone in what he imagined—quite accurately, he had to admit—his father would say. But it didn't matter. He knew Makaiden. It bothered him that she'd lied, or that she'd been forced to lie. But certain actions of hers, and her skittishness, now made sense.

He tried to address what he thought might be her fear—one she might not even admit to. "To the best of my knowledge, a GGS ship has never been boarded by any of your father's people." That's why the name Nathaniel Milo didn't have that much meaning for him.

"You don't deal in military munitions."

"Were you part of your father's operations?"

"I was on his ships growing up, but he didn't want that life for me. In the end, he didn't even want that life for himself." She shook her head sadly. "So I'd stay with an aunt or an uncle on Dock Five or on Corsau. But even that didn't work out." Her mouth twisted in a grim smile. "My family attracts trouble. So I'd end up back on the *Keeper* again, until I was old enough to be sent away to the academy at Ferrin's for flight training. That's when I went from being Kaidee Milo to Makaiden Malloy."

And then to Makaiden Malloy Griggs. He now understood why she didn't answer easily to Makaiden.

"And the only reason you need to know all this," she said, "is because in order to gain entry to those optional landing sites, Kaidee Milo has to surface again."

Kaidee wasn't exactly sure what she anticipated as Devin's reaction to the fact she was Nathaniel Milo's daughter, but she would have bet a pitcher of Trouble's Brewing's best ale that it would be something between disdain and disappointment.

Instead, he stepped closer to her. "Will that put you in any danger? Using your father's name after all this time?"

That wasn't what she expected. Nor was the gentle concern on his face.

"There are some in Port Chalo who didn't like him," she answered cautiously. Was Devin holding back his anger until it could most hurt her? Toward the end of their marriage, Kiler had excelled at that. "But there are also many who owed him favors. I'm counting on the latter."

Devin was silent for a moment, and Kaidee tensed slightly.

"Owed," he said. "Your father's no longer alive?"

"No." That answered his question. She didn't want to get into details. They had nothing to do with their current problems.

"Let's get some tea, coffee. You can tell me more about these optional landing sites. I'm not sure we'll need them. But I do know I want all the facts and the options I can get."

Talking to Devin about how smugglers and pirates operated was easier than she thought. Though as she explained the details of covert contact routines and approach patterns, she knew why. The man loved facts, data. She was simply expanding his knowledge base. Still, his lack of reaction to who her father was puzzled her.

Except, she reminded herself, *I'm no longer a GGS employee. It's not like he can fire me for lying on my personnel application.* Though it hadn't been a lie. Legally, she was Makaiden Malloy. Her father had paid a lot of money to ensure that.

"We have a day and a half yet to decide what we'll do," Devin said finally. "I still think the message from Ethan was genuine. He did say he'd update me. He might have a message pack waiting on the *Prosperity*. Plus, he knew we'd be in transit in jumpspace, and maybe, for once, he didn't want to worry me overmuch. In his own way, he might have felt he was saving me grief by leaving out details."

"Or he didn't trust the security of the *Rider*'s comm pack and just sent the basics to you via your Rada," she pointed out.

Devin picked up his mug of tea but didn't sip it. "He doesn't know we're on your ship. Last message Barty and I sent to my father was that we were bumped off a Compass Spacelines flight to Marker and had found alternative transport. I didn't know he was sending a ship at that point. And neither Barty nor I mentioned that we met you."

She wondered why but thought it better not to ask. "So he's expecting you to arrive...?"

"Probably on a commercial passenger flight, or maybe even a private one."

"Then he won't have people waiting for us at the freighter docks."

Devin shook his head. "You really think that Ethan didn't send that message, don't you?"

"You know your brother's messages. But, remember, I was one of those pilots who would be handling a pickup like this. And I can't see why someone would choose Port Chalo for you and Trippy. Why not Marker or Garno or, hell, assuming they heard about the problems on Dock Five, Calfedar? Come to think of it, since you told them you were having problems booking transport, why not send their ship to Dock Five?" She leaned forward, arms on the table. "Why Port Chalo?"

"I can only assume the *Prosperity* was already headed there. Or maybe to Starport Six—you know we have clients there. Diverting it to Port Chalo might have seemed the easiest thing to do."

"Then why not—" Noise in the corridor outside the mess area halted her words. She recognized the timbre of Trip's voice and Barty's deeper one. Footsteps followed. Devin turned toward the sounds just as Barty, leaning one hand on Trip's shoulder, shuffled around the corner.

"Should you be up and around?" Devin asked before Kaidee could.

"Trip's bragging he invented some new food and it's almost dinner. I'm tired of eating in sick bay. Actually, I'm tired of sick bay altogether. No offense, Captain Griggs," Barty added with a smile.

"We now have apples. Excellent ones," Kaidee confirmed, amused when Trip blushed at her compliment.

"There are honey-grapes too. At least, there should be," Trip said, helping Barty into the chair next to Devin. Kaidee leaned back, waiting for Trip to sit, too, but he remained standing. He glanced at Barty, then looked at Devin. "I heard about what some slag-heads did to your offices, Uncle Devin. I feel—"

"It's not your fault, Trip," Devin said.

"It's like every bad thing has happened because I left." Trip flopped down into the chair, then ran one hand through his hair in a move reminiscent of Devin's own habit.

"You'll be home soon. We'll get it all straightened out."

They would. Where would she be then? Once again, the feeling of loss washed over her. Her ship belonged to Devin, but it hardly fit with GGS or Devin's personal investments. Plus there was the not-so-small matter of her being Kaidee Milo. It might not mean anything to Devin, but she was sure Petra Frederick would be furious. And Barty...

She glanced at the man, who looked paler and thinner than he had three days ago outside Trouble's Brewing. He would know the Milo name. He also deserved to know the truth. She turned to Devin. "Do you want to go over my optional landing sites with Barty now or wait until later?"

Barty deserved the truth, but Devin had been circumspect in what he said around his nephew. She wanted to open that door, though, so that at some point Barty would be told.

Devin put his Rada on the table and tapped up the holographic screen, angling it toward Barty. "Makaiden's concerned that the message from Ethan might have been forged. Or forced. Here's the code breakdown. It looks like our genuine house code and Ethan's personal code to me. But Makaiden is worried someone might be drawing us into a trap."

"I also thought they knew you were coming in on

my ship." She caught herself after she said it. Technically, it was Devin's ship. But damn it, it *was* her ship. She shoved the problem to the back of her mind. "If it is a trap, it's possible they'd have someone at the Compass Spacelines terminal. If not there, then at the private docks at Terminal D, which is where the *Prosperity* would normally berth. Either way, I'd rather have us, not them, in control of the situation. Which means not landing at Port Chalo Spaceport at all."

"Because our IDs would be scanned upon landing," Barty put in. "And if Tage's people are behind this— which that stealth pointer seems to suggest—ImpSec would have immediate access to those files."

She nodded. "Exactly. So I discussed some, um, optional landing sites with Devin that would put us anywhere from an hour to three hours outside the spaceport. We could either contact the *Prosperity* and see who answers or grab a ground-flitter and take a look around for ourselves."

"If you're considering either Lufty's or Uchenna's, I'd go with Lufty's."

She stared at Barty, wondering if the man was some kind of human *Ragkiril* who could read minds. She'd heard whispers that human mind-rippers actually existed, but then she saw his lips curve into a smile. He *was* ex-ImpSec. But if ImpSec knew about those smugglers' ports, why were they still operating?

She noticed Devin's narrow-eyed glance at Barty too.

"Lufty's was my first choice," she said carefully. Her father always trusted the Luftowski family. "Should I even ask how you know Lufty's?"

"You may, but the story would go better in different surroundings. One that serves saltbeer and limes."

"I had saltbeer once," Trip said. "Horrible stuff."

She barely heard his comment. Saltbeer and lime was her father's favorite drink. Barty was telling her he knew who she was, and in a way that wouldn't incriminate her in front of Devin and Trip. She was heartened by his concern for her, but it wasn't necessary. "Devin knows."

"Saltbeer?" Trip asked.

"When you mentioned optional landing sites," Barty said, "I suspected he might but wasn't sure."

Trip's gaze went from Barty to his uncle to Kaidee and back to Barty again. "Would someone please tell me what we're talking about?"

"Captain Griggs's family had some interesting connections," Barty told him.

"Connections?" Trip asked.

"You knew?" Devin put in, staring at Barty.

Kaidee ignored Devin and looked at Trip. "My father's family ran a smuggling syndicate in Baris and Calth."

"Smugglers?" Trip sat up straighter. "For real?"

Devin pointed at Barty. "You *knew*?" he repeated. "And Frederick let—"

"Frederick didn't know. And I was satisfied, based on my investigation, that Captain Griggs wasn't applying for the position in order to further her family's business but was simply an excellent pilot who happened to be married to another excellent pilot, who unfortunately turned out to be a very bad husband."

"Is there anything," Devin asked, exasperation clear in his voice, "that you don't know?"

"Yes. I don't know what's for dinner. Since I'm still not too steady on my feet, Trip, would you mind making a selection for me? A cold beer as well." Barty reached over and patted Kaidee's hand. "And before you ask, yes, I cleared it with your sick bay med-unit. I'm allowed to have just one."

Kaidee smiled and gave Barty's hand an affectionate squeeze. Trust the older man to pick up on the tension floating in the air and do what he could to lighten it, as well as indicate that he didn't hold her Milo heritage against her. That would help her get through the remaining day and a half in jump. After Port Chalo, she'd be alone again, rebuilding her life once more.

Providing whoever was waiting for them at Port Chalo didn't decide to end her life first.

It had been almost five years since Kaidee had plotted a course to Lufty's—the last time was when she'd used her vacation from GGS to visit her father, and she'd sat helm on the *Diligent Keeper*. It had been a huge risk doing that. She was a GGS employee. If someone had seen her, she could have lost her job. But things were going sour with Kiler, and when her life was a mess, talking with her father was one way she had of sorting things out.

The man might have been an arms smuggler and a pirate, but he was intelligent, fair, and wise. If situations had been different, if he'd not been part of a large and struggling family out of one of the worst sections of the Walker Colonies, he might have been able to apply to the Imperial Fleet Academy, maybe even become an officer in the Fleet. But he couldn't, so instead he took a small pirate operation his uncle had started decades before and turned it into a profitable—if somewhat infamous—syndicate.

But he was so very proud of his daughter: Captain Makaiden Malloy Griggs. Except Kaidee's life with Kiler was falling apart in great, shattering chunks.

So Nathaniel Milo did the unthinkable and unexpected. He turned the syndicate over to his brother and sister and, with financial help from a friend he called Sully, went legitimate, hauling freight and paying off the few fines the government had been able to levy against him. For almost two years, while Kaidee struggled with Kiler's increasingly aberrant behavior, the *Diligent Keeper* was an honest freighter operation. And once Kaidee's divorce was final, a slot waited for her and the *Rider* in her father's new company, if she wanted it.

She did, but Kiler's death and subsequent debts delayed her. These were her problems to solve, not her father's. Plus, if Orvis found out she was a Milo, the amount of the debt would triple.

Then, six months after Kiler died, Nathaniel Milo was killed on Moabar Station. It haunted Kaidee that she wasn't there. ImpSec maintained that her father had been part of a Farosian plot to free Sheldon Blaine. She knew that was a lie, but it didn't matter. He had defended his ship with his life. The *Keeper* was still missing, even after almost a year. Kaidee didn't want to think that his ship and what was left of his crew might be stuck in jumpspace somewhere, the ship malfunctioning. But if it had been destroyed, the Empire would have announced that. Gleefully.

Kaidee wiped the dampness from her eyes and focused back on the nav display in front of her. The *Rider* would have to take a heading away from Talgarrath upon exiting the gate in order to pick up the signal from the hidden trader gates smugglers preferred to use. *Slippery space,* her father used to call it, because the old gates were often unreliable, their guidance signals fluctuating. She'd have to transit one for a few hours in order to avoid detection by Imperial beacons.

Lufty's had its own beacon, secreted inside a miners' raft that orbited Talgarrath's smallest moon. She prayed her access ping codes would work. It had been almost five years.

She saved the course to the nav comp, then entered an alternate using Uchenna's data. It was always wise to have an escape hatch.

The whine of the lift doors opening, then closing, interrupted her work and had her turning just as Devin stepped over the hatch tread and onto the bridge. She'd left him—she glanced quickly at the time stamp on a nearby screen—two hours ago in the galley with Trip and Barty. She wondered if Devin had pressed Barty for more details on her father; he hadn't seemed pleased that Barty knew who she was and hadn't told him.

"Problems?" she asked as he swung around the chair at the closest console, then sat.

"I'm not sure. It depends on your answer."

Her answer? She hadn't even heard the question yet, but she could guess. "Did I ever steal anything from GGS or pass on proprietary GGS data? The answer is no. And not because I tried and failed or because your security measures stopped me. I never tried. I had no interest in trying. I loved piloting the *Triumph*. It was," and she paused, drawing a short breath, "probably one of the best times in my life. A ship of that level of sophistication was, simply, a joy."

"That wasn't my question."

"Then what do you want to know?"

He looked down at his hands clasped between his knees, then back up at her. "Are you still in love with Kiler?"

She opened her mouth, then closed it, his question so unexpected she had to stop herself from answering with a quick *Of course not*. Because Devin couldn't possibly care whether she was in love with Kiler Griggs. Rather, he wanted to know if her love for her husband made her look the other way when he carried out his schemes.

"I had no idea whatsoever," she said carefully, "that Kiler was using—*abusing*—Guthrie property. Those last six months we flew different routes. I rarely saw him. He was assigned to Mr. Jonathan and Mr. Ethan," she said, falling back into the old GGS lingo. "I was assigned to you and Master Trip and, when needed, Miz Hannah and the children."

"That's not what I asked." His voice was quiet, but she detected a note of tension. That wasn't like him. Not Devin, perpetually calm and in control.

"You asked if I loved Kiler."

"*Still* loved."

She shook her head, puzzled. "Why would that matter?"

"Because *I'm* in love with you, Makaiden."

Kaidee's world suddenly went into free fall, as if her ship's artificial gravity had shut off. Then she felt heat rushing to her face. She had to have misheard. She glanced toward the hatchway, expecting to see Trip or Barty laughing. This had to be some kind of prank. Or...she remembered their dance lesson, his kiss. Was this another attempt to collect "appreciation" for paying off her debt?

She scrambled to put her thoughts into words that wouldn't insult the man who owned her ship. And who—damn it, yes—considered her a friend, ship's papers notwithstanding. "You don't...Okay, there seems to be a certain physical attraction between us.

Right now. That can happen when people are thrown into tense circumstances like this. But that doesn't mean...You don't fall in love with someone in three days." Her last words came out in an uncomfortable rush.

"It's been seven years." His voice was a deep rumble. "The five years you worked for us. The two where you disappeared from my life. Not three days. Seven years."

Seven years? "When I worked for—You never said anything."

"You were married. And so much in love with your husband that when he was fired, you quit your position in order to be with him."

God, yes, that's what it looked like, didn't it? "He threatened to tell Mr. Jonathan who my father was if I didn't."

Devin frowned, then briefly closed his eyes. He opened them. "Is that why you stayed with him, bought this ship together?"

"Kiler always had some grand plan. He saw GGS as a stopping point on the way to owning his own fleet. I probably should have fought him on contracting for the *Rider,* but we'd been together almost ten years, and when things are going badly, you really want them to go right. It was a stupid thing to do, but I signed on the loan. I thought, I don't know, maybe this would give him a focus. Settle him down." She laughed harshly. "I filed for divorce right after he was fired. The marriage was over, but the ship tied us together financially. Neither of us could afford to buy the other out." She looked pointedly at him. "Didn't you notice the ship has two captain's quarters?"

He lifted his chin as if he was about to say something, then nodded slowly.

It hit her again what they were discussing almost as calmly as suggested route changes: that Devin thought he was in love with her. And that she had fallen out of love with Kiler a long time ago.

But that was the Devin Guthrie she knew: restrained and in control. Not like Kiler, who was prone to sudden attacks of passion, usually in public places.

It adds to the excitement, he used to say when she felt embarrassed.

In contrast, Devin told her he loved her in that impeccable schooled accent of his, while sitting with hands clasped, elbows on his knees. Which was probably just as well. The idea of Devin Guthrie loving her bordered on the impossible. An heir to the Guthrie fortune did not fall for the daughter of a smuggler.

But it would be far too easy for a daughter of a smuggler to fall for Devin Guthrie. It would end up in heartache—hers—but at least this time she'd be going in with eyes open.

"Maybe when this is all over," she said carefully, "and things calm down, if you still want to, we could spend some time together."

"If I still want to?" He unclasped his hands, then shoved himself to his feet. Something sparked in the depths of his smoky-blue eyes. She straightened, unsure of how to read his face and his tone.

"After seven years of waiting," he said, stepping toward her, "I think I know exactly what I want."

"Devin—"

"Same rules as yesterday, Makaiden. If you order me off this bridge, I'll leave. I cannot—will not—ever make you do something you don't want to. But damn it, woman, it's been seven years." He reached for her, his voice rasping. "If I let you go now, if I lose you now, I don't know when I'll ever find you again."

No, not so in control at all.

She rose but didn't touch him, the air between them positively alive with electricity. The restraints were off. Emotions colored Devin's face, and there was a glistening in his eyes that had nothing to do with his glasses. His gaze searched hers, but the hand that reached for her fisted as if he was physically holding himself back. He was breathing hard. But so was she.

"Just tell me I have a chance." His voice was a deep, pained whisper. "Tell me you're willing to try."

Heart pounding, she closed the small distance between them with one step. She touched his cheek with two fingers, her thumb resting on his jaw. God and stars above, this was insane. Worse than insane, because insanity was permanent and this, whatever she could have with Devin, would be at best temporary. And the parting painful.

But he leaned in to her touch, his hand covering hers, and she knew she was lost, stuck in an emotional jumpspace that made the trader gates' slippery space feel calm by comparison.

She stood on tiptoe, brushed her lips over his, and shoved her fears—and common sense—out the airlock. "I think I'd like those dancing lessons. Now."

Kaidee had the presence of mind—barely—to hit the palm lock on her cabin door as Devin pulled her inside. The door closed and he pinned her against it, his mouth trailing kisses down her neck, one arm snaking behind her. She arched into him. He groaned softly, then whispered, "I've dreamed of this."

His words made her breath catch.

He pulled her away from the door, one arm still at her waist, almost as if they were dancing, then he turned her gracefully, and they *were* dancing—gliding, touching, caressing.

He brushed one hand up the side of her face, his mouth following the trail as they swayed into a half turn. Then the warmth of his touch on her skin was gone. He reached for something at his waist. Out of the corner of her eye she saw his Rada light up. Music—piano, strings, a lilting reed—filled her cabin. He slid the Rada onto the small table by the door to her bedroom, then cupped her face with his hand and kissed her with small teasing kisses, turning, swaying...

"Devin," she breathed.

He stopped, his mouth taking hers, hard, his arms almost crushing her against him. She wrapped her arms around his neck and returned his kiss with equal passion.

Calm? Restrained? Not in the slightest. There was a fire in Devin Guthrie—a fire that didn't burn her out but made her hungry for more. Like the music he'd chosen, he could be gentle and teasing, sweet and tender, or demanding. Possessive. Needy. Giving.

She tugged at the seal seam of his shirt, then ran her hands inside, over the hard muscles of his chest and shoulders. Her fingers brushed against the med-patch and she hesitated. She'd forgotten he was injured. "Oh! Are you—"

He didn't give her a chance to ask if the wound still pained him. He lifted her easily, sliding her up his body until his mouth found the hollow of her neck, then moved lower into the V of her uniform shirt front. She grasped his shoulders. He raised his face.

"Couch?" he asked. "Or bed?"

She knew what the question really was: trust. The couch would be toying with each other, kissing, touching. Not that she'd never made love on a couch. Not that they couldn't.

But the bed—*her* bedroom—meant trust.

Truth was, she didn't trust him. But that didn't stop her from wanting him.

"Bed."

His breath caught in his throat. He turned slowly, his gaze on her face. At the door to her bedroom, he let her slip down until her feet touched the floor, but he still held her. And he wouldn't stop looking at her. In the background, the notes of a piano rose, fell, and rose again.

His arms loosened around her, his hands sliding toward her wrists. He lifted her right hand to his lips, kissed each finger, then her palm. His touch was gentle yet heated. She found herself shivering with anticipation. No man had ever treated her like this, as if she was the most precious thing in the galaxy. It was as intoxicating as a bottle of Lashto brandy.

She leaned into him, grabbing a fistful of his shirt to steady herself, to bring herself closer. Her knees felt like jelly. Tingles danced over her body, pooling between her legs.

He pulled her the few steps into the bedroom, then lifted her onto her bed, kneeling over her as she lay on her back. She put her palm against his cheek and couldn't help but smile. His glasses were crooked. She tugged them away from his face, but he grabbed them and tossed them in the direction of her nightstand. She heard a clink but didn't bother to check where they landed. She was too busy looking at Devin Guthrie, who could no longer hide behind his glasses.

He was gorgeous, the smoky blue of his eyes even darker. The professional, reserved mien was gone. She traced his lower lip with her thumb. He groaned, eyes closing. He had beautiful long dark lashes. She raised her mouth to his, and he collapsed on top of her, all long, hard, hot male. Then she was pulling his shirt out of the back of his pants, and he was fumbling with her uniform's seal seam. Clothing was tossed in various directions. Boots hit the decking with mistimed thuds. None of that mattered as his mouth found her breasts, and her fingers tightened in his short, thick hair.

But he pulled away, tongue trailing down her abdomen until he nipped at the soft flesh of her inner thighs. She gasped his name, then groaned in pleasure as his tongue stroked and teased, and tingles exploded into fireworks. She couldn't help herself; she was whimpering, panting, damned near mindless. "Dev, please. I need you!"

His mouth moved up her body in a heated rush. She grabbed for him, wanting the feel of his muscles under her hands, the hard length of his erection against her thigh, and the hot slickness of him everywhere. He rocked against her in a primal rhythm and then, as the notes of a piano sounded with increasing intensity, he entered her, claiming her with a kiss that was almost savage in its passion.

"Makaiden." Her name was a hoarse plea as he kissed her again, thrusting deeper. Her body went molten, her release coming with the sounds of strings and flutes edging her higher, Devin's kisses leaving her gasping for breath but wanting more. He gave her more until his control shattered, his breath stuttering, his kisses frenzied. Chords from the piano rose, the melody of the strings expanded, and, "God help me, Makaiden. I love you," rasped harshly in her ear.

She held him tightly, feeling the rapid rise and fall of his chest against hers. The music softened, slowing to the last wistful notes of a flute. He nuzzled her neck with his face. She stroked his hair, her heart still pounding. Or maybe it was his. She could no longer tell. Nor could she say the words she knew he wanted to hear, though it would be so very easy right now. But she didn't know if she loved him. Or if she didn't.

Trusting him with her body was one thing. Trusting him with her heart was another.

Devin woke to the knowledge that he was in Makaiden's bed but that Makaiden wasn't there. It wasn't shipmorning; the illumination in the main cabin was on its lowest setting. He could barely make out shapes around him from the dim glow filtering through the bedroom's open door, but then, he didn't know where his glasses were. Two things missing from his life.

He'd settle for Makaiden. His glasses he could replace.

He sat up slowly, the sheet sliding down his bare chest. He brushed his palm over her side of the bed. It was cold.

Damn it. He scrubbed at his face. It wasn't that he was inept when it came to understanding women—okay, he was inept. He was male and he was a Guthrie. He should come with a warning label.

But he thought she'd wanted him as much as he wanted her. He knew she didn't love him. But wanting was a good place to start, wasn't it?

The soft sound of footsteps had him turning toward the doorway. A female form, backlit by the muted glow from the lav. Makaiden.

"Dev?"

Dev. She'd called him that in the heat of passion. He found himself smiling in the darkness. There were some things a Guthrie male was fairly decent at.

She stepped toward the bed. "Did I wake you?

Sorry. I usually check on ship's status during the night."

His eyes had adjusted to the darkness and he realized she was wearing his shirt. Open. That made his smile widen.

"You didn't wake me," he lied. "Everything okay?"

"I want to abort out of jump in five hours."

His smile disappeared. Then he frowned. "GGS has a strict policy against aborted jumps—"

"This isn't a GGS yacht. And I can do it. We have to do it."

"There's a malfunction?" Maybe his brain, still muzzy with sleep and lovemaking, had missed that part. Aborted jumps were dangerous, even fatal. He knew that. But a malfunction in jump could be doubly fatal. In that case, even GGS regs listed it as an option, though one of last resort.

"No. Yes." She sighed and padded over to the bed, then sat on the edge. He scooted toward her, drawing his knees up. "There's nothing mechanically wrong with the *Rider*. But there's something very wrong with GGS, and the Guthries, and ImpSec, Orvis, Frinks, and whoever else wants you dead."

"I don't think it's as bad—"

"I do. Dev, being with you has brought back five years of piloting your ships, five years of training in your security procedures. Up until this point, I've been thinking like Kaid Griggs, freighter captain. But that's not what we have here. You, Trip, Barty—you're not freight. You're passengers entrusted to my care—that's the exact phrase Petra Frederick used to hammer into us at security meetings. *Entrusted to my care.* Based on everything that's happened since Trip left his university apartment, I have to assume someone is going to be watching all traffic coming out of Dock Five and heading to Talgarrath." She faced him. "We filed a fight plan, remember? If ImpSec's involved, they have the original plan *and* the amended one for Port Chalo."

"But we had reservations on a Compass flight. No one knows we're on the *Rider*."

"Devin Jonathan Guthrie." She said his name with her teeth obviously clenched. "Your name is on the ownership papers. It's public record. We've been gone more than two shipdays. The whole slagging Empire will know by the time we hit gate exit at Talgarrath."

Shit. There was that.

"They didn't need that stealth pointer in Trip's pocket comm. You gave them a nice clean trail to follow."

He rubbed at his eyes with the heels of his hands. He'd had, what, two, three hours of sleep? "Aborting a jump could kill us."

"Coming out of jump at Talgarrath to find a couple of Imperial cruisers dead-eyeing us is just as fatal. This is a freighter, Mr. Guthrie. I have a standard tow beam and a pair of low-level lasers. Standard shields. They fire one torpedo and we're slagged."

"We could consider jettisoning some cheese casserole—ow!" He rubbed his shoulder where she smacked him.

"Five hours," she said. "That will put us nicely in range of an old trader route that the Empire will not be expecting us to use. And it might even get us there before the *Rider*'s ownership papers filed in the name of Devin Jonathan Guthrie are on the desk of every ImpSec agent and bounty hunter in Baris sector. I already have everything plotted in. That gives you about four hours of sleep before I'll need you, Trip, and, if he's up to it, Barty on the bridge."

"Three hours of sleep," he told her, pulling her back against him. He was not going to face death without making love to Makaiden one more time.

He'd argue with her about the aborted jump later.

Later came during breakfast in the galley dining area.

"Devin, look at the facts." Makaiden, now in her standard gray uniform, was standing across from him, palms against the back of the chair. Barty was on his right, Trip—looking understandably pale—on his left. An aborted jump scared him too.

"Ben Halsey is dead," she continued. "Trip shows up on Dock Five, some guy tries to put a tagger on him. When that fails, the same guy tries to abduct him. Then that fails because I show up. But those same guys find us in Trouble's Brewing when you do, and now they're shooting at you. While all this is happening, the Guthrie security net is hacked and your offices are bombed." She raised one hand, ticking off the items as she spoke. "One murder, one attempted murder, one attempted abduction, one security breach, and a bombing. In roughly one week." She wriggled her fingers at him. "And that doesn't even include the fact that Orvis is now interested in you."

"That doesn't mean Imperial cruisers will be waiting for us at gate exit," he countered.

"Are you going to tell me you're wrong about the end source of that stealth pointer? That it doesn't go back to Imperial offices on Aldan Prime?"

"No, but—"

"Then, yes, odds are excellent that an Imperial cruiser or a destroyer or, hell, a couple of heavily armed patrol ships will be watching for us at gate exit. Which is why I don't intend to exit at that gate."

"Odds are? Odds can be wrong. What are the odds of winning five consecutive hands of Zentauri—"

"That's different. If we dump out and shift to the old smugglers' routes, I think I can get you to the *Prosperity*—to *safety*—before ImpSec realizes what's happened." She glanced at Trip, then back at Devin. "I need you all on the bridge in thirty-five minutes. At forty-five, we dump out."

"Makaiden, it's too dangerous." He didn't want to pull this on her, but she was leaving him no choice. "I own this ship. No aborted jump. That's final."

She straightened, eyes narrowing. "With all due respect, Mr. Guthrie, read your own regs. In the event of an emergency, the captain of any GGS yacht or transport ship has the right to overrule any GGS executive or owner on board and employ any and all methods she deems fit in order to correct or contain that which threatens the structure of the vessel or the safety of its passengers. Guthrie Global Systems Security Policies and Procedures Manual, Chapter Three, Section Five, Paragraph One."

He peered over the top of his glasses at her. "Earlier you reminded me this isn't a GGS ship and it's not an emergency."

She switched her focus to Barty. "Mr. Barthol, how does GGS Security Policies and Procedures classify attempted murder of a Guthrie family member or GGS executive?"

"If we live through this," Barty said, a mug of coffee in his hands, "you might want to consider a career change to barrister. And, yes, attempted murder is considered an emergency situation. Though it's listed as attempted assassination." He shrugged one shoulder. "Semantics."

Devin slanted a glance at Barty. *Traitor.* He tried

another tack. "How many aborted jumps have you done, and how many in a Blackfire 225? Specifically, how many in this ship?"

That made her hesitate. "I've never dumped out the *Rider*. I've been through two on my father's ship—"

"As a child?"

"Late teens, early twenties. And, yes, I was on the bridge."

"As first pilot? Second pilot?"

"Auxiliary helm," she admitted. "But I did a dump-out on the *Triumph*."

Now it was his turn to hesitate. "Our ship?"

Her half smile was smug. Damn, she could be up-pity, and damn, he wanted to drag her across the corridor and into his bed. Except it had once been Kiler's bed. Okay, use the lift and drag her up one deck to her cabin. Better. Though it would likely get him tossed in the brig. Did the *Rider* even have a brig? There was a thought. . . .

"When?" he persisted.

"A month after Admiral Guthrie—he was Captain Guthrie then—was injured by terrorists on Marker. He was on medical leave and at your family home on Sylvadae when he was summoned to a meeting on Aldan Prime. It was easier for me to transport him there and back than wait for the *Loviti* to send a pinnace."

"So Philip was at the controls?"

He could tell she knew what he was getting at. Philip could probably handle an aborted jump blind-drunk. "I'm captain of record but, yes, he assisted."

"Get Philip here and I'll let you pull your dump-out. Until then, we stay on course to Talgarrath."

She glared down at him. "Thirty minutes. Strapped in on the bridge. No exceptions. That's an order." She spun on her heels and marched across the dining area toward the stairs.

He watched her go, his heart sinking. He knew Makaiden was a good pilot, an *excellent* pilot. He'd just learned that breaking J.M.'s rules—and falling in love with Makaiden would qualify for that—usually portended something bad happening. *One rebel in the family is enough,* his mother would say. Meaning Philip, not Devin. Not old "By the Numbers" Devin, who always did as he was told, living a safe, controlled, and orderly life. That old Devin went on sabbatical a week ago. This new Devin had rescued his nephew and found the woman he loved—and had been forbidden to love for years.

He had a feeling there'd be hell to pay for it.

Kaidee sat in the pilot's chair, her palms sweating. She rubbed them down the sides of her pants as discreetly as she could, while behind her the clicking of straps signaled that the last of her passengers—Devin, and he was late, damn him—was secure in his chair. She hadn't lied about her aborted jump experience. She had been through three, but in the merchant academy and then as a navigator and second pilot with Starways, she'd studied dozens more. Including failed ones.

None of those dump-outs had Devin on board, though. Or Trip and Barty, but to her, the biggest issue was Devin. She should never have slept with him, but she was incredibly, ridiculously glad she did. It wasn't his money or the fact that he was a Guthrie. It was that he was the man she'd known and respected for years and had, whether she was aware of it or not, grown closer to. Making love to him, letting him make love to her, just brought things full circle. It didn't destroy the friendship that had grown over five years. It deepened it.

But as much as the dump-out scared her, ImpSec scared her even more. ImpSec had killed her father. Okay, Ministry of Corrections' officers on Moabar Station had actually killed her father, but they'd acted on ImpSec's orders, ImpSec's information.

She would not let that happen again.

Devin furious with her, was better than Devin dead. He could eventually get over being furious. Death had a way of sticking around.

She glanced over her shoulder to where Barty sat at the comm console. "Shunting control of warning drones to you now, Mr. Barthol."

"Acknowledged, Captain."

Barty had assured her he had some experience with ship's communications. She accepted that as fact because she had no time and no options. A ship transiting into an aborted jump had no idea what would be in its path when it dropped back into realspace. So it not only bleated a required emergency message but launched warning drones, forward and aft.

Which didn't mean something couldn't slam into them port and starboard. But she had only two drones.

What made this dump-out particularly troublesome was that Talgarrath was close to the Baris–Calth border, midpoint between Starport 6 and Calth Prime. Legitimate freighter and military traffic in the lanes was common. Given the fact that Talgarrath was home to Port Chalo, illegitimate smuggler traffic outside the lanes could be plentiful.

She finished her enviro check. All systems operational. "Sealing all interior airlocks and hatchlocks in five, four, three, two, one...now." She tapped at her screen, knowing the hiss and rumble of the blast door behind her was echoed by other doors through the ship. If they were hit upon dump-out, a hull breach would be contained to the damaged section.

Unless the bridge took a direct hit. In which case—she shoved the thought away. She needed full ship shields during the transit in order to keep the *Rider* as stable as possible when it ripped through the time–space fabric. And rip through it would. There were no gate beacons for guidance, no gate buffers to keep the ship intact.

"Master Trip?"

"Captain?"

"Sending mirror coordinates to you now." She really didn't need Trip to monitor their position, but she knew he was scared. Watching nav data would give him something to do other than sitting, strapped in, one leg jiggling as if he could shake off his nerves.

"Got 'em," Trip confirmed.

"What's my plus–minus, Mr. Trip?"

"Plus–minus three, Captain."

"Totally apex, Mr. Trip." She turned just enough to catch his tight smile at her use of his favorite expression. "Let's keep her in that range."

She turned back to her screens, tallying the data before her. So far, so good. "Initializing sublights." Engine icons went from red to yellow. Then she ran a full systems check again. There was no way of knowing which system would shake loose some glitch during an aborted jump, but invariably one did, even though the *Rider* was a newer ship with all the required aborted-jump-transit fail-safes. Which worked flawlessly under controlled test conditions, but when was real life ever like a test lab?

She brought up their coordinates, her heart rate spiking. Five minutes to jump margins. Five minutes. She'd been wasting too much time checking and rechecking systems. Her hands moved in a flurry across the pilot's screens as she shut out all thoughts of anything other than the *Rider* and jumpspace.

She'd been through three dump-outs, but she'd never done one alone.

"Two minutes," she announced. "If you're unstrapped behind me, strap in now. We're going to hit, hard, and I'm not interested in scraping your parts off my decking."

There was an answering click. Devin. It wasn't a guess. She was peripherally aware of his leaving his seat and talking quietly to Barty a minute ago. Planning a mutiny, no doubt. But she'd activated the decking sensors around her seat. Nice little addition she'd learned about long ago from an old single-hander. If he intended to sneak up from behind and hit her on the head, he was in for a surprise.

"One minute to hard edge." Now was the tricky part of bringing the sublights fully online while keeping the hypers pulsing, with no gate buffers to ease the transition. She had to trust that she knew her ship, knew its quirks. *Work everything in proper order, don't try to anticipate,* her instructors had told her.

The *Rider* shimmied, bucking as the tug-of-war between jumpspace and realspace began.

"Transmit, Mr. Barthol." She had to raise her voice over the rumble of the engines. The emergency message couldn't penetrate jumpspace, but it would already be in process once they breached the hard edge.

"Transmitting, Captain. Warning drones standing by."

Something flashed on a screen on her left. Shit! It

was coming from the enviro and support console, systems she was controlling now because—

M. Love you. D.

—Devin was sitting there. Devin, the data-systems genius, bypassing her lockout, sending a message. His timing was terrible, but his words gave her strength.

Her palms were still sweaty. "Twenty seconds to hard edge. Hang on. Here we go."

The *Rider* screamed back into realspace, bulkheads groaning, decking thumping, and something else that sounded like thousands of pebbles churning inside a metal can. Kaidee was thrown against her straps, then, just as quickly, slammed backward. Her chest ached, and for a moment she felt as if breathing was impossible. Teeth clenched, she shut down the hypers, confirmed sublight status, and intently studied the screens for any signs of coolant leak or fuel-line rupture.

The pressure lifted, but the racket continued. Nausea hit her as the forward screens blanked, then suddenly filled with the deep darkness of space. She swallowed hard and punched short-range scanners live. "Bogey check. Starboard clear!"

"Drones away," Barty called out as the rattling, groaning, and thumping subsided.

"Acknowledged. Portside clear. Mr. Trip, confirm variance."

"Plus–minus holding at three!"

"That's my boy." She was reaching to bring long scan online when a series of tiny blips flashed over long range, then disappeared. She blinked, not even sure the pinpoints of light weren't just her body's reaction to the transit. *Seeing stars, Kaid?*

She checked long range again quickly. No ships, no overt problems. Later she'd call up the logs, see what it was, if it was anything at all. Right now she was reading out short scan and...

Holy slagging hell. She did it. They made it.

She huffed out a hard breath. Her hands were shaking. Quickly, she checked their course. Damn, she was only ten minutes out from where she wanted to be. Not bad at all! She keyed in minor adjustments as she spoke over her shoulder: "Barty, talk to me. How are you feeling?"

"You worry overmuch, Captain Griggs. Good job, by the way."

She grinned as she made one last manual check of short and long scans. Empty as the inside of a prosti's head. She tapped off the decking sensors around her chair. "Devin?"

"We may have to rewrite the oddsmaker's book."

"I accept your apology. Mr. Trip?"

"Uh, Captain, can you unlock the hatch? I think... I need...the lav."

God. Poor kid. A quick glance over her shoulder showed him to be tight-lipped, with sweat beading on his brow. She reset ship's security to passive and released the blast doors. "Relieved from duty, Trip. Go."

He bolted off the bridge, hand over his mouth.

She took one more sweep of ship's systems. A few readings were somewhat off, but nothing pressing and nothing that would kill them. Speaking of which, she located the self-destruct program for the warning drones and sent the command. No need for a warning and no need to leave a trail. She brought up the autopilot program with an undisguised sigh of relief. Adrenaline drained from her body. She leaned back in her chair, letting her head fall against the cushion. "Well. That was fun. And just think, in one hour we get to play with the ups and downs of slippery space."

Boot steps sounded on the decking behind her, then warm hands grasped her shoulders. Strong thumbs massaged at the aches in her neck. She let herself go limp, eyes closing. If she were a cat, she'd be purring.

"If you're applying for the position of captain's personal massage therapist, you're hired," she murmured.

She heard Devin's low chuckle. Then, from Barty: "I'd best go check on Trip."

And give the captain and her lover a little privacy? Smart man, that Barthol.

Devin's ministrations slowed. She swiveled her chair around, tilting her face just as he leaned down to brush her mouth with a kiss.

She pulled his hand from her shoulder and twined her fingers through his. "I already said apology accepted. But redundancy is nice."

He braced his other hand on her chair's armrest. "Let's not ever do that again."

The obvious relief in his voice made her smile. "Don't ask me to make promises I can't keep."

"Okay. Let's not ever do that again without at least Philip on the bridge."

"Why Philip? You know, with your analytical mind, you'd probably make a damned good second pilot. I could teach you."

He looked affronted. "Only second? Why not first?"

"To sit second pilot you need to be meticulous, smart, and detail-oriented. To be first pilot, you need to be meticulous, smart, detail-oriented, and crazy."

"So you're saying I'm deficient in crazy?"

"It's something you need to work on."

"I take it you can recommend a course of study?"

She gave him her best slow and sultry smile. "Come to my quarters later, after dinner." They'd be through the old trader gates by then. Slippery space was something she felt confident the *Rider* would handle flawlessly. She'd copied her father's data on the old gates when she was in the academy. Those same codes, permissions, and passkeys now resided in the *Rider's* comp. "I'll give you crazy lessons."

"Does your invitation involve either cards or cheese?"

"Nope."

"Then I'll be there."

Trip recovered his space legs by the time they approached the trader gate and willingly sat at the nav console, determined, it appeared, not only to learn all he could but to prove his worth.

"Don't fret about it," Kaidee told him when he haltingly tried to apologize for his hasty exit earlier. "You hung in longer than most. I've worked regular gate transits that have puke on the decking."

That made him grin and prevented her further explanation that the reason those crew members tossed their guts was that they'd been out drinking heavily hours before. Hangovers and choppy gate transits didn't mix well.

She also saw why Trip was fascinated with his uncle Philip. He had Philip's love of spacecraft and an unending desire to do better. Knocking Trip Guthrie on his ass only made him more determined to succeed next time.

Shame he'd be forced to fit into a corporate mold. There were downsides, she realized, to being a Guthrie.

"If you expect the turbulence," she told him after they'd crossed the gate, "it's not half as bad. If I hit an old smuggler's gate and it wasn't choppy, then I'd worry. It's not what the ship's doing but whether what it's doing is normal. Got it?"

"It's like when Uncle Ethan's sailboat heels over in a stiff wind. Your center of gravity is off but the boat's performing as it should. You accept the boat is doing what it was designed to do."

"You are totally apex, Mr. Trip."

That got him blushing again and heading belowdecks for the galley—to see if his tweaking with the food dispenser would, this time, produce redberry ice cream.

A few hours later, she lay in Devin's arms in the middle of her bed, listening to his laughter rumble in his chest. "Starship captain or chef, eh? Somehow I don't think Jonathan would approve of either."

"I'm sure Trip knows that." She snuggled more tightly against him. "But he needs to find outlets that aren't Guthrie-designed. I'm sure eventually he'll be another Jonathan or Devin or J.M.—"

"I rank ahead of J.M.? I'm flattered."

"—or whatever his corporate specialty turns out to be. But he needs to be Trip too. A little rebellion now and then is good for the soul."

He sighed, his hand absently skimming up and down the curve of her bare hip. "That can be problematic sometimes."

"If you weren't a Guthrie, what do you think you'd be doing?"

That garnered a low snort.

"No, seriously," she said. "Didn't you ever have dreams? I mean, I can't believe that when you were five or ten years old you said, oh, yes, I want to be chief financial-operations officer of Guthrie Global Financial Assets."

"If I remember correctly," he said slowly, "when I was five or ten years old, I was told that's what I was going to be."

Kaidee turned on her side, propping herself up on one elbow. "That sucks."

"There were times I thought so." He gazed up at her, his eyes half-hooded. "Right now I think it's incredibly wonderful."

She smiled and trailed her fingers down through his dark mat of chest hair and over the taut muscles of his abdomen. "Then I think it's time for another crazy lesson."

His breath stuttered as her fingers caressed the length of his erection. He pulled her face to his, his kiss fierce and demanding. Intoxicating.

Incredibly wonderful. Totally Devin.

A series of discordant chimes woke her three hours later. Ah, slippery space. It liked to invent navigational points that didn't exist. She'd already patched in one code fix to the autoguidance system. Time for the second.

"Makaid'n?" Devin's voice was a low, sleepy growl.

"Hush." She stroked his hair. "Minor nav tweak. Be right back."

He snorted something and rolled over.

She slipped out of bed, grabbed for her sweatpants and thermal shirt, and padded to the main cabin, pulling her clothes on as she went. Fifteen minutes later, she not only had autoguidance back on course but she was, annoyingly, wide awake. She peeked into her bedroom. Dev was sleeping heavily.

She went back to the main room, ordered a hot sweet tea from the slurp-and-snack, then settled into the chair in front of her data terminal. She played a few hands of Zentauri against the computer, then, bored, closed out the program and brought up the news-feed database. The bombing of Devin's office puzzled her. It seemed so unrelated to Halsey's death and the kidnapping attempts on Trip. How could someone possibly know Devin would be the one to try to rescue Trip? Or was the bombing of his office another matter entirely?

She'd been away from GGS for two years, and she hadn't paid all that much attention to their corporate machinations when she was there. So she initiated a search on all news data in the past planetary month for both Garno and Sylvadae that contained the Guthrie name. Maybe there was a merger, a lawsuit, a change of command. It could be anything where someone felt they were wronged or slighted. It might have nothing at all to do with Trip—

Grallin Emberson and Tia Delaris Emberson are pleased to announce the engagement of their daughter, Tavia Delaris Emberson, to Devin Jonathan Guthrie.

The images that jumped out at her were beautiful, sophisticated, and left no doubt that it wasn't someone else with the same name. It was Devin, elegantly suited, the perfunctory GGS silk scarf threaded through the collar of a cream-colored shirt, silver-rimmed eyeglasses framing smoky-blue eyes.

His right arm wrapped around the waist of a tall dark-haired woman who was...gorgeous. Skin the color of burnt honey, large dark eyes slightly tilted, full mouth in a poised and confident pout. She was vidstar slender, her white sweater clinging to full breasts. A seapearl-and-diamond necklace that probably cost as much as the *Rider*'s entire nav system encircled her throat.

Tavia. She remembered Devin mentioning a Tavia.

Kaidee couldn't breathe. It was an aborted jump transit, a bone-jarring and damned-near-fatal dump-out all over again. But it was happening within the confines of her body, her heart, her mind, and not her ship.

...announce the engagement of their daughter, Tavia Delaris Emberson, to Devin Jonathan Guthrie.

The date. It had to be something from years ago. Though her whirling brain couldn't remember any talk of Devin being engaged when she piloted the *Triumph*, maybe it was old news. An old entry. It was...

...last week. The announcement was dated the day she found Trip in the back corridors of Dock Five.

God. Damn. It. God. Damn...She shoved her fist into her mouth and bit down, hard, on her fingers. The physical pain jolted her, kicking her brain back into gear.

It was Kiler all over again. Kiler and his lies, his false declarations of love, telling her what he knew she wanted to hear so he could get her to do what he wanted her to do. In Devin's case, he needed a ship and he needed a pilot, and he'd paid for the services of both. Obviously his definition of services was in line with his brother Ethan's.

And why should that surprise her? More than once she'd watched Ethan in some spaceport bar, his right hand at the waist of some suggestively clad young woman while in his left he held his pocket comm, telling his wife back on Sylvadae that he loved her and missed her.

Kaidee hunched over, wrapping her arms around her midsection. God damn Devin. A man she cared about. A man she believed was honorable. This hurt. This really, really hurt.

She lifted her face and stared toward the short darkened hallway leading to her bedroom, shame washing over her. She was sure Barty knew not only that Devin was sleeping with her—oh, hell. Let's be realistic. Screwing her. Devin was screwing her, and Barty not only knew that but knew about the lovely bejeweled bride-to-be, Tavia.

Kaidee felt cheap, dirty. Betrayed. Again.

Every inch of her wanted to charge back in her bedroom, rip the sheet from Devin's body, and kick him out into the corridor. Naked. Cold. With luck, he'd break his glasses and his nose when his face hit the decking.

But then he and Barty could laugh about what low-class trash she was, punching it out with him like a common prosti.

She stared at the screen, the words of the engagement announcement blurring. She wiped at her eyes, then reached out and touched the print icon in the screen's lower left corner. The only sounds in the room were her own ragged breathing and the soft shushing of the thin sheet of paper moving across the tray below the data terminal.

With a trembling hand she pulled it out, padded softly to the bedroom, and then slipped it under Devin's glasses on her nightstand. Then, just as quietly, she plucked her uniform shirt, pants, and boots from her closet and headed for the bridge. The only place she truly belonged.

16

Devin rolled over, the slow increase in illumination bringing him to wakefulness. It was morning—or, rather, shipmorning, given where he was. Which was in the middle of something Makaiden called slippery space. Bumpy space was more like it. He stretched, reaching for her...

The sheets were cold to the touch.

He opened his eyes. No Makaiden. Then a hazy memory surfaced. Something about the navigation program. And slippery space. Next trip, he promised himself as he swung his legs out of bed, he was hiring a pilot so he and his beloved captain could at least wake up together. And continue their crazy lessons or dancing lessons or whatever their hearts and bodies wanted at that moment.

At this moment, he wanted Makaiden.

He perched on the edge of the bed, listening. No sound of movement from the main room. No encouraging aroma of tea or coffee.

"Makaiden?"

No answer.

Hell. He reached for his glasses, his fingers brushing against a sheet of paper with—

He froze. His own face and Tavia's stared back at him. He didn't need to put his glasses on to know what he was looking at: the engagement announcement his mother and Tavia had drafted. No, more than drafted. Polished, perfected, and released.

His gut clenched as if he'd been sucker punched.

No, no, Makaiden didn't understand. That was . . . not him, not his life anymore. "Makaiden!"

He shoved himself to his feet and lunged for the main room, naked, his glasses dangling from his fingers. "Makaiden!"

He whirled around, heart pounding. The room was empty.

Damn it. Damn it! He plowed back into the bedroom, grabbing underclothes, pants, shirt, pulling them on, unconcerned with what was tucked in, what was straight. He needed to find her, explain, apologize. God, what must she be thinking . . . A dozen damning things came to mind. She didn't understand. He had to make her understand.

He couldn't lose her.

He punched the palm pad next to the door, then charged into the corridor. A few steps brought him to the lift, and he almost hesitated, but, no, if she was upset she wouldn't be in the galley. He moved doggedly for the bridge.

The hatchlock was open; the bridge was in semidarkness. She was in the pilot's chair, *her* chair, angled partway toward the nav console on her right. Only the green-tinged glow from various console screens and the paler glow from the docupad in her lap served as sources of light. Her shoulders stiffened as he strode in, but she didn't turn her chair, didn't take her gaze from whatever was on the pad.

He stopped when less than three feet separated them. His throat felt tight. He wasn't sure if the pain he felt radiated from her or from deep within himself. "Makaiden."

"Request denied." Her voice was flat.

He raked both hands through his hair. They came back down to his sides, fisted. "I can explain. It's not what you think." He inhaled slowly, trying to calm his stuttering heart. He exhaled. Silence.

Then she shifted, chin raised, and regarded him from over one shoulder. "You're absolutely right. It's not *what I think*." She said the last three words forcefully. "I think you're a friend. I think you respect me. And I think that I have value in your life. So you're right. It's not what I think at all. It's what you are: owner of this ship. But you don't own me. I'm not part of the package. Now get off my bridge."

She turned abruptly back to her pad.

He grasped for something to say, but the phrases he needed refused to come. Emotions he kept tamped down for so many years coursed through him, almost paralyzing him. He felt mute, stupid. *You're wrong!* kept surfacing. But that wouldn't make things right.

"I don't love Tavia. I never have." He blurted out the words. It was a bare-bones confession and less than skillful. But it was the truth.

Then, as she stared at him, he realized it also made him look callous, shallow. "What I mean is—"

"You have so little regard for her feelings that you'd damn her to a loveless marriage?" She gave a short, harsh laugh. "You're a real prince."

"She doesn't love me either." And he never intended for there to be a marriage, just the engagement he and Tavia agreed would keep both sets of parents pacified.

"Then you deserve each other." She went back to her pad.

The truth in her statement jarred him. "Makaiden—"

"It's Captain Griggs, Mr. Guthrie." She continued tapping at the pad. "I'm working out the figures for piloting your ship from Dock Five to Talgarrath, based on the current fees as posted by the CFTC. It's a standard rate. I think you can afford it. I'll have an invoice for you when we dock at Lufty's." She glanced over at him. "Sexual services rendered this trip are on the house. But don't expect that to happen again."

Her words hit him like a slap in the face. He would have preferred a slap. He almost wished she'd come at him, screaming and punching, because that anger, that pain was something he not only felt he deserved but it was something he could understand. It would get it out of her system. She would cry and he would hold her, apologize, and this would be behind them. A mistake made, rectified, forgiven. But she'd gone cold, detached. This was services rendered in a business relationship, and there was no place for forgiveness in that.

He understood that only too well. He'd lived his life that way for a long time. But something had shifted in him when he found Makaiden, when she was no longer just an unattainable fantasy but a very real, warm, intelligent woman he'd long admired and who now could be his.

Kiler's dead. If someone had asked him what words had the capability of changing his entire life, he would never have guessed they'd be *Kiler's dead.* But they were. And they had.

And this is what he got for breaking J.M.'s rules. Hell to pay. This was hell.

"But—"

"Your rules. When I want you off the bridge, I tell you, and you comply. I'm telling you for the last time: get off my bridge."

He had told her that. And if he broke that rule now, he knew she'd believe he had no honor at all. There would be a time when he would, somehow, make her understand. This was not the time. He nodded mutely and turned away.

An hour later, Barty found him in the galley dining area, clutching a mug of tea—his ineffective attempt at breakfast—long gone cold. The older man still walked slowly and his breathing still wheezed. His eyesight and acumen were as sharp as ever.

"Why do I get the feeling that you've done something abysmally stupid?" He eased down into the chair across from Devin's.

Devin sighed and scrubbed at his face with his hands. He needed a shave. "Where's Trip?"

"Sprawled on a bunk in the crew quarters, engrossed in *Elementary Piloting Procedures for In-System Freighters*. Evidently Captain Griggs found some of her old academy vidtexts and uploaded them to his bookpad."

"Captain Griggs found my engagement announcement to Tavia in the last data feed."

"Ah." Barty leaned back, drumming his fingers on the table. "I saw your mother working on it. Can I assume you neglected to inform our dear captain of that situation?"

"It honestly slipped my mind."

"Slipped? Or avoiding confrontation?"

He couldn't deny that. But when would have been the right time in the past two, three days to tell Makaiden that, *oh, by the way, I have an engagement party waiting for me when I get back home*? When he was dancing with her, trailing kisses down her neck? Or when he was tangled in the bedsheets with her after one of her "crazy lessons"? He nodded slowly. "You've known me a long time. I'm not comfortable with conflict."

Barty shoved himself to his feet, then patted Devin on the shoulder on his way to the galley. "That may be true. But then, some women are worth fighting for."

Kaidee put the half-eaten cheese toast back on the plate and pushed the tray away. Not much of a dinner but, as with her soup-in-a-mug lunch, she'd eaten only to have something to do. She turned back to her ship's data, scrolling, blinking, and occasionally beeping across her console on the bridge. There was really nothing to watch, no reason she should still be here other than she wasn't yet ready to face her quarters, and she had again braved the galley only long enough to grab the toast and flee back up to her pilot's chair.

She needed sleep. She was bone-tired and, worse than that, emotionally exhausted. How could things go so well—discounting being threatened and shot at—and then go so horribly wrong?

And in only three or four days?

It was only three or four days, a little voice chided her. A brief fling, an affair. *Get a grip, Kaid. Grow up. Women your age have flings all the time.* Hell, Pops's daughter back on Dock Five was younger than Kaidee, and she had a new lover every few weeks. She probably assigned them numbers.

If Devin had been a number, it wouldn't have bothered her. Trouble was, Devin was Devin. She knew him—*had* known him—for years.

As she'd known Kiler for years. Obviously, both her long-range and short-range personal scanners sucked miserably when it came to finding trustworthy men.

So? It's not as if this Tavia will find out about what happened. It's not as if you're going to be invited to the wedding. Plus, it's already history. And he is just a number: an invoice number. By end of tomorrow you can file him away under PAID *and forget about it.*

There was one slight hitch in that plan: he owned the ship. That meant end of tomorrow she was likely out of a job and out of a place to stay. She'd have to hire on wherever she could at Lufty's, or even maybe through the cargo docks at Port Chalo. Who knew? Starways might have an opening for a former employee. She was not, she told herself firmly, without options.

Just without hope.

The whine of the lift doors and then boot steps started her heart pounding. She didn't want his explanations. She didn't even want to see him. She was still reconstructing her emotional armor, and if he—

"Hey, Captain Makaiden? Sorry to bother you."

"Trip." She kept the relief out of her voice as she turned. "You're not a bother."

"I finished those two training manuals. Do you have any more?"

"We're going to be hitting the gate exit fairly early tomorrow. You might want to get some sleep."

He shrugged with an elegance uncommon in someone his age. It reminded her of—

"I was just going to my cabin." She got up from her chair, pushing those unwanted thoughts to the back of her mind. She could turn systems over to autoguidance just as easily from the console in her main room. "Let me see what else I can find to challenge your brain."

He tagged along behind her to her cabin, fiddling with his bookpad while she brought up the ship's library database and searched it for another basic-level text. She actually might be doing his uncle Philip and the Alliance a disservice by returning him to the Guthrie household. He was a quick study, a natural. She hoped he had the guts to stand up to his father and grandfather and follow his dream.

She found something that might interest him and uploaded a copy to his bookpad.

"Do they have a flight-training program at your school?" she asked as he closed his pad.

"Yeah, but..." Another shrug.

"Your father thinks it isn't a good idea."

His mouth quirked wryly. "I don't think my father will think anything I want to do is a good idea, once I get home."

"Not right away, no. You're going to have to take responsibility for your actions. But the time will come when you can make your own decisions. Don't..." She hesitated, not sure what to say to this man–child who was heir to a fortune beyond her comprehension.

"Don't let your family's expectations dictate your heart's desire," said a low male voice from her open doorway.

She tensed, then turned stiffly toward Devin, who was leaning against the bulkhead jamb, arms crossed loosely over his chest. He was still in the same shirt from this morning, though now it was tucked in and no longer crooked. Dark patches on his jaw told her he hadn't shaved.

The air in the room suddenly felt thick, heavy, and she wasn't the only one who noticed it.

Trip stepped for the doorway. "You both, um, probably want to talk. Or something." He nodded to Kaidee. "Thanks for the manuals, Captain."

Devin shifted to his right. "Actually, Trip, I need your help. Barty's already asleep and my med-patches need changing. I can't reach the one in back."

"Oh, sure, Uncle Devin. No problem."

He sidled past Devin and disappeared into the corridor.

Devin didn't move. Kaidee felt trapped by his gaze like a ship in a tow field.

"It was never my intention to hurt you," he said quietly.

A lump formed in her throat. She wanted so badly to hate him. She shrugged, swallowing hard. "It's better this way." Her words came out haltingly. Damned lump. "It would never have worked out. Not really." She tore her gaze from his and stared at the datascreen with its library listing, seeing nothing.

"It would; it still could work—"

"Uncle Devin?" Trip's voice echoed slightly in the corridor, then boot steps sounded, returning.

Devin swore something unintelligible under his breath.

When Kaidee finally found the courage to look at the doorway, Devin was gone.

Ping! Ping!

Kaidee hated when morning came early. She hated it even more when shipmorning came early. Her body clock, usually so well tuned to her ship, was reset by the weeks spent on Dock Five, which functioned more under planetary rhythms—albeit artificial—than ship routines. With nowhere to go and nothing to do—other than check the CFTC offices to see when the embargo would end—she'd fallen into the habit of sleeping through the night.

The past few shipdays had shot that to hell.

Well, that and Devin Guthrie.

Ping! Ping!

With a groan, she rolled over on her side and slapped at the alarm. But silencing it didn't help. Her bedroom was now at daylight brightness.

Gate exit in one hour. Then a good four hours at max sublight to the Lufty's beacon. After that, it was anyone's guess. Lufty's could clear her in a half hour or make her wait for days. It depended on whether the Luftowskis still ran it. And whether the Milo name still held some clout.

She showered the lethargy out of her pores, dressed, and then chanced a quick trip belowdecks to the galley for some of Trip's newly invented fruit. The pain, her anger at Devin, hadn't faded, but what she'd been through with Kiler taught her how to compartmentalize things.

Thank you, Kiler Griggs.

If she ran into Devin, she'd deal with it. But the galley was empty, belowdecks quiet except for the usual ship noises and, now that she concentrated, the sound of a shower running in the crew lav. Then she remembered there was a more-than-decent slurp-and-snack in Devin's cabin. It was the original captain's quarters. He had everything he needed right there.

She wondered briefly if he'd keep the *Rider* and, if he did, if he'd use the original captain's quarters for himself.

It was none of her business.

She trotted up the stairs with her bowl of sliced apples and a mug of coffee, then settled in to recheck all systems and go over course options. Just in case there were unfriendlies or questionables in the lanes after they cleared the gate.

The thump of the lift doors sounded from the corridor behind, then the harder, quicker boot steps she recognized as Trip's. Devin had more of an athlete's fluid movement. Still, she could be wrong—

"Captain Makaiden?"

She wasn't, and let out the breath she'd been holding as she swiveled around.

Trip, hair damp, with the sleeves of his blue round-necked thermal shirt pushed up to his elbows, strode all loose-limbed and grinning onto the bridge. "Would you mind if I—"

"You're late, Master Guthrie." She put the stern tone in her voice that her flight instructors had used. "Your assignment is second pilot."

"Second?" He gulped. "Second. Whoa, so totally apex!"

She pointed to the chair at the nav console behind her to the right. "Let me activate the piloting function on the console." It hadn't been used that way since Kiler was on board, and it hadn't occurred to her to let Trip train on it until he'd walked on the bridge a few seconds ago. He was so eager, so positive. She needed to ride the wake of his emotions for a while.

"It's similar to the one in the manual you have," she said as he took his seat. "It should be on now."

"It is."

"Take five minutes and familiarize yourself with the location and reaction of the screens and controls. Do you want to go get your bookpad?"

"Nope." He tapped his forehead. "Got it all here."

"We're twenty minutes out from gate exit. I'm going to make the first announcement on intraship now; then, when you're ready, I'll go over what your duties will be."

"Yes, ma'am. Captain."

She turned back to her console, falling easily into the routine she had for years when flying for GGS. She opened intraship with a tap of her thumb. "This is the captain. In a few minutes we'll be fifteen out from gate exit. Whatever you have loose, strap it down. Whatever's open, close it. This is slippery space, and gate exit will be choppy. Your next and final advisory will be at five minutes out. At that point I want everyone strapped in a bunk or cabin chair. No exceptions. Captain out."

She didn't add an invitation to be on the bridge and hoped that part of her message was clear. If Devin came up here, she would just have to tolerate it. She couldn't demand he leave the bridge and yet permit Trip to be here.

Hell, she'd survived for months with Kiler on the ship. This should be only a few more hours.

Anxious to get rid of him? She didn't have to identify *him* to that annoying voice in her mind. And, yes, she was, because seeing him only prolonged the heartache.

And it won't be heartache losing your ship?

But she was going to lose it anyway. Better to the Guthries than to Orvis.

Yet it wasn't just her desire to put distance between herself and Devin that fueled her impatience. She knew how long it took messages and data to get from Dock Five to Aldan Prime. She hadn't been trying to make Devin feel guilty when she'd told him that by the time they hit gate exit, the whole damned Empire would know he owned the *Rider*. It was fact. Devin said the stealth-pointer program in Trip's pocket comm reported back to an Imperial office, and she believed him. Therefore she also believed that they had a very small window of three, maybe four days before whoever was tracking Trip learned they were on the *Rider*. Whoever was in that office didn't have to send a ship from Aldan. Imperial cruisers were all over the sector. One could intercept them in a matter of hours.

They had to get to Lufty's, had to get out of the space lanes before that happened. They needed to disappear from the Imperial Traffic Control databases completely. Their entry to the gate after they left Dock Five was recorded. She couldn't change that. But her aborted jump transit made sure there'd be no exit signature for Griggs's *Void Rider*.

That also meant they couldn't upload or download any data or messages from any Imperial beacons they passed. That would be annoying—they needed to know more about the bombing of Devin's offices.

Everything would have to wait until they got to Lufty's.

There was safety in silence.

Exiting through the gate with slippery space still grappling for the *Rider* wasn't half as problematic as what happened ten minutes later. At least, that was Kaidee's way of looking at it.

It was bad enough having Devin in the close quarters of the bridge. But the real—and unexpected—problem turned out to be Barty.

"If we access the beacon, someone might be able to trace us. You know that." She pointed at Barty, lounging at the comm console, but her words were also directed at Devin—standing behind Barty. For the past five minutes, Barty had been the one detailing his requests. Devin had just stood silently behind him, like his hired muscle. She thought of Frinks and his Taka. Not good.

Trip, at second pilot, was looking as if he wanted to shrink into his seat, with his hands clasped tightly at his knees and shoulders hunched. After a stellar performance going through the gate, he now had discord on his first command.

"If I don't pick up whatever answers my queries back on Dock Five have generated, someone tracing us will be the least of our problems. They may have already traced us."

"Not to Lufty's."

The older man regarded her with a narrow gaze. "Captain Griggs, ImpSec could take down Lufty's anytime the emperor or Tage wants it. The only reason Lufty's or Uchenna's still operates is that it serves some purpose. *Undercover operatives* are two words that come to mind."

Kaidee couldn't deny that. It was long accepted that the reason Dock Five still existed—and its notoriety predated Tage—was because the emperor and his people felt a known den of thieves was better than an unknown one.

"You were concerned," Barty continued, "about Imperial cruisers waiting for us at the Talgarrath gate. I agreed with that. But that would be Fleet acting as enforcer, not ImpSec. ImpSec rarely moves that overtly."

"And we need to warn whoever's piloting the *Prosperity*," Devin added.

"And if that pilot is there on Tage's orders?" Kaidee countered.

"Then Ethan's message to me would have read differently."

They'd been over that point. Though she had misgivings, Kaidee recognized that Devin was probably right. Whatever Ethan might be—an annoying womanizer at times and too full of himself almost constantly—he was a Guthrie. He'd never risk Devin's and Trip's lives.

"Give me some ways we can minimize detection." She looked at Devin. Okay, she was caving. They won. But she wouldn't make it easy on them. "I take it that's your job?"

He leaned back against the edge of the comm console, his body flanked by the two pale yellow screens. "To be honest, I'm not as familiar with the system as I'd like to be. I've never had a reason to investigate Imperial protocols. I know banks, other commercial communications systems, because I've worked on the other end. In order to prevent hackers, you need to know how they get access." Devin shrugged. "At worst, if I can't delete traces of our uploads and downloads, I might be able to muddy the IDs so they won't know who we are."

"Might?" Kaidee never liked the sound of *might*. "And if they already have a watch out for us, don't you think a null ID is as much of a clue as if we used our own? Can't you make us read as someone else?"

"The only other codes I have available to me are other GGS ships. I think they'd figure it out."

Kaidee didn't like that. "Barty?"

"In order to get workable codes, I'd have to use the datalink." He smiled thinly. "I believe we're caught in a bit of a loop."

They were, and she didn't like it one bit. "We're about thirty-five minutes out from the next-closest data beacon. Do what you can to make *damned* sure whatever you send and receive doesn't also put us on some Imperial cruiser's targeting screens."

"We'll make it to Lufty's," Barty said, rising.

Yeah, us and who else on our tail?

But she didn't say that, she just swiveled her chair around and brought up system stats on her armrest screen. It made her look busy without requiring real concentration. She didn't want to give Devin any opening to stay and talk.

The chair on her right squeaked. "Thanks for letting me sit second, Captain Makaiden."

She glanced over her shoulder, aware that Barty was leaving. Aware that Devin was not. "You did good, Trip. Keep studying."

She caught his shy smile as he turned and hurried to catch up to Barty.

She waited for one more set of departing boot steps. Devin said her name instead. "Makaiden."

She forced herself not to look at him. "You're down to thirty-two minutes to work your hacks. Unless what you have to say involves that, you'd better get moving."

The last set of boot steps headed for the corridor.

Twenty minutes later, though, the men came back— this time Devin and Barty. Hoping there was some good luck somewhere in the galaxy with her name on it, Kaidee turned over the comm console to Devin, then went back to her files on Lufty's and Uchenna's. She listened with one ear cocked to the men—Devin swearing under his breath now and then, Barty grunting from the seat next to him. Keeping the *Rider*'s identity secret was not an easy task. Tampering with a ship's ident programs was something that had put more than one freighter captain—and a handful of smugglers stupid enough to be caught—in starport lockups.

She wanted the news feeds and messages—incoming and outgoing—as badly as Devin and Barty did. She still had people at GGS she considered friends. Devin's reminder—*we need to warn whoever's piloting the* Prosperity—had struck a chord. What if Nel was on board? With Halsey's death, Petra Frederick might send Nel, who didn't look like the tough bodyguard she was. And what if the pilot was Bixner or Kimber-An? Kimber-An had a husband and small children.

A light blinked on her screen. "Five minutes until we're in range," she announced.

"We're good to go," Devin answered.

She swiveled part of the way around. "I've set the link to go hot automatically. It's pretty much the same system as on GGS ships. News and trade feeds will upload without any prompts. Personal stuff, it'll flash you for passwords."

Devin was nodding as she spoke. "How long before we make Lufty's?"

"Lufty's *beacon* is about four hours out. If we end up there." She hadn't written off Uchenna's completely. If she started seeing traffic on her scanners that she didn't like, she'd change course. "Clearance into Lufty's could be immediate, or they could stall us for several hours if they're swamped or don't like my answers. The latter could cause problems. It's no fun being a sitting target."

"Before we do this again, we're going to upgrade your weapons systems."

"We're not doing this again, Mr. Guthrie."

His only response was the slight uplifting of one eyebrow before he turned back to his console.

"Link is hot," Barty announced. "Let's hope and pray we have some good news."

And that no one was tracking their retrieval of it.

There were messages waiting. And data. But unscrambling and decoding took time, because Devin couldn't in all good conscience let the packets go further into the ship's systems, and eventually to his microcomp or Barty's, without first authenticating and checking each one for worm programs. Bombs destroyed offices, but worms destroyed data—and, given their current circumstances, could also destroy systems on the ship. Both were equally lethal but, at the moment, there was only one he could do something about.

His concentration—admittedly—wasn't the best. Makaiden was doing everything she could to push him away, and his mind kept searching for options while he worked on the packets. He needed to find a way to bring her back to him. He needed to pay attention to what he was doing.

He released a packet of data to Barty, then rewarded himself for a minute by staring at Makaiden's profile while his memory brought up images of her body, naked, curved next to his. She was not remotely perfect, and if a director was casting a new vid, she'd never be the star. There were flaws in the symmetry of her face; her mouth was a little too wide, her nose, a bit too broad at the end. Her hair was an unremarkable color somewhere between medium blond and light blond. One eyebrow was crooked. She was of average height and weight.

Jonathan once referred to her as "passably pretty." Devin thought she was gorgeous, and he loved every average, crooked, flawed, passably pretty inch of her. He had for seven years. He found the width of her mouth expressive, and her crooked eyebrow impish, playful. On her, the utilitarian blue GGS pilot's uniform looked both professional and sexy as hell—damned odd combination. Her plain, rumpled freighter grays made his fingers itch to pull them off.

He recognized that Tavia was considered beautiful, yet he could easily go weeks without touching her. Every time he looked at Makaiden, he wanted to bury his face in her neck and shove his hands under her clothes.

Not an easy task when she was barely willing to talk to him—not that they'd had a sufficient block of time that didn't also involve trying to stay one jump ahead of whoever was behind them. But he had tried, and she had rebuffed.

He went back to the comm console. *Clear another packet and you can stare at Makaiden again.*

"Munton Fetter! Well, I'll be damned."

At Barty's startled exclamation, Devin took his gaze from the jumble of numbers and letters on the comm console. The older man was leaning back in his chair, the DRECU angled in the air so as to bring attention to it. "I guess I shouldn't be surprised," Barty continued.

Makaiden was also looking over her shoulder, eyes slightly narrow. "Munton Fetter? Person, place, or thing? Sounds like a Takan meat dish."

"You called him Fuzz-face."

Her narrowed eyes went slightly wider. "You knew him?"

"Knew of his brother, Danniel. Wild man—too wild for ImpSec. Pulled one too many stunts, washed out of training. He operated as a mercenary for a while." Barty looked down at his datapad. "So did his brother, Munton. Both have also done strong-arm guard work on Garno."

The images of the holes blown into the GGS offices flashed through Devin's mind. "So one chased down Trip on Dock Five and the other stayed behind to set off explosives in my office?"

Barty shook his head, still reading. "Evidently Danniel's dead. Ritualistic murder about a year ago. Sounds like he got on the wrong side of one of the Stolorth clans and they sent a death angel after him."

"What's a death angel?" Makaiden asked, swiveling her chair around.

"*Ragkiril,*" Barty said, as Devin said: "*Kyi-Ragkiril.*"

Barty dipped his head slightly. "I bow to your expertise."

"Not mine, my aunt's. She's done extensive studies of the Stolorth culture. Jonathan's been talking about expanding into Stol for about a year, so I was given some required reading." But permits and permissions to trade with the Stol Empire had become increasingly elusive—not so mysteriously—after Philip's abrupt departure from the Imperial Fleet. Devin knew that was one of the reasons J.M. had been trying so hard to curry Tage's favor lately.

"I know what *Ragkirils* are," Makaiden said. "I just never heard the term *death angels.* Mind-rippers, mind-fuckers, sure. And there's an Englarian temple on Dock Five with some horrible paintings of one."

"In Danniel's case, mind-ripper was almost literal." Barty tapped the screen of his microcomp. "The only thing they ever found of his body was his head."

"Get a big discount on a burial casket that way," Makaiden intoned.

Barty snorted.

Devin held back a grin. Some of Makaiden's spunk was returning. He hoped that was a good sign. "So the brother...?"

"Munton," Barty supplied.

"Munton. Thank you. This Munton takes over the business and comes after Trip. Who's paying him?"

"I don't know. Yet." Barty tapped the datapad again. "I have about a dozen more pages to sift through. This was pulled from three different sources."

Makaiden leaned one elbow on the arm of her chair. "Tage has entire squads of assassins on call. Why would he or his people hire someone from outside?"

"We have no concrete proof it was Tage. But if it was, or if it was on his orders, then it might be so that it wouldn't be traced to him or Imperial Security," Barty said. "But they'd usually hire someone a lot better skilled than this. The only thing I could say for this Munton was he was persistent."

"Trip said the guy tried to put a tagger on him," Makaiden continued. She frowned slightly. "But you," and she raised her chin at Devin, "said there's a tracer program in his pocket comm, and that's something we're very sure came from Tage or ImpSec. Duplication of effort, or are we looking at a new player here?"

"Redundancy is good," Barty said before Devin could answer. "But, as I said, this Munton falls short of the usual standard for an outside hire."

"And Munton called him Jonathan, not Trip," Devin put in, remembering the story he'd had Trip relate at least three times.

"Someone at GGS, then?" Makaiden offered.

"Or at the university." Though Devin had a hard time finding logic in either. Trip had been called Trip for so long, there were people in GGS who had no idea Jonathan's son's real name was Jonathan Macy Guthrie III.

"May I keep reading?"

In answer to Barty's question, Makaiden swiveled her chair around. Devin went back to decoding the messages onto his Rada. Makaiden, he guessed with fair accuracy, was checking news feeds.

There was nothing from Ethan, nothing from Jonathan. Devin didn't know if that was good or bad news. With the security problems Ethan had reported at the Guthrie estate, Devin thought the chances of hearing from Jonathan were slim. Still, he thought his oldest brother would have tried...something. After all, it was his son who went missing.

Ethan's silence was also troubling.

And it all could be simply a security glitch. He could easily see Petra Frederick shutting down communications. And Ethan had already told him where and when to expect the *Prosperity*. Duplicate messages increased the chance of interception. Devin didn't like it, but he recognized that silence right now was probably a wiser course.

"Well, here's something. I think," Makaiden said. "Alternate news source—a university student gossip network. There's a report of a murder at a student apartment complex at an unnamed major university in Aldan. Victim is unidentified except for his occupation: bodyguard to a student—and I quote—*who is from a wealthy, well-known, and well-connected Imperial family. Reports state the student is missing and that law enforcement has received significant information on the suspect in both the murder and possible kidnapping.*"

That was too close to the facts not to be a reference

to Trip. But why were the regular news outlets avoiding the story? And why did even the student report shy from names? If anything, the student sources were more likely to take detailed rumor and innuendo and run with it—loudly. Devin raised his index finger as soon as Makaiden looked up from her screen, catching her attention. "Send that to my Rada. I might be able to work further with it."

"Sending. But as for working it further, we're out of range of the beacon, and I'm not looking for another one."

"When we get to Lufty's," he added.

"You can—"

An alarm wailed suddenly, and whatever Makaiden was going to say was lost in its shrill sound and her terse "Shit!"

Devin's heart rate spiked. "What is it?" He didn't expect an answer—at least, not immediately. Her intense focus and the way her fingers flew over her console told him this was trouble. He just didn't know how big or if it was in here or out there.

He glanced at Barty, who was leaning forward, frowning. A thudding sound behind him told him Trip would be on the bridge in seconds.

"Long range?" Trip slid into the seat at navigation as Devin angled around toward him. Out there, then. His nephew had been studying the manuals.

"Four to five hours out," Makaiden confirmed, and though to Devin that sounded like a very safe distance, he knew military ships could move at speeds a common freighter could not. That four to five hours could shrink quickly. "I'm still pulling data. Looks like the bastard's running a scrambler net forward. It's playing hell with my scanners."

Trip's console and screens lit up. "Yeah, I see that."

Devin swung his chair forward again. "Do they see us yet?" he asked the back of Makaiden's head.

"Maybe, maybe not," was her answer. "I've been deliberately running in that beacon's shadow, though our thermal signature's larger and more distinct." She hadn't turned around but continued to work her console. "But their initial sweep could pick us up as only a stutter—unless they have really, really good equipment, or they're Fleet and can pick up a range boost from any Imperial data beacon, in which case they probably know that my mug of coffee here needs more sugar."

"Let me look." Barty pushed himself out of his chair and headed to where Trip sat. "Do you have a database of ship signatures we can compare this to?"

"If it was a freighter in the CFTC database, scans would have already squawked out the ID. Same with any known commercial spaceliner." Her voice was tense. "That means they're military or mercenary. Or pirate."

A series of yellow lights blinked over the console to her left. "Looks like we're not a stutter anymore. They're probing us. Damn it." She tapped at her screens.

"But they're still five hours behind us," Devin said.

"Four hours forty-one minutes. And, yes, before you ask, I've got a damper on our energy discharge. With luck we'll look like we're an old clunker and not worth bothering with."

That sounded like something that would work against pirates but not the Imperial Fleet. Their objectives would be different.

"Why would Fleet come looking for us here?" Devin remembered her objections to using the regular Talgarrath gate: to avoid Fleet.

"They don't have to come looking. Fleet has ships everywhere in Baris. Or have you forgotten we border the Alliance?"

"No, but—"

"Okay, yes. I told you using the smugglers' gate would decrease the chance of running into a Fleet cruiser. I didn't say it was foolproof. If ImpSec got notice of your buying this ship, then Fleet knows. I felt fairly sure we'd have a day or two more before they found out. Evidently, I was wrong." She shot a glance over her shoulder in his direction, then went back to her screens. "Put it this way—Orvis knows. As lien holder, he was notified. I can see him selling that info to ImpSec if it served some purpose."

"He's cut deals in the past," Barty put in.

No good deed goes unpunished. All Devin had wanted to do was solve Makaiden's problems, fix her life, make it better. It never dawned on him that by so doing, he might actually make it worse. And risk their lives as well.

He'd always considered the Guthrie name as protection. Now it made them a target.

"Four hours ten minutes," Trip announced. "They're picking up speed."

"And changing course to match ours," Makaiden said, annoyance and frustration clear in the tightness of her voice. "They need to confirm whether we're the ship they were sent to find."

Devin grasped for something positive. "In four hours we should be at Lufty's beacon. If we get clearance—"

"If whoever this is manages to close the gap, if they get an hour or two behind us, Lufty's will know. And if this is Fleet, Lufty's will not be happy and will not answer my pings. We need them to go away."

"If this is Fleet," Barty said from where he leaned over the back of Trip's chair, "they'll try to disable us and board us long before that."

Fleet could also destroy the *Rider*, Devin knew. If Tage wanted revenge on Philip, this would work nicely. "Couldn't they just be another ship going to Lufty's like we are?"

"Sure, but why run a hot probe on us? If you're out here minding your own business, then you don't go minding anyone else's either." She glanced over her shoulder at him. "That's one of Captain Milo's rules." She turned back, but not before he saw the shadows under her eyes.

"So this could be a pirate, looking for cargo?" Devin asked.

"That's always an option."

"And if they realize you're not carrying any?"

"Depends who they are, how big their ship is, how many weapons they have, and how many crew." She reached to her left, tapping at databoxes on one screen, then made three quick taps to another. A grid on the screen enlarged, showing, he guessed, the other ship's position or configuration. "There are only four of us on board. This ship itself could be a prize. And if they board us and realize who you and Trip are, we could have a real kidnapping and ransom demand on our hands."

It would almost be better, then, to pray the ship behind them was Fleet. But, no, it wouldn't. Between Philip's notoriety and Tage's insanity, Fleet posed as large a danger as pirates. That stealth program in Trip's pocket comm was an Imperial device. Pirates would likely just want money. Tage wanted their lives.

Devin turned his Rada over in his hands as his mind ran in circles. Then he stopped, suddenly realizing what his microcomp contained. "Would they board an Englarian mission ship?"

That got Makaiden looking at him again. Barty and Trip too.

"How would you—"

Devin held up his Rada, halting Makaiden's question. "One of the suppliers involved in a big business deal GGS has in Baris is an Englarian agri co-op. I downloaded specs of three of their ships right before I left for Port Palmero. I don't know why I didn't think of it before. GGS has to have their ships' idents in order to coordinate them with our depots."

"Fleet has standing orders not to interfere with the Englarians," Barty said. "At least they did when the Admirals' Council had more power. But I suspect there's still something of a look-but-don't-touch rule on the books. It could work."

Makaiden switched her gaze from Barty to Devin. "Do you know how difficult it is to change a ship's sealed ident?"

"Haven't a clue in a bucket, but it looks as if I'm going to find out. If you think it's an option worth pursuing."

She arched one eyebrow—the crooked one—then sighed. "Pirates, for the most part, leave the Englarians alone. Too many have Takan crew who are devoted to Abbot Eng." She flicked one finger in the direction of the corridor. "Use my quarters. Door's unlocked. You'll need to isolate the ID packet, make a backup—"

"And copy the primaries to an impenetrable location. Yes, love. I know." He returned her arched eyebrow with one of his own.

She dropped her gaze and turned away from him, but not before he caught the rise of color on her cheeks. His use of the endearment was deliberate. It was a common enough expression—Audra, his parents' cook, called everyone "love."

But he didn't, and he guessed with fair accuracy that Makaiden knew that.

He felt he'd given her enough time to get over the shock of his so-called engagement. Time to return to the negotiating table.

But first he had an extremely critical program to unravel. And, judging from the increasing intensity of the beeping and blinking on Makaiden's console, not a hell of a lot of time to do it in.

"At their current speed, we've got forty-five minutes before whoever that is might be able to tag us with an ident sweep. If we're supremely lucky, an hour. They're still several hours behind us, but they're hauling ass," Makaiden told him, leaning on the back of one of her dining-table chairs. She hadn't followed him into her cabin when he left the bridge but appeared ten minutes later. He'd been about to contact the bridge and ask her how much time he had to reset the *Rider*'s ID when she knocked on the open doorway jamb.

More proof, as far as he was concerned, that he and Makaiden were on the same datastream, as the saying went. Tavia never would have inquired. Tavia would have had no idea what he was even attempting to do.

"Can you do it?" she asked.

He shot her a quick glance, then went back to the small bits of code on his screen. He was moving and backing up files at this point—boring work, but incredibly necessary. "Depends if you're willing to share your knowledge."

It was strictly a guess on his part. GGS pilots weren't supposed to know illegal procedures like changing a ship's embedded identification program. But the little she'd let him learn of her real history, and the large amount of time he'd spent watching her negotiate her way around Dock Five, only cemented his belief that there was a lot more to Makaiden Milo Griggs than Petra Frederick could ever guess at.

He wanted to prove to her that those things were neither a detriment nor an impediment. He could still hear her *It would never have worked out. Not really.* He was so unsettled at the time she said it, he hadn't considered her reasoning behind it. But dealing with Makaiden wasn't all that much different from being at the negotiating table with an unwilling or insecure CEO of some business that GGS wanted to acquire. As long as the focus was on what didn't work, negotiations would go downhill. The focus had to be on the strong points, the strengths of the merger.

Those strengths included her knowledge and his skills.

Besides, he really needed to kiss her again. Soon.

Her gaze avoided his. "I don't—"

"Don't go all proper and by-the-book on me now. I need you." That could be taken in several ways, and he meant all of them. "And we have only forty-five minutes."

She swore softly under her breath, then swiveled around the chair on his left and sat. "I've never done it. I've seen it done two, three times on ships my father's crew, um, appropriated. Never on a Blackfire. What I saw, what I know, might be outdated."

"It's more than I've seen. I only know what they do in those action vids Trip's so addicted to."

Alarm flashed in her eyes. "But you know—"

"Code theory and program structure? Totally. But this is an Imperial government-created program and fail-safe."

"Government issue? Well, hell, Dev," she drawled. "That should make it easy."

His laugh was a half snort, half chuckle, and then she was grinning too. Until he held her gaze for a little too long. Then her smile faded. "We're wasting time."

"We have"—he glanced at the holographic display hovering over the edge of the Rada—"four more minutes to waste. Backup's still in progress. Tell me the biggest problem I'll encounter and we'll go from there."

"This is a legit freighter, not a pirate rig or conversion. Tampering with an Imperial ident program can trigger the complete lockup of ship's primaries. Backups won't reinstall. Engines shut down. Systems we need—like lights, grav, enviro—quit. We drift until we run out of air and die. Unless we freeze to death first."

That was a big problem, although the idea of wrapping himself around Makaiden's body to keep her warm held definite appeal. He stared at her a long moment. Those problems weren't the ones he expected. Threat of jail times, fines, okay. GGS was always facing the threat of fines for some alleged and often imagined discrepancy. But the fact that the ship itself would turn into judge, jury, and executioner...

He saw Tage behind this. It was brilliant and horrific at the same time.

"Our chances sound better if we face whatever ship is behind us. We don't have to do this."

She leaned both elbows on the table. "Chances are, if the worst happens—and knowing you, I'm betting it won't—whoever's behind us won't let us drift and die. We have about five hours of air on board once we kick in backup enviro. We blow the engines and regular enviro, we're no worse than if they ID and board us. But if we make them go away, that increases your chances of getting to the *Prosperity* and home." She leaned back.

"This all comes back to my registering this ship in my name, doesn't it? Makaiden, I'm sorry."

A shrug preceded her answer. "You're not used to Dock Five."

"I've dealt with marginal business operations before. It wasn't that." He hesitated for a second. Guthrie men were horribly inept at expressing their feelings. He abandoned all the romantic avenues he'd tried to this point—and failed with—and went for plain honesty. "It was finding you. Nothing's ever been so important to me before."

That brought her arms crossing protectively over her chest.

"I know you don't believe me and that a big reason is because of my relationship with Tavia. In a way, you were right when you said she and I deserved each other." He shook his head with a short, derisive laugh. "She always said that by being together, we were saving two other people from heartache. She's a barrister with aggressive political ambitions, and she's very up front about wanting only a low-maintenance relationship. And I . . . I thought you were happily married." He paused. "I know it sounds cold, shallow. But Tavia or I aren't so cold and shallow that we'd fake loving someone when we didn't. We also had an agreement. If either of us found someone we loved, the relationship would end. No problems, no rancor." The slight narrowing of her eyes signaled her suspicion. "When we get back to Garno, you can ask her."

Suspicion wavered, Makaiden's lips parting slightly. Devin hoped that was a good sign.

"When we get—" But her sentence ended when the panel on the bulkhead chimed.

"Captain Makaiden? That ship's three hours forty-five minutes out. They're really moving."

Makaiden reached back and tapped the comm button on the panel. "Thanks, Trip. We're just finishing backups here. Alert me to any more changes. Captain out." She tapped it again, then turned back to Devin. For a very long moment, she was as quiet as he was before. Then she sucked in a long breath. "Okay. Truce for now. We have to get working on this ID program. Because if we don't, it won't matter how we feel about each other. We won't be alive long enough to enjoy it."

The acknowledgment—albeit oblique—that she did have feelings for him made him smile. "That's the most encouraging dire prediction I've ever heard. Backup's done." He expanded the *Rada*'s holoscreen and motioned Makaiden closer. "Let's take a closer look at that program."

A closer look was both encouraging and discouraging. The encouraging part was that Imperial identification programs hadn't changed all that much in the past decade or so. The discouraging part was that the program was full of fail-safes and traps, many of which seemed innocuous on first inspection. Devin knew this was no time for distraction. If anything, he needed a cool head and a large dose of inspiration. To him, Makaiden was both. One part of him wanted to send her back to the bridge. The other wanted her here.

He found justification in the latter with the fact that she'd seen this before. He hadn't. He needed all the

help he could get. The holoscreen before him was a
jumble of numbers, letters, and icons that made up a
ship's systems codes. This wasn't the same as unravel-
ing a financial account-protection program. Lives
were involved. In spite of all the things that had happened, he'd come to rather like his life. And he was responsible for Barty and Trip. And for Makaiden,
though he doubted she'd acknowledge that.

He managed to break down the first two levels of
security guarding the program in about fifteen minutes. But then he was staring at a string of coding he
didn't like and didn't fully understand—and that made
him like it even less.

"Out of my realm," Makaiden admitted. "Maybe
Barty can help?"

He hated to lose her presence. A lot of the anger
he'd sensed from her hours ago had faded. Their former camaraderie—while not back—felt as if it might
consider returning.

"Make sure he brings his DRECU," he said, not
without a bit of reluctance.

She pushed herself out of her chair, then headed for
the corridor and the bridge. The room seemed a little
colder, a little less bright, without her. Moments later,
heavier footsteps sounded through the open doorway.

"Trouble?" Barty asked as he stepped into Makaiden's
quarters.

Devin shot a quick glance toward the corridor. No
Makaiden following behind. Disappointment fought
with practicality. She'd been off the bridge for a while
and deserved to sit in command of her ship. "Sorry to
take you from your work."

"The illustrious Fetter brothers, though interesting
reading, can wait. Nothing I've come across so far

points to why Fuzz-face came after Trip. What's your problem here?"

"This looks like object coding. But if it is, it doesn't belong here. I'm thinking it's a shunting bug." Error or deliberate, he couldn't tell, but if he popped it, whole parts of the program could dump or shunt over to a wrong location.

Barty took the chair Makaiden had vacated and stared at the Rada's display. "I haven't seen this before, but perhaps I have something in archives." He slid his microcomp next to Devin's, tagged the offending data, then started searching.

Devin went back to the ID program, trying another bit of wizardry to see if he could unearth a back door—a deliberate security hole often inserted by a program's creator, ostensibly for ease-of-maintenance purposes by restricted, authorized techs. Or sometimes for more nefarious purposes. He was hoping for the former. The latter could set off alarms within the program and disable the *Rider*.

"Try this," Barty said, turning his screen toward Devin. "It's a sample code string from an Imperial ID verification program that's been used on Starport Six and Marker."

Devin snagged the sample from Barty's smaller DRECU. Maybe, just maybe. He thought he saw a pattern but didn't want to be overconfident. He chose a different section of code, copied it, studied it. Maybe...

"Devin?" Makaiden's voice sounded through the cabin's comm speaker. "That forty-five-minute window you had is now less than twenty. I need answers."

Shit. He rose, but Barty was already reaching back, tapping open the comm-panel speaker. He slumped back in his seat. "Acknowledged," he said, knowing she could hear him. He wiped his palm over his face, but that didn't help clear his mind. "I'm not where I want to be with this program. Maybe in two, three hours—"

"We don't have two or three hours."

"I know." He glanced at Barty. The man didn't look happy either. "Makaiden, can you spare three minutes to look over what I've done?"

"Be right there."

This time the lighter, quicker footsteps in the corridor were the ones he wanted to hear.

She leaned on the table, palms flat on the top, and studied the Rada's display for just about the three minutes he'd allotted. Then: "This is far from my area of expertise. But what you have there," and she pointed to a section he'd highlighted, "looks like the stuff my uncle would do. I recognize some of the same commands. But more than that, I don't know." She pulled back from the table and shoved her hands in the back pockets of her pants.

Barty nodded. "I say we go with it. A lot of the Englarian mission ships aren't that sophisticated and have been cobbled together from donated parts. They have older comm packs, older ID programs. As long as whoever's behind us doesn't scan us as the *Void Rider,* I think we can bluff our way through anything else."

Devin arched an eyebrow at Barty, the realization of exactly who they had to masquerade as hitting home. "And if they demand visual contact? You can impersonate an Englarian monk?" Devin knew with fair certainty he couldn't. He'd been raised in traditional Celestialism: a monotheistic religion that much of the Empire followed. Englarians were...different. Where he prayed to God, they prayed to Abbot Eng, who, his followers believed, would intercede with God on their behalf. They also had a whole list of ritualistic blessings that they could spout off on command. If they weren't communing with the abbot, they were blessing somebody. Their unflappable placidity made him itch.

As he watched, Barty's expression transformed from its normal penetrating stare to a bland, almost beatific mien. "Praise the stars, brother. It's clear the abbot has brought you to me as a divine sign. So how may I be of service to you this blessed day?"

Makaiden let out a low whistle. "Damn, he's good."

Barty turned toward her. "Through the divine guidance of our beloved Abbot Eng, I always seek that which is beneficent." His voice was soft, almost sweet. He brought his hands together in a prayerful motion that was graceful and fluid, looking as if he'd made the gesture for decades.

He *was* good. Devin had no problem blocking out his emotions, but it was his choice when he did so—not because some old man in a flowing robe decreed he should act that way. And he'd be damned if he knew how to look so benignly—and divinely—besotted.

"I think I have a tan blanket or sheet somewhere I can use to make you a robe." Makaiden stepped toward the corridor. "That is, a robe for Brother . . . ?"

"Brother Balatharis," Barthol said with a slight incline of his head. "Your humble servant."

Devin snorted out a laugh. Thank God for Barty. *Pun intended.*

"Fifteen minutes," Makaiden called out over her shoulder. She stopped, angling halfway around in the open doorway. "Can you amend the ID in that time?"

Devin's expression sobered. "I have to."

She studied him. "You'll do it. I have faith in you."

Then before he could wonder further about the softening in her expression, she headed down the corridor, out of his sight.

Ten minutes later, he had the small snippet of code that would alter every mention of the *Void Rider* to the *Veil of Relief*, showing ownership by the Order of Devoted Missionaries on Calfedar. The order was real, according to Barty, who provided the data that would make everything look authentic. The ship's name wasn't on the order's roster; however, it was one of the few that would not only work in their guise as a missionary ship but—more important—fit decently into allocated spaces in the code strings of the ID program.

It was a good bit of code. In any other circumstance, he'd have absolute faith that it would do what he wanted it to. But this wasn't any other circumstance. And he was up against Imperial and ImpSec techs who had no qualms about triggering the destruction of a ship because one of their programs malfunctioned.

It wasn't the back door he wanted, but it was the one he would use: put the communications system in a ten-second emergency shutdown. When it came back up and the ship's main computer segued with it, the ship should think it was the *Veil of Relief*.

He found his palms—annoyingly—sweaty as he took the seat at the comm console on the bridge, then slotted in the small archiver. Trip was still at nav, Barty in the seat behind Devin.

"Blast doors closing, fifteen seconds," Makaiden announced as she tapped commands into the screen angled out of her armrest. It was a security precaution—if the ship's primaries failed, there was a limited backup enviro for the bridge and the captain's quarters. But that was all. No sick bay. No galley.

As the doors clanged shut, Devin noticed that Trip had his bookpad on the decking by his boots. His nephew's younger sister knew him well. Trip went nowhere without that pad.

Devin touched a series of icons on the screen on his right. "Initiating comm failure."

The lights on his console blinked. A warning siren bleated softly.

"Ten seconds, Devin," Barty said. "Nine..."

Devin launched the program from the archiver, the display on his Rada—linked to the *Rider*'s main system—alive with data.

"Seven, six..."

It had to find that back door, that security hole. Numbers, symbols flashed by. Everything looked right, but he'd thrown this together so quickly. But, yes, okay, the communications program shifted over to a seek-and-repair mode. Just as he thought it would. His back door should be...

There! Yes. His fingers flew over the Rada's suspended display, forcing the communications program to recognize his altered code as what it sought.

The program stuttered, his Rada's display wavering. His heart thumped in his chest in the same erratic movement. *Damn it, damn it, no!* It was running a bypass, sequestering his codes as if for later reference. He must have missed—

But, no, it wasn't sequestering. It was authenticating. Hell's fat ass, it was authenticating, accepting the false data as its—

The bridge plunged into darkness just as the rumble of the sublight engines beneath his boots died.

Kaidee *hated* when her ship didn't work. Dead in space was not a place she liked to be. Especially with an unknown bogey on her tail, closing at a disturbingly fast rate of speed that made her heart pound in her chest and her throat go dry.

"Devvvinn?" She drew out his name in a long question as she flipped open the small panel cover on the pilot's console that housed the bridge's backup enviro. The resulting whoosh of air through the overhead ducts was encouraging—but it would be encouraging for only five hours. The silence and stillness beneath her boots was not encouraging at all.

"On it!"

He was—or at least his super-expensive microcomputer was—still working, its holo display pulsing with data. She glanced over her shoulder, catching the odd reflection of the display in the lenses of Devin's eyeglasses. It was almost as if she could see into his brain, as if the green-tinged images were coming from his eyes.

Other screens glowed around her. Not her ship's—those were dead. But Barty's military DRECU and Trip's bookpad provided small sources of light.

The silence and stillness around her screamed louder.

Deep breath, Kaid. Long, deep breath. This wasn't the first time she'd gone dead in the lanes. It had happened once on the *Prosperity* and twice when she'd flown for Starways. All three times it was simply a matter of correcting a power-overload problem: *when the power goes out, seek first the source of the power.* That was from the official Starways manual, chapter and verse.

That wouldn't help her. Some unknown fart in her ship's power source wasn't the problem. This was known, and she'd helped to cause it.

Hell of an epitaph.

She forced her gaze away from the Rada's bright glow and stared out the darkened viewport, letting her eyes adjust. This time when she glanced down at the decking, she could just discern the small emergency lights set at the base of her chair and—she swiveled around away from where Devin was—at the hatch-lock to the corridor. There would be more guide lights there. Those would all fade eventually if they didn't get the damned ship up and running.

"Here's one good thought." Barty's low voice broke into her thoughts. "We probably disappeared off their long-range scanners."

"That would work only if we could go stealth and still have maneuverability," Trip replied. "Since we're drifting on the trajectory of the last known coordinates their scanners have on us, all they need to do—"

"Trip, you might want to shut down your book-pad," Devin said, without turning around. "Conserve power. We may need it later."

Devin didn't have to interrupt Trip's comment. Kaidee knew the answer anyway. Yes, they'd gone cold. But if their pursuer stayed on course, it wouldn't be long before short-range scanners and sensors defined that there was an object in their path that matched the specs and configurations for a medium-size jump-rated freighter like a Blackfire 225.

She pushed herself out of her chair—her console was useless—and headed for Devin as the dim glow of Trip's bookpad winked out. Devin's glasses still reflected the Rada's display and highlighted his frown and the tightness around his mouth. He didn't like whatever he was looking at.

"Reinstall the primaries," she said. "We'll take our chances, try to outrun them." *Try* being the operative word. She doubted they could. But maybe there was another smugglers' gate—someplace they could play duck-and-hide until she could get Devin, Trip, and Barty to the safety of the *Prosperity*. Something that was starting to look less and less likely.

"I just tried a reinstall." Devin's voice was too calm, too emotionless, and he didn't move his gaze from the Rada's display. "It's not taking."

Her gut clenched. "Backups—"

"I made two copies. Working with the second now." He moved another section of code on the display.

Two copies. Good idea, in case the first backup was somehow corrupted or viewed as an illegal program and attacked by the security system. She remembered her father and her uncle talking about that. She searched her memory for more, for anything that might help.

Anything to keep from thinking about the ship coming toward them as they drifted, helpless. "Are you coming in on the maintenance or command authorization?"

"Maintenance. It's usually allocated as a residual power draw for systems-failure situations. I found its back door. A legitimate one. But it refuses to accept the initialization command."

Barty pushed his microcomp closer to Devin's Rada as he scooted toward the edge of his seat. "Let me look."

Kaidee rested her hand on the back of Devin's chair and watched Barty copy data, searching for answers. She suspected with fair certainty he had several files of Imperial code hacks at his disposal.

Devin was glancing back and forth between the suspended display and the DRECU. "That's a possibility," he said, pointing to the DRECU's screen. Then his fingers were moving blocks of data on his display, and his conversation with Barty was reduced to snippets of jargon that made only the barest sense to her.

She checked the time stamp in the lower left corner of the Rada. Eleven minutes had passed since her ship went dead in the lanes. The ship pursuing them was now eleven minutes closer, or more if it had continued to gain speed. And if it had, it could be a mere two or three hours before they felt the impact of a tow field or the hard jolt of grappling clamps.

She took a quick mental tally of the weapons on board—L7s and Carvers. It was a pitiful list if they were to defend themselves against pirates. Futile if the ship behind them was Imperial, with ImpSec assassins. But then, she'd never considered she'd have to do either. She was a legit hauler who worked legit contracts. Even Kiler had agreed to that and, after his death, she'd been doubly cautious.

Until she saw Trip Guthrie—alone and definitely out of place—on Dock Five. She stared at the sealed hatchlock at the far end of the bridge and fought the urge to throw herself at the thick metal doors and pound her head against them. How could doing the right thing—*the morally right thing*—bring her so much damned trouble? *No good deed goes unpunished* echoed annoyingly in her mind.

Barty, on her right, coughed twice. The third time his cough was more strained, drier.

"You okay?" She didn't like the sound of that. In the dim lighting, he was a slightly paler shade of green than Devin.

He nodded. "Just a little dryness."

"Would water help?" Enviro should be on in the corridor and her quarters, and she had a few bottles of water in her galley cabinet. She stepped back toward her chair.

"If you don't mind."

He did sound raspy. Kaidee checked the small enviro emergency panel. Deck 1 was secure. She was reaching for the blast door release when she caught herself and shook her head. *Idiot.* The rest of the ship was on manual. "Give me a minute to get the doors open. Trip, can you help?"

"Sure, Captain Makaiden."

The emergency-access panel was to the right of the hatchway. She slid the cover up, then showed Trip where the handle and crank were. Behind her, Barty coughed again.

Definitely not good. But then, emergency enviro usually did a piss-poor job of filtering.

Trip put his weight on the crank and, as the doors creaked slowly open, she could hear Devin talking softly to Barty but couldn't make out the content of their conversation. More computer tech talk? Or was Devin as worried as she was about the older man?

"There's one more blast door mid-corridor and then the door to my quarters," she told Trip as he rose, a tall shape in the dimness. He followed her, their boot steps sounding eerily hollow in the silent ship. "Same thing," she said, guiding his hand to the crank behind the open access panel.

"If Barty needs sick bay, can we get him there?" he asked as he worked the crank.

"Not unless your uncle can get ship's power back on." She caught his worried tone clearly. "I have a small med-kit in my lav, though." She shoved the blast door into the bulkhead slot as Trip grunted, somewhere down by her knees. She reached down blindly and found his shoulder. "Halfway's enough. Come on."

They repeated the procedure at her doorway. "Wait here," she told Trip. "I know my way around. I don't want you falling over a chair."

She slipped quickly past the chair and low table and headed for the dining alcove along her main room's outer bulkhead. She kept one hand out before her and felt the edge of one of the dining chairs. The slurp-and-snack—useless right now—was on her left. A small cabinet with mugs, a few dishes, and assorted condiments and nonperishables was below it. Her fingers found its recessed outlines. She slid the door open, then groped the interior, past the cardboard box of sweetener packets and another that held sealed packages of a dried-fruit-and-nut snack. The latter she often stuffed in her pockets when she knew she'd be waiting in line at some dockmaster's or customs official's office. It could take two hours to get a five-second signature of approval on a manifest. Those little snack packages not only helped pass the time but often helped her make friends with other captains in line.

If Devin couldn't get ship's power back up, those snack packets and the bottles of water—she finally found them—might be all they had to live on. Until the air ran out.

Ever the optimist, Kaid.

She moved through the darkness back to the open doorway and Trip, catching the dim pinpoints of the emergency lights on her right leading to her lav and her bedroom. "Take this back to Barty," she said, handing him a bottle. "I have a handbeam in my nightstand. I'll meet you back on the bridge. Unless you want to wait—"

"I'll get this to Barty."

"Don't forget those blast doors are only halfway open," she called as his boot steps thumped quickly away.

"Not to worry, Captain!"

If only . . . Shaking her head at her own dismal thoughts, she headed back into her cabin, one arm out, fingertips skimming the walls, eyes straining to see the small dots of light on the decking.

Her bedroom was small, the edge of the bed easy to find. She sat on it, then rolled on one hip toward her nightstand, trying unsuccessfully not to think about how it felt to be rolling around on this same bed in Devin's arms. That wasn't going to happen again. She wasn't going to let that happen again. And not just because of the lovely Tavia waiting for him back home. But because he was going back home, to Garno or Sylvadae, and she didn't belong in either place.

She pulled out the handbeam and—after scraping her knuckles against the inside of the drawer—the spare power pack and was swinging around to stand when the hard thudding of boots against the decking sounded from the corridor.

"Makaiden?"

It was Devin. Hope rose. Maybe he'd gotten

through that code-laden back door and her ship's primaries were already reinstalling. That would mean they'd lost twenty, thirty minutes at most. Maybe, just maybe, they could make it to Lufty's beacon before the other ship tagged them with an ident sweep. Maybe, just maybe, someone at Lufty's could help, send a ship to do an intercept.

"Here!" She flicked on the handbeam and had gotten as far as her bedroom door when Devin's tall shadowy form reached her.

His hand closed firmly around her arm. But there was a tremor in his voice when he spoke. "Barty collapsed again. Trip said you have a med-kit in here. We need it now."

Kaidee, kneeling next to Barty's quiet form on the decking in front of the communications console, angled the small medical analyzer's screen so Devin and Trip could see it. "The infection in his lungs is back. He really needs to be in sick bay. Best I can do is... Here, hold this." She shoved the medalyzer into Devin's open hand, then rummaged in the kit by her knees for an inhaler. "Trip, give me some light."

Trip pointed the handbeam at the open med-kit. Kaidee spotted the palm-sized triangular unit slotted into the side of the kit and grabbed it. She fitted it over Barty's nose and mouth, then tapped it on. His eyelids fluttered slightly, but he didn't rise to consciousness. And his breathing, even with the inhaler, was labored.

Her own chest felt heavy. Damn it, she should never have listened to Kiler and agreed to move the sick bay to Deck 2, behind the galley. But he'd been insistent on having a cargo area near the bridge, and it never occurred to her she'd be facing a total lockout of her own ship. In a normal power failure, emergency systems would power sick bay.

Trouble was, tampering with a ship's primaries didn't trigger a normal power failure. It triggered a catastrophic one. Which meant that even if sick bay was where it belonged, on Deck 1, there would be no power to run its medical units.

Devin held the analyzer unit down by the side of the inhaler and frowned at the data on the screen. "How long will this breathe for him?"

"At current output?" She studied the screen, her heart sinking. "A little more than two hours. It's only meant to be a temporary measure, just enough to get the patient to sick bay or the closest hospital."

"But..." Trip said, then fell silent.

"But two hours wouldn't get us to Lufty's, even if we had full sublights," Kaidee finished softly for him. "I know, Trip. I know."

"Isn't there a way? Can't we just open the blast doors to Deck Two?" Trip moved the beam of light from Barty to the corridor, then back again. "The air will flow down there."

"Aside from the fact that the air ducts seal in a total lockout, the air we're breathing here is all the air we have. You open up Deck Two, you're splitting an already limited volume. Plus, even if we had air, there's no power to run sick bay." A short sigh of frustration escaped her lips. "I'm sorry."

"Is there anything we can do?"

Kaidee rose. "We can make him more comfortable. You have the handbeam. Go pull the cushions from my couch. You'll find a spare blanket in the closet near the lav. Bring them back here." It wasn't much, but it was something.

"Would he be better off on the couch or the bed in your cabin?"

Kaidee shook her head. "Someone would have to stay with him. That would split us up. If we get boarded, I want all of us together here on the bridge. You understand?"

"Yeah, that makes sense." Trip nodded, then headed doggedly down the corridor for her quarters. Gone was the bright-eyed young man who'd found her diversionary tactics on Dock Five to be so "apex!" Trip was maturing, and it clearly wasn't a pleasant lesson.

Kaidee took the few steps to the pilot's chair and, crossing her arms, leaned them against the chair's high back. Weariness and frustration washed over her. Then strong arms encircled her waist, drawing her back.

"Devin. Don't." She didn't sound terribly convincing, but she was too tired to care.

A masculine sigh, half growl, half rumble, filled her ear. Warmth cascaded down her neck. Her heart sped up, which only added to her frustration. To be betrayed by her own body. How slagging annoying.

He turned her in his arms until she faced him in the darkness of the bridge. "Maybe you don't need this. But I do." He clasped her against him, one hand threading up into her hair. His lips brushed the side of her face and came to rest against her left ear.

And that was all. This was not, she realized as she melted into his warmth, a sexual encounter. It was one of comfort, a touching of two souls amid desperation and disaster. Devin just held her, and she remembered the guilt he must feel—the changes to the ship's ident program were all his doing—and that Barty was his friend. *Had* been his friend for decades.

She hugged him, stroking the strong planes of his back. "We'll get through this somehow," she whispered. She didn't believe that, but she had to say it because, in saying it, she had a better chance of believing.

At the sound of Trip's approaching boot steps, she pulled away from him.

Devin sighed. "I have a few more things to try with that program yet. Get Barty as comfortable as you can."

She knew Devin slid into his seat, because the chair at the comm console had a distinct squeak and because his face was again a silhouette limned in green. He took his glasses off, rubbed them on his shirtfront, then put them back on and tapped a databox, moving it to the right. Then he reached for Barty's DRECU, swiveling it toward him.

"Lucky he left this on," Devin said, as Trip put the stack of cushions on the decking, the light from the handbeam brightening the bridge slightly. "There's no way I could access it. I don't know his codes."

Kaidee took the blanket from Trip. "If that's an Imperial ship out there, we should probably destroy Barty's microcomp before they board us. The less they know about him, about us, the better."

"Will they get here before his inhaler runs out?" Trip asked.

"If it is a Fleet ship, there's a chance," she said. The real question, though, was would the Empire restore him to health so they could sentence him to death? Likely, in Kaidee's opinion, but she wouldn't voice that. Devin probably already knew. Trip, at his age and for all his impending maturity, didn't need to know. ImpSec was rarely kind to those who left its ranks. And Barty didn't have the Guthrie name to protect him, though she knew Devin would try every avenue. But too many things pointed to the Empire's involvement in the attacks on Trip on Dock Five. Kaidee held no belief that an appearance of an Imperial ship—if that's what was out there—equaled rescue.

"Let's put the cushions against the bulkhead, in the corner over there." She guided the handbeam Trip held toward the rear of the bridge. "That will help steady him."

The three of them moved Barty carefully, then Kaidee showed Trip how to monitor Barty on the small medical analyzer and check his inhaler. The unit would assist his breathing for another hour and forty-five minutes.

"You have EVA suits on this deck?" Devin asked, kneeling next to her.

She pointed to a locker in the opposite corner, even though Devin probably couldn't see her fully. "Two. But the breathing apparatus is different."

"I might be able to rig something using one."

"Get those primaries installed and we won't need it."

"Yes, Captain," Devin said, but as he pushed himself to his feet, he leaned forward and brushed the side of her face with a kiss.

She shook her head slightly, as if by so doing she could shake off the emotions that rose every time he came close to her. She wished she didn't like him—*genuinely* like him—so much. It would make it far easier to push him away or ignore him.

She turned back to Barty, tucking the blanket around his hips a bit more snugly, because it was something to do and she felt useless. Then she pushed herself to her feet. "I have some supplies in my quarters we might need. Trip, stay with Barty. I'll be back in a couple minutes."

Kaidee reclaimed her handbeam and made several trips, bringing the rest of the bottled water, the snack packets, and her bed pillows, then heading back down the corridor for her cold-weather gear and extra blanket. Ship's temperature was already dropping.

If they had to, they could conserve their air supply and heat by shutting down the rest of Deck 1, staying confined to the bridge and the small lav adjacent to it. It might buy them another half hour or so, stretching their five-hour limit to a bit more.

If it comes to that, why bother? She didn't know. Tears pricked her eyes—unusual for her. She wasn't the soggy sort. But she was and always had been a fighter. A survivor. Maybe in that extra half hour—if it came to that—they'd think of something. Devin would work one more miracle.

But Barty might be dead by then.

All because she'd decided to rescue Trip Guthrie. And because she hadn't had the sense to walk away from Devin. *You own this ship now? Fine; you fly it.* That would have stopped the whole thing right there. They'd still be on Dock Five, where she had friends, options, resources.

But what if Devin had hired another pilot? Dock Five's brimming with them. Then he'd be gone, maybe in the same circumstances, and he'd be dying. And you'd never know what really happened. Just like with your father. Just like with Kiler.

Was she destined to be the death curse for the men she loved? She stripped the blanket off her bed, folding it carefully for no reason other than it felt better to be doing something.

You don't love Devin.

Yeah, I do.

Idiot.

No argument there.

She pulled her heavy coat and a thick sweater from her closet, folding them neatly and placing them on top of the blanket. Neither would fit Trip, Devin, or Barty. And the ship would get colder, the air less breathable. She had some towels, could maybe even use her bedsheets as a buffer against the cold, but when it all came down to it, did it really matter? An extra ten minutes before they froze to death or ran out of air?

She dropped the handbeam on her bed and sucked in a harsh breath. She would not cry. She would not collapse. She would not give in to the fear gnawing at her like a mad, ravenous *crigblarg*, insatiable, unrelenting...

Boot steps behind her. She recognized them, knew them by heart already, knew the way Trip loped and the way Devin strode. This was Devin. She did not want him here right now, not with tears streaming down her face and her breath coming in hard hiccups.

She scrubbed hurriedly at her face but it was too late, because he was saying her name and, when his arm slid around her waist, she realized she was trembling. And wanted nothing more than to be held by him forever.

"Hush, Kaidee, hush." He nestled her face against his shoulder and rested his head against hers.

She gave a little half laugh, half sob. "It takes all this to finally get you to call me Kaidee?"

A sad chuckle rumbled in his chest. "I always thought that when I called you Kaidee, I was sharing you with everyone else who did. When I call you

Makaiden, then you're mine alone." He brushed a light kiss over her forehead. "But I know you don't like it—"

"Actually, I like it too much. I like *you* too much, Devin Guthrie." She made a fist with one hand and rapped him on the chest before pushing away—as far as his arm around her waist let her. "I'm sorry. I'm not usually like this." She swiped at the wetness on her face. "This has been the best and the worst couple of days in my life. I feel like, I don't know, I'm in free fall. Plummeting into a gravity—"

She stopped, her own words suddenly blazing in her mind.

Plummeting into a gravity well.

Gravity.

She looked down at her boots and Devin's—what she could see of them in the glow of the handbeam. She stamped her foot, hearing the thud, feeling the thud. She couldn't believe her own stupidity. How could she not have realized?

"Makaiden?" Devin was frowning.

"Gravity. *Gravity,* Dev."

"What about it?"

"Ship's artificial gravity is working." She couldn't keep the excitement out of her voice. "It's *still* working."

"Why . . . ?"

"Artificial gravity should have gone off with the sublights when the primaries crashed. It's *supposed* to go off. But it didn't. That means—"

He stepped back, grasping her shoulders hard. "There's power. We have a power program functioning normally outside the parameters of the lockout."

"Can you use that to reinstall the primaries?"

"Hell's fat ass, yes!" He yanked her back to him, his mouth covering hers in a kiss of joy and passion.

She clung to him, knowing they were wasting time but not wanting to let him go. It was just a few extravagant seconds. A celebration. A reaffirmation.

If he got the primaries reinstalled, they might make it to the *Prosperity,* to GGS, to the Guthrie estate on Sylvadae. She was sending him back to Tavia.

Hell. She'd deal with that crisis when she had to.

19

If this works, Devin mused, carefully overlaying his code strings onto the *Rider's* main-system databoxes via the Rada's display, *I may have a new career. Just in case when I get home J.M. decides to fire my ass for running off after Trippy without permission.*

Neither he nor Makaiden could figure out why artificial gravity had remained on after the systems lockout. An Imperial oversight? Or maybe the horror stories about tampering with a ship's ident programs were just that: horror stories. But whoever created the trap code to snare Devin's attempts to enter into the sealed unit software didn't figure in the firmware—or that Devin's Rada was sensitive enough to notice the firmware didn't go down under lockout when the software did.

Though enough had gone wrong—definitely. But the artificial-gravity system remaining functional left a huge pathway for entry through a firmware link with his Rada or even the DRECU. It was a primary system. And it was operating. That meant the primaries weren't in a true lockout. Just . . . sleeping.

All he had to do was wake them up.

Carefully.

He glanced over at Makaiden, who sat with legs crossed, elbow on the chair's arm, and chin resting against her fist. She was mostly silhouette in the bridge's lack of lighting. But his memory filled in what his eyes couldn't, and his mouth still tasted their kiss. Makaiden. *His* Kaidee.

And if he was wrong about this program and the back door he'd found through the firmware, he could be condemning her—condemning all of them—to death.

"Okay." He blew out a hard sigh through tense lips. "This is it. Systems should come back on in their usual order, but I can't guarantee it."

"We need enviro, sublights, and shields," Makaiden said. "Anything else is a blessing. Trip?" She leaned to her left, looking past Devin. "The ship may kick when sublights come on. Make sure you're braced and Barty's secure."

"Got it," his nephew said, a slight tone of nervousness in his voice.

Devin understood. He tugged on his safety strap, checking the clasp. "Here we go." He dragged the last databox across the display and sent the initialization command.

The display flickered. Screens on the communications console in front of him winked on, then went out. A loud humming noise started, stopped—and Makaiden swore out loud. "Damn it, no. No!"

"Wait!" Teeth gritted in frustration, Devin held up his left hand, his right hand dragging databoxes, rearranging bits of code. He had it, he almost had it. He had to remember that this was a ship, not a banking facility. Files were more than files—they were almost living instructions, constantly communicating with one another, with the ship. With other ships. With maintenance bots. With—

"Okay. One more time . . ."

He held his breath.

Console screens flickered on, off . . . on. On. Stayed on. A distant humming grew to a rumble beneath his boots. Makaiden let out a whoop as overhead lights winked on. Warm, fresh-smelling air wafted across his face.

"We're on, system is on!" Makaiden had pushed the smaller armrest screen to one side and was working with both hands on the main screens in front of her.

Devin let out the breath he'd been holding. His heart started beating again. He watched Makaiden work her ship.

"Shields are restructuring. We're at sixty-five percent. Sublights are half power, but everything looks good. Damned good. Retracting all blast doors now. Sick bay should be fully operational in about two minutes." She glanced over her shoulder at Devin. "You and Trip get Barty down there, get him on the emergency med system. If nothing else, he'll be stable until we reach Lufty's. They have a full med-unit there."

Devin had already unlatched his straps and was standing. "Lift works?"

She glanced at her screens, then back at him. "Yep."

He motioned to Trip. "We can use the blanket as a stretcher."

"Intraship's up," Makaiden said. "Any problems, call me. I'll be right down."

"Don't touch the Rada. I have it running as a mirror in case we hit any more glitches." He held her gaze for one more long self-indulgent moment, then hurried to help Trip with the unconscious Barty.

Corridor lights flickered on around them as they trundled Barty into the lift. When they hit Deck 2 and exited, there was more humming and thrumming, systems cycling up to full power. The air on this level smelled slightly stale, but his fears that sick bay might be sluggish were unfounded.

He was surprised by Trip's sure-handedness with sick bay's instrumentation.

"I found a couple equipment manuals, read them," his nephew admitted as they watched Barty's medical readings level out. "Uncle Philip always said a good officer knows more than just which chair his ass belongs in."

Devin snorted. That was Philip, verbatim.

"Barty's stable," Trip continued. "This"—he pointed to a databox in the upper right of the wall screen—"is monitoring the infection levels in his lungs. Anything over three-fifty is considered serious."

"Four eighty-five," Devin read out loud.

"The unit will keep him unconscious until he's back down to around three hundred or so. He uses less air when he sleeps. There's less irritation in his lungs."

Devin arched an eyebrow. "Sure you don't want to pursue medical school?"

"Starship captain, ultimately. But I'd take patrol-ship captain, like Aunt Chaz."

Devin clasped him on the shoulder. "Let's get home first. Then maybe I can try talking to your father about letting you take additional courses at—"

"Devin?" Makaiden's voice, sounding worried, came through the intraship speaker in sick bay. "I need you on the bridge. Now."

Devin's gut clenched as he jabbed at the speaker button. "On my way." He turned to Trip. "Stay with Barty. Make sure he's secure. Sounds like we have trouble."

He knew the minute he hit the bridge and saw the pulsing icon on the *Rider*'s scanner display that they indeed had trouble.

"Who is it?" He slid into the seat at the comm console in front of the Rada, then angled around toward her.

Makaiden glanced over her shoulder. "Fleet. At least, I'm ninety percent sure, based on scanner data. They're close enough now—about two hours out— that I can fill in the gaps. That means they can too. They just started probing us again about three minutes ago. I don't have a confirmed ident on them yet, but they're either Fleet or a merc group running an old Fleet ship. Either way," and she waved one hand toward the corridor, "you need to change clothes."

That last bit wasn't what he expected to hear. "Change clothes? To what?"

"There's a tan blanket on my bed and scissors in the galley. Bring both. I need to turn you into a monk. Brother Balatharis is listed as church administrator and ship's liaison in our docs, and whoever is out there will want to talk to him."

Devin stared at her. No. She couldn't possibly want him to . . . "Balatharis?"

"You did more than get us up and running. You altered ship's ID. We're the *Veil of Relief*, in service to the Englarian Church. Unless you tell me Barty's awake and talking, you're the only chance we have to convince whoever it is out there that we're not who they're looking for. And that they need to go away and leave us alone. The last thing we need is someone following us to Lufty's."

Devin had several fantasies that involved Makaiden taking off his clothes—though she'd removed only his sweater, not his thermal undershirt. None of those fantasies included her draping an old blanket around him and turning him into a monk.

Monks were celibate, weren't they?

Neither celibacy nor Englarianism was in his plans, but it looked as if there wasn't a damned thing he could do about the latter. Barty was ill and unconscious. Someone had to play Brother Balatharis. That someone, much to his consternation, was Devin.

He stared at the info vid on Trip's bookpad as Makaiden snipped and tucked and adjusted the blanket robe. It was a news interview with two Englarian monks that Trip had been required to watch as part of his comparative-religions class at the university. The class lasted an entire semester.

Devin had never taken comparative religions. He now had about ten minutes to absorb enough to convincingly impersonate a soft-spoken holy man who believed in a mystical connection between the stars and an elderly fanatic named Abbot Eng.

"Praise the stars." Trip paused the vid. "They say that all the time. And *Blessings of the hour.*"

Makaiden was tucking the blanket's edge into the collar of his thermal shirt, her fingers brushing his neck and shoulders. He fought the urge to press his mouth against her palm, then nibble his way up her arm. He knew it was partly from relief that they weren't going to die—at least, not from the primaries going into full lockout.

But partly he just wanted to nibble his way up her arm before she disappeared from his life again and he lost the chance.

"And sometimes," Makaiden was saying, "it's *Praise the stars in the abbot's holy name.*"

"They meditate a lot," Trip said, starting the vid

again. "Listen to how the monk answers the question about an incident on a starcruiser."

Devin listened, ignoring the question, focusing on the answer and the monk's totally innocent demeanor, which, yes, made him itch with its overwhelming placidity.

"I was deep in meditation at that point," the man said, his voice soft and melodic. "I regret I can offer no information as to what transpired on the ship. But I will pray for guidance on the matter from our revered abbot."

It was almost word for word what he knew he'd probably be saying if their pursuers wanted to question him. He had a sinking feeling, though, that it would only invite more questions. He needed to have answers for when it did. "What if they want to know our mission? Barty set it up that we're in service to the Order of Devoted Missionaries on Calfedar. How do I justify that we're on a course to Lufty's?"

"We don't tell them we're headed for Lufty's. As far as they're concerned, we're on a course to Port Chalo, which is a veritable den of iniquity." A half smile tugged at the corners of Makaiden's mouth. "Wouldn't Brother Balatharis go where there were hundreds of souls in need of saving?"

Devin shook his head. He should have thought of that. He hadn't. That, too, worried him. In financial matters, he was never at a loss for a counterargument. This was decidedly not his area of expertise. "You'd be a lot better at this than I would."

"But Barty didn't set me up as Sister Makerra. I'm Captain Makerra in the docs. And Trip's too young to hold the rank of church liaison."

He knew that. But it didn't make him comfortable

in this role he had to play—no, more than play. There was too much at stake to consider this play.

A pinging noise had her turning away from him. She leaned one hip on her seat, then swung her armrest screen around and studied it. "Shit. They tagged us and pulled our ID." She shoved herself the rest of the way into her seat, tossing the scissors into a cup holder secured to the edge of the console. "Let's hope they don't go poking around too deeply into it."

He stepped to her side. "Do we know who they are yet?"

"Working on it." She was tapping commands back and forth between two different screens. "They'll be in visual comm range in about twenty minutes. We'll know for sure then, but it looks like they're Fleet. Arrow-class destroyer, based on mass and configuration."

Arrow-class meant nothing to him other than *big* and *deadly*—though if Philip was here, he'd be spouting weapons capabilities and maneuvering limitations. Some of his incomprehension must have shown in his eyes.

"It's about twice our size," Makaiden said, "and ten times as deadly."

Twice as deadly was deadly enough. He didn't want to contemplate ten times.

He hiked up the bottom of his blanket robe and headed for communications, taking the seat in front of his Rada again. "Okay, so there are a lot of lost souls out there. I need workable specifics I can toss at them if they demand details."

Trip flopped into the seat next to him and paged through his bookpad. "Give me a few minutes. I think I have an Englarian charity-project analysis from that class."

"Do we have a few minutes?" he asked Makaiden, who had turned in her seat, one arm propped on the back of her chair.

"Keep researching until they contact us. Even then, I can stall. They don't know what our shiptime is. I can say you're sleeping, in meditations, whatever works. Just keep in mind there's a limit to how long they'll wait."

She turned back to her console. He stared at the comm screens, willing the incoming-transmit chime not to sound, as he waited for Trip to find the report. *Praise the stars. Blessings of the hour. By the divine guidance of our revered Abbot Eng...* He ran the catchphrases through his mind. His only saving grace, as he saw it, was his excellent memory. But remembering phrases was different from reciting them with the proper and convincing cadence.

"Here." Trip shoved the bookpad at him.

Devin shut out everything else around him, committing to memory every fact that could potentially be useful: names and locations of Englarian temples in Aldan and Baris and their head guardians, locations of educational centers and clinics, sources of charitable funding. He wasn't surprised to see Guthrie Global on the list. Jonathan had mentioned that when they'd discussed the Baris–Agri deal and the role of the Englarian farming cooperatives.

But Devin's job was numbers, not people. He'd never met the representatives from the Church. That was Jonathan's specialty. Now he wished he had. If he'd spent actual time with a few of the monks, he'd have a personality template to call to mind.

He read the rest of the report. "Where's that interview again? I want to watch—"

The incoming-transmit chime pinged.

Shit.

Makaiden swung around. "How much time do you need?"

There was little to be gained by a ten-minute delay. "Let's get it over with."

She nodded. "Trip, I need you off the bridge. It's about time for you to check on Barty anyway."

Devin handed the bookpad to Trip as he passed by, then looked at Makaiden. "Should I be here?"

"Up to you. Like I said, they don't know shiptime. You could logically be up here, compiling reports to send to Calfedar. Or you can wait in my quarters and I could call you on intraship."

And walk down the corridor only to trip on his makeshift robe and fall flat on his face? Sitting seemed safer. "I'm compiling reports to send to Calfedar." He lifted his chin slightly. "Answer them."

"Remember I'm Captain Makerra."

"Captain of the *Veil of Relief*."

She flashed him a tense smile, then tapped the up-raised screen on her armrest. "I'll angle this so they can't see you when I talk to them. Same thing. They won't see me in the background of your camera. But shut down the Rada's display. I don't think they're going to believe someone donated that."

He was already doing so. Then there was a lower-pitched chime as Makaiden opened the comm link from her console. "Makerra of the *Veil of Relief*, in service to the Englarian Order of Devoted Missionaries."

An image flashed on the screen in front of Makaiden. Devin could barely make it out from where he sat—only that it was a gruff-looking human with short hair. Male, he thought, but couldn't be one hundred percent sure.

"Thurman Anibal, captain of the *Nola Tran*, Imperial Fleet, Baris." A man, then, with an equally gruff voice that sounded as if he enjoyed chewing rocks. "I have your ship's docs here, as I'm sure you know, Captain Makerra. Out of Calfedar?"

"We are. Is there a problem, Captain Anibal?"

"I was going to ask you that. We thought we picked you up on long range a few hours ago. Then you disappeared."

"No, sir. We've been on course to Talgarrath the entire time. We did, however, have a power failure in the starboard generator and went cold for about twenty minutes so we could do repairs."

"I see."

Devin wondered if he did. He had no idea of the merits of Makaiden's excuse, no idea if a generator failure would require taking the entire ship offline. He trusted she was pulling the story from an actual experience. Something else that happened when she flew for GGS that he'd never heard about?

"We appreciate Fleet's concern for our safety," Makaiden said, "but we don't anticipate any further problems."

"I see," Anibal said again.

Devin had the feeling Anibal was only half listening, perhaps reviewing ship's docs or getting information from one of his officers. He didn't know if that signaled disinterest or a need for further probing on the Fleet captain's part.

"You have a Church liaison on board?"

Further probing. Damn.

"Brother Balatharis. That should be in our docs."

"You're not Englarian, Captain Makerra?"

"Contract pilot, sir. But my services are a donation through CFTC Outreach."

That made Devin raise his eyebrows. He had no idea if that was true or not and hoped Makaiden wasn't trapping herself in a string of lies.

"Outreach usually assigns Takan pilots."

True, then.

"Yes, sir. I swapped assignments with the pilot because his wife's due to give birth to their first child."

"I see."

Devin saw the man's repetitive comment as a space filler—a way to keep the conversation going without really participating. He had to be receiving information from another of his officers. They'd found some error, some incongruity in the ID Devin had constructed for the *Rider*. Or the upload had skewed something. The fact that he wasn't even aware that the new ID had taken hold surfaced again in his mind. Was there some kind of hidden secondary program, something that would grab any altered program and, instead of destroying it, save it and send it—tagged as a hacking attempt—to the first Fleet ship it found?

It was exactly the kind of security program he would have designed. He'd scanned for something like that, but he might not have been as thorough as he should have been. Damned time constraints—

"Put Brother Balatharis on the comm," Anibal said suddenly.

Devin's gut tightened. *Here we go.*

"If you'll hold for a minute, sir, I'll transfer you to him."

There was a soft double chime, which Devin knew meant voice and vid functions were paused.

Makaiden half-turned in her seat. "Something's up. I don't like it."

Devin nodded. "Too many *I see*s. He's either running a verification program or I screwed up somehow."

"Can you handle it?"

"Promise me you'll let me take you to dinner tonight, fanciest and most romantic location Lufty's or Port Chalo has." The *Prosperity* could wait. In fact, he'd even toyed with the idea of not going back on the ship, of sending Trip and Barty to Sylvadae without him. That would give him time with Makaiden, time to convince her that she belonged with him on Garno.

A short exasperated sigh. "Devin—"

"Promise."

She studied him, emotions flickering through her eyes, which had turned dark, serious. "I promise."

"Then I can handle it."

She swung around, reaching for the armrest's console. "Captain? I have Brother Balatharis for you now."

Devin straightened his shoulders, then relaxed them slightly. That wouldn't do. That was Devin, not Brother Balatharis. He tapped open the comm link and tried his best to look benign, dreamy, and a little befuddled. He wasn't sure how to play monk, but he could definitely play absent-minded professor. He'd had more than a few in his college and postgraduate days. "Blessings of the hour to you and yours. How may I be of assistance?" He saw Anibal clearly for the first time: a leathery-faced man with close-cropped curly hair and eyes narrowed in suspicion. Figures, out of focus, moved behind him, but Devin could see that those figures wore Imperial uniforms.

"Blessings of the hour to you, Brother."

To Devin's surprise, Anibal inclined his head in a gesture of reverence and respect, and his voice was minus some of its gravelly undercurrents.

Oh, shit. A frightening realization hit Devin, more frightening than the fact that the Imperial destroyer could blow them out of the space lanes. Captain Anibal was Englarian.

Devin wasn't.

His mind stuttered. He plastered on a weak smile he remembered Professor Creel's face often wearing and grasped for the dialogue from the Comparative Religions' class vid. "Praise the stars that we are both safe and well. I apologize for not greeting you immediately. I have been deep in meditations. I find my time out here so peaceful." He made an aimless gesture with his left hand to denote *out here,* then lowered it quickly. He didn't think Englarian monks wore expensive wristwatches, and he'd almost flashed his.

"The abbot be praised your ship wasn't hampered by the power failure."

How much would Brother Balatharis know about the ship's systems? When in doubt, obfuscate. "We're blessed with an excellent captain and crew. Surely Abbot Eng watches over those who do his work."

Anibal glanced down, then back up. "Port Chalo, I see. I hope...Please don't take this as a criticism, Brother, but the temple there has not received the attention it should."

If Devin had any doubt that Anibal was Englarian, that dissolved it. The man had been to the temple on Port Chalo. Devin hadn't. He'd never even been inside an Englarian temple. He splayed his hands in what he hoped was an understanding gesture, careful not to reveal his wristwatch. Or his ignorance. "So many projects, so little time."

"Then your reason to be in Port Chalo isn't to restore the temple?"

Was it so bad that it was in need of restoration? And did Anibal mean the physical structure or some problem with staff? The name of the temple guardian came into Devin's mind. "We're always aware of Guardian Whitte's needs and hold him and the temple in prayer daily. My reasons for traveling to Port Chalo, though, are many. And, of course, due to privacy issues, I'm not at liberty to discuss them here."

As he said the last few words, he stiffened. Too much corporate Devin. Too little beneficent Balatharis. Plus, to make matters worse, his damned blanket robe itched.

"Brother Balatharis." Anibal dipped his face again...but with a little less reverence this time? Devin couldn't be sure. "If you'll grant me a minute, I'd like to move this conversation to my office."

Devin did his best to look humble and unperturbed. "As you wish, Captain."

The screen blanked in pause mode. Devin swung to his right to find Makaiden watching him. Good. It saved him the trouble of bellowing her name in abject panic.

"I—"

Her raised hand silenced him. She glanced down at the armrest console she'd pulled against her side, tapped something, then nodded. "Safe. Go ahead."

"I fucked up. Big time. I'm sorry."

"We don't know that—"

"I do. I went into corporate mode. Damn it!" He slammed one hand on his chair's armrest, thoroughly annoyed at his own stupidity.

"We don't," she repeated, spacing her words, "know that. The guy's a believer. Factor that in. To him, you're part of the woo-woo hierarchy. He's not."

"I don't know a *crigblarg*'s ass about his religion!"

"It doesn't matter. Just keep assuring him you'll pray for him. Praise whatever he says. Tell him he's divinely inspired. In short, lover, kiss ass."

Lover. She called him lover. That brought heat to his face and a tightening to his groin. Bad timing. Monks were celibate.

The comm link chimed.

"He's back on," Makaiden said. "You feel you need out, take off your glasses. I can manufacture a fritzed comm signal. That could buy us a few minutes to regroup."

Dear God, woman, how have I lived without you for all these years? The words he wanted to say caught in his throat. There was no time. He held her gaze for one long moment, then turned to the comm console and keyed the link live.

"Captain Anibal, blessings."

"Brother Balatharis. Pardon the disruption. But we need to continue this conversation in secure surroundings."

Secure evidently meant the captain's office, judging from the little Devin could see behind Anibal. He wondered whether *secure* also meant the short downtime was enough to upload some kind of probe through the comm link. Or upload confirmation that there was no Brother Balatharis.

Devin tossed his fears and insecurities out the airlock. Makaiden had faith in him. She'd said so. "All our intentions are known by our beloved abbot. The only security we need is that of his divine care. What is it that troubles you, my friend?"

Anibal went silent, but his gaze didn't waver.

I've overplayed it. Ethan was always the one with the talent for the stage. Not me.

"A great number of things about our meeting trouble me," Anibal said finally. "Your being here, heading for Port Chalo. Your ship malfunctioning just long enough for us to find you. I've been in the lanes too long to be a believer in coincidence."

Devin was aware of Makaiden shifting in her seat—the slight rustle of fabric against plastic and metal. He was also aware of his fingers clenching, wanting to reach for his glasses. But a two-minute communications glitch wasn't going to save them if Anibal had penetrated their farce.

There was nothing for him to say. He waited, fingers knotted.

"I have my duties as a Fleet officer," Anibal continued. "It's not often they coincide with my personal beliefs. But here, they have. Brother Balatharis, this area of Baris is known for pirate traffic. You've already experienced mechanical failure. I'd be remiss in my duties, not only as an officer but as a believer, if I didn't see you and your ship safely to Port Chalo. If you'll have your captain contact my exec, we'll set up a course so we can escort you to safe harbor. We'll keep your ship constantly on our screens. The slightest whisper of trouble, and we will act swiftly."

Devin sat, stunned. And not totally convinced. It could all be an elaborate ruse. Anibal could be the consummate actor. Having a Fleet ship tail them to Lufty's...

No. Shit. *Shit!* A Fleet ship tailing them meant there was no way they could go to Lufty's. He had to dissuade Anibal. Now.

"Your words are a true blessing to my ears, Captain. But greater duties await you, I'm sure. The blessed abbot watches over all of us, and while I agree this meeting was not by chance but by divine inspiration, I also know...more than that, I *feel* in my heart you're meant for much greater missions than to escort this lowly and humble ship."

Anibal lowered his mouth to his fisted hands, then looked up. "Brother, at the risk of sounding too bold, I have to disagree. This is why I needed to speak to you privately. My officers know this is a dangerous area. They'll accept my decision to escort you. But truth is, I have been . . . remiss. I've fallen from the blessed and beloved path this past year, and I *must* do this. I believe our meeting is a sign. A sign to bring me home again. As you said, our meeting was not by chance. This was divine inspiration and divine intervention." He straightened. "I'll give my exec the order to coordinate with your captain. Then I feel a great need to retire to prayer."

Devin bowed his head. Hell's unholy fat ass. Makaiden was going to kill him. If Captain Anibal didn't do so first.

There was no way they could go to Lufty's.

Captain Anibal wasn't protecting them. He was delivering them to the enemy. Devin had no doubt either Tage's agents or Orvis's operatives were waiting for the *Void Rider* in Port Chalo.

And it didn't escape him that Anibal might know exactly that.

20

"Maybe the Farosians will attack Starport Six and they'll be called away." Makaiden had pulled her right leg up underneath her in the pilot's chair. Now and then her left boot heel thumped softly against the chair's base. "Barring that, I'd say we're stuck with them until we're picked up by Talgarrath Traffic Control."

"Makaiden, I'm sorry." Elbows on his knees, Devin sat hunched over at the comm console, his monk's robe an untidy lump on the decking by his boots. The heavy fabric no longer tortured him. His handling of Anibal continued to. "Anibal blindsided me with that escort offer. I'm a better negotiator than that. But I've never had to pretend to be someone else in negotiations. I lost focus and dragged us into further problems."

"Not necessarily. We do legitimately read as the *Veil of Relief*. Tage's people, if they're there, will be looking for the *Rider* or a ship with Guthrie ownership docs. Same for Orvis or whoever else has pulled ship's records from Dock Five by now. We'll be coming in as an Englarian mission ship with a Fleet escort. A bit more fanfare than I'd like, but at least nothing about us screams *owned by a Guthrie*."

He'd considered that. But there was a downside. "Unless Anibal knows exactly who we are and this is just a ploy to deliver us to Tage without raising any alarms."

"Fleet's too regimented to run that kind of stunt."

"The Fleet that my brother Philip knew, yes. But things have changed. I don't even remember Philip mentioning a Thurman Anibal. For all we know, he's an ImpSec operative." Devin wished Barty was conscious. Barty would know, if not who Anibal was, at least if this was the kind of game Tage's people would play.

"And you're a Guthrie. Whatever Tage's motives are behind tracking your nephew and maybe even engineering a fake kidnapping, he still has to deal with that fact."

"It didn't stop him from trying to kill Philip."

Makaiden went silent, elbow on her armrest, mouth leaned against her fist. Then: "We have three hours before we hit the beacon and are picked up by Talgarrath Traffic Control. Assuming we're not being led into an ambush, that give us three hours to work out some options. Including the shortest, quickest, and safest way to get you, Trip, and Barty transferred to the *Prosperity* once we get there."

He considered waiting to tell her, springing it on her at the last moment, and probably would have done so if Barty hadn't been ill. But Barty was, and that bespoke additional—and likely somewhat complex—planning. His selfish desire to give her as little time as possible to say no collapsed under the weight of the responsibility of the lives of Barty and Trip. "I'm not going back to Sylvadae on the *Prosperity*."

She frowned, then slowly arched that one asymmetrical eyebrow. "You think J.M.'s going to have you shot on sight?"

She'd heard his and Barty's recounting of the confrontation in his father's library. He gave her a wistful smile. "He'll have a few choice words." *Though maybe not before breakfast.* "But I think you and I should go to Tal Verdis."

The frown was back. She shrugged. "You own this ship. But unless Tage has changed his restrictions, I don't have clearance to cross the A–B. I could file for it, sure, but that could take weeks."

He mimicked her shrug. "I'll wait."

"And your family? Your projects?"

"Talgarrath's serviced by TransNet and Zipcomm. GGS has accounts with both. Once the security issues are cleared at the estate, talking to my family from Port Chalo wouldn't be all that different from talking to them from Garno. And my office has dealt with me being off-planet many times."

Her eyes narrowed slightly. "It's not like you to dodge your responsibilities."

"I'm not dodging my responsibilities. I'm trying to keep you in my life."

"Devin—"

"We *have* something, Makaiden." He had to make her understand this, now. He feared there wouldn't be time later. "Something that's been building for years. Something I've wanted for a long time. I've spent too much of my life doing what others expected of me, rationalizing that it was my job to handle those responsibilities that Jonathan was too busy to do, that Philip wasn't around to do, and that Ethan didn't want to do. So I did them, and to a great extent I'll probably always do them. Just like I will make sure Trip and Barty are safely on their way home.

"But this chance to have you in my life, it's my one great rebellion. It's my making a choice because you are what I want. I don't walk away from my responsibilities. But I'm tired of walking away from my dreams."

Her lips parted as if to say something, but then she closed them and, with a small shake of her head, looked away.

"You don't believe me."

She turned back, her expression softening. "No, idiot that I am, I do. It's just that . . ." And she stopped.

He heard a slight quavering in her voice. It was all he needed to shove himself out of his chair and cross the short distance to where she sat at the front of the bridge, arms now crossed defensively over her chest.

He touched her shoulder, then cupped her face with his hand before she could pull back. "You're not an idiot. I could never fall in love with an idiot."

Something flashed in her eyes, then she sighed. Confusion? Frustration? Capitulation? He couldn't tell.

"I can't . . . deal with this right now, Devin. I have an Imperial destroyer an hour behind me and closing, Talgarrath two and a half hours in front of me, and no idea what's waiting for us when we get dirtside. *If* we get dirtside."

He leaned down and brushed her mouth with a kiss—a kiss he was encouraged to note she responded to without hesitation. Then the kiss deepened and— praise the stars!—it was her choice to do so. She leaned up into him, one arm curling around his neck. A rush of heat shot through him. He grasped her shoulders tightly, then ran his fingers up her neck and into the silk of her hair. He wanted nothing more than to drag her into his arms and down the corridor into her quarters. He wanted her naked in bed, the feel of her heated skin on his, the scent of her in his nose, the sweet taste of her in his mouth.

But what he wanted would have to wait. There was

an Imperial destroyer loaded with weapons an hour behind them.

Still, there was no way he was going to be the one to break that kiss.

She pulled back with a reluctance that matched his own.

He cleared his throat and ignored how his body wanted her straddling him in that pilot's chair. Another fantasy for another time. "I'm going to check on Barty and Trip, make sure Trip gets something to eat. We've missed a few meals. Then I'll bring back some soup or casserole for us, and we'll take our problems, and our options, one by one." He tapped her chin lightly with his index finger. "Don't mistake this for our promised meal. I intend to have that romantic dinner with you, Makaiden. And I want to dance with you again."

Kaidee waited until she heard Devin's boot steps fade and the lift doors close before slumping in her chair, her head thumping against the seat back. GGS was known for its single-minded persistence in pursuit of success. Now she knew where that came from.

Her defenses were down, her concentration fractured because of the seriousness of their situation. And here he was, closing in. Literally. It was a brilliant strategy. With all that had happened—their mad escape from Dock Five, Barty's illness, her ship's malfunctions, their damned dancing lessons—she barely had time to catch her breath.

Then Devin would kiss her, leaving her even more breathless.

Damn him.

She straightened, shoving all that away, and pulled

up her data on the spaceport at Port Chalo. It looked like she was going back to the one place she never wanted to see again.

The place where Kiler died.

The aroma of melted cheese wafting in from the corridor—and the sound of familiar boot steps—made her pull her concentration from the data on her screens and turn. No surprise: Devin with a tray.

"Barty's infection is receding, but the med-unit's unhappy with his continued collapses." He put the tray on an empty chair at navigation, then handed her a mug of soup. "Trip negotiated with it"—Devin's mouth twisted in a wry smile—"and it will begin bringing Barty back to full consciousness once we hook up with Talgarrath's controllers. He should be mobile by the time we reach the spaceport."

She swallowed her mouthful of soup, suddenly aware of how hungry she was. She'd missed lunch, and the apple slices she had for breakfast were a faint memory. "I'm fairly sure we'll be directed to the general aviation terminal there, but, other than that, I have no idea where they'll hangar us. Probably not with the luxury yachts. It could be quite a hike for us to find the *Prosperity*. Will Barty be up to that?"

"Couldn't you send a message to their comm? Find out where they are?"

"This isn't a GGS ship. The *Prosperity* won't automatically recognize our signal. We'd have to go through the general port comm links, which leaves a record, and I don't want to risk someone tracing our message. It would be easier and safer, once we get dirtside, if you use your Rada or Trip's pocket comm to reach Ethan on board."

"He won't be on board."

"Ethan's not meeting you?" This surprised her.

Devin was shaking his head. "He gave no indication he would be, no. And with all that's going on at home, I doubt he'd leave. You read his last message. He has his hands full."

She had and remembered that the estate's security was compromised. That, coupled with the bombing of Devin's office, would require Ethan's presence at GGS—not chasing through Baris after his nineteen-year-old nephew, who already had one uncle and one longtime family employee as escorts.

Ethan didn't know about Fuzz-face. Or Orvis. But she did, and until she got Trip, Barty, and Devin to the *Prosperity* and under the care of GGS staff, she wasn't sure she could guarantee their safety. "We can't discount that someone might be watching the ship. We're going to have to literally cruise the hangars to find her."

"She might be locked. Whoever's been sent with the *Prosperity* will probably be waiting at the passenger terminal. You know I was never able to update Ethan that we were coming in on the *Rider*."

"They'll have to come back to the *Prosperity* eventually. Once we know where the ship is, we gain access, then use ship's comm to reach the pilot. Unless your father gave orders to lock you out and changed all GGS ship codes, the security program will recognize you. Which is why you should be going back on the *Prosperity*," she added softly. "You're needed at home, Devin."

Another firm shake of his head. "If I'm needed anywhere, it's on Garno—a good reason you should take me there. As far as my family and the estate, Jonathan and Ethan are on site. So's Marguerite." He cocked his head slightly, as if some thought amused him. "Sometimes I think she's smarter than Jonathan. And they have Petra Frederick and her people. They can do without me for a few weeks. And," he said, as she started to launch her counterargument, "the *Prosperity*'s security program will definitely recognize Trip."

"What if Frederick is part of the problem?" It was a stretch for Kaidee to believe Petra Frederick would turn against the Guthries, but the possibility had been raised before, and she had to make Devin see why he had to leave.

"Then my returning to Sylvadae would leave no one outside their trap. If Frederick is working with Tage in trying to flush Philip out, or if my father has truly gone over the edge, the one place I don't need to be is in their grasp."

He was right, damn his logic. But his logic and the whole discussion about the *Prosperity* might be useless. "We have to get out of Anibal's grasp first. We're assuming he is who he says he is and that his sole purpose in escorting us is that he's looking to find religion again. None of that may be true. We need to work out options if there's an unwelcome welcoming committee waiting for us ahead."

He turned his soup mug in his hands. "Tell me what this ship can and cannot do if there is an ambush."

"We can't make a run for it and we can't shoot back. Especially against an Imperial welcoming committee. Our best bet would be negotiations once they take us into custody. The biggest thing against us will be the ship's altered ID. I've been giving that some thought. I think—and hear me out—that laying the blame for that on me is our best option."

"I'm not going to let—"

"You are, and here's why. I can prove that Orvis has

been after me. From what Barty says, Fleet has no more love for Orvis than I do. That gives us a common enemy. We go with the story—which isn't that far from the truth—that I ran into you on Dock Five, convinced you to buy my ship to help me get away from Orvis. In exchange, I got you to your meet point with the *Prosperity*. But because of the way the sales transaction was handled, I got paranoid that Orvis would find us. So I changed ship's ID. This leaves you, Trip, and Barty out of that whole mess."

"Other than impersonating an Englarian cleric?"

"I forced you to do that. I didn't believe the ship tailing us was Fleet. I convinced you we had to play this game or we'd all die."

"How about you bribed me with sexual favors?" His mouth was twitching.

She knew he was using humor to undermine her argument. "If that's what it takes to keep you, Barty, and Trip safe, fine. Tell them whatever you want."

The hint of a smile faded. "I'm not letting you take the blame."

"Yes, you are, and for the same reason you told me it's unwise for you to go back to Port Palmero: that leaves no one on the outside to go for help." She straightened, the look of surprise on his face supremely satisfying. She'd used his own argument against him.

"They could still decide to lock up the whole lot of us."

"But you can always roll over and offer evidence against me. Cut a deal. Use those negotiation skills you brag about."

He slid his soup mug onto the console's ledge, then folded his arms across his chest. It was a casual movement, but she remembered how to read Devin Guthrie.

When he was calm, that was when there was the most danger.

"Our primary objective," she continued, "is to get Trip to safety. That's what spurred you to leave Port Palmero. That's what prompted me to chase after him on Dock Five. Almost everything that's happened somehow relates to him: from Halsey's death to Fuzz-face Munton. Orvis even picked up the scent and tried to get in the game.

"If we have some Fleet ships waiting out there, I'm going to guess they've been told to stop us but not why. We're going to have to employ diversionary tactics. Make them think this whole thing is over ident tampering. Get them to let you, Trip, and Barty go. Then, when you get home, if you want to throw a couple of high-priced barristers over to Starport Six or wherever they're holding me to defend me, I won't complain." She gave him the same quirked smile he'd offered her earlier. Then she leaned back in her chair, reached for her casserole, and ignored him while she stirred the cheese and chunks of vegetables. It smelled delightfully spicy. Trip had evidently been playing chef again.

She took a bite, savoring it. It could well be her last meal in freedom.

By the time the soup and casserole were gone, she and Devin had debated the pros and cons of a few other scenarios. Trip showed up, took the seat at nav with one leg flung over the armrest, and added a few ideas. Finally all three of them agreed that no one scenario held all the answers. There was too much they didn't know—mainly, were more Imperial ships waiting for them at the Talgarrath beacon?

They were getting close to finding out. Trip went back down to Deck 2 to finish reading another of Kaidee's flight instruction manuals while he waited for Barty to regain consciousness.

"He's growing up," Devin commented after Trip left, a mixture of pride and wistfulness in his voice. "The past week may subdue his adventurous streak for a while, but it's also shown him what he's capable of. Jonathan's not getting back the same son."

"That's not a totally bad thing."

A series of tones had Kaidee turning. "Traffic's picking up." She tapped long-range scan to see what data she could get on the newest blip on her screen. Five minutes ago there were three ships on a similar vector for Talgarrath. Now there were four. Normally that wouldn't concern her. But things weren't normal, so everything concerned her.

Devin left his chair to lean on the back of her seat. "Another freighter?"

"Don't know yet." The fact that the other three *were* freighters didn't stop her from keeping tabs on them. They could still be trouble.

Some workable data came a few minutes later. "Commercial spaceliner," she told him, pointing to the other ship's ident. "Compass."

"Could be the flight we were supposed to be on."

"Having Ethan's people waiting at the Compass terminal might even work in our favor. Especially if they're in GGS uniform. Anyone watching for you or Trip would follow them." Chimes sounded behind her. The readout on her armrest screen upped her pulse rate a notch. "Speaking of uniforms, grab your robe, Brother. Captain Anibal is requesting an audience."

"Shit." Devin's comment was low, but she heard it. The rustle of fabric behind her and another low but muffled epithet told her he was pulling the heavy blanket over his head. She angled the pilot's chair so her comm screen wouldn't show Devin's image, then she opened the link.

"Makerra, captain of the *Veil of Relief*."

Anibal's image smiled at her. From the lack of movement behind him, she guessed he was in his office. She offered him a bland smile in return, very aware that bared teeth could also bite.

"Blessings of the hour," he said. "Is Brother Balatharis available?"

"I'll be glad to check for you, Captain. A moment, please." She froze the vid screen and muted the audio functions, then turned. "Ready?" she asked Devin, who was looking rumpled and grumpy at the comm console.

"What do you think he wants?"

"If we're lucky, a personal blessing from the divinely inspired Brother Balatharis before he hands us off to Talgarrath."

"I'm not going to let you take the blame for this, Makaiden."

"I have faith that your devious mind and incomparable eloquence will have my ass out of the brig in no time."

His lips thinned. She knew he wanted to argue. She also knew he knew this wasn't the time to do so.

He closed his eyes and, even over the low thrumming of the sublights and the constant hum of the bridge consoles, she heard him draw in a long breath. His shoulders relaxed and, when he looked up at her again, the tension and grumpiness were absent from his face. He'd put on more than the robe. He'd put on Brother Balatharis.

"Good job," she said softly.

"Don't distract me, love." He swiveled the chair toward the comm console and tapped the screen. "Praise the abbot's holy name this fine hour, Captain Anibal. How may I be of assistance?"

Kaidee kept half her attention on Devin's conversation with Thurman Anibal and half on her short-range-scanner screens. This close to Talgarrath, long range was of little use. Plus it was Anibal she was concerned about, not something five hours away. If he was going to make a move—if he knew the *Veil* was really the *Rider*—then it was going to come very soon and, she knew, happen very quickly. It could be anything from the *Nola Tran* lobbing some torpedoes her way to a phalanx of Imperial patrol cruisers suddenly on the *Rider*'s vector, with weapons ports hot.

It could also come with threats and ultimatums. That was the only thing they could, honestly, handle. And it would be up to Devin to do so.

At the moment, the conversation was about Guardian Whitte, head of the temple at Port Chalo. Kaidee couldn't tell if Anibal was sincerely concerned with the temple or if this was a test, a trap to make Devin reveal his ignorance—and his true identity.

"The Port Chalo temple is one of many blessed locations in Baris that we have slated for improvements," Devin said, his voice mild, betraying none of the nervousness Kaidee felt and was guessing he did also. "Without my notes in front of me—and unfortunately I have just stowed them away—I'm unable to go into specifics discussed and prayed over with Guardian Whitte. But I assure you, every issue is taken into prayer for guidance for the continued good of all."

"So are you saying, Brother, you're not aware there

was no Peyhar's celebration this year due to an air-filtration breakdown?"

"Now that you mention it, the problem does sound familiar. But..." Devin reached up to rub the bridge of his nose under his glasses and, for a moment, Kaidee thought he was signaling for a comm cutoff. Her fingers hovered over her screen, but his glasses stayed on. He cleared his throat. "My apologies, Captain. I'm coming off a somewhat debilitating illness, and even with my healing time in meditation during this journey, my memory is not what it should be."

"I see. Well, that would explain why you wouldn't be that familiar with Guardian Whitte's problems."

Kaidee didn't like the sound of that. But if Anibal knew who they were, or even suspected they weren't an Englarian mission ship, why was he toying with them?

Short range flashed. Two more ships. She quickly tagged them, running their data through the *Rider*'s system, looking for idents. A friendly freighter out of Dock Five would be nice—except, no, it wouldn't be. She wasn't the *Rider* right now. They wouldn't know her. They wouldn't come to her aid.

Devin was still calmly and politely dancing around Anibal's questions about Whitte and the temple, praising stars and noting blessings left and right.

This was going on far too long for her liking. She checked short range again. Null idents, both. Shit. That could mean Fleet. It could also mean pirate, but what kind of slag-headed pirate would approach knowing a Fleet ship was in short range?

Unless the Fleet ship wasn't a Fleet ship. Or unless the pirates weren't pirates but Fleet. Or unless—

"Brother Balatharis, please excuse me." Anibal's

voice suddenly took on a hard tone. "I have a pressing matter I must attend to."

The comm link chimed again. Link broken, transmit ended.

Kaidee spun her chair around. "We got two good-size bogeys coming in short range on our starboard axis."

Devin straightened. "Fleet?"

"Unknown."

"What else could they be?"

"Pirates, mercenaries. Farosians. Hell, Stol could be invading Baris."

"Is that Anibal's 'pressing matter'?"

"I'd say that's a strong possibility. But I don't know if it's because they're friends or enemies."

Devin raised his chin, peering toward the screens on the pilot's console. "How far are they from us?"

"Forty-three minutes, and, yes, if that's Fleet, they can close that gap fast." She swung back to her console. "I don't want it to look like we're trying to escape," she said over her shoulder. "But I'm pushing the sublights to max. We can't outrun them. But maybe, somehow, we can outthink them."

She opened intraship. "Trip, we may have company coming. I'm going to take ship nonessential functions down to half power to give the sublights and shields more boost, but I won't pull from sick bay. Make sure Barty's secure. If he wakes, fill him in."

"Yes, ma'am, Captain," came the reply. "If you need me—"

"I'll holler. Right now I want you with Barty in case he wakes. Captain out." The sublights' thrumming increased through the decking. Overheads dimmed.

"Can we make it to Lufty's?" Devin asked.

She glanced at him. He had one arm pulled out of

the robe and was about to yank it over his head. "Keep that on. Anibal may contact us again, especially if those are mutual unfriendlies."

He lowered his arm, tugging the robe back on.

"As for Lufty's," she continued after a quick check—so far so good—on ship's status and location, "wish we could. We can't. We're closer to Port Chalo. Like it or not"—and she didn't—"that's where we're going."

"What do you need me to do?"

"Sit comm. Anibal may contact us. When Talgarrath Traffic does, I'll handle it. Keep in mind we're an Englarian ship. I've never done Church work, but I have friends on Dock Five who have. Traffic may or may not want to talk to you too."

"And if Anibal asks questions?"

"You tell him whatever works. We have a scheduled meeting with Guardian Whatshisname—"

"Whitte."

"—and can't be late. Or it's been moved up. With those two out there, I don't think he'll be checking transmit trails to see if we've really heard from the temple." Data flashed on the screen on her left. Her skin chilled. "Shit."

"What?"

"Just got a positive on one of our new friends. Null ident, but she's a P-75. That's an Imperial patrol ship."

"It could be routine patrol."

"It could. I'm not going to hang around to find out."

"What's Anibal doing?"

She tapped her console, switching views, bringing up the newest data. "Looks like . . . yes. Changing course to meet them."

"Away from us? This is good news?"

"Away from us, yes. Good news? Depends on what the other ships do. If *they* change course to intercept us or to cut us off, no. They could be trying to box us in. Remember, this is a freighter. Those are warships. They have speeds I don't." And weapons. Torpedoes were even faster. And deadly.

21

Chimes from the comm console had Kaidee reaching quickly for her armrest screens. "Traffic control," she told him, then opened the link. At this range it was audio only. "Captain Makerra, *Veil of Relief*, in service to the Englarian Order of Devoted Missionaries. Inbound for Port Chalo Spaceport."

"*Veil of Relief*, this is Talgarrath Traffic Control," a man's voice replied, with what sounded like a drawling Dafirian accent. "We're just downloading your docs. We see you're a..." There was a pause. Makaiden's heart thumped in her chest. Had Anibal been in contact with traffic control? Had the false ident skewed?

"You're a Blackfire 225. Is that correct?"

"That's affirmative."

"Sending that data to Port Chalo Ground Control now. They're going to want to know duration of stay for hangar assignment."

Hangar assignment. *Hangar assignment.* Makaiden had never heard two more beautiful words in her life. *Hangar assignment* meant that docs and ident were cleared. "Two to three planetary days," she answered. Actually, she'd depart as soon as Trip, Barty, and Devin were transferred to the *Prosperity*. She did not intend to stick around, in case ship's docs unraveled. But a quick departure wouldn't make sense in their guise as a missionary ship.

"Two to three, *Veil*. Got that. You're cleared to our inner beacon. Stand by at that location for dirtside permissions and hangar assignment. Talgarrath Traffic out."

The comm link signaled with its disconnect chime. Makaiden took one quick check of Anibal's ship and the two newcomers—they weren't yet heading for her—before she pumped her fist in the air with a whoop.

"This is good?" Devin asked, rising as she angled around in her chair toward him.

"They're granting us permission to land. They're assigning us a hangar. Devin, my darlin', this is not only good, this is *damned* good." Relief poured through her. They were going to make it. "You're a slaggin' genius. You ever want to ditch GGS and turn pirate, my friend Pops can find a half dozen ships that'd love to pay you very well for your skills. You found a back door in an Imperial security program that got by both an Imperial ship and traffic control. You have no idea how much that's worth on the black market."

He grabbed her hand and pulled her out of her chair and up against him so quickly that she almost stumbled, but then his arms came around her, steadying her, enveloping her, leaving her no room for escape. His mouth came down hard on hers, and she didn't want escape. She wanted his kisses, his body, his passion. She wanted his clothes—especially the godawful blanket robe—off.

For the second time in the past hour, she pushed from her mind the fact that he was a Guthrie, that he owned her ship, and that he had some high-class woman named Tavia waiting for him. She pushed away every reason why Devin Guthrie was so very wrong for her. She would think of those things later, tomorrow, when he was safe on board the *Prosperity* and she was on her way to Lufty's—with or without the *Rider*.

Right now she lost herself in his kiss, in his lips on hers, in the feel of the hard muscles of his body under her fingers.

A short, quick double ping. Then another.

Shit. *Shit!* She jerked back. "Short-range scanner." She lunged to the console, not bothering with the pilot's chair. She wanted the big screens. She wanted to know what was suddenly going wrong.

Devin's hand rested on her shoulder. "That's the P-75?"

"Changing course along with its friend. Still a null ident, but I've got a configuration on it now. Heavy cruiser, eight-hundred-fifty ton. That's Imperial warship tonnage."

Another chime. Comm link. She shoved herself back in her chair, swung the armrest screen around, and checked the readout. They were five minutes out from the inner beacon. "Port Chalo Ground Control," she told Devin. "Let me see if I can't get us bumped up for immediate clearance before those Imperial ships decide to use us for target practice." She opened the link. "Captain"—she hesitated, almost saying, *Griggs*— "Makerra, *Veil of Relief*. If you have a slot open, we need it. Having a little problem with enviro here."

"*Veil of Relief*, Port Chalo Ground Control," a woman's voice said. "Acknowledging your situation. Give me a few minutes. Stand by."

"Standing by." She ran one hand through her hair in frustration.

Devin grabbed her wrist and planted a soft kiss. "I'm not the only genius here. We'll make it."

She pulled her hand free and went back to her screens. "If we're not cleared, I'm going to head full out for those freighters. Hopefully, Anibal's friends won't start shooting before I get there. Hopefully, if we get there, Anibal's friends will think twice about shooting. Damn it, I hate this," she added. She did. Heading for the freighters could save their lives, but it was putting others—innocent others—at risk.

"Do you know them?" He pointed to the freighters' icons on her screen.

"Not personally. They're showing CFTC affiliation, though. Keep in mind that we aren't right now. But I'm not going to ask them for help or use them for cover. This isn't their problem. I just want to make Anibal hesitate long enough that we can get...I don't know. We're two hours out from Lufty's beacon from here. I don't know if we have that much time. Quickest way to dump off Anibal's screens would be to go dirtside blind, but I've never done that. Sometimes you get lucky, you find an isolated bit of terrain that's not on planetary security grids. Sometimes you're not lucky, and planetary security puts a missile up your ass when you hit heavy air." She was being brutally honest. She had to be.

"You've decided surrender's not an option? I know I can talk—"

"They're not here to talk." She jabbed one finger at the Imperial ship icons. "You don't bring in a P-75 and an eight-hundred-fifty-ton heavy to talk. You bring them in to punch holes in a ship's hull."

Devin straightened. "You have charts for Talgarrath?"

"At nav."

"You keep an eye on those ships." The nav chair squeaked as he dropped into it. "I'll find us that isolated hidey-hole in their security grid."

"Don't put us down in water, Dev. This ship won't float and I can't swim."

"Not to fret, love. We're going dancing tonight. It might be under the stars on a desert island, but this I promise you. We're going dancing."

"I'm going to move us onto the beacon's far side, closer to those freighters." She fired thrusters. "If we get clearance, we're still within range of the port."

"What's Fleet doing?"

"Anibal's still heading for his friends. His friends are still heading for us. Find me that hidey-hole."

"Got two possibilities. But I need to double-check Talgarrath's security-grid specs." He pushed himself out of the chair and headed for the Rada at the comm console.

Kaidee watched as he brought up the holo display. "You have Talgarrath's grid specs?"

He shot her a smile that was both devious and sexy as hell. "Garno has the same system."

"How would you—"

"GGS manufactures some of the components, designed a key bit of software, and provides upgrade support," he said, moving databoxes around quickly. "Have to have schematics for the whole in order to make the parts."

It crossed her mind then that Devin—the Guthries— had access to a lot of Imperial information that the Farosians or, hell, even Stol might want to obtain. She doubted Devin could make the planetary security defensive scanners go down, but apparently he could find holes. Or make them. That might be why Tage—

The comm chimed again. "It's Port Chalo. We're either going dirtside legally or the next few hours are going to test my piloting skills and your devious brain."

"Yes, ma'am, Captain Makerra."

She hesitated for only a second then flashed him a tense smile as a thank-you for the reminder of who she was. "Makerra. *Veil of Relief.*"

"Port Chalo, Captain Makerra. We have you cleared for descent. Transmitting landing coordinates and hangar assignment now."

Kaidee muted the comm quickly, huffed out a whoosh of air, then turned it back on. "Makerra here. Thank you, Port Chalo. Data is in. Thank you."

"We'll pick you up when you hit heavy air, Captain. Enviro malfunctions are serious problems. We're here to help. Port Chalo clear for now."

Kaidee tabbed the link off and snorted. "Serious problems, my ass. They're putting together huge estimates for repairs right now. Port Chalo is the one place you do not want to use to fix your ship." She opened intraship. "Trip, we're cleared for descent. If Barty's awake—"

"I am, thank you," sounded in the background.

"Glad to have you back, Mr. Barthol." She was. Hearing his voice gave her an unexpected emotional boost. "Gentlemen, strap in, please. To quote every jumpjockey I've ever known, descent is hell. It'll be sweaty for a while. This is a freighter, not a passenger liner. Captain out."

"Where are Anibal and friends?" Devin asked as she prepped the ship to go dirtside. He was standing, stripping off the heavy blanket. Good idea.

"Far enough away that we'll be off their screens before they can reach for the firing button. Strap in, lover. I'm trading off pretty for time this trip."

Descent through planetary atmosphere was not pretty. It never was. At best, it made you feel like you were trapped in a can of rocks strapped to a *crigblarg*'s back in the middle of a mating frenzy under a really hot sun. Kaidee had flown Devin to dirtside spaceports on Garno and Sylvadae many times, but the *Rider* wasn't a GGS luxury yacht. The required S-curves to bleed off speed were steeper, and there were no buffers to ease the body, human or otherwise. Gravity toyed with the ship's mass, and Kaidee had to make repeated adjustments to the *Rider*'s extended flaps, stabilizers, elevator, and ailerons. It was never a painless transition as the ship morphed from a deep-space craft to a heavy-air one.

She was more worried about Barty, but he'd refused her offer of sedation, preferring to review on his DRECU the events he'd missed while unconscious.

No one shot at them on descent. No one fired surface-to-air missiles as she brought the *Rider* in on final approach. She didn't know if it was luck or they'd simply arrived before their enemies could react. She didn't care. She'd never been through a more harrowing, exhausting, stressful day, ship or dirtside. She taxied her ship to their assigned hangar off Runway 27R, on the spaceport's perimeter, went through all the required post-flight checklists, and, when still no one had launched a missile at them, threatened them, or challenged their docs—or commed them and asked for a blessing from Brother Balatharis—she let her head drop back onto her seat's headrest and closed her eyes.

"I need a drink."

Devin's strong hands massaged her shoulders. "I've heard that Port Chalo is the city that never sleeps. I'm sure there are plenty of bars open."

"There are." Damn, that felt good. She leaned her head forward, letting his fingers work the knots on the back of her neck. They were the size of asteroids, she was sure. "We need to find the *Prosperity*. The Empire never sleeps either."

The sound of the lift doors opening and closing came from the corridor. That was followed by boot steps. She let out a long sigh and pulled away from Devin's talented hands.

Trip crossed through the hatchlock, followed by Barty. A pale, slower-moving Barty. Kaidee had no idea where the GGS ship was. Even if it was in the next hangar, she didn't know if the man could make it without an AG chair.

He raised one hand as he sank into the chair at the comm console. "I'm better than I look."

"We're not running anywhere in the next ten minutes, so relax," she told him. "We don't know where the *Prosperity* is. Or who's watching her. We need to find that out first."

"Anibal's not ImpSec," Barty said. "I know you were worried about that. I don't know him personally, though he's been a Fleet officer for more than twenty-five years. Bit of an oddball. If he's captain now, it's only because the ranks have thinned."

"He may still be coordinating with a team dirtside," Kaidee pointed out. "Plus I told Port Chalo we have an enviro malfunction—"

"I listened to the logs. Well done."

"—so someone may show up with a repair estimate." She would also eventually have landing, refueling, and other fees to deal with. But she knew that wouldn't happen until the morning, dirtside time. Another advantage of coming in when they did. "I need this ship dark to discourage the curious and money-hungry, but I also need her secure. Barty, no offense, but you're a better shot than a scout right now."

"I agree. No one will get past me."

"Trip, you're young and strong, but you're also the one people keep trying to kidnap. I can't watch you and watch my back. I need you here, with Barty. This ship is a valuable asset. I'm not even going to ask your uncle's permission to tell you this. I'm telling you this. If you're threatened, you shoot to kill. Do you understand? Can you handle that?"

"He does and he can," Devin said before Trip could answer. "Philip trained him, just as he trained me. But Makaiden's right. Out there, you're bait. We don't want bait at this point. We want to know where the *Prosperity* is and make sure she's not under a threat."

"I can handle it, Captain Makaiden." Trip's voice was strong, with a hint of Devin's calmness. And not even a "totally apex" at being given permission to kill. He *had* grown up.

"Good. Now, in most other spaceports, I could request a listing of ships in port. But this is Port Chalo. It's a sanctuary zone, something the Empire has been chipping away at, but some rules are still enforced. That means I have to register to get that list and sign all kinds of waivers and disclaimers, and that's something I can't and don't want to do." Barty was nodding as she spoke. She knew he was well familiar with this, but Devin and Trip weren't. "So Devin and I need to take a walk."

She turned to him. "Dark clothing. Armed. Bring the Rada. Any ID or credit chips, put them deep. Port Chalo is also a pickpocket zone."

He grabbed the Rada from the comm console. "Meet back on the bridge?"

"No, at the main airlock." She pointed toward the corridor. "Five minutes. Barty, keep the DRECU running. Devin synched the Rada to it. That's probably our most secure means of communication as long as we're in range. I know where the luxury yachts are usually parked."

"Concourse A," Barty said.

She nodded. "Overflow at C, but only the last three hangars. We're in D, so we'll check C first. Once we find the *Prosperity*, we'll make sure we can get safe access." She motioned to Trip, then Barty. "Get your gear packed, be ready to move on short notice."

She followed Devin out into the corridor, but where he headed right for the lift and stairs, she went straight to her quarters. Only as she stepped into the main room did her brain suddenly replay what had just transpired on the bridge: Makaiden Malloy Griggs, giving orders like a seasoned drill sergeant.

Where had *that* come from? Then she knew: her father. Nathaniel Milo was a large, affable man, but when it came to ship and crew safety, he cut no corners. She'd been through evacuation drills, boarding drills, fire drills, hull-breach drills . . . She hadn't realized how much had stuck with her.

She also hadn't realized how frightened she was. She'd told Trip Guthrie to kill anyone who threatened him. And she meant it.

She stripped off her gray shipsuit, then tossed it on the bed, trading it for a pair of dark-gray pants and a black thermal shirt. She should feel safer. They were dirtside. The *Prosperity* had to be in one of the nearby hangars. They had the advantage of night. And no one had any way of knowing the *Veil of Relief* was the *Void Rider*.

Right?

There was a black-brimmed cap on the top shelf in her closet. It would work well to cover her hair. She strapped on her utility belt with the handbeam and short-bladed knife, then added her weapons belt with her L7, spare power pack, and pocket comm. ID and credits she secured in her jacket's inside pocket.

She was ready.

No. She ducked into the lav and found her med-kit. There were two painkiller hypos left. She took both, along with some anti-infective patches.

You're overreacting, Kaid. This isn't a slagging war. They don't weigh anything. Shut up.

She dimmed the lights in her bedroom, then in the main room, and stepped out into the corridor.

And almost plowed into Devin.

She stared up at him, startled, her right hand pointing down the corridor. "The airlock's down—"

He pushed her back against the bulkhead, pinning her there as his mouth covered hers with a fierce insistence. His hands tightened on her shoulders. A sudden heat jolted her, and then she was returning his kiss with equal passion, clinging to him as if he was the source of her life. Her hands slid under his jacket. She could feel the pounding of his heart, the rise and fall of his chest. She grabbed a handful of his shirt, wanting him closer even though closer wasn't possible.

He broke the kiss, wrapping his arms around her, pulling her tightly against him as if he knew her need. His lips rested against her forehead. She nuzzled his face, the scent of his skin enveloping her.

"Okay," he said, his voice low and rough. "Now we can go."

She felt his absence acutely when he released her. *Get used to it.*

Kaidee had been raised on ships and stations. It always amused her that dirtsiders thought their night was dark. Dirtside night was dim, shadowed, but it was never really dark. Not like the dark of space or the darkness of a cargo hold in a dead ship. The spaceport was close enough to Port Chalo that the glow from the city lit the sky. Vehicles—land and air—streaked by with headlights, taillights, and strobes. Night here was not dark.

What bothered her more was the wind. There was no wind on a ship, no wind on station. And the wind here carried smells, acrid and burning and oily. It was like Pisstown on Dock Five, except you couldn't go up one level and escape it.

She hunched her shoulders under her jacket and turned up her collar. Tonight the wind was also cold, and it blew relentlessly through the cavernous hangar's wide entrance. She could close the doors. It could provide security, but it could also trap them. So she'd opted to leave them open.

She and Devin stood in the shadows at the edge of the entrance, listening to the *Rider*'s ramp retract and close behind them. There were five other hangar bays here in Concourse D. Two were occupied—she'd done a visual check as she taxied in. But lights were on in neither.

In the distance, past the rest of the hangars, lights glowed in the building that housed General Aviation's fixed base operator's office. But they were dim.

General Aviation—being mostly private passenger craft—was less active at night. Cargo—where the *Rider* normally would have been assigned—never stopped. But their bogus church affiliation and the fact she was carrying passengers got her an assignment that worked out exceedingly well—considering General Aviation was also where the *Prosperity* should be.

"I somehow thought there'd be more hangars for private ships here," Devin said. "More people."

"Cargo—which is on the other side of the spaceport—is triple this size." That was where the *Rider* usually parked when Kiler came for his meetings with the people from Nahteg. "But there's tie-down space for seventy just behind the row of hangars, including fixed-wing aircraft. We were assigned a bay because I said we needed repairs. Most people use Lufty's or Uchenna's. You'll know why when you see the bill."

A small glow pulsed against Devin's hand. If she hadn't been halfway watching for it, she would have missed it. It was his Rada, secure on his belt under his jacket but angled out slightly as they waited for the all-clear signal from Barty on the bridge.

"They're set," Devin said. "Let's go."

She stepped out into the wind, Devin at her side.

"Would be nice if they're hangared next door," Devin murmured.

"This bay next to us is locked—I saw the signal lights on the way in. The one next to that was open and empty." She quickened her steps. "Still is. Right now I'll discount any locked bays. The *Prosperity* has to know you'd be looking to leave quickly."

"I'm not leaving."

She let his comment pass. She wanted to listen. For night, the spaceport was noisy. Machines, land vehicles, whirred in the distance, along with incoming freighters and heavy-air jets. The wind against the hangars' metal walls made its own sound—a whooshing almost like a hyperdrive coming online. All of that covered the sound of their boots against the pebbled asphalt. She hoped it also didn't cover anyone following them from behind. Or attacking from the side.

They checked the first three bays in Concourse C. None held a 220-ton Splendera.

"She's in Concourse A, then," Devin said.

"Unless, figuring you were coming in on a Compass flight, they finagled gate space at the main terminal." The Guthrie name and Guthrie money could do those kinds of things.

Devin turned his face, staring at a gap between the hangars toward the main spaceport in the distance—a long, snaking, brightly lit glass-and-metal structure. "Barty would never make it there. I'm not even sure he'd make it to the end of this row."

"You can't walk there. There are runways and taxiways in between. We'd need to use the monorail. I've got a small antigrav pallet stowed in Cargo Four that could carry him to the station, but we couldn't bring it on board. Canvassing the main terminal could take hours."

They pressed on, staying in the shadows at the edges of the large hangars but other than that walking normally. It was late, but it wasn't unusual to see crew coming and going at all hours. Especially in Port Chalo.

Lights flared suddenly, striping the wide taxiway in front of them. A four-wheeled land vehicle rumbled toward them, its headlights two intense beams spearing the darkness. She tensed, her heart beating rapidly, but Devin kept moving, slowing only long enough to drape his arm over her shoulder, pressing her against his side. "We're on our way to find a decent pub, right, my darling? Keep walking, minding your own business, and they'll mind theirs."

A waist-high power panel jutted out from the side

of the hangar, just short of the next set of bay doors. She wanted to duck behind it, hide, but that was crazy. The darkness provided more-than-decent cover. And crew used this taxiway all the time to get to the monorail.

She tugged the brim of her cap lower, dropping her gaze as the vehicle passed. Relief flooded her as the rumbling faded behind them.

Devin loosened his grasp on her shoulder. "Security?"

"Don't think so." She chanced a quick glance in the direction it had gone. "Someone going to a ship out on the tarmac. Security would have been moving a lot slower." And might have stopped to question them.

Devin dropped his arm from her shoulder, then moved his jacket aside, checking on his Rada. "All quiet," he said, as they crossed the narrow alleyway between the looming buildings. "This is B. Do we bother?"

"The bays here are too small to house a Splendera. It's got to be A."

"Or the main terminal."

"Then we're dealing with the monorail."

"Or we borrow a truck." Devin slowed as they came upon a large, dark boxy shape parked to the left of a locked bay.

"I doubt the owner left it unlocked with its code pack on the console."

He flashed her a grin. "Don't need it. You forget. I'm your resident genius."

She punched his arm playfully, then: "Lights ahead."

The next bay door was open, and as they approached, a whirring and humming grew louder. "Repairbots," she said, slowing.

He urged her on. "I told you. Keep walking, minding your own business."

"And they'll mind theirs. I know. I know." Still, she gritted her teeth.

They stepped into the wide shaft of light spilling from the bay. Repairbots floated up and down the length of a ship half the size of the *Rider*. No one else was in sight.

"BGR-150," she told him.

"Too cramped, don't care for it. Rather have a Blackfire 225."

"You already do."

"Just checking." He took her hand as they darted across the last alleyway leading to Concourse A.

For reasons she couldn't quite pin down, her heart was pounding rapidly now. Part of it was the fear that wouldn't go away of someone coming up behind them, dressed in an Imperial uniform, weapon in hand. But part of it was that finding the *Prosperity*—if they found the *Prosperity*—meant it was all over. Trip would be safe. The ship would head back to Sylvadae, hopefully with Devin on board.

Or not.

She was torn. Ending it now meant never having to deal with Tavia or the disappointment and disapproval she knew she'd see in J.M.'s eyes when Devin tried to bring her into his family gatherings, as she knew he would.

But ending it now meant never seeing him again. He might try, but there were ways to disappear—at least for a while—and she would use them. She needed to get her head on straight, her life back together, her ship's ID reset. Ending it now made sense.

It also hurt.

She wanted to stay with Devin. Like an idiot, she'd

started to fall in love with him, and she wanted that chance to find out if this could turn into real love. It might not. It often didn't. But she wanted that chance.

She pulled her hand out of his, slowing as they reached the first set of hangar-bay doors. Those were locked, but the next ones weren't. As in Concourse B, a soft glow filtered out from the wide opening. More repairbots? Or was someone waiting for someone to return? The land vehicle that so surprised them could have pulled out of here. They'd been too far down the row of hangars at the time to be able to tell, but now she wondered if that's where it came from.

She tugged at Devin's sleeve. He slowed. "That vehicle that passed us ten minutes ago could have left from here." She motioned to the open hangar.

"Crew going out for a drink or coming back in?"

But they were heading away from the monorail, she almost said—but they were at the edge of the open bay. She stopped, ears straining. *Shit!* She heard noises and what might be voices. "Someone's there," she whispered.

"Repairbots or crew." Devin patted her shoulder reassuringly. "We glance in as we walk by, then keep going and check the next one."

"Right." *Get a grip, Kaid. If it's the* Prosperity, *that's good news. If it's not, we keep looking.* Girding herself with false confidence, she pushed past him into the opening. And froze. The large sleek form of a Pan-Galaxus Splendera filled the hangar, its polished white hull gleaming even in the diffuse light from the hangar overheads. A distinctive crest of two intertwined-Gs was clearly visible on its starboard flank. A servobot hovered by the ship's extended ramp, but it wasn't the ship, the familiar crest, or the blinking 'bot that stopped her heart from beating.

It was the dark-haired man on the rampway in GGS blues, arms crossed casually over his chest as he stared up into the *Prosperity*'s airlock.

He didn't see her. But she saw him.

Kiler Griggs. Her ex-husband was alive.

22

Devin recognized the familiar outline of the *Prosperity* emblazoned with the Guthrie crest the minute he stepped up behind Makaiden. Relief flooded him. Here was Trip's ticket back home, to safety. He grabbed Makaiden's arm—she was almost frozen in place, no doubt as surprised at their good luck as he was.

"We found her!"

The look on her face wasn't one of surprise but horror. And she wasn't looking at him.

He followed her gaze to the ship's rampway, where a crewman in GGS blues leaned against the ramp railing, watching someone in—

The man suddenly swung toward them. Dark brows lifted, then dipped into a frown Devin had seen before, on a face he shouldn't be seeing now.

Kiler Griggs. Makaiden's husband.

Fucking impossible. Denials raced through Devin's mind. Kiler couldn't be here. Kiler was dead. Unless Makaiden had lied. . . . But, no, Devin couldn't accept that. Didn't want to accept that.

Makaiden shook off his grasp and took a few steps toward the ship. "Kiler? *Kiler?* What in hell is going on?" Her voice held a slight echo in the large hangar.

"I've missed you, too, sweetheart. I'm sure you have questions about the past year. Come on board and I'll explain. You, too, Mr. Guthrie."

Something's very wrong here. Devin tamped down his shock and confusion and forced his mind to analyze. Kiler alive was one thing. Kiler alive in a GGS uniform was almost as if they'd gone back in time.

That was impossible. But the possibility that Makaiden had lied about Kiler's death wasn't. Except Kiler had just acknowledged that Makaiden would have questions *about the past year*. So she hadn't known he was alive. That was the only good news Devin could find at the moment. He studied the former GGS pilot, then put a blank expression on his face and a bland tone into his voice. Give nothing away. "Who hired you to fly for GGS again?" He really didn't care about the answer. He only wanted to keep Kiler talking so he could try to make some sense of the situation.

"That's another interesting story. It's cold out here and a lot warmer in there." Kiler swung his right hand toward the *Prosperity*'s airlock, but his gaze stayed on Makaiden. Then his chin lifted, as if he was looking past them out into the darkness.

Not into the darkness. *At* someone. *Shit*. Devin slipped his hand under his jacket toward the Carver in his shoulder holster. He should have pulled it the minute he saw a dead man who didn't belong.

Something cold and hard with a distinctly metal feel pressed against the back of his neck. "Don't try it, Mr. Guthrie." The man behind him yanked on his arm. "Keep that out there."

"Don't even think about it," Kiler said, his friendly tone a moment ago replaced by a firmer one. And underscored by a pistol in his hand.

Devin splayed his hands outward in a casual gesture. Under his jacket, his muscles bunched. Rage shot through him—at his stupidity, at this insanity. He tamped it down. Two drawn pistols right now trumped two pistols still in holsters that the opposition knew were there. He had to keep his mind clear. With the barrel of a weapon pressed against his neck and one aimed at Makaiden, it was the only option he had right now.

"Kiler!" Makaiden switched a pained, confused look from her ex-husband to Devin, then back to her ex-husband again.

"Don't you think about pulling a gun either, my sweet wife. Keep those hands out. Good girl." He stepped quickly toward the bottom of the ramp.

Makaiden's arms were out to her sides but she was shaking her head. "Kiler, this is crazy. The Guthries aren't your enemy. There's no reason to do this. Put the gun away. Tell Fuzz—your friend to back off."

Fuzz. Devin didn't think her verbal stumble was an error. She'd just told him the identity of the man behind him. Fuzz-face from Dock Five. The man Barty knew as Munton Fetter.

Devin's mind raced with scenarios, pulling clues from the exchange between Makaiden and Kiler. Did Kiler have some long-standing grudge against GGS because he'd been fired? Was that the impetus behind all the problems with Trip?

"Put the gun down, Kiler," Makaiden repeated, more strongly this time.

Kiler ignored her. "Find that weapon he was reaching for, then check her for an L7. I've got them both covered, and as Kaidee can tell you, Guthrie, I'm a damned good shot."

"What do you want?" Devin asked Kiler through gritted teeth as Fuzz-face groped under his jacket, finding the Carver. He wanted nothing more than to slam his elbow into the man's windpipe, but the gun against his neck and the one pointed at Makaiden told him that was unwise at this point. "Who put you up to this? The Farosians?"

"What the hell do I care about them?" Kiler's mouth twisted in a sneer.

Then it wasn't a political move against GGS—or himself as Philip's brother. Both ideas had surfaced quickly and were now discarded. Devin needed data, facts to work with. And the only way to get them was to keep Kiler talking. The former GGS pilot was only a few feet from Makaiden now, and that fact shot a bolt of white-hot anger through Devin. He didn't like the look on the man's face, which was one of possession. Makaiden didn't belong to Kiler.

"What the hell do you care about us?" he countered harshly. "Why the guns, the threats?"

The pressure of the gun on his neck was suddenly absent. Fuzz-face sidled up on Devin's left, a Stinger in one hand and Devin's Carver in the other.

Kiler smiled, his eyes narrowed. "Because it's fun to be rich."

"You want the *Prosperity*? That's what this is about?" Had he and Makaiden interrupted a simple ship heist? But that wouldn't explain Fuzz-face's presence on Dock Five.

Kiler ignored him, his focus on Makaiden. "I'm taking that L7 now. You as much as blink, sweetie, and Guthrie's dead. Understand?"

"No, I don't, damn you!"

"Honey, I invited you on board. You waited too long." He plucked the small laser pistol from Makaiden's weapons belt. "And look what I found here. A knife." Both went into his jacket pocket. He nodded to Fuzz-face. "Give me the Carver and check him for other weapons."

Fuzz-face shoved the muzzle of the gun in the side of Devin's neck and pulled at the front of his jacket.

Devin locked his gaze on Kiler as Fuzz-face patted him down with jerky movements. "Griggs, if this is about money—"

"Isn't everything?"

"If it's about money, let Makaiden go," Devin persisted. "I'm worth a hell of a lot—"

"You trying to bribe me? We'll just add that to your list of crimes for when the stripers get here."

Devin would love to see a squad of stripers right now. Except something in Kiler's tone and the haughty mien on his face told him the encounter would not go as planned.

That made no sense either.

"Holster's empty. No knives," Fuzz-face reported. "Nice microcomputer, though."

"Leave it for now." Kiler waved the pistol again. "Up the ramp. Let's go."

As Kiler moved behind him, Devin managed a brief glance at Makaiden, catching her attention. She was pale, but anger flashed in her eyes. He gave his head a small shake, hoping she understood. *Not now. Wait.*

Then he did a quick analysis of what he could see of the hangar while Kiler and Fuzz-face pushed them toward the ship. Fuzz-face had friends on Dock Five. Their whereabouts now concerned him greatly. On the ship seemed likely, but if they were, why hadn't they disembarked to help out? Or were they to play the part of the stripers, to force Devin to . . .

He didn't know. His mind frustratingly could come up with nothing.

Think, Devin. Analyze.

If they were up against just Kiler and Fuzz, the situation was bad but not impossible. Two against two was a fair fight. Two against four—or more—was not. And he would not go down without a fight.

Damn it. Of all the scenarios Philip had put him through, the ones he hated most were ones with hostages—and it looked as if that was where they were headed.

Their boot steps thumped hard on the rampway, then they were through the main airlock and into the familiar plush surroundings of the ship. Kiler moved quickly between Devin and Makaiden, the threat clear, but it was the only threat. The main cabin, with its three seating groupings forward and large dining table aft, was empty. No stripers. No Dock Five cohorts. Yet.

No crew. Was Kiler really the pilot or had he killed the GGS crew? Devin did a cursory examination of the cabin for signs of a struggle as they were herded toward the rear of the main room. Either they'd had time to clean up—he thought of Trip's apartment and his family's contention that ImpSec also acted as housekeepers—or there'd been no confrontation.

Unless they were locked belowdecks in one of the cabins. He expected that's where Kiler was taking Makaiden and him—he hoped that's where Kiler was taking them. He knew this ship. More than that, he knew her systems, her computers. And he still had his Rada.

"Sit," Kiler ordered suddenly. "Behind the table. Seats against the bulkhead."

Devin hesitated long enough for Kiler to bring his pistol—a powerful Stinger—up to Makaiden's head. "Don't be stupid."

Devin slid into the bulkhead chair as directed, his back to the outer bulkhead. Makaiden sat catercorner to him, her back against an inner dividing wall. The galley was behind her. Devin understood Kiler's setup: the large, heavy polished wood table—bolted to the decking, as were the chairs—served as an effective barrier to prevent Devin from lunging at either man.

But it also hid his hands. He folded his arms across his chest, rumpling his jacket front, and dropped the lower arm down to his lap. Keeping his gaze locked on Kiler, he brushed his fingers against Makaiden's thigh. Her hand found his only long enough for a quick, reassuring clasp of fingers.

"What now, Kiler? This is crazy, you know that." She raked her other hand through her hair. Good distraction. The eye—in this case, eyes, both Kiler's and Fuzz's—followed movement.

Devin released her fingers and found the Rada in its holder. He tapped a quick-start low-function button he'd customized a few months back, when participants in meetings were often distracted by the Rada's holographic display or when he simply found it convenient not to let them know he had the microcomputer on. One tap and it would record and, at specific data-load intervals, automatically transmit to GGS archives via whatever signal it could grab. If the *Prosperity*'s comm system was active—and he suspected it was—it would also upload to ship's logs.

Whatever happened, someone somewhere in GGS would find it.

"We wait," Kiler said, in answer to Makaiden's question. "We have Guthrie. Saves us a lot of time. Shortly we'll have Trippy and the old bastard, Barthol."

We. Then there were others. A chill raced up Devin's spine. He shoved it away. He had to get ahead of Kiler's thought processes here.

"If you're looking for ransom," Devin said, "my

presence is more than sufficient. Aside from what GGS will pay, I have personal funds. Let Makaiden go. Leave Trip and Barty alone."

Kiler snorted. "There's no ransom where you're going. As for Kaidee," and he tilted his head as if a thought had occurred to him, "that's up to her. Yeah, I like that. What do you say, Kaidee doll? We had some great years. I'm willing to forget the divorce if you are. It's just a stupid legal document anyway."

Stony silence was his only answer.

That silence was broken by the sound of hard boot steps. Someone—or several someones—coming up the ramp. Makaiden, beside him, stiffened. She knew as well as he that the odds were rapidly moving in a bad direction.

"Griggs, got your message." A man's voice boomed through the airlock. "I'll contact Tage and tell—"

Devin sat upright and, for the second time in less than an hour, his mind reeled in disbelief. And not because of the mention of Darius Tage. But because it was his brother Ethan who said the name.

"Ethan!" Devin half-rose out of his seat, which made Fuzz step closer, laser pistol aimed at Devin's face. But Devin remained half standing, fists planted on the tabletop, the shock of Ethan striding into the *Prosperity*'s main cabin almost freezing him in place. Pieces of facts—hard, ugly suppositions he desperately didn't want to be true—began to assemble in his mind. If Ethan was talking about contacting Tage, then Ethan was not here to help. And he'd known Kiler Griggs was on board.

"D.J.?" Ethan's widened eyes narrowed quickly. He slowed, then, with one fist clenched, spun on Kiler. "Why the fuck aren't they locked in a cabin, Griggs?

You damned well better tell me Trippy and the old man are below."

Some of Kiler's bravado wilted, his shoulders dipping under the blue uniform. Then he lifted his chin. "You said not to leave him alone, where he could get at ship's systems."

"Put Gerker—"

"Gerker and Vaughn haven't come back from the cargo terminal yet."

Devin dropped back into his chair as he listened to the exchange. He forced himself to shut down his emotions, to ignore the fact that—for some bizarre reason he couldn't yet grasp—his brother Ethan was involved in all this. Kiler was taking orders from him.

No, not a bizarre reason. Ethan had revealed one very important clue when he said the name Tage. Tage wanted Philip, wanted revenge. Trip's disappearance might well be the catalyst to bring Admiral Guthrie across the border, back into Imperial space.

But why would Ethan do that? Pain wrenched Devin's heart. For God's sake, they were brothers. Family.

"Do they have the kid?" Ethan asked Kiler.

"You have any idea how many freighters park at cargo?"

They were looking for the *Void Rider*. Devin's rash action in not only buying the *Rider* but in using his own name, was not only the catalyst but the key. Ethan knew they'd been bumped from their reservations on Compass Spacelines but expected them to catch another flight. Somehow he found out—Orvis came to mind—that Devin had bought a ship. A freighter that would normally dock on the other side of the spaceport. He remembered Makaiden saying so.

A freighter that was now only a few hangars away on the far end of General Aviation.

"Ethan." Devin put a hard but cold tone in his voice, pulling his brother's attention away from his argument with Kiler Griggs. "What in hell's going on here?"

His brother turned to him, a thin smile curving his lips. "You really don't know, do you? So tell me, how does it feel to be the one left out of the plans? Don't like it, do you?"

Devin stared at him, hearing the petulant undercurrent that surfaced every time Ethan thought he was slighted by J.M., just as it had in the library before Devin headed for Dock Five.

Just because I don't have all the degrees you and Devin have doesn't mean I'm stupid.

That was Ethan's constant complaint, that he was never viewed as smart or as worthy as Jonathan, Philip, or Devin.

So because of some childish sibling rivalry, he tried to kidnap Trip? And why would Tage want any part of that?

"I don't like having guns pointed at me," Devin replied evenly. "But whatever problem you have with me, fine, we'll work it out. Makaiden has nothing to do with that. Neither does Trip or Barty. Let her go. Send them"—he motioned to Kiler and Fuzz—"away, and we talk. We'll solve this together," he added, then winced internally at his unintended condescension. But this was Ethan, and that's the way one talked to Ethan.

Which was evidently why he was sitting here. To Jonathan, Philip, and Devin, it was childish sibling rivalry. To Ethan, it was his life. Some of Devin's anger cooled. A good negotiator fully understood the opposition's position.

"Let Makaiden go," Devin repeated. "Put away the guns. You don't need them."

Emotions flashed over Ethan's face, the tightness of his mouth relaxing. Abruptly, he turned away and stalked toward the dark-blue half-circle sofa that curved out of the port bulkhead.

He spun back. "No, not this time. Not anymore. You're not talking me out of it, shoving some mindless business assignment at me, sending me to this office or that, just to keep me busy. Keep Ethan out of trouble." His voice rose in a false and bitter mimicry. Then he sobered. "Big changes are coming to GGS, D.J. Power is shifting and, guess what? It's shifting to me. Father's been trying to get concessions out of Tage for years. He failed. Tage won't even talk to Jonathan. But I did it. Me. Ethan Guthrie." He jabbed his index finger at his chest.

"Ethan, you can't—" Devin caught himself before he said, *You can't make deals for GGS with Tage or anyone. You're a corporate officer only on paper. You have no authority.*

Ethan knew all that. Too well.

"You can't think we wouldn't be proud of any important deal you made," Devin amended. But it was too late.

Ethan laughed. "You're such a fucking liar." He looked at Kiler. "Where in hell's Gerker? I need the kid here before the stripers show up."

Kiler shook his head. "No, you don't." He pointed to Devin. "You have him. Let the stripers get the *Rider*'s location out of him. You just hand them proof he killed Halsey and funded Trip's kidnapping. They'll do the rest."

"Proof I did *what*?" This time Devin shot to his feet, heart pounding, mouth suddenly dry.

"Sit *down*," Ethan bellowed. Fuzz lunged forward, teeth bared.

Devin stood his ground, but inside he shook with rage. This was crazy. Ethan was crazy. Why would they want it to look as if he was the one who wanted to hurt Trip? Then he remembered the small news article Makaiden had unearthed, the one stating the police already had leads in the case. Leads Ethan provided them? "I had nothing to do with Halsey—"

"You paid for an assassin." Ethan's voice was oily. "I have copies of the financial records. Records you tried to destroy by ordering the bombing of your own offices while you went after Trip yourself."

"There are no such records. There never were!"

"There are if you know the right codes to gain access and create them."

Devin stared at the man who was his brother, no longer recognizing him. This was not the Ethan who challenged him to swimming races as a child or traded music vids with him as a teen. This was not the Ethan he'd shared breakfast and dinner with almost every day of the first twelve years of his life and almost weekly for a decade thereafter. This was not, *could* not, be his brother.

Makaiden leaned forward on the table, her hands clasped together. "You sabotaged the security and communications systems on your father's estate," she said quietly.

Ethan's smile made Devin feel ill.

Just because I don't have all the degrees you and Devin have doesn't mean I'm stupid.

Ethan wasn't stupid. Desperate, yes. Twisted, yes. But he wasn't stupid. Devin thought of the other hacker he'd intercepted a few days ago poking around in Trip's accounts, just as he was. Ethan.

Devin lowered himself into his chair. The last thing he wanted to do now was appear threatening, and, even though he was younger, he was taller than Ethan. He took a cue from Makaiden—pull back, speak softly. Analyze. Gather facts.

"Why, Ethan? Why me?"

"Father was going to give you the entire Baris division. Hell of a wedding present. You didn't know that, did you?"

GGS–Baris? That was a multitrillion-credit enterprise. Being Garno CFO was one thing. But owning the entire Guthrie operation in Baris—the manufacturing facilities, the export centers, the raw-materials acquisition and distribution... Even to Devin, that was staggering.

And wrong. "Father would never split up GGS—"

"An inoperable brain tumor makes you do funny things. He didn't know I overheard his conversations with his doctor and Chanoy from Legal. He's got six months, maybe a year. He changed his will. Jonathan gets GGS–Aldan. You get GGS–Baris. Philip gets GGS–Marker, and Trippy—*Trippy*—gets GGS–Garno. He's fucking nineteen years old.

"And do you know what I get? The Guthrie Commerce Development Center in Port Palmero. That's it. A goddamned conference center with, what, a dozen hotels? Two dozen office complexes? J.M. makes me a goddamned landlord, unless... unless"—he leaned on the edge of the table, bringing his face down to Devin's—"unless you die or are incapacitated. Then I get GGS–Baris. Okay, I have to share it with Marguerite and Hannah, but I can get around that. Tage is going to help me get around that." He shoved himself back, his smile smug.

"You're going to kill me." Devin couldn't believe he was saying those words.

"I don't have to. You're going to be tried and convicted of murder and attempted kidnapping. Probably arson too." Ethan shrugged. "You'll sit in maximum lockup for the rest of your life. And I get Baris." His eyes narrowed. "I deserve Baris."

"You're going to kill Jonathan and Trippy? Marguerite too?"

Another shrug. "Tage has a timetable. I have plans for GGS. He has plans for the Empire. We work well together."

"And does any of this involve delivering Philip to Tage?"

"Philip's a traitor to the Empire. A blot on the Guthrie name. Father should have disowned him."

Tage is the traitor, Devin wanted to say but didn't. It wouldn't do any good.

A pocket comm chimed softly. Kiler pulled the small comm off his belt and held it to his ear, his Stinger still in his right hand.

Ethan glanced at him. Kiler shook his head, then frowned.

"Vaughn," Kiler said, holding the pocket comm in Ethan's direction. "You'd better talk to him."

The table in front of Devin jiggled slightly. He shot a glance at Makaiden and felt her foot tap his. She wanted his attention on something. Her chin was propped against her left hand, elbow on the table. Her right hand—

He realized she was leaning to one side, collapsing into herself as if she was afraid, tired.

He dropped his left hand to the chair's edge, felt her

fingers grab his and tug. He angled forward, wiping one hand over his face to cover the movement. Then his fingers found the metal centerpost and, with her guidance, the locking metal ring that secured the table-top to the post.

A ring that could be unlocked—*was* unlocked—to remove the top for repair or maintenance, just like the deck-locked chairs and sofa.

The wooden top was heavy but unlocked. He and Makaiden could lift it. Shove it. Laser fire would penetrate it, but it would also give them the element of surprise. And maybe, just maybe, knock Kiler and Fuzz off their feet, pin them to the decking. He could handle Ethan.

He gave her hand a quick squeeze, then leaned back. She'd given him an option, a diversion. Their only recourse. But they'd have to do it before Gerker, Vaughn, and the stripers arrived.

Ethan turned his back on them and, pocket comm still to his ear, stalked toward the front of the ship. Kiler glanced once, then again, after Ethan's retreating figure. Whatever Kiler heard on the pocket comm had him worried. And distracted.

They wouldn't get another chance.

Devin crossed his legs, lifting the tabletop off the post with one knee. Makaiden was leaning on it, then her weight suddenly disappeared. She continued to feign distress, but her hand under the table helped to hold the top steady.

Kiler looked over his shoulder again.

"Now." Devin breathed the word.

He shoved the wooden tabletop up and out, dropping back into a crouch the minute he felt it leave his fingers. It slid hard over the backs of the deck-locked dining chairs opposite him, then jettisoned forward.

He lunged. Makaiden lunged. The table slammed into Kiler's back, knocking him to the decking, but it only clipped Fuzz.

And Ethan was shouting, running back toward them.

23

Kaidee had one goal and one goal only: get a pistol. Any weapon. Her arms and shoulders ached from lifting the tabletop, but she didn't care. She wanted a weapon, and she was going to kill that slagging bastard Ethan. If Devin didn't do it first.

She landed hard on her knees, then on one elbow, pain searing through her, but she pushed up in a tight crouch like a competitive runner. Kiler was sprawled, groaning, to her right. Devin was next to her but the next moment he was a blur, launching himself at Fuzzface. She heard a crash, a thud, hard breaths, and low grunts.

She lunged for Kiler, seeing the glint of her L7 just under his shoulder. She put her knee in the middle of his shoulder blades and snatched the L7, flicking it from stun to kill. There wasn't time to aim. She fired at the man barreling toward her.

Ethan dove to the right, ending up behind a couch. The laser's energy flared past him, scarring a forward bulkhead.

She took aim again, approximating his position. A hand grabbed her ankle. Kiler. She kicked him, falling on her ass as he clawed his way up her leg. She jerked the L7 around.

His eyes went wide and it was as if time stopped, the grunts and thuds receding, her vision narrowing, and it was only Kaidee and Kiler.

"Kaidee. Please." His voice was pained. The tabletop still covered the lower half of his body. But his

GGS uniform—the one he had no right to wear, the one he'd forced her to lose—was clearly visible.

"You son of a bitch." She flicked the L7 to stun and hit him with the full charge. He went limp, his hand falling from her ankle.

She found she was shaking and grateful to be sitting down. *Don't make me regret not killing you.*

A body slammed into her from behind, then yanked her back. Ethan. His arm locked around her neck, catching her in a choke hold. She rose halfway up on her feet, gasping, flailing at him with her left hand.

"Give me the pistol!" He grabbed her arm.

She let the force of his movement send the L7 sailing across the main cabin.

"Bitch!" He dragged her, squirming, to her feet.

Only then could she see that Fuzz-face was a bloody, beaten mess under Devin's knee, his gaping mouth showing teeth missing. The Stinger in Devin's hand was pressed against Fuzz's temple.

Ethan's breath was harsh in her ear. "Drop the pistol, D.J., or she dies."

Blood trickled down Devin's forehead from a cut near his hairline; there was another cut on his left cheek. His glasses were skewed. But his lips thinned, and his eyes were hard. His voice carried an unmistakable deadly note. "If she dies, he dies."

"I don't give a damn about him." Ethan kicked Kiler's still form. Kiler's head rolled to one side. Devin's Carver was underneath. "She hits the decking, I grab that, I kill you. Simple."

Kaidee didn't like the sound of simple. She locked her hands around Ethan's arm, yanking it away from her windpipe. His muscles were like metal rods. All those years of sailing, pulling heavy sheets and riggings, had paid off. She dug her nails into his skin. He didn't flinch.

Neither did Devin. His gaze never left her face.

Ethan jerked her upright another painful inch. "Your call, D.J. Drop the gun or I break her neck."

Kaidee pulled again on Ethan's arm but this time slipped one hand inside the upper pocket of her jacket. The cylindrical hypos were slick under her fingers, but she'd done this a dozen times before, reaching blindly into a med-kit to help an injured crew member. She palmed a hypo, thumbing the cap off, then swung her hand up and rammed the dispenser into his forearm, holding the tab down to send all five doses into him.

Ethan roared as the sedative flooded his system, but she was already fumbling in her pocket for the other one. This one she flipped over, dispenser down, and, as he pounded his fist into her midsection, rammed it— gasping, choking, eyes streaming—into his thigh.

He arched back, lifting her feet off the decking, but it was enough for her to wriggle free. She dropped to her knees, sucking air, tears blinding her, and grabbed for the Carver. The whine of a Stinger set to kill sounded over her head.

"Makaiden!" Devin's voice was raw. Ethan hit the decking with a sickening thud as Devin lowered the Stinger.

Wrapping her fingers around the Carver's muzzle, Kaidee dragged herself up on one knee. And saw darkness descending. "Behind you!"

Devin spun, catching Fuzz in the neck with his elbow. The man collapsed against a dining chair with a horrid gurgling sound, then went limp, falling to the floor.

It was suddenly quiet, except for her own rasping, rattling breath and the blood pounding in her ears. She shoved the Carver into her weapons belt, her hands shaking.

Dear God. The inside of the *Prosperity,* one of the most beautiful ships in the GGS fleet, looked like a war zone.

Devin holstered the Stinger, then grabbed her arm, bringing her to her feet. His hands roamed quickly over her body, as if he was assuring himself she was really alive. "Are you hurt? You're all right?"

"Fine. You?" Even as she said the words, she felt stupid. God. Ethan was dead. And here they were, exchanging inane pleasantries. "Dev, I'm so sorry."

His expression tightened with pain. "He would have killed you. He would have killed me. And it wouldn't have stopped there."

"I know," she said, as he propelled her toward the airlock. Away from Ethan's body.

He stopped just short of the hatchway to the ramp and sucked in a breath. "I have this overwhelming need to kiss you." His voice rasped. "Hell, I have this overwhelming need to make love to you until the goddamned universe implodes, but we don't have time. Security's headed here to arrest me, and Kiler's thugs are looking for the *Rider.* I hope to God Trip and Barty are still on board. Can you get us off-planet quick?"

"Can you punch holes in traffic control's security grid?"

He tapped the Rada strapped to his side. "I can."

"Then I can." She pushed him ahead of her through the hatchway. She didn't ever want to see this ship again. "Go!"

They ran more than halfway to the *Rider,* the cold air searing her lungs, the whine of the wind covering all but the loudest of their boot steps but also hiding noises of anyone behind them.

Her head ached, her chest ached, and various parts of her anatomy were pummeled by small explosions of pain. But she was alive, and Devin was alive. She'd think about the carnage back on the *Prosperity* later.

Devin slowed her at the Concourse C hangars, pulling her into the shadows. "I won't be ambushed after all this."

"You said you could contact Barty's DRECU with your Rada. If someone's on the bridge, with or without them, would that give away too much?"

"With the tech that stripers usually carry, no. ImpSec is another matter. They could track my signal." He brought the microcomputer up and stepped into a recessed doorway. Kaidee stood at his side, blocking the glow from the screen. "But I can muddy it. They'll unscramble it eventually, but by then..." And his voice drifted off as he concentrated on a short line of numbers.

By then, Kaidee knew, they'd either have rescued Trip and Barty or died trying. Tage's assassins wouldn't make the same mistakes as Ethan.

"What are those numbers?"

A pained laugh preceded his answer. "Something only Barty or I would know. The date of the first time I beat him at basketball. The second is the last time he and I played a game."

"What should his answer be?"

"The scores."

She stepped closer, a shiver coursing through her body. The temperature was dropping. She could see her breath now.

New numbers flashed in a small databox at the bottom of the screen.

Devin's breath stuttered out. "Thank God. They're safe. Unless they've got a mind-ripper in there, reading Barty's brain, they're safe." He shoved the Rada back under his jacket. "Keep the Carver out, just in case."

The wide bay doors were still open. Devin slipped around the corner first, with Kaidee close behind. She hesitated as he did, scanning the darkened hangar as he did.

"Go," he whispered.

They ran, boots thudding hard on the cold floor. Kaidee focused on the ramp strut and its security panel under the ship. It would take at least a minute to deploy the ramp. If someone was waiting in ambush...

Light speared the darkness from overhead. Her breath caught, her boots skidding, but Devin had her arm. "Keep going! It's Trip. Ramp's on the way down."

The grinding, chugging sound of the ramp extending was the most beautiful sound on the planet.

Then they were scrambling up the ramp, Devin shoving her ahead of him.

"Seal the airlock!" she told Trip as soon as their boots hit the decking. Barty was there as well, Carver in hand.

"You need sick bay?" he asked.

"Bridge," she told him. "We're doing an unauthorized departure as soon as Devin scrambles their security air-grid."

Barty followed her. "I have some interesting information on Kiler you'll want to hear, when we have time."

She glanced quickly at him.

"Nahteg—that corporation Kiler was doing business with when he supposedly died?"

Supposedly died. That stalled her footsteps. "You knew Kiler was alive?"

"My datapad picked up the feed from the Rada. I was honestly shocked, but then not, considering the data I found. And who Kiler was really working for. Think about it. Nahteg. N-A-H-T-E-G. It's *G Ethan* spelled backward."

"Kiler and Ethan go back that far?" She started walking at a good pace again.

"This has been a while in the making. I have a fairly detailed report that you and Devin will need to see. Later," he added, as she spun the pilot's chair around and slid into it, bringing her armrest screens up. Seconds later, Devin was at the nav console on her right, synchronizing the Rada, its bright-green holographic display once again sending reflections dancing over his glasses.

Barty sat at comm; Trip, at second pilot. Kaidee brought all systems live, her hands flowing rapidly from screens to touchpads to screens again, her mind replaying Barty's words. She didn't know if she was more disturbed by the fact that Ethan and Kiler had been planning this for some time or that, through Barty's DRECU, Trip had listened to his uncle Ethan trying to kill Devin and herself. As well, he had to have heard Ethan brag about his connection to Tage. Trip had to know what that would mean for GGS and his family. It was a heavy burden for a nineteen-year-old.

It had to be a huge burden for Devin. Ethan's betrayal and Ethan's death. His father's terminal illness.

He would have to talk about it—later. Now he had work to do, intense work, and that, she realized, was a blessing.

He didn't have to think about Ethan.

She wondered if she should have killed Kiler. He'd already been declared dead once. Why did he do that? Was it part of Ethan's plan? She might never know. The only clue he'd given was money. He wanted to be rich. So someone, maybe Ethan, had paid him well to pretend to die.

She powered on the heavy-airs, sending a rumbling through the ship. "I'm going to taxi her out in black-out mode. Trip, I need you up front, your nose literally on the viewport. My bow cameras might miss something small- to medium-size." Like a truck.

Trip moved quickly to her console, bracing himself against the edge.

"I want to dim bridge lights. Devin, can you still work?"

"Not a problem."

She tapped bridge lights down to three quarters and turned off all nonessentials. The *Rider* had cleared the last row of tie-downs when Port Chalo Ground barked out commands.

"Unidentified ship on Taxiway T Seven, cut engines now! You're not authorized to—"

Kaidee tabbed the volume down. "Barty, monitor local traffic. I don't want to hit anybody. Devin, we're getting airborne as soon as I'm sure we've got clear skies. If you can't find us a hole, I can—"

"Got one. Sending data now."

Databoxes flickered on her screen. "That's two."

"First one's the best. Second is backup."

"Barty?"

"Ground control is pitching fits, but they're holding up all traffic. There's not that much at this hour anyway."

"I'm not looking for the usual traffic. It's ImpSec I'm worried about."

"I'm listening in on three private ship-to-ships. No one's reporting bogeys."

"Trip, you should be strapped in, but if they throw something out on that runway, I want to know about it."

"I'm braced pretty good here."

She swung the ship around to the last taxiway, the *Rider* now in full heavy-air mode. "Barty, announce our immediate departure on ship-to-ship as a courtesy. I have a feeling ground control already knows."

Then she punched the engines, sending the *Void Rider* roaring off into the frigid Port Chalo night sky.

Descent was hell, but ascent was no paradise either. The planet always seemed reluctant to let a ship go, with gravity extending its long, sticky fingers into the atmosphere. She was sure something pursued them at one point—the long-range scan trilled, showing bogeys that were almost two hours behind. But they were closing in on one of Devin's artificial null zones in the security grid. She guided the ship through and knew the *Rider* had just disappeared from Talgarrath's screens.

They would probably assume she'd crashed and would send scoutbots out seeking wreckage. Let 'em seek. It would keep them busy.

Eventually someone might discover where she'd slipped through—though not how—and figure out their trajectory. She wanted to be firmly in the space lanes by then and heading for the smugglers' gate to Calfedar. It seemed the safest place to go right now, and the ship, with its Englarian registry, could blend in.

Trip seemed unusually subdued. Granted, being squashed back into your chair as the ship pulled away from the planet didn't often make people chatty. But Trip always had questions, comments. Now he had none. But then, Barty's DRECU had picked up much of what was said on the *Prosperity*, and Trip likely had heard it all. Or, in his case, too much.

They broke free of the planet's pull and the *Rider* made its final morphing changes from heavy-air to space vehicle. Kaidee ran a status check. Sublights had picked up a little wobble, but she knew that would smooth out in about twenty minutes. It hadn't been the most textbook-perfect launch. She glanced over her left shoulder at Barty, who still had the commset ringing one ear. He raised his chin slightly, acknowledging her gaze. She gave her head the minutest of tilts in Trip's direction.

Barty nodded slowly, his mouth grim.

She understood. Trip's world was coming apart. He was worried about his parents, his siblings, his grandfather. And he'd already admitted several times that he carried guilt for running away, for being a catalyst for all that happened afterward.

Except he wasn't. Ethan, with Tage's help, had put things in motion before Trip left Aldan Prime.

She swiveled around to face Trip and Dev at the starboard consoles. "Trip, Devin and I need to hit sick bay. Your uncle's bleeding on my decking, and I think I have a cracked rib." Or three. "I'm turning the con over to you."

That brought Trip's head up, life finally flashing in his eyes.

She unhooked her straps and pushed herself out of her seat. "But before we go below, I need you to think about one thing. You weren't the cause of all this. If you'd stayed in your apartment, if you were kid-napped by whoever Ethan sent, very likely Ethan's plan would have succeeded. Your uncle Devin and your parents might be dead. Tage would be control-ling not only GGS's resources but its funds.

"I'm not saying your bolting off for Dock Five was the right thing to do. But you saved lots of lives. In-cluding your own."

He nodded slowly. "Thank you. I'm...This is not an easy thing for me to understand right now. I'm working on it." He hesitated, then: "Thank you for your faith in me, Captain Griggs."

She gave his shoulder a reassuring squeeze—he was growing some good muscles there—as she passed. Then she stopped in front of Devin. "Let's go get you patched up."

They made it into the lift before he dragged her into his arms, his mouth hard and demanding on hers, his hands roaming her body with a fierce possessiveness. He pinned her against the lift wall. The intensity of his kisses had her heart racing, her breath coming in gasps. The doors pinged, opening onto the lower level. Devin reached back blindly, slapping the lift's emer-gency shutoff, then returned to kissing her again.

She pulled her mouth away slightly. His lips moved down her neck. "Devin, I need to get you to sick bay."

"My cabin's closer. I need to get you in bed."

She framed his face with her hands, bringing his gaze to hers. "We're not safe yet. Not until we get through the jumpgates. Even then...God, Dev. I'm so sorry about your brother. Your father. I really am."

He closed his eyes, wrapping his arms tightly around her, his face buried in her hair. They stood that way for a very long moment. Then his body trembled against hers. He didn't want to cry. He was fighting the emotions. She could feel that, because she'd been there.

She stroked his back.

He'd killed his brother. And, like Trip, he had family in serious danger, including a father who was dying. There was nothing he could do to help—not right away. They could send warnings from the first data beacon they hit, but Tage was still out there, as were the falsified charges that Devin had Halsey murdered, had planned Trip's kidnapping. He might never be able to clear his name.

He might never be able to go home again.

"I'm okay now," he said roughly, releasing her.

She brushed the dampness from his face and knew that was a lie, but it was one they'd live with for a while.

The medalyzer confirmed her guess: two cracked ribs. The unit hummed against her skin as it started the bone-regeneration process. Devin was in front of sick bay's small mirror, sticking anti-infectives to his face.

Both their bodies would bear an interesting variety of black, blue, green, and yellow bruises. As soon as they were safe in jump, she intended to explore and kiss every single one of Devin's, and told him so.

He shot her a lecherous grin over his shoulder. "In addition, I think we might—"

The wail of alarms erupted through the ship. Kaidee froze, heart leaping into her throat. Then she tore off the med-unit and bolted for the corridor, Devin's hard boot steps pounding behind her.

"Bogeys, Captain Griggs!" Trip's voice echoed on

intraship as she and Devin raced up the stairwell. "Short range shows a warship, a big one. And a P-75. Closing fast."

Shit. Anibal's friends were back.

Trip moved out of the pilot's chair. She slid back in, raking her straps over her chest, swinging the armrest screens in front of her face. The gate was three and a half hours away. The warship with its ominous null ident less than forty minutes behind them.

They'd never make it.

Her heart sank lower than she thought possible. "Listen up. This is not good news. They must have been waiting for us." Now she knew why there'd been so little pursuit on the ground. "How they knew we'd come out here and not on the planet's dark side, I don't know. But they did. Gate edge is three and a half hours away. We run, I can almost guarantee they will shoot. But I'm willing to try it if you all fully understand that risk." She looked at Devin. "There's no option for negotiations anymore. Our bogus ship's docs are not why they're here."

"There are always options," Devin said firmly. "If we run, we die condemned by lies. As long as we're breathing, we have a chance. I'm not saying it's going to be easy, and I'm not saying it won't take time. But there are worse things than waiting." His hard expression softened. "I've waited years for you, Makaiden. I'm not giving up now."

Tears pricked at the back of her eyes at the raw emotions in his voice. "Just my luck to fall in love with a damned optimist." Her voice cracked.

His gaze went intense, heated.

The incoming comm link chimed. "It's the warship," Barty said, his voice tight.

Kaidee swiveled around, nodded at Barty, then

centered her chair to the pilot's console again. "I'll take it here." She opened the audio link. "This is Captain Makaiden Griggs of the *Void Rider,* in service to Guthrie Global Systems."

"This is Admiral Philip Guthrie on the Alliance flagship *Hope's Folly,*" a deep masculine voice boomed. "It's *damned* good to hear your voice again, Makaiden. If you'll change course to intercept, we can lock you down to one of our exterior access bays and get you safely out of here. Now let me talk to that conniving, systems-hacking genius brother of mine."

Devin rose from the chair in the *Folly*'s now near-empty ready room and, with typical Guthrie awkwardness, accepted Philip's embrace. They were the last to leave—Makaiden, Trip, and Barty had just headed down one deck to their assigned cabins on 2 Forward, giving the brothers some privacy in which to share their grief. It had been an intense three-hour debriefing after an equally intense—but exhilarating—hour and a half of intercepting the 850-ton Stryker-class warship, coordinating hullside docking, securing the *Rider* to the exterior access, and the long, final walk—okay, they'd damned near run—down the narrow airlock corridor to where Devin's silver-haired brother waited for them in an impeccable Alliance officer's pale-gray uniform.

With his wife, Rya—also in uniform, a long laser rifle slung across her back.

Devin had no idea Philip had remarried. Rya was not only more than a dozen years his brother's junior but was the daughter of a former commanding officer. But Devin immediately sensed that spark between Philip and the tall young woman with the curly brown hair—and not just because, in addition to the rifle, she had two more pistols in her weapons holster and the hilt of a knife peeking out of the top of her left boot. Definitely a woman who could claim Philip's heart.

"Congratulations again on your marriage." Devin patted Philip's arm, stepping back.

Philip's smile was thoughtful. "Rya's phenomenal.

And congratulations on finding Makaiden again. Focus on what you two have, not on what we've lost."

They'd lost more than just Ben Halsey and Ethan. Their father, J.M., was dead—not from illness but murder. That was a deep loss—a searing pain Devin knew would take a long time to heal. They'd parted on bad terms. Things felt unfinished. And his father might have died believing Devin was responsible for what happened to Halsey and Trip. As long as he lived, Devin would hate Tage for that.

But Ethan wasn't blameless. Tage's assassins had gained entry to the Port Palmero estate after Ethan destroyed the house's security. Petra Frederick had died defending the old man. Other security and servants were dead or wounded.

But others lived, though their lives were about to change drastically. Their mother, Valerie, along with Jonathan, his family, and Ethan's wife and children, were on their way to Kirro Station, on board a sleek, damned-near-impossible-to-find luxury-yacht-turned-pirate-rig called the *Boru Karn,* with Philip's ex-wife, Chaz Bergren Sullivan, in command. In tandem with the *Karn* was the *Triumph,* with key Guthrie staff and the children's pets on board.

Philip had been coordinating the rescue effort with Gabriel "Sully" Sullivan, Chaz's husband, when the *Karn* intercepted messages going to the *Prosperity* about the plot to frame Devin for the death of Ben Halsey—a plot started weeks ago by Ethan and Tage.

The *Folly* and her P-75 escort under Captain O'Neil's command spent a shipday playing hide-and-seek with Captain Thurman Anibal's *Nola Tran* before O'Neil was able to put two small torpedoes into the hull near the *Tran's* jumpspace engines. The *Tran* fled, and Philip once again picked up the *Rider's* trail.

Now the *Folly* would head for Kirro, where another family reunion would take place.

"It'll be good to have you on board," Philip said. "Makaiden too. We have a top-notch Takan helmsman—he's not much older than Trip. He'll help her and Trip get familiar with ship's systems. You and Con Welford can swap illegal computer hacks that I don't even want to know about."

"You going to put me through boot-camp training first?"

Philip snorted. "You mean again, don't you?"

"Just as long as I get to be an admiral."

"Stay out of trouble in boot camp and you might make lieutenant commander." Philip's voice was stern, but his mouth was twitching. He nodded toward the corridor. "Makaiden's waiting for you. Relax, get your bodies synchronized to shiptime. Dinner's in the executive mess in"—he glanced at the time stamp on the ready room's wall screen—"three hours."

"My body tells me three hours is just about time for breakfast."

"My point exactly," Philip said. He reached the door—gray metal, very utilitarian, just like everything else Devin had seen so far of the *Folly*—and pushed the palm pad. "I'm going to spend a little time with Trip—he has a lot of adjustments to make—and then check in on Barty in sick bay. Three hours, executive mess, Commander Guthrie. That's an order."

"You are such a pain in the ass, Philip," Devin murmured, following his older brother into the corridor.

"I give demerits for insubordination."

"I'm not worried," Devin said, as they took the stairs down to Deck 2 Forward. "I'll just hack into your files and wipe my record clean."

"That will piss off my chief of security. Not to mention your sister-in-law."

"They're the same person."

"Then you're really in trouble."

A large white cat with a black tail and one black ear suddenly raced toward them down the corridor, heading for the stairwell they'd just exited. Devin didn't know if he was more surprised by the cat or by the fact that Philip saluted the beast. "What in hell's that?"

"*He* is Captain Folly. Show respect to your superior officers, Commander. You've just earned another demerit."

"You're joking, right?"

"About the cat or the demerit?"

"Both."

"Nope."

This corridor, unlike the bridge deck above, was carpeted—gray again—though bulkheads were plain, unless power panels and conduit counted as decoration. They stopped in front of the cabin temporarily assigned to Trip and, when he came out of sick bay, Barty. "Welcome to the rebellion, Devin," Philip said, his eyes suddenly serious. He tapped the palm pad, and, as the door opened, Devin heard no small excitement in Trip's voice: "Awaiting your orders, sir!"

Devin smiled to himself, took the few steps to the next cabin door, and put his hand on the pad. The door opened and he strode in.

Makaiden stood in front of the long viewport, framed by the blackness of space and the few visible pinpoints of light. Distant stars. They were as far away as his hopes, his dreams had once been. But everything he'd ever wanted was now only a few feet in front of him.

She turned. She'd stripped off her jacket but still

wore the same dark thermal shirt and now-ripped pants she'd put on—was it only six hours ago?—before they'd gone to find the *Prosperity*. She looked battered, bruised, and tired. But something he thought he'd never see lit up her eyes.

Makaiden loved him. And he, with every bit of his being, loved her.

He extended his hand as she took a step toward him. "Dance with me."